JOURNAL OF A
UFO INVESTIGATOR

JOURNAL OF A
UFO INVESTIGATOR

A NOVEL

DAVID
HALPERIN

VIKING

VIKING
Published by the Penguin Group
Penguin Group (USA) Inc., 375 Hudson Street, New York, New York 10014, U.S.A. • Penguin Group (Canada), 90 Eglinton Avenue East, Suite 700, Toronto, Ontario, Canada M4P 2Y3 (a division of Pearson Penguin Canada Inc.) • Penguin Books Ltd, 80 Strand, London WC2R 0RL, England • Penguin Ireland, 25 St. Stephen's Green, Dublin 2, Ireland (a division of Penguin Books Ltd) • Penguin Books Australia Ltd, 250 Camberwell Road, Camberwell, Victoria 3124, Australia (a division of Pearson Australia Group Pty Ltd) • Penguin Books India Pvt Ltd, 11 Community Centre, Panchsheel Park, New Delhi – 110 017, India • Penguin Group (NZ), 67 Apollo Drive, Rosedale, North Shore 0632, New Zealand (a division of Pearson New Zealand Ltd) • Penguin Books (South Africa) (Pty) Ltd, 24 Sturdee Avenue, Rosebank, Johannesburg 2196, South Africa

Penguin Books Ltd, Registered Offices:
80 Strand, London WC2R 0RL, England

First published in 2011 by Viking Penguin,
a member of Penguin Group (USA) Inc.

1   3   5   7   9   10   8   6   4   2

Publisher's Note
This is a work of fiction. Names, characters, places, and incidents either are the product of the author's imagination or are used fictitiously, and any resemblance to actual persons, living or dead, business establishments, events, or locales is entirely coincidental.

LIBRARY OF CONGRESS CATALOGING IN PUBLICATION DATA
Halperin, David J. (David Joel)
Journal of a UFO investigator : a novel / David Halperin.
p.   cm.
ISBN 978-0-670-02245-8
1. Teenagers—Fiction.   2. Unidentified flying objects—Fiction.
3. Mothers—Death—Fiction.   4. Pennsylvania—History—20th century—Fiction. I. Title.
PS3608.A54925J68 2011
813'.6—dc22   2010034999

Printed in the United States of America
Set in Celeste with Briem Akademi
Designed by Daniel Lagin

To Rose
who taught me to believe

CONTENTS

JOURNAL OF A
UFO INVESTIGATOR

PART ONE
FOLLOW THE MOON

(JANUARY 1966)

CHAPTER 1

THE UFO FELL FROM THE SKY ON THE NIGHT OF DECEMBER 20, 1962, *the week of my thirteenth birthday. The event itself, after more than three years, I recall with perfect clarity. Many of its circumstances, however, have blurred in my mind.*

I can't remember, for instance, where I'd been that evening. I was certainly coming home from somewhere, maybe a meeting of some sort. I see myself standing before the house, on the front lawn, just a little off the sidewalk, ready to go inside yet looking steadily into the sky. It was very cold, and it must have been late, certainly after 10:00 P.M. Orion was high in the southern sky over the house, Sirius not far below and to the east. All the stars were extraordinarily clear, their colors very marked. I could make out the red of Betelgeuse, the ice-blue, diamond-blue glitter of Sirius. There was no moon.

The object appeared in the east. I don't know what called my attention to it. I was not surprised to see it. I'd been a UFO investigator for two months, since the fourth week in October. I knew such things were there in the skies, if only I was ready to look toward them.

It was a disk, glowing deep fluorescent red. Darker at the edges than near the center. Apparent size about twice what the full moon's would have been if the moon had been visible. It moved westward at a leisurely pace, toward me, briefly obscuring the stars as it passed beneath.

My camera was in my bedroom, third dresser drawer. My father's binoculars were on a shelf in his den. I was torn whether to run into the house to get them, knowing the thing might be gone when I came out. I suspected it wasn't likely to register on film. While I stood trying to decide, it came to a dead stop over the house.

How long it stayed motionless, I don't know. I didn't think to look at my

watch. Suddenly it began to flutter downward, in a classic falling leaf maneu-
ver, as if to land or crash on top of me. I tried to run; my feet wouldn't move.
They tingled as if electricity were running through them, the way the body
tingles when lightning's about to strike. Or when a nightmare begins and I
don't yet know how it will end.

My legs crumpled. The frozen earth, its winter-brown grass red in the
blood-colored light, slammed against my body. I lay in a twisted S, my face
turned upward, the back of my head wedged against the ground. The disk—
solid, heavy, bigger than a bus or even a boxcar—fell quivering a few hundred
feet above me. Its crimson glare pulsated, darkening slowly, all at once bright-
ening. It swallowed up the sky.

My hand at least would move.

I felt around my pocket for my key chain, found the thick metal triangle,
the Delta Device. I squeezed—

The disk stopped. Hung in midair.

Not because of the Delta. It can't have had that power. But after a few sec-
onds I felt the gadget vibrate in my hand, and I knew: yes, this works, just as
Jeff Stollard and I had planned. Another moment, and I might be crushed to
death. But not in silence.

And the disk—

"Danny!"

—spoke to me. The words it said I have forgotten. Maybe they weren't words,
just sensations, images or feelings perhaps, stimulated within my brain—

"Danny!"

The door opens. She comes in.

My mother. She leans on the dresser, just inside the doorway to my bedroom,
breathing hard from the strain of walking twenty feet.

"I've been knocking. Didn't you hear me?"

"No," I lie. But it's not quite a lie. I heard her knock but didn't entirely hear
it, just as I see her every day, but not entirely. Right now I hardly see her at
all. My desk lamp is the only light I have on. Outside its circle, she's in
shadow.

She shuffles over to me, in her bedroom slippers. She always wears her
bedroom slippers.

"Danny. Do you know what time it is?"

I glance at the last words I've written—*images or feelings perhaps, stimulated within my brain*—and move my hand to cover the paper. A mistake; I've called her attention to it. I look at my watch. "About eleven thirty," I say.

"Almost a quarter to twelve."

"Eleven thirty-seven." I correct her.

"It's a school night. You know that."

"I know."

She persists: "Christmas vacation is over."

Oh, yes, don't I know it? January once more. Wake with the alarm before it's light, ride the school bus through the bitter gray morning. Try to do the reading I didn't do last night. Then stagger from class to class, boredom to boredom, my eyes foggy with all the sleep I haven't gotten. Eleventh grade now. I turned sixteen last month.

She stands beside me, resting her weight on the back of my chair, touching my shoulder with her fingers. I lean forward. It makes me nervous when my mother touches me. I smell the sour sickness of her body. I don't turn around, but I can see her in my mind: spindly limbs, gaunt, peaky face. Her thick cat eyeglasses, the lenses like teardrops. I wear glasses too.

"What are you writing?"

"Oh . . . something for English class."

"English was my best subject," she says.

When she was in high school, I guess. English is my best subject also. When I write, the teachers tell me, I sound almost like a grown-up.

"A story?" she says, leaning over me, trying to read what I've written.

"Sort of. We're supposed to write . . . a kind of journal." I'm making this up as I go along. "Of somebody who we are. Who we might be."

"A story," she says, as if that made it so. As if she still knew me from inside out, top to bottom, the way she did when I was little.

But this isn't a story. And it has nothing to do with any English assignment. Writing a story, I know the twists and turns in advance. I know how it's going to come out. This . . . journal, I guess, comes from a place I don't yet know, and it unfolds itself inside me, bit by bit, so I can't see beyond the next folding.

"You know it upsets Daddy," she says.

"What upsets him?"

"You staying up to all hours like this. Night after night."

And not even out on dates, like a normal teenager. I know the way my father thinks. Sixteen; at that age I ought to go out with girls. I don't; therefore I'm weird. Abnormal. Not really his son. I investigate UFOs; that makes me weird. I study the Bible too; that makes me weirder. He has no idea what I'm going through.

Neither does she, though most of the time she's nicer about it. I touch my hand to my pants pocket; my wallet's there. When she's gone, I'll take it out, look at the card.

"Danny!"

His voice, irritable, calls from the den. "What, Dad?" I yell back.

"How much more you gonna be up?"

"Maybe another half hour."

I hear him grumble to himself. I hear everything that goes on in this house—this little matchbox the three of us live in, all the rooms jammed together, no doors except for the bedrooms and the bath. We moved here ten years ago, after the heart attack, because the house is all on one floor. My mother can't climb stairs.

She nods at me, as if to say: *You hear that? A half hour. You promised.*

Does this story—journal, whatever—come from some UFO world? An alternate reality, where I'm still Danny Shapiro, and Jeff Stollard and Rosa Pagliano are still people who've been in my life? Where nevertheless we say things, do things, experience things that have a weight beyond ordinary reality?

It's possible. I've read articles about automatic writing, ouija boards, communication through our souls from the beyond. Mostly I don't believe those articles. They're written by crackpots. I'm a scientific UFOlogist. If we're to solve the mystery of the disks, as we surely will, if only we keep working at it, ignore the idiots who ridicule us, it will be through scientific research and analysis. Nothing else.

The images rose within me this afternoon, as I rode home on the school bus. It seemed half a dream, yet I know I was awake. The other kids' songs, their teasing, their yelps of laughter at jokes I don't quite understand washed around me like water around my bubble of air. It was like remembering things I'd known, but for years had barely thought of.

—images or feelings perhaps, stimulated within my brain. And while I tasted the relief that I wasn't going to be squashed after all, at the same time pondering how remarkable it was that this disk, this alien craft, should descend over me like a spider on its thread and speak to me mind to mind—

My mother eases into bed. I hear her through the wall that separates her bedroom from mine.

—the object pulled up, lifted back into the sky, shrank to the apparent size of a silver dollar held at arm's length. Then a quarter. Then a dime. It moved away, continuing its interrupted path westward, until it vanished in the distance—

My hand stops writing. All on its own; my brain just watches what's happening, perplexed, marveling. I lay my pen down. I know I can't force this. I pull my wallet from my pocket, and there's the card, hidden behind the driving learner's permit that arrived yesterday in the mail.

The UFO Investigators

Member _____

shall be accorded all privileges

pertaining to that post

signed _____

Headquarters OR9-3781, OR8-0496

The first phone number was mine. The second—"ORegon 8-0496"—was Jeff Stollard's. Still is, though now they've made it all numbers. In eighth grade, and the summer before that, Jeff and I were best friends. That fall we wrote our science paper on UFOs together; we got all excited, agreed we'd keep on until we found the truth, write a book about it. What are UFOs? Where are they from? Do they come to help us or to conquer and destroy? I still search for answers. Jeff no longer cares.

Christmas vacation of eighth grade—just before New Year's 1963. I walked the mile and a half to Jeff's house. There'd been snow, but the weather had turned sunny, a bit warmer, the sidewalks awash with the melt. Jeff and

I ran off the cards on his toy printing press, and in homeroom after vacation we announced our club. Rosa Pagliano came up right away and told me she wanted to join. Me. Not Jeff.

Wherever she is—does she still have the card I signed for her?

I imagine Jeff threw his away long ago.

But I have mine, softened and worn from three years in my wallet. On the back is the heart I drew, pierced with an arrow, *DS & RP* written inside. *This time*, I told myself, *I'll turn it over, look at the heart, bring back my old dreams*. I can't. It hurts too much.

DS could stand for *Dumb Shit* as well as *Danny Shapiro*.

I wish I'd written my initials out in full, DAS.

The *A* is for Asher, my mother's grandfather, who died in the old country. That's why I read the Bible, so I can understand the old man I never met and know the reason his name is in mine. I don't believe in God. I pray when I'm desperate, *Please, dear Lord, let it not be too late for me*. Too late—to be normal. To be invited to parties, have friends and girlfriends; the feeling deep in my soul says I was half, now I'm whole. No more hunger and thirst . . .

That's my only prayer. Seldom do I resort to it. I know there's no one listening.

I investigate UFOs because unlike God, they are real and can be seen.

"Danny!"

My father sounds louder now, and angrier. How would it be to live in a house that's dark and quiet sometimes, where parents go out together and I can be alone? But my mother's too sick. We go out only as a family, to visit my grandmother for the Jewish holidays. Until the break-in we hardly even locked our door. My mother was—she *is*—always home.

"Yes, Dad?" I call out.

"Will you turn off that goddamn light and get to sleep? It's past midnight, for God's sake!"

And only now have I picked up my pen. I should begin to be frightened. Not of his walloping me when he comes storming in; he's never done that. But of the tidal wave blindness of his rage, the bitter words that burn like lava, that will leave me scorched and desolate and sleepless afterward as I struggle to swallow what the three of us spend our lives pretending isn't so. Namely, that he hates me and everything I am.

I run my free hand over my face. No pimples, at least none ripe for lancing. So tonight the worst is unlikely. "Yes, Dad," I holler. "In a minute."

It'll be a lot more than a minute. I can't help myself. It's flowing again, pouring through my pen, and will take me, if only I can follow, toward the place of truth, the heart of all secrets—

Shivering—from the chill, from the terror of the death that had hovered above me and now was gone, at least for now—I pulled myself up from the ground. I brushed bits of dirt and grass from my heavy coat. I felt in my pocket for my keys and let myself into the house.

It was dark there . . .

. . . and very quiet, except for the phone on the kitchen wall, ringing loudly over and over. It had been ringing even as I opened the door. My watch read 11:37.

"Hello?"

"Danny! Are you all right?"

Jeff Stollard. I pressed the receiver against my ear, breathing hard. "Damn near crushed me," I said, as soon as I could speak.

"What? What crushed you? What are you talking about?"

My parents must not have been home. Lucky for me. I could almost hear my father: *Don't your friends know better than to phone you in the middle of the night?* But he wasn't around, nor my mother. Jeff and I could talk freely, as long as we needed. Like the summer before, between seventh and eighth grade, when one or two evenings a week we sailed off on our bikes into the softening light, and when tired of riding, we walked the bicycles, no parents to eavesdrop, until we'd talked through everything we cared to understand. Religion, mostly; how his being Baptist made him different from me, me different from almost everyone in our school. What happens to us, if anything, after we're dead.

"So you got the signal?" I said.

"Told you it'd work."

My keys were still in my hand, the Delta Device attached. The Delta rested in my palm, a shadow among shadows. I ran my thumb over it. Two small triangles of sheet metal, their edges hammered into curves and soldered together, the wiring pressed inside. It pained me to feel the lumpy, splattery soldering, to remember how the gun had jumped and trembled in my hand.

Jeff had done his better, smoother. In metal shop he always did better than I did.

"But what was the emergency?" he said.

I tried to tell him. My teeth chattered; I had to stop and take a few breaths before I could go on. "Whoa, whoa," he said. "Are you trying to tell me this thing actually landed?"

"No, it didn't land! My God, if it had landed—"

"I'm not your God, Danny."

"For God's sake! I just meant—"

"I just meant, don't take the Lord's name in vain!"

"I'd have been squooshed like a bug!" I screamed, and felt my saliva spray over the receiver. I felt myself getting demerits, over the telephone wires, for being hysterical. "It was bearing down on top of me," I said. "And—and—"

"And?"

"It spoke to me."

"Really? What did it say?"

A serious question? Sarcastic? Jeff can be both, and you usually don't know, even from his expression, until afterward.

" 'Until the seeding,' " I said.

"The *seeding*?"

He spelled the word out, and I confirmed it. *The seeding.* Even as I wondered how I'd earlier lost the memory of what the disk said and why it just popped out now, talking with him.

"What's *that* supposed to mean?" he said.

I couldn't tell whether he was going to laugh or have me exorcised, try once more to convert me so I won't go to hell when I die. "Until the seeding," I repeated, and felt the electric tingling shoot up through my legs, my thighs, the two currents meeting in my belly and running upward. My hand shook so I could barely hold the receiver.

"It was heading westward," I said. "Toward Braxton."

He didn't answer, and I knew what he was thinking. Rosa Pagliano lives in Braxton. Would the disk stop over her house, as it had over mine? Descend to her, speak to her? Take her inside? I thought of how she'd smiled at me in music class, while everybody was singing that song "And I'll not marry at all, at all, and I'll not marry at all . . ." And then I really began to shake.

"Do you think—you know—I should phone Rosa? Let her know—to go outside—she might see it too—"

"You wouldn't dare," Jeff said.

"Don't be mad—"

But he'd hung up. I stood, receiver in hand, and felt my heart going *thumpa-thumpa-thump*, the way it does in sentimental books. Only this was for real, very unpleasant, and I wanted it to stop, to be as I'd been before I saw the UFO, before I knew there were things in the sky besides moon and planets and stars, airplanes and birds, the ordinary stuff a little kid might know. Once or twice I heard my father yell, "Will you turn off that goddamn light and get to sleep?" It had to have been my imagination. My father wasn't even home—I could not hear him mumbling in his sleep from the bed he'd set up for himself in the den, because he couldn't stand lying next to my mother anymore—and besides I hadn't turned on any light. I hung up the receiver. After a few minutes I lifted it again. With trembling fingers I dialed Rosa Pagliano's telephone number.

CHAPTER 2

TWENTY-NINE DAYS LATER CAME THE BREAK-IN. IT WAS FRI-day night, January 18, 1963. My parents and I had gone to Trenton, to my grandmother's, to eat her dinner in honor of the Sabbath, which she had kept on observing in the religious way after my grandfather died, long after my father and even my mother had stopped doing that kind of thing. It's a twenty-minute drive from Kellerfield, Pennsylvania, where we live.

We got back after eleven. My father was the first one in the house.

"All right," he said. "Which of you two left the door hanging wide open, so anybody in the goddamn world can just walk in and help themselves?"

It wasn't me. When we left home, I'd helped my mother out to the car; she was bundled up against the frigid night in two sweaters and her heaviest winter coat and a blanket draped around her. I made sure she didn't slip on the ice patches in the carport. My father locked up after us. Or, it seemed, didn't lock up.

I was about to point this out. But then my father switched on the kitchen light, and we had other things to think about besides whose fault it was.

My mother took one look, let out a weak scream, and shuffled off as fast as she could move. "I can't look!" I heard her say. The kitchen was ransacked. We didn't dare see what they'd done in the living room. We followed her to her bedroom. It was the same there as in the kitchen: all the drawers open, contents dumped on the floor. She collapsed onto her bed, sobbing, wailing.

"Don't they know I'm *sick*?" she blurted out between sobs.

Burglars should have known not to break into the home of a sick woman. My father stood looking at her, shaking his head, an expression of disgust on his smooth, handsome face, as if at a loss to imagine why having your house broken into should have that effect on anyone. Or maybe I was the one who felt disgusted. He hurried out to the kitchen to phone Sy Goldfarb, our family doctor, to find out what he should do in case this brought on another heart attack. Meanwhile I went to my own room to see what was gone from there. And, at first, was relieved.

My drawers, like my mother's, had been emptied onto the floor. Hardly anything, though, seemed to be missing. Later, when things calmed down, we did an inventory and found practically nothing had been stolen. The burglars had even left the TV in the living room, which surely any thief would have wanted. It wasn't clear how they'd gotten in. My father insisted he'd locked the door, and no windows had been broken into.

The only thing taken was my briefcase, out of my closet, with a chunk of my UFO files—my report on my sighting the month before, the first three chapters of the book Jeff Stollard and I were writing together— inside it.

"So now they can read what you wrote about them," Jeff said to me. He handed me a sheaf of crinkly, smeary onionskin papers with *CHAPTER 3: THREE MEN IN BLACK* typed at the top of the first page. I'd worked long and hard on that chapter; good thing I'd made a carbon copy, kept it separate from the original.

"Jeff, I told you. It wasn't the three men who broke into our house."

"Says you."

"Says the police."

Eight days had passed since the robbery. It was the last Saturday in January—sun just up, sky a flawless blue, yet windy and cold enough to freeze my fingers inside my gloves. Jeff and I were at the Kellerfield shopping center, on the bus about to leave for Philadelphia. The police investigators had come to our house, dusted in vain for fingerprints, filled in their forms, and gone. My mother could again sleep most of the way through the night. "If it isn't the Bobbsey twins back again," the bus driver said as we climbed aboard, our dollar bills extended for change. "We're not twins," Jeff said. "Not even brothers." The two of us do kind of look alike—same thick horn-rimmed glasses, same quiet, reserved air. But Jeff is a few months older and more sturdily built. His eyes are pale blue; mine are brown. My hair is darker than his too. He's always made a lot of these differences.

"The police told you it wasn't the three men?" he said. "You asked them that, in so many words?"

"No, of course not—"

The driver put the bus in gear, and we were on our way. One more research trip to the microfilm archives in the Philadelphia library, just like its predecessors, only today with a difference I didn't think I was very comfortable with. Or rather, that I knew I was damned *un*comfortable with.

"Jeff, you sure this stops in Braxton? It didn't two weeks ago."

"They've added a stop. Improved service. Look, you can ask him"—he gestured toward the driver—"if you don't believe me." But the driver was bending over the wheel, swinging the bus onto the Philadelphia highway. I opened my new leather briefcase, replacement for the one they'd stolen, and slipped the Three Men in Black chapter into it.

Jeff sat in front of me. We each had a full seat; hardly anyone else was on the bus. Soon, when we reached Braxton, he wouldn't be alone in his seat. I, unfortunately, would. "I'm through with this too," he said, passing me a slim gray book with *Flying Saucers and the Three Men—Albert K. Bender* printed on the cover. "Didn't believe a word."

"Neither did I."

"Yes, I gathered," he said, and grinned, as if I'd done something funny. I flipped through the pages, filled with my marginal notes. This was Albert Bender's tell-all book, just published. Only what it told was mostly nonsense. As far as I was concerned, the book was itself part of the cover-up.

For there really had been three men in black suits; that much was documented. They'd first appeared in 1953, in Bridgeport, Connecticut. Bender, an internationally known UFO researcher, had stumbled on the secret of the flying disks and was about to reveal it. The three men came knocking at his door. They left him too sick to eat, too scared to speak.

"And now they've come for you," said Jeff.

"It wasn't them. The police told us. They think it was teenagers, probably from Braxton"—because Braxton was an older town, a poorer town, that had been here sixty years before anyone thought of putting up a suburban development called Kellerfield. Yet Rosa Pagliano, lovely and smart, like the rose in Spanish Harlem in the song, was from there. "That coed didn't have anything to do with it either. She probably was a Temple University student, just like she said."

"A likely story."

Jeff wasn't serious. He didn't really believe Bender's three men had bur-gled our house, any more than he believed a UFO had dropped from heaven and said to me, "Until the seeding." He'd have laughed if I'd told him how I'd taken to scanning our street through the early winter dusk for a strange car with three riders, coming back to our home to finish what they'd left undone. I imagined them slender and impossibly tall, like shadows at sunset.

"If that girl was really from the college," said Jeff, "how come she didn't give her name?"

"She did. My mother couldn't remember, is all."

"We're getting into Braxton," said Jeff.

I looked out the window. He was right; we'd left the highway. Must be a new stop along the Philadelphia route. Peeling weather-beaten houses stood on either side of the road. The sidewalks were broken and dirty.

"The break-in was twenty-nine days," I said, "after the night of my UFO."

"So?"

"That's almost exactly a lunar month."

"So?"

Tell him about the phone call I'd received? For the dozenth time I de-cided: better not. The bus slowed. A tingling, mostly unpleasant, spread up-ward from my lower abdomen. "There she is," Jeff said.

There she was. Standing beside a grimy, graffiti-spattered bus stop sign, wrapped in a gray coat that looked as if it hadn't been bought for her—the girl Jeff and I both were crazy about. Rosa.

"Scoot over, will you?" she said to Jeff.

The driver pulled away from the Braxton stop, as if in a hurry. My heart, which had begun its damned *thumpa-thumpa-thump* the instant I saw her at the bus stop, began to calm down. She turned in her seat, gave me a smile, and it started up all over again.

Rosa liked me. We'd been friends since seventh grade, when she was the cute, petite girl sharing a desk with me in social studies class. In eighth grade she was still petite but had blossomed. I don't have to explain what I mean by "blossomed." Jeff noticed it, though, before I did. Her brown eyes were huge, her lips full, yet her face overall put me in mind of a kitten.

Maybe it was her cheekbones. Her honey-blond hair tumbled in curls around her cheeks. She wouldn't wear a hat, cold as it was. Or maybe she didn't have one.

"*Brrr*, it's cold! How much longer, huh, guys?"

"How much longer what?" Jeff said to her.

"Having to take these stupid buses."

There were places she wanted to go, Rosa told me once, that couldn't be reached by local bus. The tickets couldn't be paid for out of babysitting money. Jeff started to talk about getting our driver's licenses in another three years, but she wasn't interested. What she wanted was for us to make our own UFO to travel in. Now.

"Come on, guys! We can do it. So I won't freeze my poor hiney off at bus stops."

I may have blushed at the mention of her hiney. She may have noticed me blushing. One time, in seventh grade, she'd pulled up her dress halfway when the social studies teacher wasn't looking, to show me— But these were painful thoughts. Dirty ones too, and I didn't want to think them. "*Brrr*, I'm cold!" she said again. Jeff put his arm around her shoulders and squeezed her to him.

Surely I'd turned redder than Rudolph's nose. I looked out the window so Rosa wouldn't see . . . and wondered once more whether the busy signal I got when I phoned her, the night of my UFO, had been Jeff calling her up.

I never knew. I couldn't bring myself to ask. For all I know it was Rosa's mother on the line with one of her alcoholic "suitors," complaining about the latest child support payment that hadn't arrived.

Probably, though, it was Jeff.

What did he say to her that night? I've lain awake, sometimes for hours, imagining. *Danny's seen a flying saucer!*—he must have begun. *Poor old Danny—in and out of his dreams. Hardly even knows what's dream and what's real!* Then his smug chuckle; and Rosa would have laughed with him.

Or maybe not. She's stood up for me more than once when the kids made fun—of my wearing glasses, dreaming my way through gym class, missing school for Jewish holidays. But how can I know?

From the seat in front of me I heard what I thought was a kiss. I willed my head not to turn, my eyes to stay focused on Braxton's unappealing sights. I wondered what these streets would look like if there'd been war last October. If the Russians hadn't backed down and pulled their missiles out of Cuba.

I kind of almost wished it had happened, so none of us would be here. I wished I were somewhere else. Just where, I couldn't have said. Only not here, not with these people. Not on this bus.

The Monday before our break-in, a girl knocked on our door. I was at school, my father at work, my mother just up from the bed rest she needs to digest her lunch. "Zaftig," my mother described the girl. Pretty; or she might have been if not for her ugly thick glasses. Studious, my mother called her. A bookworm—well, like me.

She told my mother she was a sociology major at Temple, doing fieldwork for a class project on the postwar suburbs. My mother gave her tea. They sat and talked.

That Friday night the burglary. Coincidence? I couldn't decide.

"All right, Danny," I heard Rosa say. "Hand over that book."

The semiurban winter landscape, built up yet desolate, whizzed by outside the bus window. *Flying Saucers and the Three Men* lay on my lap. "I told her about it over the phone last night," Jeff said, grinning.

They'd chatted for hours, no doubt. Jealousy, sick and ugly, filled my mind; I willed it away. Jeff's fingers played with one of Rosa's curls. She looked like she enjoyed the touch yet moved herself apart from him, very slightly. I gave her *Flying Saucers and the Three Men*. She opened it, began tearing through it, one page after another, until I wondered if she was going to read the whole book right there on the bus.

" 'Preliminary evaluation,' " she read from the handwritten note on the back page. " 'Account is a hoax.' Don't need to know more than that, do we? Two whole paragraphs proving it's a hoax. Signed with initials: DAS. What's the *A* stand for, Danny?"

"Asher," I said.

"It was his great-grandfather back in Poland, or Russia, or something," said Jeff.

"Lithuania," I said. "But, guys—"

"Your great-grandfather was a rabbi, wasn't he?" said Jeff. He smiled his tight little needle-Danny smile, as when he makes some joke like that my eyes are brown because I'm full of shit up to my eyeballs. "And your grand-father's a rabbi too. Isn't he?"

"*Was*," I said. "He died when I was four."

I remembered my mother's father, though. A gentle old man, sitting on the porch of the big old house in Trenton where we lived until after my mother's heart attack, reading yellowed and crackly old books in Hebrew. "And he wasn't a rabbi," I said. "Just a sort of Bible scholar"—as if it made a difference, as if a Bible scholar's grandson would somehow be less alien in Rosa's eyes than a rabbi's. "Now, come on, guys. Please . . ."

"Much shorter note now," Rosa said. "In a different handwriting. 'I agree completely. JDS.' Now those initials: could they possibly stand for—"

"Jeffrey Duncan Stollard," I said. I put the emphasis on the *Duncan*, and most especially the *Dunc*.

Rosa gave a loud sigh. She closed the book and handed it back, not looking at me. She rested her head against the seat, closed her eyes. Had she slept the night before? That mother of hers; what had she been doing now? If Rosa were to bare her legs like in seventh grade, would I see once more that crazy woman's marks upon them?

Meanwhile Jeff was talking, trying to get her attention.

The three men, who according to Bender's new story were glowing-eyed aliens from another solar system, had given Bender a small metal disk. He could contact them by squeezing the disk and saying the word *Kazik*, sort of like our Delta Devices.

"Bender says"—Jeff laughed, as though this were something funny that maybe he could get Rosa to laugh about too—"they kidnapped him, see, and took him on board their spaceship. Then they implanted something in his brain. So any time he even *thought* about telling anybody who they were, what they were doing to him, he got these terrible headaches. And if he *did* ever tell anybody—"

"Yeah?" said Rosa, her eyes wide open.

"*Poof!* He'd disintegrate, right on the spot!"

"His whole *body*?" said Rosa. "It'd just *disintegrate*?"—

—I've got to stop writing. I should never have put these things on paper. Mom will find them, on one of her prowls through here while I'm at school.

She'll see how I'm describing our break-in, which happened, sure, but not the way I'm telling it—

She'll know what I've thought, felt, imagined about Rosa Pagliano, the shiksa.

Will my mother disintegrate like Bender, once she knows?

Or will it be me who's turned to powder, in an instant's blinding flash?

CHAPTER 3

WHEN WAS I FIRST IN LOVE WITH ROSA?

I ask myself that after I've gone to bed sometimes, when I can't sleep and I toss and turn, hearing my mother do the same on the other side of the wall. Probably Thursday, December 20, 1962, the night Jeff and I had our meeting at the Kellerfield library to put the final touches on our science paper on UFOs.

That was a good paper, A or A+ for sure. We'd started it two months before, the same day Kennedy announced the blockade on Cuba, and we joked that if there were war, we'd never have to hand it in, because we'd be dead and so would all the teachers. Now it was finished. We proofread it together, and when we were done, we gathered up our books and went outside the library and stood by the bicycle rack. Talking.

It was very cold that night. No moon; the stars clearer than I'd ever seen. They looked almost like the twinkling lights on the Christmas tree I'd wanted so badly when I was little, but my mother had always said no. We talked about Rosa.

"I like her," Jeff said.

"I like her too," I said.

"Then you're my rival," said Jeff. "How shall we settle this? Duel to the death?"

I felt pained, as if I hadn't been understood. I looked toward the stars— the red of Betelgeuse, the ice-blue, diamond-blue glitter of Sirius. That's what the Christmas tree is, a ladder winding its way up through the stars, toward the biggest star of all. Happy are they who climb it.

"I didn't mean I liked her *in that way*," I said.

"I did mean I liked her *in that way*," said Jeff.

I swallowed hard. Maybe I did kind of like Rosa in that way. But a girl whose name proclaimed shiksa? Living in Braxton with her mother, a dyed-haired divorcée who did awful things to her when no one was looking? My mother's not a snob, or a bigot either, but she has her feelings. Also, Jeff had spoken first.

There were new things in this sky that I hadn't read about in my astronomy books or found on my star charts. I didn't know what they were. . . . That very day, in music class, we'd sung the song about the girl who wouldn't marry at all, at all, and Rosa sat behind me to my right. She sang loud, clear, and I thought how pretty her voice was. Then I turned around, and what did I see but those warm brown eyes looking straight at me.

She laughed as she sang:

> O I'll not marry a man who's shy
> For he'd run away if I winked an eye . . .

At first I thought she was laughing at me, telling me the song was right, that boys who are shy like me aren't worth marrying. Then I realized it was something very different.

She's gone. But still I see her laughing. I see her waiting, sweaty and bold, for me to decide whether I'll dance with her. And I call myself *fool, fool, fool*, and I can't go to sleep.

The break-in at our house was Friday, January 18, 1963. Four days afterward the phone rang in our kitchen.

"Jeff?" I said, picking up the receiver.

"Count the days."

The words came out in a weird croak, as if whoever was calling had a high voice and he was trying to make it sound low, adult, mature. "Jeff," I said, "knock it off, will you? This isn't funny."

No answer. I realized this wasn't Jeff, or anyone else pulling a prank, but something serious and very strange. Could this be the same voice that had said "Until the seeding"? But that had been less a spoken utterance than a resonance within my mind. These were words coming from a throat, from vocal cords I assumed were human.

I waited, feeling something like bugs crawling over my skin. The caller, whoever or whatever he was, also waited. Finally I said: "I don't understand. Count the days from what? *To* what?"

Again silence. Had he hung up? I didn't think so, though I couldn't hear any sound from the receiver. "Count them forward?" I said. "Or backward?"

"Backward. Follow the moon."

Then *click!* and I knew I'd heard all I was going to. I started to dial Jeff's number, so I could tell him what just happened. Then I stopped. This was something private to me that I had to work out for myself. It was late afternoon; I was alone in the house. I walked over to the calendar on the kitchen wall and confirmed what I'd remembered. There were twenty-nine days between my UFO sighting and the break-in. A lunar month is twenty-nine and a half.

Follow the moon.

Jeff and Rosa held hands as we walked to the library from the bus stop, past the Logan Square fountain. In his fine tenor he sang songs from *Brigadoon*. Jeff is crazy about musicals; even back then he knew dozens of show tunes. He mocked my terrible voice when I tried to sing too. So I stopped trying. "There's a smile on my face for the whole human race," he sang to Rosa, and I wished I could chime in with the refrain, "It's almost like being in love." But the words would have come out a tuneless croak, as if one of the bronze frogs ringing the fountain had come to life. I walked, silent, behind them.

It was so cold the fountain had frozen. The frogs, which normally spouted arches of water through their mouths, grew icicle beards instead. "Like Santa Claus!" Jeff hooted, and I tried to laugh. But the whiskered frogs reminded me of my great-grandfather in Lithuania, whose face I knew from the picture that hangs in my grandmother's house. Shame chilled me through my winter coat. What would saintly, gray-bearded old Asher think of me—his son's grandson, the bearer of his name—riding buses and subways on the Sabbath with his friends the sheygetz and the shiksa, the girl whose pale, tender face hovered in my half dreams like a rising moon?

My mother put a lot of the old ways behind her when she married my father. This one she didn't. It was OK that I had Gentile friends, even girls. But that was when I was little and the girls were just friends. Not anymore. "All the music of life seems to be," Jeff sang, holding Rosa's hand but gazing off into the frigid cloudless sky, while she threw me a backward glance, her lips skeptically puckered. "Like a bell that is ringing for me . . ."

The microfilms were kept in the library's Newspaper Room, on the ground floor below street level. With much laughing and touching, Jeff showed Rosa how to thread them onto the spool. So now there were three of us, not just him and me like the weeks before. For hours we sat at the microfilm machines, our index cards filling with UFO sightings from the archives of obscure newspapers all over the country. Luminous disks in the nighttime. Silvery by day, sparkling in the sun as they weaved among the clouds. Egg-shaped UFOs, cigar-shaped UFOs. UFOs of fluorescent red, and every other possible color.

Patterns eluded us. It took faith to believe they'd emerge. With cramped hand and weary eyes I looked up from my work toward Rosa. She and Jeff sat in front of her machine, not writing, not reading, just holding their hands in the green-tinged light over the screen. Jeff put his hand on top of Rosa's. Then she put her other hand on his, then his over hers. . . . In a minute they were giggling at their game, and I tried not to watch while I hoped a librarian, some elderly scold, would come over to remind them this was a library, a quiet place for solemnity and seriousness.

I turned back to my own machine. I cranked the handle; I watched the pages of long-destroyed newspapers whiz by under my nose. When I stopped, I saw the newsprint on the screen beneath me, looking so real it seemed I could reach out and touch the paper.

But there was no paper. There was only the screen. If I held my hand close above it, the newsprint appeared on the back of my hand as well as the surrounding screen. My hand then took on a ghostly appearance, not invisible exactly but transparent, as though my bone and flesh had become unreal. The only things real were the letters and words of the long-forgotten stories, shining upon my skin.

CHAPTER 4

Somewhere in Chicago, it is reported, there is an apartment house where the elevator stops conventionally at the basement level. But it also goes down, down, *down* to a much lower level, when the down button is pushed in a certain coded manner. . . .

AND IN A TINY TOWN IN PENNSYLVANIA LIVES A METALWORKER named Richard S. Shaver. He receives through his welding gun—or maybe his memories—revelations from under the surface of the earth. Of beings called dero, survivors of an ancient race of space travelers abandoned on Earth when the sun turned poisonous. Its rays made the dero mad; their madness made them evil. They live underground, in a network of hidden caves. The UFOs are their secret airships. They are the devils of the ancient myths.

"From immemorial times," Shaver was told, "the dero have had their Hells in the underworld, and it has never ceased. You see, you surface Christians are not so far wrong in your pictures of Hell, except that you do not die in order to go there, but wish for death to release you once you arrive. There have always been Hells on earth, and this is one of them."

Crackpot stuff, I always thought. *Only a nutcase could believe it.* Now I'm not so sure.

After lunch I left Jeff and Rosa in the Newspaper Room and took the elevator to the Rare Book Room on the third floor. "Follow the moon"—and to do that,

I needed to find Jewish calendars because the Jewish year is lunar. I was told they'd be in the Rare Book Room.

In the elevator I was alone. I pressed the button marked "3." As soon as the doors closed, I began pressing buttons rapidly and at random. I don't remember which ones I pressed. To my relief, or maybe disappointment, I didn't go down, down, *down*. The elevator car shuddered and paused. I thought I was going to be trapped between floors. Then it moved again and stopped back at the first floor. Three young men who looked like college students got in. Again I pressed "3."

I'd never been in the Rare Book Room before, and I was curious and a bit excited about what I might find. At the entrance was a turnstile. Just inside, to the left, were a desk with a sign saying J. MARGULIES and, behind the desk, several file cabinets. No one sat at the desk or at the large reading table in the middle of the room. Rows of books were locked behind a thick chain-link barrier, ceiling to floor. No windows; no apparent sign of life.

I'll leave, I thought, *and come back later.*

But the turnstile would go only one way. I didn't feel much like climbing back over it. My best bet was to wait and see if this "J. Margulies" might turn up.

Framed exhibits, pages from old manuscripts and books, hung on the walls. One of these caught my eye. The page within the frame was about twelve by eighteen inches. Dense lines of writing, in a delicate undulating script that I supposed to be Arabic, surrounded a beautifully colored central picture. The picture's focus was something that looked like a winged horse with a human face, flying through the night sky. Its rider wore a turban and ornate, flowing robes. Above horse and rider, enormous stars glared out of the deep indigo.

The exhibit to the right was also interesting. Here again was a central picture framed by the mysterious, delicate writing. A large, voluptuous woman, with huge black eyes and flowing hair, grasped the clothing of a smaller, young-looking man. The artist had dressed both of them elaborately but managed to leave much of the woman's bosom naked.

I examined the picture closely. I read both labels. The one, of the winged creature that had first attracted me, read: Miraj-Nameh, Persia, fourteenth century. The other was labeled Joseph and Zuleikha, Mughal India, sixteenth century.

"*May* I help you?"

I turned, startled, to see a young man towering over me. That at least was my first impression. It took me a moment to realize he was a teenage boy, just a few years older than myself. He was tall, well over six feet, and extraordinarily thin. He had brown hair and slightly buckteeth. He was neatly dressed, in a blue blazer, a dark tie, and a white shirt that looked heavily starched. How he'd gotten so close without my hearing him, I couldn't imagine.

"*May* I help you?" he said again.

"Yes, certainly." That was all I could say. I could not for the life of me remember what I'd come here for. Then it came back to me. "They told me this was the place to find Jewish calendars."

"Jewish calendars? You mean, those things the funeral homes put out? Well," he said. Then he said: "What do you want *those* for?"

I hadn't expected the question. Could I tell him I wanted a moon-based calendar to "count the days" backward in lunar twenty-nine-day cycles? Suburban burglary . . . UFO encounter . . . and so on, back through the cycles, through the years, until unexplained events of every sort were brought into the pattern? Impossible. I'd be packed off to the loony bin for sure.

"Never mind. None of my business, is it?" He threw himself into the swivel chair that was behind the J. MARGULIES desk, spun around in it, and began rummaging through one of the file drawers. "What years do you want?"

"Ohhh . . ." I started to say, *Back through 1947.* That was when the UFOs first began to appear, two and a half years before I was born. But he looked up at me and frowned, suspiciously, I thought, and it seemed wiser not to ask for too much. "Let's just try the last few. Start with 1960."

"Hmmm." He leaned back and stretched as he pondered this. The chair, which wasn't in the best condition, lurched backward. "That means we need to go back to Rosh Hashanah 1959. What year is that in the Jewish calendar, do you remember?"

I didn't. Still, it was some comfort he'd heard of Rosh Hashanah and seemed to know it falls a few months before everyone else's New Year. "Let's see what we've got," he said, leaning forward again. "Here's 5723, which looks like this year. And 5722, which is last year. These are the years reckoned from the Creation, aren't they?"

I nodded.

"How quaint. Not to say ridiculous. *Tantum malorum*, et cetera and so forth. That's Latin. I don't suppose you've learned any Latin, have you?"

"Huh? What?"

"Old saying. *Tantum malorum religio suadere potuit*—'So many evils has religion brought about!' Tribal morality, for instance. Also obscurantism, like thinking the world was created six thousand years ago. Or there's no life anywhere but the skin of this planet. Now I've probably offended you. I can see it by your face. Don't tell me you're religious? Studying to be a rabbi, or something?"

Creep. I suppressed a grimace. "No," I said, "I'm not at all religious. And about those calendars . . ."

"Yes, yes. That's what you're here for, the calendars. Not to listen to me chatter. Here's 5723, here's 5722. And 5721, which takes us back to September 1960. That's all we have, I'm afraid."

"That'll be fine." I scooped up the three calendars. "Why do they keep these in the Rare Book Room anyway?"

"Lord knows," he said, glancing at them. "The deathless artwork, I suppose. Got your library card with you?"

I gave him my card. He looked at it, looked at me. I thought I saw him nod, and that made me uneasy. He ran the card through a machine and stamped the calendars. "Building use only," he said, handing them to me. "Give them back at any of the library desks before you leave today. You don't have to come back up here."

"Got it."

I flipped through the most recent of the calendars. It advertised a different funeral home from the calendar hanging in my grandmother's kitchen but otherwise seemed pretty much the same. Each month was accompanied by a gaudy Bible illustration. I didn't recognize most of the pictures. I'd loved Bible stories when I was little, but lost interest in them a long time past and mostly forgotten them. September's picture, *JACOB'S DREAM AT BETH-EL*, was of an enormous shining, undulating staircase, its top hidden in distant clouds. Angels in robes climbed their way to and from the endless heights. Below it was printed: " 'And he took one of the stones of the place, and put it under his head, and lay down in that place to sleep. And he dreamed, and behold a ladder set up on the earth, and the top of it reached to heaven; and behold the angels of God ascending and descending on it'—Gen. 28:11–12."

"He*llo*-o? You haven't gone off to some other world, have you?"

I looked up from the picture, my skin all goose bumps. "It's just—something I remembered," I said, trying to explain. But the memory eluded me, and what did I need to explain to this weirdo anyway? I put the calendars in my briefcase and started to go.

"Not so fast. I've got to inspect your briefcase before I let you out. Nothing personal. Standard company policy."

I hoisted it onto the desk. "Nice briefcase," he said.

"Thanks."

"Looks brand-new."

"It is. Somebody stole the old one."

"What a pity. Nothing important in it, I hope?"

"Just the manuscript of a book I'm writing."

"Well. That *is* a pity. You should keep those things at home, in a secure place."

"It was at home. In a place I thought was secure."

He shook his head. "Seems like we're not safe in our own homes anymore. Assuming we ever were." All the while he'd been searching through the briefcase. He pulled out the book I'd carried to Philadelphia with me. "Well, well, *well*," he said. "Albert K. Bender, *Flying Saucers and the Three Men.* Tell me. How is dear old Al, these days?"

I stared at him while I tried to think of an answer. Of course I had no idea how Albert K. Bender was. I didn't know anyone who might know anyone who knew Bender. For me he was a remote, almost legendary figure, like Jacob and his angels on the shining stairway.

"And *how* are Al's three friends?" the boy went on. "From the planet—Kazik, or whatever its name was? The ones with the dark suits and the dark faces and the bright, bright eyes. Their eyes *shone like flashlights*, didn't he say?"

My mouth hung open. I tried, not very successfully, to force it shut.

"And how about the three *women* in black?" he said. "Only they don't wear black, do they? Tight uniforms, can't remember what color. You remember them, don't you? They're the ones who bring him onto the spaceship. Right before the brain implant. They paralyze him. They strip him naked. They massage every part of his body *without exception.* Italics mine."

"Wait a minute," I said. "How do you know about all this?"

"*Please*. Think you're the only person in the world who reads books? What I want to know is, *Why* do they all have eyes that shine like flashlights?"

"I—I—"

"Do their eyes just make it easier for Bender to see them? Or do *they* see better with glowing eyes? 'Why, what glowing eyes you have!' 'The better to *see-e-e* you with, my dear.'"

He gave a very effective horror movie laugh. I felt my flesh crawl. This was not a laugh, I thought, that should have emanated from a human throat. "Look," I said. "I really don't think we need to take Bender's book all that seriously."

"But we do need to take the three men seriously, don't we? And Harold Dahl's man in black. Remember him?"

Harold Dahl. 1947. Harbor patrolman at Maury Island, off the coast of Washington State. "The *man* in black," said the boy. "Just one. The other two must have been on missions to other galaxies. He pays Dahl a visit. He tells him he saw something he shouldn't have. Tells him word for word everything he saw. Warns him: if he loves his family, he won't *whisper* about it to anybody."

"Now, hold on," I said. "That Maury Island business was a hoax! Wasn't it?"

"Of course it was a hoax. Do you seriously believe a flying disk crashed into Puget Sound? Dropped slag into Dahl's boat? Killed his stupid dog? Do you think *anyone* believes that?"

"Then why are we even talking about it?"

"Because of the *people*. Don't you understand? The *people* involved. Harold Dahl is a man worth knowing. Before Maury Island he was in the dero caves. Fought his way out with a submachine gun. Marvelous story; vintage Harold Dahl. I'd arrange for the two of you to meet, except we lost track of him."

"Lost track?" How strange that this boy, met by chance, should know the people and things I wanted so badly to know myself. *Was* it chance? I began to feel frightened; I touched my hand to my pocket. The Delta Device was still there. "You lost track of Harold Dahl?"

"Completely vanished. Somewhere in the Southwest, New Mexico, I think. All of a sudden he's gone. Disappeared. So lost even God and the Internal Revenue Service can't find him."

"Who are you?" I said.

He must have been waiting for me to ask. He reached into his inner jacket pocket and whirled out a business card. "Julian Margulies, of the SSS. And, on alternate Saturday afternoons, of the Philadelphia Free Library. *At* your service."

I examined the card. A name, a Philadelphia address, and a telephone number crowded together at the bottom. Most of the upper part consisted of a sixty-degree angle, trisected, with an ornate capital *S* in each of its three segments. In each upper corner was a slender, pointed black oval, beginning near the trisected angle and rising outward toward the edges. If the ovals had been vertical, I'd have thought them the slit pupils of a cat's eyes. Horizontal, they'd resemble two flying disks seen from the side. As it was, they gave the impression of being the slanted, almond-shaped, wide-apart eyes of some humanlike but unspeakably strange creature.

Whatever—I didn't want to look at them. Their effect was hypnotic; I wasn't ready to be hypnotized. I forced my eyes down to the bottom of the card, to the name printed there. "What's the *A* stand for?" I said.

He looked baffled. "In your *name*," I said. " 'Julian A. Margulies,' it says here."

"Oh, *that* A. I'd forgotten. I don't use it very much. But it stands for Arcturus. If you must know." He looked at me solemnly, then raised his eyebrows a few times, rapidly, comically, as if doing a takeoff on Groucho Marx.

"Julian Arcturus Margulies?"

"That's right. I come from the *sta-a-ars*, don't you know?"

"And this SSS," I said, looking at the trisected angle. "What does that stand for?"

"Initials of the three men in black. Sigmund, Sandor, and—uh—Sammy. But you have the advantage of me, sir."

"Huh?" I said. "Oh." I fished in my wallet for something that might serve as a business card. The best I could find was a blank membership card for The UFO Investigators.

"How cute," he said. " 'The UFO Investigators.' Do I have the honor of addressing Mr. OR9-3781, or Mr. OR8-0496?"

I felt myself turn red. "I'm Danny Shapiro."

"Danny Shapiro. Of course. It was on your library card. How stupid of me.

Well, Danny Shapiro, I regret that we meet under these circumstances. With me dressed so informally, that is. I do own a black suit—"

"So do I," I said untruthfully.

"But I only wear it for funerals. And, of course, for terrorizing UFO investigators who've found out *too much*. I haven't yet got the hang of making my eyes glow like flashlights, however."

"I've got to go," I said.

I turned to leave. But then I stopped. "You know that picture you have on your wall," I said. "The one with the winged horse, or whatever the animal was, and the man riding it. I was looking at it before you came in. It—it fascinated me."

"The *Miraj-Nameh* illustration? It fascinated you? You don't say. You seemed a *lot* more interested in Joseph and Zuleikha. Mostly Zuleikha."

I blushed. I looked away. I could not stand to see him do another Groucho Marx imitation with his eyebrows. "Who was Zuleikha anyway?" I asked.

"Potiphar's wife. The lady who was always trying to get Joseph into bed with her. The Bible doesn't say what her name was. That's the Arabs for you. They think they know lots about the Bible that the Bible doesn't say."

"So that writing is Arabic?"

"Arabic or Persian. You'll have to ask Rochelle about that. If she can read it, it's Arabic. If not, it's Persian. Or maybe Urdu. I don't think Rochelle's ever learned Urdu."

"I have to ask—who?"

"Rochelle," he said loudly, as if I were bound to know who Rochelle was if only he pronounced her name distinctly enough. "Oh, that's right. You don't know Rochelle."

He looked at me closely. Suddenly, for no obvious reason, he broke into a grin. "No," I said. "I don't know Rochelle."

"Well, then. You ought to come over for dinner sometime."

"Dinner?"

"Yes, dinner. Why do you look so suspicious?" He didn't wait for me to answer, to explain I wasn't used to total strangers inviting me to dinner. "At our place. So you can meet Rochelle. Don't worry, you'll like Rochelle. You and she will have a *lot* to talk about."

"So Rochelle is your sister?"

He seemed to find the question extremely funny. "No, she isn't my sister," he said, laughing, mostly through his nose. He threw himself back into his chair and laughed some more. "*Not* my sister," he said again. He pushed a button under his desk; there was a loud click from the turnstile. "The phone number is on my card," he said. "Give me a call. We'll arrange something."

"Thanks," I said. I was about to put the card into my pocket but suddenly dropped it back onto his desk. There was something dangerous about that card—maybe those eyes printed on it, which I hoped sooner or later I'd be able to forget. If I took the card, my life would be changed in some way I could not foresee or undo once it had happened. "Well, see you around."

"Hey, wait, wait—"

I dashed out. The third-floor elevator was a few steps away from the entrance to the Rare Book Room. I heard him calling me; I had the sense of missing something. I was so eager to be gone I didn't stop to think what. I ran inside the elevator and pressed the button marked "G." I went down, down, *down*. From the elevator I rushed into the Newspaper Room.

And found no one there.

CHAPTER 5

THE ROOM WAS EMPTY. CAVERNOUS.

No Jeff, no Rosa. No shabby middle-aged men at the long brown tables, reading the current newspapers. The fluorescent ceiling lights were on as usual. But the microfilm machines were dark and deserted. Coats, notebooks, pens—all gone. Chairs neatly beneath the tables, newspapers back on their racks. There was no librarian.

My first thought was my watch had stopped. I hadn't been in sight of a window for hours. Somehow it had gotten to be past five; the library had closed. Outside the building it was dark and cold. The last bus to Kellerfield had left without me.

But the clock on the wall read 3:35, and the second hand swept around its face.

I stepped up to the long, curving counter. RING BELL FOR SERVICE, read a hand-lettered sign. I struck the bell with my hand, listened to it echo through the empty room. I waited. No one came.

I rang again, waited again. My fingers felt for the Delta Device. I forced my hand out of my pocket, back to the counter. Not yet time for that. Nothing was falling from the sky on top of me. Not yet.

For a minute or two I kept on pounding the bell. When I couldn't stand any more of its ringing, I ran out, down the winding corridor, up the stairs. Then up more stairs. Everywhere was neat. Still. Empty.

No librarians . . . no readers, browsers, borrowers . . . no guard at the main exit checking bags and briefcases. The late-afternoon sun shone through the windows of the high-ceilinged reading rooms, onto the carpeted floor. On the spines of silent rows of books, the gold lettering glittered.

Oh, God. It's begun.

UFO invasion? Nuclear war? The missiles that should have been fired last October: were they on their way?

"Jeff," I called out softly. Then, louder: "Kazik! Kazik!" Before I knew it, the Delta was out of my pocket and I'd squeezed it, hard. The soldering popped open. The wiring crammed inside the sheet metal casing erupted onto my palm.

I stared down at it. I tried to push it all back in, to force the gadget together long enough to send out a signal. All I managed was to cut my thumb on the metal's edge. The mass of curls and coils, spilled out, refused ingathering. The Delta was ruined, wrecked for good, useless as a teddy bear in a thunderstorm. I tossed it somewhere among the long tables and began to run.

At the elevator I jabbed the up button. The arrow of the dial above the sliding doors jerked its poky way along the ring of gold-colored numbers. If it didn't come soon, I'd go insane.

Julian Arcturus Margulies, sitting at his desk, seemed unsurprised to see me.

"That's the remarkable thing about rare books, isn't it?" he said. "You fall under their spell, you just can't stay away."

"*Julian.*"

"You don't have to be so alarmed. Your nice new briefcase isn't lost. You left it here next to my desk. I called after you, but you were in such a hurry, you just didn't hear—"

So that was what I'd had the sensation of missing. I no longer cared about that briefcase. "*Julian!*"

"Yes?" He peered at me with an expression of kind attention.

"Did they close early today? Or what?"

"Of course not. Why should they close early?"

"*The library is empty.*"

"What are you talking about?"

"Nobody's here! I went down to the ground floor, to the Newspaper Room, and there was nobody. Not in the reading rooms! Not anywhere!"

He looked puzzled. Only for a moment. "Oh, *that*," he said. "That happens sometimes. It'll be all right." He walked around the desk and put his hand on my shoulder. "Danny, you've got to stay calm. Are you listening to me?"

I nodded.

"You know the elevator you just got off?" He pointed down the hall. I nodded again. "Go back there. When you get in, push the button for the basement. The one marked 'B.' As in *boy*. Not 'G,' this time; the floor below it. Have you got that?"

"I think so," I said.

"When the doors open, walk out and turn to your left. Go about fifty feet, and you'll see a small door to the outside. To Nineteenth Street. It's below street level, though. Are you listening?"

"Uh-huh."

"Go out that door. Climb to the sidewalk. Directly up the slope. It's icy, but I think you can make it. You've got that?"

"Uh-huh."

"Then go around to Vine Street, to the front entrance. Come in again. It'll be all right."

I started off toward the elevator. "Danny!" he called.

"What?"

"Don't forget your briefcase."

I pressed "B." I rode down to the basement. I forced myself, faint with dread, down the dimly lit hallway. On either side of me boxes were stacked nearly to the ceiling, such that I could barely make my way through the passage. The door was where Julian had said it would be.

I slipped more than once, getting up that slope.

At first, when I reached the sidewalk, it was the library all over again. Nineteenth Street was empty, still, silent. But then I began to feel the rush of traffic, to hear the honking of a taxicab. I saw I'd wandered into the street and leaped back to the sidewalk. I leaned against a building, catching my breath. A man in earmuffs and a thick overcoat marched past, glaring.

It was a few minutes past four when I walked back through the library's entrance hall. Filled, as usual, with people. I wasn't ready for the Newspaper Room. I walked into the general reading room on the second floor and sat down at one of the long tables. I opened my briefcase. I pulled out Bender's *Flying Saucers and the Three Men* and the three Jewish calendars. I began flipping through the calendars, mostly looking at the pictures.

My eye fell upon Saturday, December 22, 1962. My thirteenth birthday, by the Jewish calendar. The day that should have been my bar mitzvah—

When I should have proclaimed myself a man.

Only my mother was too sick, so we couldn't—

I stopped leafing. I thought of all the things over the years that we couldn't do, I couldn't do, because she was too sick. She couldn't go outdoors; needed rest, needed quiet. Needed me to stay with her, read to her. My friends, when I had any, had to be hushed. Asked to leave the house if they couldn't be still . . .

Sadness transfixed me. I could not move so much as my eyeballs. I don't know how long it was before I felt a hand on my shoulder.

"You all right?"

Rosa Pagliano. Some kind of hallucination? Her touch was real, though, or had been before she took away her hand. Relief flooded me; happiness too. But also confusion. "What are you doing here?" I said.

"I wouldn't leave with Jeff. He wanted me to. You wouldn't believe the fight we had. They almost threw us out of the library, we were screaming so loud."

"So the bus *did* stop in Braxton—"

Of course it had. And today she'd come with us, not just me and Jeff. She'd climbed onto the bus at Braxton, told Jeff to move over, wiggled into the seat beside him. . . . Each detail so vivid; how had I forgotten, even for a moment? "Rosa," I said, and felt my tongue curl around her name.

"Where *were* you? Why didn't you come back to the Newspaper Room? We waited and waited."

Rosa slipped into the vacant chair beside me. She carried a book, which she slid into her lap, where I couldn't see it. I caught a whiff of her perfume, strong stuff, the kind the sexier girls in our school wear, but I'd never before noticed it on Rosa. Why hadn't I?

"Jeff got sick of waiting," she said. "He started carrying on, the way he always does when he doesn't get his way. Got himself so worked up, that finally—"

"I did come down. You were gone. The room was empty."

"Wha—a?" Her lips parted. "I understand," she said after a second, which was enough time for my eyes and mind to have glued themselves to those lips. Not quite rose red, as the poets say. Yet red enough, and luscious, without benefit of lipstick. I was too hypnotized, those few silent moments, to ask what it was she'd understood. "Finally he says to me, 'Come on! The hell with Danny! We're going home.' I told him to screw himself."

"You told him what?"

"To *screw himself.*" She broke out of her whisper. "Go home and listen to records of his stupid musicals, for all I cared. I wasn't going to leave you alone."

A librarian frowned at us, finger to her lips. Another minute and we *would* be thrown out. Rosa put her hand on my knee. "So he left by himself," she said. "Now listen to me, Danny—"

"Could I have your attention, please? The library is closing in twenty minutes. Please bring all materials to the checkout desk . . ."

And on and on, while I thought about Jeff, and what he'd do without Rosa as his girlfriend, and whether she liked him all that much to begin with. Whether after this we could still be friends. Our Delta Device, once the link between us, now a piece of junk, a silly, lumpish toy from eighth-grade metal shop—

"What's that book you've got?" I said when the loudspeaker voice finished.

"One of theirs."

It was still in her lap. I tried to make out what it was, then looked up, embarrassed. She'd think I was peeking under her skirt. As she snatched it away, I glimpsed the jacket picture: a battered, twisted rag doll, stringlike hair tumbled around its averted face. Also the title, *The Scandal of* something. "It's about—" I said, and felt myself turn red, because I knew what that "scandal" had to be but didn't yet know a name for it.

"That's right. So I'll know why Helen does to me like she does. I'll take it when we go."

Helen was her mother. I'd never heard Rosa call her by her first name. "Take the book? You have a library card? Will they let you—"

"No, I don't have a card. And I said 'take,' not 'borrow.' That clown who checks bags won't look under my sweater. . . . *For chrissake*"—in a whisper, with a grimace better suited to a scream—"quit looking at me like that! Such a damn goody-good! You don't know what I live with."

"And me: do you know what I—"

She put her finger to a scab by the corner of my mouth, where a pimple once had been. I pulled away. I didn't want to be reminded of what had made that scab. "It's not easy for you either," she said. "I *do* know; I'm not blind. But listen to me now. There's something you need to hear."

She pulled her chair close. Her voice sank. "It was in one of those old newspapers. From Florida. Don't worry, I've got it all written down for you, the exact place and date and source and all that stuff. It scared me. More than anything I've ever seen."

My arm, which I might have put around her, lay on the table. Too heavy to lift.

"There was this disk. Glowing red. Just like the one that came down on top of you last month. The people didn't see it flying, though. It was on the ground when they spotted it."

"So it must have landed!"

"If it was ever in the air. Shhh—in a minute you'll see what I mean. They saw it sitting in a field. For a while it didn't do anything. One guy got into his car, to go for the sheriff. And then the disk—it—it—"

"Took off?"

"No. It didn't take off. It sunk into the ground."

She took a deep breath. She'd never looked this shaken. Not even that time in seventh grade, lifting her skirt to show her wounded legs. Was it really the newspaper story that had spooked her? Or was it me, and what I'd just been through, which she understood even though I had not?

"Down into the ground," she said. "Like an elevator, they described it. And I thought of that story you and Jeff tell each other, like it's some big joke, about the elevator in Chicago—"

"Into the ground?"

"Like it was sitting on the ocean, and it went down into the water. Only there wasn't any water. Just solid ground." She closed her eyes; she breathed. "Danny. You've got to promise me—"

"What?"

"If your UFO comes back and drops all the way down and stays there, you won't—you won't—"

"What?"

"Get inside."

"*Attention. The library is closing in ten minutes. Closing in ten minutes . . .*"

She jumped up, sparing me the need to promise. When I make a promise, I don't break it. "My things are downstairs," she said. "I'll get yours too. You shouldn't move. You look sick."

"I'm all right." But already she was gone.

Before me on the table were the three Jewish calendars. Also my copy of *Flying Saucers and the Three Men*. A business card protruded from it like a bookmark. Of course—Julian's. The one I'd left behind. I pulled it out and quickly turned it over, so I wouldn't have to look at those eyes. On the back was written, in an ornate, nearly Gothic script: **SSS—Super-Science Society. "Science is a turtle that says that its own shell encloses all things"— Charles Hoy Fort.**

I picked up the Bender book. I was about to slide it into my briefcase. On impulse I opened it and turned to the last page.

There was my "preliminary evaluation," dismissing the book as a hoax. There was Jeff's "I agree completely." And below both, in the same handwriting as the back of the card, was a third annotation.

**There are more things in heaven and earth, Horatio,
than are dreamt of in your philosophy.**

PART TWO
SUPER-SCIENCE SOCIETY

[FEBRUARY 1966]

CHAPTER 6

"SO YOU DON'T BELIEVE IN THE PLANET CLARION," SAID JULIAN
Margulies. "My, my. What a hardened skeptic you are. Next you'll be telling
me you don't believe in the dero and the underground caves."

"I don't, not very much," I said.

"But you do, just a little bit?"

He eased up on the accelerator and downshifted. Our Pontiac still came
up fast on the huge truck wheezing ahead of us in the right-hand lane of
the Schuylkill Expressway, vomiting foul black exhaust. It was the first
Saturday afternoon in April 1963, warmer than I'd have expected; we had
opened the windows wide to catch the breezes. Nearly three years have
gone by since then. It's February now, and the year is 1966, and I'm in
eleventh grade instead of eighth. And it's been forever since I've felt a
spring breeze.

Julian braked lightly. A stream of cars in the left lane zoomed past us. A
fat red-faced man leaned through the right window of one of those cars,
shaking his fist at us and screaming something I couldn't make out.

"He should save his language for the truck driver," I said.

"I'm delighted they've finally passed us," said Julian. "They've been on our
tail since we passed through Fairmount Park, maybe even earlier. I was
afraid they were following us from the library. In their black car. How many
black cars do you see on the road these days?"

"Did you see who was in the car?" I asked.

"I *think*," he said carefully, "there were perhaps *three* of them. Three *men*.
Dressed so *oddly*—all in black, I think. And their eyes looked so very . . .
very . . . *strange*."

I didn't respond. The man I'd seen had worn a grayish white jacket over a hideous red sport shirt, and his eyes were barely visible, his face was so puffed with rage.

"Well," said Julian after a moment, "there's no law saying the men in black always have to dress in black. Or that they always have to hang out together. Actually there were only two of them. The wife was driving, uglier looking even than the man, and very aggressive behind the wheel. Bound to be an accident down the road, and I hope we're not around when it happens. They did have me nervous for a while, though. You didn't have somebody tail us, did you?"

"Of course not." I may not have said this in the most convincing tone. I've never been very good at lying, and the truth was I'd indeed had us tailed, though not quite in the way Julian imagined. Fortunately he'd chosen that moment to try to pass the truck himself and wasn't paying full attention to me. He glanced over his shoulder, eased into the left lane, and a moment later we were around the truck and in the clear.

"Murderous traffic," I said.

"My *dear* Mr. Shapiro, you don't have to make it quite so obvious you're from the suburbs. To a Philadelphian this is hardly traffic at all. You should see the expressway on a weekday. Of course I've had a chance to get used to it; I've been driving for ages. I'll be sixteen next July."

"Ages? And you'll be sixteen next July?"

He laughed. "Aren't you glad that black car didn't turn out to be an unmarked state trooper? I can see us now, pulled over to the shoulder. Huge hulking cop marches over to us. 'May I see your license, please, sir?'"

"What would you do if that happened?" I asked.

"I'd show him my license, of course." He fished his wallet out of the inside pocket of his jacket, flipped it open, and handed it to me. Sure enough, there was a driver's license, marked with the Pennsylvania keystone emblem, in the name of Julian Arthur—not Arcturus—Margulies. The photo wasn't very flattering, but it was unmistakably Julian. He stared straight ahead, blank, unsmiling, his buckteeth very prominent. The license had been issued nearly two years before. I closed the wallet and handed it back.

We were getting out of the city now, and the traffic began to thin. Every now and then I caught a glimpse of the Schuylkill River to our right, glistening in the late afternoon sun. I had only the vaguest idea where we were headed.

It was a house in the country, he'd told me, out in Montgomery County. This was the headquarters of the Super-Science Society.

More than six weeks had passed since I'd met Julian in the library, without my taking him up on his dinner invitation. I wasn't sure, to begin with, how seriously he'd meant it. Also, there was something about him that unnerved me, gave me the feeling he was best avoided. I still went to the Philadelphia library most Saturdays, sometimes with Rosa, never again with Jeff. Of course the bus stopped in Braxton; it always had. I stayed clear of the Rare Book Room. I made sure to leave the library a half hour before closing time, so as not to run into Julian as he left work.

The last week of March he phoned.

It was late in the morning, just before lunchtime. I was working at my desk, trying to keep my eyes open; I'd slept till almost ten, but it hadn't helped. My mother drifted around the house, forlornly singing her song about "sailing along on Moonlight Bay, we could hear the voices singing, they seemed to say . . ." I kept the door to my room closed, tried not to listen. She loves that song; it reminds her of her and my father's courting days. For me, it's like fingernails dragged across a blackboard.

"You have stolen my heart, now don't go 'way . . ."

It was Tuesday, but I wasn't in school. A freak snowstorm the day before had forced the schools to close and put my father into an even nastier mood than usual.

He'd come into my room about eleven the night before, complaining about the racket I was making, typing up UFO sightings on file cards. I promised I'd do something else that didn't make noise. But he sat down on my bed to talk, starting out calm, reasonable. The way his inquisitions usually do.

He just wanted to *understand*, he said. How was it a bright kid like me could piss away my life on this UFO garbage?

"So it's been fifteen years of flying saucers," he said when I'd answered his questions about the dates, the numbers. "There's been three thousand or God knows how many sightings of these stupid goddamn lights whizzing through the sky. None of them ever crashes. None of them ever manages to leave anything solid behind—"

That's simply not true, I told him.

"What?"

UFOs have at times left physical evidence, I told him.

"Yeah? Like when?"

I didn't want to get into the Maury Island UFO crash of 1947; that was almost certainly a hoax. There were vague rumors of a crash somewhere in New Mexico, also in '47, but I'd never been able to find any details. So I began to describe the New Haven case from August 1953, when a red fireball about a foot in diameter tore through a billboard—

"Piloted by *very* little green men. Right?"

He sweated, grinned. His eyes were furious. I kept on. Many people in New Haven, I told him, heard the terrific noise the fireball made, scared one woman so much she had a miscarriage—

"And what did this red ball of fire leave behind? If I may ask?"

I was just getting to that. The fireball left some metal by the hole in the billboard. It was analyzed, determined to be copper with some copper oxide—

"Copper and copper oxide. You tell me something now. Why in the god-damn fucking hell would an interplanetary spaceship have left behind it copper and copper oxide?"

I tried to tell him: I didn't *know* why it was copper and copper oxide. I knew the facts; I didn't know what they meant. That was what I was trying to find out, why I dedicated myself to UFO research—

"WHY COPPER AND COPPER OXIDE?"

He was on his feet, his face swollen with fury, bellowing over and over that same meaningless question. "I don't *know!*" I cried. "I'm not one of the UFO pilots! What do you want from me?"

"I want—" And then he turned, stormed out of my room. At the doorway he glared back at me. "Lucky husband!" he snarled. And then he was gone.

From her bedroom my mother gave out a wail. She'd pretended to be asleep through all this, though I'd known she was awake, lying rigid in bed, hearing every word. She knew, just as I did, what he meant by "Lucky husband!" The man married to that lady in New Haven who'd miscarried when the fireball came through. If something like that had happened to my mother—if she hadn't insisted, against medical advice, on carrying me to term—what might their lives have been like?

Would they still be singing to each other about Moonlight Bay?

The front door to the house opened, slammed. She let out another cry, of such misery and terror it chilled me to hear it. She's always been afraid of this: that I'll exasperate him so much he'll tear out of here and won't come back. I waited to hear the car start up; I'd forgotten about the snow. Probably he had too.

He came back in. With steady, even steps he came to my room. He pulled open my door. His face was grim, stony, righteous.

"Let's see that pimple."

It had sprouted that morning on the tip of my nose. I'd hoped, absurdly, he wouldn't have noticed. I stood up to give him a better look; I was nearly as tall as he was, not that it meant anything. "*Suivez-moi*," he said as he led me to the bathroom by my shoulder. I suppose I'm lucky it wasn't my ear.

I didn't protest. I'd protested before. It had done no good. By the bathroom's white fluorescent light he reinspected my face. Silently he dipped his needle into the alcohol.

When it was over—the needle triumphant, the pimple yielded up its pus-filled guts—I was dismissed to bed, a dab of bloodied toilet paper stuck to my nose. There I lay, shaking and sleepless, until nearly dawn. I was just grateful the snow had saved me, that I wouldn't have to get up in another hour for my stupid lousy school. It was later that morning, as I sat going over my file cards and trying to forget, that Julian phoned.

"Didn't lose my card, did you?" he said.

I'd picked up the phone in the kitchen, on the eighth ring. My mother should have answered it; she hadn't. Had she gone somewhere? Drifted, after her own dreadful night, into a sleep too deep to hear the ringing? I was in the house alone.

"Not at all." On the contrary: I'd been keeping the card on my desk and could not begin either my UFO work or my schoolwork without picking it up and fiddling with it. "Sorry I haven't phoned. It's just that things have been . . . so crazy," I said, hoping he wouldn't ask what "things" were or in what way they'd been crazy.

"Well, that's the way it is these days. Everybody's busy. All the teachers think theirs is the only class you've got homework for. The science teacher doesn't realize you have English papers to write, et cetera and so forth. Not like the dear old days of first grade, when you were doing good if you knew the alphabet. Got any plans for Saturday, a week and a half?"

"I imagine I'll be in Philadelphia. Doing research in the library."

"Good. That's my week to work Rare Books. We'll meet after they close. I'll drive you out to our house."

"Your family's house?"

"Of course not. The SSS house. Old farmhouse, in the country. Take the Schuylkill Expressway, past West Conshohocken. We'll have dinner, do some observing if conditions are good. Jacket and tie, please; we all dress for dinner. Rochelle will be there. One of us will take you back to—where is it you live?"

"Kellerfield."

"That's on Route Seventeen, isn't it? About ten miles out of Trenton?"

"Uh-huh."

"Back to Kellerfield, then. Or if it's late, we'll set you up a cot."

I began to regret saying yes about three seconds after I hung up the phone. I imagined myself stepping into Julian's car and vanishing without a trace. No doubt I would be used as victim for some grotesque experiment, involving needles or other sharp instruments, in this crumbling farmhouse in the middle of nowhere, where my screams could not be heard and no one would know what was happening to me.

This was where Rosa could help.

We would go to the library together as usual that Saturday, I told her. But she would leave early and wait at the corner by the main entrance until she saw me and Julian come out. Then she would follow us, unobtrusively, to Julian's car. She would note down the license number and a description of the car. If I wasn't back by two in the morning or hadn't contacted her in some way, she was to call the police.

"Bullshit," Rosa said.

This was the way she talked all the time, since breaking up with Jeff. Her mother had gone from being "Helen" to "the old bitch," and when my face must have shown my distaste—awful as the woman was, she was still Rosa's mother—she snapped: "Goddamn it, yours is too!"

"But all I'm asking you to do—"

"If you're afraid of what's going to happen to you once you get into that boy's car, then don't get in!"

We argued, even yelled a little bit. Eventually I brought her around. When Julian and I left the library together that afternoon, Rosa was on the corner, looking like she was about to cry. Of course I didn't say hello. I didn't nod to her, and I looked at her as briefly as I could as Julian and I walked past. But

I glimpsed her shining brown eyes fixed on me and was seized by a ghastly certainty that this was the last time I'd ever see her. Sadness weighed on me so heavily I could barely pick up my legs to walk. Julian meanwhile chattered away about "Clarion," the tenth planet hidden behind the dark side of the moon, whose slinky space brunettes—centuries old yet ageless—pick up lucky and not exceptionally truthful earth males for rides in their UFOs. As far as I could tell he'd seen nothing at all.

The heat was unusual for the beginning of April. Even with the Pontiac's windows opened wide, the breeze blowing in, I felt myself sweating. I touched the knot of my tie. I wished I could take it off or at least loosen it. Julian looked perfectly cool, dressed in a blue blazer very much like the one I was wearing. I'd half expected him to wear his black suit, but this was evidently not an occasion for it.

"How do you manage to have a driver's license at age fifteen?" I asked him. "I thought you had to be sixteen even to get a learner's permit."

"That's not a commandment from Mount Sinai, you know. It's not even a federal regulation. There's plenty of states out west where everybody has a license by the time they're fourteen. Sometimes even twelve. The farm boys and girls need to be able to drive the machinery into town. Otherwise the work won't get done."

"What farm machinery do you need to drive in Philadelphia?"

"Ha-ha. How witty we are this afternoon. The fact is that the commonwealth of Pennsylvania has taken a *very* considerable interest in the research of the SSS. All private and discreet and off the record, of course. If we're to continue this research, which they very much desire we should, we need our mobility. Which means *auto*mobility, the way things currently stand. So exceptions are made, though naturally we all take care that the general public doesn't hear about it."

"Exceptions—" I wondered whether such an exception could be made for me. How wonderful to drive, take my car wherever I pleased. It wouldn't make a difference then whether the bus stopped in Braxton or not. But could I learn? Would I be safe? My mother used to drive, almost like my father though without his confidence, until once when she was pregnant with me she wrecked his car in what she calls a "moment of inattention." I take after her, she's told me often, with my dreamy ways.

"Matter of paperwork," Julian said. "We ought to see about getting it done for you. You already know how to drive a car, I assume?"

I swallowed. I shook my head.

"Really? That surprises me. We'll have to teach you then. I wouldn't worry about it. Anybody over the age of ten or eleven has the motor skills to drive. The only thing people our age lack, most of them, is judgment and responsibility."

"And the state of Pennsylvania trusts you to have judgment and responsibility?"

"Of course they do. So does the library administration, when they put me in charge of our rare books. You cannot imagine how valuable some of those items are, or how fragile. We have sixteen bound manuscripts, one hundred and forty-seven incunabula. Somehow the library trusts me—"

"One hundred and forty-seven *what*?"

"Incunabula. It may now be one hundred forty-eight, actually. Depending on whether we were able to bid—"

"Julian."

"Hm-*hmmm*," he said encouragingly, after a moment.

"Julian, like—isn't an incunabulus—I mean—isn't it—isn't it— Well, *you* know what I mean."

"No, I don't know what you mean. No idea at all, in fact. Why don't you give me some help here?"

"I mean, I thought an incunabulus was a demon, or a ghost, or something. Isn't it? Something that gets into bed with people who are sleeping alone, I mean, and— and—"

"Fucks them? Screws them? Balls them? Has carnal knowledge of them?"

"Well . . . yes!"

"I seem to have the general idea then," said Julian. "To answer your original question, yes, we do have one hundred and forty-seven of them in the Rare Book Room. In the file cabinet behind the librarian's desk. We give them out on overnight loan to our hornier patrons. Just one more service from your Philadelphia Free Library."

"*Seriously*, Julian!"

"*Seriously*, Shapiro, your problem is that you've got sex on the brain. An incunabu*lum*—with an *m* at the end, please—is a book printed before the year 1500. What you have in mind is an incubus. Or maybe really a succubus. Probably *much* more a succubus than an incubus."

"What's the difference?"

"An incubus, dear sir, is a male demon who fucks, screws, et cetera and so forth, women ripe for his attentions. The succubus is female, does all of the above but to some lucky man. Or lucky boy. Especially if he's sleeping on his back. Sleep on your back in succubus territory, my friend, and you're asking for trouble."

I took a few seconds to digest this.

"Julian," I said finally, "you remember Antonio Villas Boas?"

Villas Boas was a Brazilian farmer, abducted a few years earlier by a UFO with a spacewoman on board. "Remember?" said Julian. "How could anyone forget?"

"Would she have been . . . sort of like a succubus?"

"Interesting thought. Blond, wasn't she?"

"Whitish blond hair," I said. "Long slits for eyes—"

I shifted in my seat; below my belt I felt myself hardening. High and well-separated breasts. Thin waist and small stomach. Wide hips and large thighs. These were other details Villas Boas had given of the alien who'd taken him captive and twice had used him. I didn't want to repeat them to Julian; I didn't even want to remember them. But did I have a choice?

"Well," he said at last, and I wondered if he'd been thinking the same things I had. "If you've got to be kidnapped by an extraterrestrial, I suppose you could do worse. Still, there's a lesson there for us."

"Which is?"

"Next time it's dark, and a red fluorescent disk flutters down into your cabbage patch, don't wait around to take pictures. Just drop your hoe and run like hell."

"Huh? Red fluorescent disk?" Somehow I'd forgotten that detail. "What did you say?"

"I said, *we're at our destination*," Julian said loudly, as though I were hard of hearing. He signaled, braked, and turned off the narrow two-lane road— we'd left the expressway long before—onto what sounded like a gravel driveway. "Our own little observatory, laboratory, and think tank. Otherwise known as Super-Science Society headquarters. Isn't it a beauty?"

There was a house at the end of the driveway. In the gathering darkness I could barely make out its shape, but it seemed to be large, at least two stories. There was a tower, looking something like a silo, attached directly to the house. I could not see how high the tower was. For all I could tell, its top might have reached unto heaven.

CHAPTER 7

THE FIRST THING I SAW AS WE WALKED INTO THE HALLWAY
was the staircase. It impressed me; I don't know quite why. There was something about the width of the brown wood stairs, or the heaviness of the banister, that gave the feeling of an immensity suggested rather than seen.

Hanging on the wall by the foot of the stairs, framed in wood so dark it was almost black, was the trisected angle, the SSS emblem from Julian's card. It was painted starkly in black on what looked like parchment. Next to it, similarly framed but in brilliant color, was a manuscript page like the one I'd seen in the Rare Book Room, of the man flying the winged horse.

Equal impossibilities—magical flight and trisecting the angle? Was that what the artwork was supposed to communicate? Before I could ask, Julian led me down the hall and through the doorway of a large, comfortably furnished living room. There was an ornate fireplace, without any fire, in the wall opposite us. Close to the fireplace, lit by the warm yellow light of a standing lamp, a chessboard lay upon a small square table.

A girl sat at the table, studying the chessboard.

She wore a long black evening gown of some velvety material. The chess game, to judge from the positions of the pieces, was in its middle stage. There were four chairs at the table, hers included, but no sign of whoever it was she was playing against. Her tawny blond hair fell almost to her bare shoulders. I saw at once she was attractive, but I didn't realize how attractive until she looked up from her game, smiled, and rose to join us. She was just about my height or maybe a shade taller. Julian towered over both of us.

"Allow me to introduce—" Julian began.

"Rochelle Perlmann," the girl said. She held out her hand, and I shook it.

Her grip was firm and strong. I gazed into her face, partly to keep from staring at her bosom.

"I'm Danny Shapiro," I said.

"Pleased to meet you, Danny."

"One, two, three," said Julian, pointing to Rochelle, me, and himself in turn. "But where is the fourth?"

"Tom? He's up in the lab. We heard the buzzer go off, and he went to check."

"Is everything all right?" Julian sounded worried.

"We'll know in a few minutes."

She turned to me, smiling. "We've been having some trouble with the vacuum tubes," she said. "Last Wednesday one of them just went and *shattered*. There wasn't any danger from the force field radiation, not at the levels we've been using so far. But the glass was *everywhere*. We were up till three in the morning cleaning it up, can you imagine?"

"Sounds pretty awful," I said.

"Oh, it *was*. Where do you go to school, Danny?"

"Abraham Lincoln Junior High, out in Kellerfield. I'm in eighth grade."

"Eighth grade? Really? I would have thought you were at least in ninth, to look at you. I'm in the eleventh grade at Dag Hammarskjold High, in Bala Cynwyd. Don't look so *scared*," she said, laughing. "I'm not that much older than you. I skipped a grade at the beginning of junior high."

"She would have skipped two or three," said Julian, "except her family kept moving her all over the world."

"Yes, and aren't we glad of that?" said Rochelle. "If I'd skipped two grades, I'd be off to college next fall."

"And then what would the SSS do?" said Julian.

"I imagine Julian's already told you," Rochelle said. "He's in tenth grade in the Philadelphia schools. So is Tom. You'll meet Tom in a minute."

Julian said, "Danny saw that *Miraj-Nameh* picture in the Rare Book Room and was quite taken with it. I told him you were the expert."

"*Really*, Julian. I can't even read the text. It's all Persian, except for a few quotations from the Quran in Arabic. Danny, I hope you didn't come all the way out here for that. I'm bound to disappoint you."

"He also was interested in Joseph and Zuleikha," said Julian.

"Oh, yes, Joseph and Zuleikha." A frown passed across her face. "The virgin boy; the seductress. The older woman. *Oh*, yes."

"Old enough to be his mother, wasn't she?" Julian smirked.

"*Jool*-yan!" She glared at him. He put his finger to his lips, made a zipping gesture. The smirk remained. "Come, Danny," she said, turning to me. "Let's see what we can make of the *miraj*."

She took my hand and led me back into the hall, to the picture of the winged horse hanging at the foot of the stairs. For a moment she examined it. Then she pointed to a few squiggly words, indistinguishable to me from all the rest of the squiggles. She read them aloud, with some relish I thought, moving her finger from word to word.

"Arabic?" I said.

She nodded.

"It's written from right to left?"

"Uh-huh. Like Hebrew."

She looked at me, and we both grinned, as if we'd shared a secret, a hidden link between enemies or at least aliens. My heart began to beat faster. She turned back to the text. " 'Praise be to the One,' " she translated, " 'who carried His slave by night from the Sacred Mosque'—that's in Mecca—'to the Most Distant Mosque'—that's the Dome of the Rock in Jerusalem—'whose neighborhood We have blessed, in order that We might show him some of Our signs.' That's from the Quran," she said. "The only place in the Quran that mentions Jerusalem."

I must have looked confused, because she said: "Oh, don't you know the story of the *miraj*?"

"The mirage?"

"No, no." She laughed. "The *miraj*." The word still sounded to me like *mirage*, although there was something she did with it at the back of her throat that made it a little bit different. "That's the 'night journey.' When God carried Muhammad to Jerusalem in the middle of the night, on the back of a winged horse. Or maybe it was a winged donkey. You see it's a sort of hybrid, a winged animal with a human face."

She might have been giving a tour of their lab, explaining her latest experiment. Was that the sort of thing they did here—bred together horses and donkeys, eagles and people, until they got the kind of animal shown in the picture? It didn't fit very well with vacuum tubes and force field radiation.

"What was that?" I said.

"That? What?"

"I thought I heard—from upstairs—"

A noise like a cat's howl, but to musical accompaniment if that were possible. She shrugged.

"He got off in Jerusalem," she said, "and he stood on the rock. He saw a ladder. He climbed it into the heavens. . . ."

I looked up the staircase. Darkness. Suddenly from above, I heard a cry, almost a shriek—"I gotta have yuh now or my heart will break!"—and a burst of ugly music. A chorus, something about not being too young to get married. Beyond the top of the stairs, a door closed. And again silence.

"Tom," she said, nodding to me. Then, as if there'd been no interruption: "He left his footprint on the rock. They say you can still see it there. I never could, though. That's why the Muslims built their dome around that rock, where the Jewish Temple used to be."

Used to be . . . no longer is . . .

Jerusalem Is Destroyed.

Where had I seen those words?

The memories flooded back. Of the sunlit bedroom, second floor of my grandmother's house, where my mother lay recovering from her heart attack. She'd propped herself up with pillows; I sat on the bed beside her. I held, so she could look at it with me, the Jewish calendar I'd brought up from the kitchen.

JERUSALEM IS DESTROYED.

That was August's picture—a somber painting, done in gray, of walls and arches and pillars sliding into rubble. Even at age five I thought it unlucky, not to be dwelt upon. I hurried on to the next month, the next picture. JACOB'S DREAM.

My small mouth fell open. It was the same picture, though in a different year's calendar, that I was to see years later in the Rare Book Room. Immense swirling stairway, rainbow arching over its top; winged angels going up and down the golden steps. And I was there—five years old, dreaming with Jacob. Longing to climb that ladder into the sky.

My mother gazed from her pillows, at me, at the calendar. She burst into sobs.

"I'll never be able to walk up all those steps," she said.

———

"Danny?"

All the while Rochelle had been talking. About the golden Dome of the Rock, now in the place of the Temple, and its red and green carpets and the huge rough rock at its center. Within the rock a cave; beneath it yet another cave, which no one's ever seen. Well of Souls, that hidden hollow is called, because the spirits of the dead come there to pray. . . . With half an ear I'd caught what she said, and a great yearning came over me as when I was five, staring with my mother into Jacob's dream.

"I'd love to see it," I said. "I'd love to visit Israel sometime."

"Silly, it's not *in* Israel. You can't even get there from Israel. It's in the Jordanian part of Jerusalem. You know—there's a border dividing Jerusalem in half, between Israel and Jordan. It's been that way fifteen years, since Israel was created. If you've been in Israel, you've got to pretend you haven't before the Jordanians will let you in. And if you're Jewish, it doesn't matter where you come from. They won't let you cross the border."

"Well, *that's* not very fair!"

"Well, that's the way it is. We had to act like we were Episcopalians when we lived there. Just like Mama, she really *is* an Episcopalian. We went to church every Sunday at St. George's— Oh, there's Tom."

Footsteps. Creaking wood. A short, plump boy with dark blond hair, dressed like Julian and me in jacket and tie, came down the stairway. "Everything all right up there?" Rochelle asked him.

"Fine. Don't know why the buzzer went off. I took a few minutes to adjust the force field. I think I was able to get the lines smoother, at least if you judge from the filings."

She seemed to have forgotten I was there. Then she remembered. "Danny," she said, "this is Tom Dimitrios. Tom—Danny Shapiro."

We shook hands. His hand felt soft and slightly sweaty. I'd noticed, with some satisfaction, that his voice was nowhere near as deep as mine. "I know you," I said. "I can't remember how or when, but I've met you somewhere."

"Never seen you before in my life."

He seemed very certain, and I decided to take his word for it. Julian meanwhile had materialized in the hallway beside us. "Tom is our expert technician," he said to me. "Tom, do you have any notion what the viewing conditions are going to be like tonight?"

"They had the weather report on Wibbage," Tom said. "They said there's a front coming through later this evening. Should get rid of all this haze, I think."

Wibbage. WIBG, the Philadelphia rock station. No wonder the music had been so hideous. And that was what the Super-Scientists listened to? The same rock and roll as the dumbest, gum-chewing, greasy-hair-combing kids—the Braxton types—in my school? A fantasy died, painfully, inside me. These were just teenagers, after all, and I'd wanted them to be something more. So we could be friends.

"Well, then," said Julian, "let's have our dinner first. Afterward we'll go up to the observatory and see what can be seen. Danny, let's make the salad. We'll let the young lovers finish their chess game."

CHAPTER 8

I FOLLOWED HIM INTO THE KITCHEN. IT WAS BRIGHTLY LIT and filled with a wonderful smell of roast beef. Julian took off his jacket and tied on an apron. He tossed a second apron over to me. *What am I supposed to do with this?* I thought as I caught it, then realized: *Dummy, put it on.*

"The potatoes are fine," Julian pronounced, peering into a pot on the stove. "And the beans are coming along. So I *think*, Mr. Shapiro, we can dig out the greenery and get to work."

There was a cutting board beside the sink, another on the counter opposite. Julian waved me to the counter and handed me a colander filled with mushrooms. I began, awkwardly, to slice them. He rinsed a bunch of scallions, laid them on his cutting board, and decapitated them all with one grand flourish.

"Well now," he said, "what do you think of Rochelle?"

"She's—" I groped for the right word, to convey how she'd affected me. "*Gor*-geous!" I exclaimed; and my voice, which I'd thought safely matured, jumped a few octaves on the first syllable.

Julian laughed. Waggle-waggle went the eyebrows. "Ah, you dog, you! *Two* of them! First your secret admirer and now Rochelle. Who will be next, I wonder?"

"My secret admirer?"

"That pretty little blonde with the curly hair who followed us to the car. Don't tell me you didn't see— Careful, Danny! We don't want you slicing off your finger in our kitchen."

I looked at my left index finger. At first I thought I hadn't broken the skin. But then the blood began to well up, firm and globular at first, then breaking and running all over my fingertip. I went to the sink to rinse it. Julian gave me a dish towel to press against the cut. "I can't believe you didn't notice her," he said.

"How do you know she wasn't *your* secret admirer?" I said.

"She only had eyes for YOU-U-U," Julian sang, very much off-key. "A pity. I rather admired her myself."

"Anyway, didn't you say Rochelle was Tom's girlfriend?"

"Really? Did I say that?" He looked down at the floor. *"Out of here, Mehitabel!"* he cried. A coal-black cat with blazing eyes, who'd been sneaking around our feet, looking for a convenient spot to jump up onto a counter, retreated a few steps. Then she lay down on the floor and emitted a faint whine. "That's Mehitabel," Julian told me. "The cat."

"Mehitabel the cat?"

"Mehitabel. The cat."

"Where does that name come from?" I asked. There was something familiar about Mehitabel the cat. But I couldn't quite put my finger on it.

"Somewhere in the Bible, I think." He went back to his scallions. The cat began to rear up—*"Down, Mehitabel!"*—and she lowered herself, hissing ominously, pressing first her head and then her belly and hindquarters against the floor. From that position she glared first at Julian, then at me. "I forget," he said, "have you read the Bible? Who was Mehitabel in the Bible?"

"I used to read the Bible when I was little. Then I stopped. Now I've started again. And I haven't come across any Mehitabel. I think it's from somewhere else, some other book—"

"Maybe. I wouldn't know. Why did you start reading the Bible? You're not getting religion, are you?"

"No. It's not about religion. It's more like history, like where I come from."

And why that pretty little blonde had to remain my secret admiree. Why there wasn't any way Rosa and I could go on dates even if she wanted to, sneaked kisses the way the kids around us did. The Bible and its history had made me different. The others were the goyim, the shiksas. Reading the Bible, maybe I'd grasp how this came to be.

"And Ezekiel's wheels," said Julian, convincing me he hadn't the slightest idea what I was talking about. " 'Ezekiel saw the wheel,' " he sang. " 'Way up in the middle of the air.' UFO sighting, if I've ever heard one.... Uh-oh. Here she comes again."

The cat was in motion. She trotted up to Julian, then stopped and pressed herself against his leg. He inserted the tip of his shoe under her belly, lifted her slightly, and sent her flying four or five feet. She let out a terrific yowl and ran from the kitchen. "If she tries that with you," he said, "that's what you do."

"I just hope she doesn't claw my pants leg off."

"She probably would, come to think of it. Mehitabel's been with us a year and a half. Showed up on our doorstep one rainy night, hungry, bedraggled, pregnant. We fed her, cleaned her, found homes for her kittens. Now she's sleek, well fed, more little ones on the way. Fifth time now. Lord only knows where she finds the toms. Or what we're going to do with the current batch of kittens."

"Why don't you have her—what's the word?"

"Spayed?" he said. "Neutered?"

"Yes, that's it. Neutered."

"What? And deprive poor Mehitabel of one of the great pleasures of a cat's brief life? Egad, sir, what a heartless brute you are. No, no, there's already two tomatoes in the salad. You don't need to cut up a third. And with this, I *think* we are just about ready to eat."

CHAPTER 9

I CARRIED THE SALAD BOWL TO THE TABLE IN THE DINING room. Julian followed with the potatoes, the green beans, a basket of rolls, and finally the roast. Rochelle and Tom came in a few minutes later. They didn't say whether they'd finished their game or, if so, who had won.

Julian carved. Rochelle uncorked a bottle of red wine and poured it into four large wineglasses. She smiled at me charmingly. "One of the benefits of having friends old enough to buy liquor," she said.

I wondered who those "friends" might be. Mostly male, for sure. Older, with experience I could only read about, in books I mustn't get caught looking at. To distract myself, I sipped the wine, which surprised me with its dryness. I'd expected it to be sweet, like the wine my grandmother served for the Passover Seder. Then I sipped some more.

"Take it *easy*," Rochelle said. "We can't let you pass out on us during dinner. You'll need a clear head when we go up to the tower for observing."

"What am I going to observe?" I asked.

"You won't know till you've observed it," she said mischievously. She and Julian laughed.

"We've been studying the moon," Tom said.

Follow the moon. Had these people too gotten a telephone call? I looked closely at Tom's pudgy, unsmiling face. He was right: I'd never seen him before. Yet he was also familiar somehow, and I didn't know how.

"There's things on the moon," he said, "that shouldn't be. Not according to the textbooks. Lights, shadows. Craters that are there when they shouldn't be and aren't there when the maps tell you to expect them. We've all seen them for months now."

"But . . . ?"

"We don't all see the same things."

Which, I supposed, was where I came in. "Have you written to M. K. Jessup about this?" I asked. "I mean," I said—because Tom was staring at me as if I were about the dumbest idiot in the state of Pennsylvania—"you really ought to try to get in touch with Jessup. I know he's interested in UFOs and the moon. He spent about half *The Case for the UFO* talking about that."

Tom let out a snort, cut off a large bite of meat, and stuffed it into his mouth.

"His other books too—" I began.

"Oh, Danny," said Rochelle. "If you know how to get in touch with Morris Jessup, you be sure and tell us. I don't think the mail goes where he is. And they haven't figured out how to connect telephones there."

I felt my skin crawl. I knew exactly what she meant. Since age five I'd lived with hints at death, used when the word itself was too near and terrible to be spoken. "Jessup's dead?"

"Four years ago," she said. "This very month. Mama still cries when she thinks about it."

"Killed himself," said Tom.

"Maybe," Julian said. "Or maybe not."

"He killed himself," Tom said. "His wife had left him, he couldn't get his books published, he was itching to do that radio séance. Him sitting in the afterlife, and the whole damn audience of WOR radio trying to make contact with him. Every insomniac in New York City closing his eyes and saying, 'Jessup, Jessup, Jessup.' Almost worth killing yourself for."

"You didn't see the terror on his face," Rochelle told him.

I stopped eating, put down my fork. "And you did?"

She nodded. "We lived in Coral Gables then. In Florida, right outside Miami. We were back from the Middle East for the first time, beginning of '58. Daddy knew Morris through his navy connections."

"Navy?" I said. "What did Jessup have to do with the navy?"

"The invisibility experiment," said Rochelle, as if I'd know exactly what she meant. "And the marked-up copy of *The Case for the UFO* that the Gypsies sent to the Office of Naval Research."

"That's the book Rochelle found on the car seat," Julian said. "Next to Jessup's body."

Car seat? Gypsies? Invisibility experiment? All this was new to me; none of it hung together. I must have looked as bewildered as I felt. "Hello?" Tom said to me. "The year 1943? Philadelphia Navy Yard? Ring any bells?"

"Wasn't it something—" I groped in my memory for something I'd read once or maybe just heard about. "Wasn't there a rumor about a ship . . . made to disappear—"

"A destroyer," said Tom. "Disappeared from the navy yard here. Then it turns up again, maybe two minutes later, offshore at Norfolk, Virginia. See what I'm saying?"

"Not exactly—"

"You can't *get* from Philly to Norfolk in two minutes!" Tom said loudly. He looked exasperated at my slowness; patience, I gathered, was not his strong point. "Any more than you can get to the earth from—I don't know, from Zeta Reticuli or wherever—fast enough that the trip'll be worth making. *Now* you understand?"

"I guess . . . what you're trying to say is—I mean—"

Tom gave an angry, bitter laugh, almost a cough. I wanted to grab him by his tie and shake him until he explained just what about me he found amusing. "No," I said, "I don't understand. I don't have the slightest idea what you're talking about."

He shook his head, tore a roll in two, and began mopping up the gravy on his plate.

"Danny," said Rochelle very patiently, "in 1956, Morris Jessup started getting incredibly strange letters, from a man he was never able to track down. About an experiment in the navy yard thirteen years earlier, during the war. . . . So!" She broke into a smile. "Lights going on inside, I see!"

They weren't really. But at least I wasn't getting any more confused. "Go on," I said.

"The letter writer sounded half crazy," she said. "But only half. That was what got Morris all excited. Most of the people in that experiment, the men who'd been made invisible, had gone insane from it. They'd become paralyzed, frozen. Sometimes they'd catch on fire too. 'They burned for eighteen days.' The whole experience was 'Hell Incorporated.' That's what the man who wrote the letters said. *Hell Incorporated.*"

" 'The experiment was a complete success,' " Julian said. "Remember that, Rochelle? 'The men were complete failures.' "

Rochelle shivered and grimaced. "Yes, Julian. I remember. That's from one of the letters," she said to me. "No, I don't know what it meant. Neither did Morris. But it seemed like the kind of thing you know is true, even if you don't have one speck of evidence for it.

"And the man claimed to have more evidence than anyone could possibly want. He kept asking Morris to put him under hypnosis, to bring back all the details he'd forgotten. Morris couldn't wait. He thought this was the clue to antigravity. How the UFOs fly. How *we* can fly, if we've a mind to."

I thought of Rosa. How flight was practically the only thing on her mind these days, and how excited she'd be if she were here with us. And that I was glad she wasn't, I didn't know why. I really must ask to use their phone, give her a call. . . . "Think of it this way," said Tom. "The Philadelphia experiment was to Einstein's unified field theory what Alamogordo was to $E = mc^2$. Only without the mushroom cloud."

"So did he?" I asked Rochelle. "Did Jessup ever hypnotize the man?"

"Danny, he never could *find* the man."

"Or maybe," said Julian, "they found him."

He drew his finger across his throat. His eyebrows jumped up and down in comic Groucho mode, just like in the kitchen. Only here the effect was macabre, chilling. Over the empty dinner plates I looked from Julian's face to Rochelle's to Tom's. Then back to Rochelle. What exactly would I tell Rosa when I did phone her? That I was safe, I could trust these people, we wouldn't need the police? Was I sure of any of this?

"Morris got a call," said Rochelle, "from the Office of Naval Research in Washington. Someone had sent them a copy of his book *The Case for the UFO*. Not just the book. There were annotations all over the pages. Three different people had written notes to themselves and one another, all through the book. It was like they were passing Morris's book back and forth among them, underlining passages, writing comments like 'Now he's getting close,' or sometimes, 'He doesn't understand, none of the gaiyars can understand.' "

"Gaiyars?" I said.

"A word Gypsies sometimes use for people who aren't Gypsies. That's why we think they were Gypsies, these three men. They talked like they were some secret society, the ones in the know. About the invisibility experiment—they had a lot to say about that—and about the UFOs, and all the kinds of things we want to know. I mean, we, the SSS. The government too, most likely. Though they'll never come out and say it."

"And that book," I said. "Have you seen it?"

"Yes. I've seen it."

She moved her empty wineglass back and forth, as though she were writing some invisible message to herself on the tablecloth. The clock ticked loudly in the silent house.

"How to tell it?" she said. She stared into the glass. "We found out Morris was dying from the Dade County police. Most of the deputies were Daddy's friends. They phoned him that evening, as soon as they found Morris in the park. There was nobody else they could phone. His wife had packed up and left him. He lived all alone in the house at the end of our street.

"I'd never seen Daddy drive like that. He must have run three or four red lights on the way to the park. I don't think he'd run a red light in his life before that evening."

"Your father took you with him?" I felt a strange creeping sensation, as though something were beginning to crawl over me, into me, through me. As when my father had taken me—

"The sun was setting when we reached the park," Rochelle said. "Morris's car was there, the way I'd seen it a million times in front of his house. He was behind the wheel, the way he always was. But he was slumped back in the seat, dead, his eyes staring open. Danny, you have *never* seen eyes looking like that.

"He looked like he'd been gasping for breath," she said. "He *was* gasping for breath, actually, when they found him. That was what the deputy said. He'd run a hose from the exhaust pipe in through the window, the police said, and cranked up the car."

"Or somebody did it for him," said Julian.

Rochelle nodded. "The hose was still there when we came supposedly. I didn't see it. I couldn't look at anything, except Morris's face. And the book on the seat next to him."

"The book—" I said.

"Yes, Danny. Morris's *Case for the UFO*. I'd read it a few years before, when it first came out and I was nine and we lived in Jerusalem. That was about all I had to do with myself those summers in Jordan, sit in the garden and read books from the British Council Library. That, and learn Arabic and French. Wasn't like I had any friends to play with . . .

"And now there was that same book, lying next to his body. Only it *wasn't* the same. Be patient—you'll understand in a minute what I mean. I stole it."

"You what?"

"I was pretty good at stealing, even back then. The deputy wasn't paying attention. He was yelling at Daddy. 'What'd you bring her here for?' he kept hollering. And Daddy yelled back that it was important I be there, important I see this, that I *see*—"

—and "What'd you bring him in here for?" the bundle on the bed had croaked out when my father brought me into her room—so weak, but still I could hear her; I let out such a howl—

"I think I would have gone insane," I said.

"Maybe you would have," said Rochelle. "Maybe I did. Anyway, they were so busy screaming at each other, Daddy and the deputy, they didn't notice me. And they'd left the car door open.

"I reached in. I grabbed the book.

"I was wearing a big, loose smock then, like an artist, and a pair of jeans. I stuffed the book into the front of my jeans, under the smock. And I took it home with me, and Daddy never saw it. I stayed up all that night, with my flashlight under the covers, just like in the comics, reading it.

"Because this wasn't the ordinary book, Danny. Not the one I'd read in our garden in Jerusalem. It was the special copy, the marked-up copy, that the Gypsies or whoever had sent the Office of Naval Research, and afterward they passed on to Morris for his reaction. With all the annotations. And the drawings.

"And I read it all. That was when I first knew—really, really *knew*—the UFOs are real. Them and the invisible ships. The disappearing people. How you get a ship, or a person, or anything you want to vanish. Yourself included."

Rosa . . . how worried she must surely be getting . . .

"And the different kinds of UFO beings!" Rochelle said. "The ones that are more or less harmless, and the . . . others. Antigravity. How they travel to the stars and back, faster than that ship got from Philadelphia to Norfolk. Go up by going down . . . You sink into the earth, and there's the moon below you—"

"Down, down, *down*," I said. "Underground, to the caves of the dero."

It was as if the words were inside me and just forced themselves out, in a voice that sounded strange even to me. The others sat and stared.

In the silence that followed I listened to the clock ticking.

"Listen, Rochelle," Tom said finally. "Suppose Jessup was murdered, by the three men in black or whoever—"

"I never *said* it was the men in black."

"Or the three Gypsies or whoever—"

"I never said it was the Gypsies either."

"Well, whoever," said Tom. "Why did they leave the book in the car for you to find? If the annotations were so important. Doesn't it stand to reason they would have taken it with them?"

"I don't *know*. Maybe they didn't know about the annotations. Probably they thought it was just one more copy of *The Case for the UFO*. I didn't know about the annotations when I took it. I just took it because—well, it was Morris's book. How proud he always was of having written it."

"Where is it now?" I asked.

Silence.

"You don't have it, I gather?"

Again silence. Julian seemed to be smiling to himself, and that made me more uneasy even than the finger across the throat. *Jump up from this chair right away*, I instructed myself. *Demand to be led to the telephone. Call Rosa. Tell her to find some way to get me away from here, right now.*

I didn't move.

"The police came for it the next day," said Rochelle. "They'd noticed it was missing. They knew Daddy and I had been there. The deputy came out to our house. At first I lied about it, but then he said he was going to arrest Daddy, so I broke down. He took the book."

"What did the police do with it?"

"Nobody knows," said Rochelle. "They say they have no record."

"So it's gone now? Lost?"

Rochelle looked me full in the face. Her smile had turned strange, crafty. A lot like Julian's. "Maybe lost," she said. "Maybe not. Hard to find, maybe. But maybe not impossible."

She had a plan; I was part of it. What I was supposed to do I didn't yet know. I would not be the same after it was done. I had the feeling a crevasse was opening before me in the earth, or possibly the sky, and I was about to fall in.

"Not all that's hard is impossible," she said. "There are things people call impossible that people like us really ought to try. That's what the SSS is about."

I tried to speak. No sound came out.

"That's why I'm here right now," she said. "Not out parking with some twelfth-grade boy, listening to him talk about his college board scores while he's trying to unhook my bra. That's why we took for our emblem the trisected angle."

And the winged horse? I wanted to ask. I might have been relieved, heartened by the contempt with which she spoke of those boys. If the crevasse in front of me hadn't just opened about a hundred yards wider.

"When do you get your driver's license?" she said. "No, I don't mean when you're sixteen. Julian's already told you what we do about that."

She looked toward Julian. He nodded. I must have been blushing. I wished I could hide somewhere until the blush subsided.

"Get your license," she said. "Get it as soon as you can. Then we can head off for Coral Gables and vicinity. We'll see what we can find, you and I."

"It might mean missing a few weeks of school," Julian said to me. "You can live with that, can't you?"

Oh, yes, I could manage. A few weeks less of tedium, of mockery. Of feeling there was no one else like me in the world. Rochelle stood up, stretched. She arched herself back, her hands clasped high over her head. I turned my eyes away from her pushed-out breasts, even while knowing that was precisely where she wanted me to look.

"I can't do all the driving myself," she said.

CHAPTER 10

THE TOWER ROCHELLE HAD MENTIONED, WHICH WE WERE SUP-
posed to go up to for "observing," was the silolike structure I'd seen when
we first drove up to the house. A spiral staircase led up through it from the
second floor. There weren't any lights in the staircase; Julian had to go before
us with a flashlight. The steps were high and narrow, and there were no land-
ings. By the time we reached the top and stepped out onto a circular platform
under the sky, I was completely out of breath.

Good thing there's a railing, was my first thought as I looked about the
moonlit platform. *You could walk right off otherwise on a darkish night.*

I was so disoriented, so distracted by my surroundings that it took me a
few moments to realize the others had disappeared somewhere and I'd been
left alone. I began to panic, to be afraid they'd locked some door behind me
and I was trapped here in the moonlight. I was about to call out. But just then
a light flashed from within a small domed hutlike structure at the center of
the platform. From inside I heard laughter.

I started toward the doorway of the hut. I caught a glimpse, inside, of two
bodies twisting against each other. I thought I heard clothes softly rubbing.
There was another laugh. A gleaming white hand appeared, pressed against
the back of a neck, amid short blondish hairs.

Julian stepped around the hut. Evidently he'd been outside too, on the
other side of the hut from me. "Tom's setting it up for you," he said. "On the
northwest quadrant."

I wasn't sure what he meant. At that moment I could not have cared less.
All I felt was my stomach clutching with grief and disappointment, at the
knowledge that she was Tom's after all.

Rochelle and Tom stepped out through the doorway. The entrance was low; Rochelle, but not Tom, had to stoop to come out. They held hands. Tom's hair was mussed, and one strap of Rochelle's evening gown had fallen off her shoulder. Tom gave a loud, harsh laugh and went back into the hut.

Rochelle replaced her strap and smiled at me.

"Isn't it *awful*," she said. "There's only room in there for two people, one at the telescope and one at the table. Some nights you could just *freeze*, waiting out here."

I looked up at the moon. I didn't trust myself to say anything.

"All right, Danny," said Julian. "You can go in now. Go in, and see what you can see."

Tom sat at a wooden table, a large notebook in front of him. A kerosene lamp burned on the table. From the telescope came a loud ticking sound.

"See where the eyepiece is?" Tom said. "I'd adjusted it for myself. You may have to bend over a little."

I put my right eye—or, more exactly, the right lens of my glasses—to the eyepiece of the telescope. I saw only a featureless lunar glare.

"Take your glasses off," said Tom. "It's better that way. Focus with the eyepiece. That'll make up for your not having the glasses."

I took off my glasses and tried again. I could feel my eyelashes brush against the eyepiece when I blinked.

"Try to relax your eyes," said Tom. "You'll see better. I can cover the lamp, if that's disturbing you."

I turned the eyepiece first counterclockwise, then clockwise. Craters and ridges seemed to emerge from the blur, then sink back into it. Finally I hit the right spot. The features stood out with almost uncanny clarity. I had no idea where on the moon I was.

"I think I've got it," I said.

"Good," said Tom. "What do you see?"

"There's two big craters. The one on the left looks a lot deeper than the one on the right. There's a lot of little pockmarks around them, particularly the one on the left."

"Good. Anything else?"

"Something kind of like—like a W shape, I think. Underneath the crater on the right. If the whole thing were upside down, it might be kind of like a curved eyebrow. With the two craters as two eyes."

"Good," said Tom. "Damn good. That eyebrow, or W, is Schröter's Valley. The crater it's under is Herodotus. The one off to the left is Aristarchus. And actually the whole thing is upside down. Everything you see through a telescope is upside down, did you know that?"

"I didn't."

"See anything inside Aristarchus?"

"Something right in the middle of it, I think. Looks very bright."

"That's the mountain peak in the middle. Lots of craters have them. You're a damn good observer, you know that?"

"Thank you," I said, and felt myself blush with unwished-for pleasure at the compliment.

"Anything else there?"

"Some lines, or stripes, I think, running from the middle of the crater to the outside. And there's—wait a minute."

Something was happening in Aristarchus that even I could recognize as extraordinary. Just inside the crater's rim, on the upper left, a pinpoint of bright red had suddenly appeared. As I watched, it blossomed into a shining red globe, very much like the drop of blood that had welled up from my fingertip earlier that evening. I waited for it to burst, to run, to wash the crater floor with blood. But nothing happened. The drop, or whatever it was, remained stable.

"I'll be damned," I said. "I'll be *damned.*"

"What? What?"

"A shining red spot. Or maybe a sphere, I'm not sure. It just sprang up out of the side of the crater. Want to take a look?"

"No. By the time I get the eyepiece adjusted it may have changed, and you need to see it. Just be damn sure you remember what you see."

"It's starting to fade now."

"OK, OK." I heard his ballpoint pen scribbling in the notebook. "God*damn* it, I forgot to write down when you first saw it. How long have you been looking at it now?"

"I'm not sure. Not much more than a minute, I don't think."

"And it's fading, you say?"

"It's practically gone now."

"Show's probably over then."

I stood up from the eyepiece and stretched. "There's a chair over by the wall," said Tom, "if you want to sit down."

I slumped into the chair. I felt drained, as if I'd just seen something the watching of which demanded all my strength. Bathed in moonlight, Rochelle stood in the doorway. "Danny had a sighting?" she said.

"A real doozy," said Tom.

"What was it?" I said to her.

I don't know why I expected her to know.

She shrugged. " 'The earth hath bubbles,' " she said, " 'as the water has. And these are of them.' "

"What?"

"*Macbeth.* Act One, Scene Three. We studied it in English class last month."

"And the moon has them too?"

She didn't answer. She looked off into the distance.

"Why don't we take a walk?" she said to me. "In the moonlight."

She walked toward the railing. I began to follow her. Then I stopped.

"Come on," she said. "What are you afraid of? That I'll push you over the edge?"

The thought had crossed my mind. I plucked up my courage and walked to the railing. She was leaning on the railing, and I leaned there too, beside her. I imagined we were standing together on the deck of a ship sailing through a midnight sea, only this was the middle of the air. I didn't dare look down toward the ground.

"What did you mean," she said, "at the dinner table when you talked about going down to the caves of the dero?"

"Oh . . . I don't know. I think it was just a joke. It just came out of me. I don't know why I said it."

"It's not a joke. You know that."

Everything inside me turned cold. I clenched both my hands around the railing, for safety.

"The dero caves are not a joke," Rochelle said. "Richard Shaver's welding gun—or whatever was talking to him—was telling him the truth. Mostly the truth anyway."

"The dero are real. Is that what you're saying?"

"Them. Or something like them. I wouldn't want to swear to the name. Shaver sometimes calls them the *abandondero*, you know. The abandoned ones."

Richard Sharpe Shaver. The Pennsylvania metalworker, his name so comical, his messages from the subsurface world so relentlessly horrid. The world of those left behind when the Elder Races—

"Left for the stars," said Rochelle. Without realizing it, I must have spoken my thoughts aloud. "They knew they were being poisoned by radiation from the aging sun. They were withering; they were dying—"

" 'They seemed to age quickly,' " I said. Like a certain woman I knew: prematurely aged, withered, though I seldom noticed unless I looked at old photos. " 'Girls of twenty soon appeared to be old women.' "

Rochelle nodded. "Oh, yes," she said. "You know more than you let on, don't you? You know the Shaver literature; you can quote it by heart. So you know that's why the Elder Gods left earth in their spaceships. They left the dero behind them here to absorb the radiation poison. That's how the dero got so weird. But you knew all that already."

I thought: *I didn't know it was true.*

"I won't swear to the details," said Rochelle. "Or exactly what kinds of things these . . . things . . . are. There's a continuum. We still don't know the—what's the word?—*taxonomy* of what lies along it. We get only glimpses here and there. I doubt if Shaver really understands it. I'm sure he doesn't, actually. He's not a great thinker. I know; I've met him."

Where? How? But these people seemed to go everywhere, know everybody. "And the things they do?" I said. "To the ones they kidnap—into their caves—"

"Yes. It's true. The thirst, the burnings, the impalements—all of that's true. But don't ask for details. Please. You really don't want . . ."

Her voice trailed off. Her features twisted in pain and sorrow. I thought I saw her trying to frame the word *No!* with her mouth. But no sound came out. Her face wrinkled and withered and fell away, like an old woman's, so that at last only her eyes, huge and unblinking, remained her own, staring at me through a layer of unshed tears.

Shaver was wrong, I thought. *It isn't the sun that poisons us. It's the moonlight.*

"We're going back down," Tom called out. "Anybody who wants to come is welcome."

The light in the hut was off. Julian, carrying the flashlight, had already disappeared down the spiral staircase. Tom followed.

"We'd better go," said Rochelle. I looked back at her and was relieved to see once more the beautiful girl who'd sat beside the chessboard.

"They'll leave us here," she said. "That's just the way they are. And I don't have a light."

CHAPTER 11

THE STAIRWELL WAS DARK WHEN WE FOLLOWED TOM AND
Julian through the door. Their flashlight was small and faint beneath us. I couldn't see, and hadn't remembered, the high step at the very beginning.

"Danny!" said Rochelle. "Are you all right?"

"Twisted my ankle, I think. Why aren't they stopping?"

"Don't worry about it. Hold my arm, and lean on me. We don't need their flashlight. I've been up and down this staircase a couple of hundred times."

So I hobbled down step by step, in total darkness, for what seemed like half an hour. When she led me at last into the second-floor hallway, it no longer felt like the same house we'd left earlier in the evening.

"Where are Julian and Tom?" I asked.

She peered carefully to her left. "Not *here*, it doesn't seem like. And not here *either*," she said, looking to her right. "Where do *you* suppose they are?"

"I really wouldn't know," I said.

"Then I wouldn't know either."

She stood facing me, very close. She smiled, warmly, enticingly. It was as if her weird transformation hadn't happened at all.

"You know," she said, "you didn't have to let go of my arm."

I tried to lift my hand, to take her arm again. It would not move.

"I've been wondering all evening," she said, "how you'd look without your glasses."

She reached up and took them off. "Oh, *nice*," she said. "Very, very *nice*." She raised her left index finger to my eyebrow and lightly traced the outline of my eye socket. "Marvelous socket. And a *scrumptious* curve here," she said, moving her finger up the bridge of my nose and then down to the tip. "And you cover it all up with glasses. Why do you *do* it?"

"I can't see without them," I said.

"Ever hear of contact lenses? Ever read the Bausch and Lomb brochures? My glasses are twice as thick as yours, I'll bet, when I'm not wearing my contacts."

"I've worn glasses since I was almost six," I said.

"Doesn't mean you have to keep on wearing them."

I don't know where she laid my glasses. She didn't move her one hand from my face, yet the other was behind my neck, pressing me gently toward her. Something furry, which after a moment I recognized as Mehitabel the cat, rubbed against my leg. I didn't look down, didn't kick it away. I stroked Rochelle's smooth, shining hair and bare shoulders, down to the edge of her evening gown.

"There's a zipper there somewhere," she murmured. "Might be worth pulling on, just to see what happens."

She began to kiss me, delicately running her tongue over my lips, back and forth against my teeth.

" 'Bout time you learned to unhook a bra," she said.

"Aren't you Tom's girlfriend?"

"Maybe," she said, very softly, very sleepily.

She took my lower lip between her teeth and pulled on it gently. Then she let it go. Again she bit it softly, again let go. Her hand moved slowly down my back and around the front of my thigh.

"Oh, my," she said, feeling between my legs. "We *do* have a boner here, don't we?"

I began to shudder, to whimper. I thought I heard the cat cry out. I felt myself filling with pleasure beyond my control, beyond my comprehending. Rochelle smiled. . . . And from the glow of her smile appeared the image of Rosa Pagliano, shining in the darkness like the smile itself.

Rosa laughed, her head thrown back in delight. In her eyes was a little bit of anger. She sang, "And I'll not marry at all, at all, and I'll not marry at all . . ."

"That's all there is," said Rochelle. "It wasn't so bad now, was it?"

"I'm all *wet*," I said. "And it's all *sticky*."

"That's just the way it is. There's nothing to feel bad about."

"But, Rochelle, that's all? *All?*"

Raw, bewildered, half blind, I stood beside her in the darkened hallway. After a moment she took my hand. Gently she led me to the stairs.

"Come," she said. "Let's play a game of chess."

PART THREE
MIAMI AIRPORT

(MARCH 1966)

CHAPTER 12

MONDAY, SEPTEMBER 9, 1963. THAT DAY, TWO AND A HALF years past, comes as plainly into focus as if I were living it now. The beginning of the first full week of ninth grade. First-period bell about to ring, calling us maybe to English class? Social studies? Algebra II?

I don't know. I wasn't there.

Instead I was on my way to Miami with Julian—yes, Julian—to track down the book that had lain beside Jessup's corpse. The sun rose as we crossed the state line into Florida. All night we'd been traveling. My leg ached from hours of keeping my foot steady on the gas. Palm trees, which I'd never seen before, emerged in the brightening light on either side of the highway. In the passenger seat Julian shook himself awake. After a minute he finished yawning.

"I had a dream yesterday," I said.

"So did we all."

"But it's in my head now. I can't stop thinking about it."

"And I'll bet I'm about to hear it."

I laughed, waited for him to object. He didn't. All for the best, really, that it was Julian and not Rochelle on the seat beside me. This dream, so to speak, I could never have told Rochelle.

"It was this past June," I said. "The eighth-grade end-of-year dance. The night was pretty warm, and everybody was in the school gym dancing. Except me and some of the other kids . . . like, I've never learned to dance—"

Had Julian? My guess was that he danced, if at all, as miserably as he sang. But we never talked about such things; there'd been no time. Evenings, all that summer, I rode off on my bicycle to meet him at the Kellerfield shopping center, about a mile from my home. For the next hour or two, in Julian's old blue Pontiac, we practiced highway driving and when to go through a yellow light, three-point turns, and remembering to put in the clutch while braking so as not to kill the engine. I learned slowly; he was patient. When the time came to test, he was my only examiner.

"Go on," he said.

I hadn't realized I'd been silent so long, sunk in memory. "It was hot in that gym," I said. "They were playing the song 'I love him, I love him, and where he goes I'll follow, I'll follow . . .' You know that one?"

"Sure. Peggy March." He sang, " 'From now until forever, forever,' " in an unrecognizable tune. "Now back to the dream."

"And this girl came up to me"—she was Rosa Pagliano, but I didn't want to say her name. That would be bad luck. "She's cute, and very smart. Also kind of—you know."

"No, I don't know. Tell me."

"Wild," I said, and felt myself blush.

"Aha," said Julian.

This wasn't really a dream, but he couldn't have known that. I remembered the gym lit all pink and purple and how it smelled of perfume and sweat. My gut stirred when I saw Rosa and realized it was me she was walking toward. I wanted to run away. I wanted to go to the bathroom. Jeff was with me, and some of his buddies, but she paid him no attention. Didn't say hi to him, even though he'd liked her first. Even though, until the December night when he and I talked outside the Kellerfield library, I hadn't known I could like any girl *in that way*.

That's one reason he and I fought after she was gone.

"On her lip," I told Julian, "she had little beads of sweat. Her dress was damp at the armpits. I could smell her ten feet away," I said, and remembered how I'd been stirred by that raw scent of her.

"Awful lot of detail, for a dream."

"Do you want to hear it or don't you?"

"Sorry. Of course I want to hear."

"And she said—she said to me, 'Dance?' "

It sounded trivial, anticlimactic, when I said it. It hadn't felt that way at the time. Though my eyes were fixed on Rosa, I felt Jeff watching to see what I'd do. I felt my mother also watching, from the rafters of the gymnasium. Maybe that was why I did what I did.

"And then?"

" 'And then' nothing. I woke up."

"Ay-ay-ay!" Julian's groan turned into a massive yawn. He stretched, arching his long body up from the seat; his knuckles pressed against the roof of the car. "And I thought this'd be a dream worth hearing! You say she's a looker?"

"Prettiest in our class," I said, maybe exaggerating a bit. *You've seen her, Julian*, I wanted to say. *She followed us to your car that day back in April.* But I didn't.

"And wild?"

"Yeah. I guess wild."

"In what way?"

I felt queasy and hopeless. I didn't want to talk anymore. I wished it were Rochelle in the car with me, the way it was supposed to be. I just grunted and hoped he'd catch on and leave me alone.

"Come on, you've got to tell. You can't leave me hanging like this."

"For God's sake, Julian!" It was stupid to yell; I was worn out from the long drive and irritable. I tried to keep my voice under control. "Two days after that dance she stole a bunch of money from her mother's purse and hitchhiked to Florida. To be with her father, I think. Or maybe—"

In homeroom, the last week of classes, we heard the news. Until school ended, nobody could talk about anything else. There were rumors about somebody else she'd gone to Florida to be with—a boy from her neighborhood, older, seventeen or eighteen. A Braxton kid.

"When did she come back?" Julian said.

"She never came back."

The road sign, JACKSONVILLE 14 MILES, whizzed by. I glanced at Julian and saw him staring at me. "It wasn't my fault," I said. "It was her mother. That crazy lady beat her with the buckle end of a belt. She'd been doing it for years. Once she lifted her skirt—this girl, I mean—and showed them to me."

"Showed you what?"

"The welts. From the beatings."

Also the other marks, which I thought were probably cigarette burns, though Rosa never mentioned anything about that. "It wasn't my fault," I said again.

"Of course it wasn't. Whoever said it was your fault? All you did was dream about her, didn't you?"

Yes. I only dreamed. Sometimes ordinary dreams, sometimes wet ones. And when it was time to do something, and she was in front of me saying "Dance?" all I could do was make a dumb joke. "Never touch the stuff," I said, and she laughed, as if that might conceivably be funny, and turned and marched off, stiff and deliberate, and I thought of those legs beneath her summer dress and how shapely they were. I never saw her again.

Jeff and I talked about her, first week of summer vacation. It was the last time we rode our bikes together. It hit me, as we talked, how much I'd lost at that dance and how I'd never have it again. Right in front of him I burst out crying. I tried not to; I couldn't help it. Jeff laughed, the way I knew he would.

"What the hell you sobbing about, you little crybaby? I'm the one who liked her! You were too chickenshit even to dance with her, when she asked you!"

He didn't have to say that. I kept on crying, all the harder for struggling to hold it in, and I screamed things I shouldn't have. Later I apologized, and he said it was OK. But it wasn't. When I phoned him to go riding again, he said he was too busy. Always he was too busy. And I don't have a friend anymore.

I was at the wheel when Julian and I hit Washington, on our way south. It was afternoon rush hour. I woke him to ask if he wouldn't like me to pull over so he could drive.

"Why would I want to do that?" he said, and went back to sleep.

So I saw us through the maze of D.C. traffic, swinging from lane to lane, my eyes darting from inside to outside mirror and back again. There were no "moments of inattention." Somehow I managed not to get us killed. Julian didn't wake up.

Then it was Virginia, and to cope with the heat, we traveled by night and slept by day. Even at night it never really cooled off. We drove with the windows open to catch all the breeze we could.

Each place we stopped, after we crossed into Florida, I got hold of a local phone book and checked it for the name Pagliano. I took care to do this when Julian wasn't looking. In Jacksonville there was a listing for "Pagliano, Joseph." Her father, maybe? I phoned that morning from our motel room, just past the town, while Julian was in the shower.

"Yeah?"

"May I speak to Rochelle, please?"

"Rochelle?"

"Rosa. Sorry—I meant Rosa. Is she there?"

What would I have said if she'd picked up the phone? Explained that I'm Jewish and she isn't, and that was why I couldn't dance with her, because my mother is sick and I don't want to do anything to make her get sicker? Rosa's always known I'm Jewish. We started to be friends in seventh grade, when one of the boys made fun of "*Jew*-dism" in front of me, and Rosa glared from under her thick eyebrows and called him a prejudiced bigot. She wouldn't speak to him until he took it back.

On the other end of the line—silence.

I started babbling. "I'm a friend of hers from school, and I know she's in Florida, but I don't know where, and I thought you might be her father—"

"You got the wrong number, mister."

A loud click; that was all. From the bathroom the shower roared. Julian began to sing.

Julian also made phone calls. He made them from motel rooms in the late afternoons, after he'd gotten up and I was still more or less asleep. His voice drifted into my mind, weaving its way among my dreams. I kept imagining I heard him tell the operator to charge the calls to Albert K. Bender.

Bender? The Bender of Bridgeport, Connecticut, who'd been silenced ten years earlier by the men in black? Why should he be paying for Julian's telephone calls?

Julian made a call from Jacksonville, before we were to begin the final night's drive to Miami. "Good news," he said when he hung up. "Rochelle's flying into Miami tomorrow night. Ten-oh-four P.M. We're to pick her up at the airport."

I sat up in bed. Thirty seconds before, I'd been asleep. My dream—of school, of the kids, of a classroom without Rosa anymore—was already vanishing, like a balloon floating up out of reach. I didn't know whether my heart was pounding because of the dream or from what Julian had just said.

"From New Mexico?" I said.

"That's right. She's finished in New Mexico. She said there's nothing for us there."

"What did she expect there to be?"

Julian didn't answer. The night before we left Pennsylvania, he'd phoned to say I'd be traveling with him, not Rochelle, as we'd planned. I felt relief, then disappointment, then relief once more. Rochelle had been called to New Mexico, he said, on urgent business. He never would tell me what. Probably, if I'd asked, he would have told me the thing I really wanted to know: whether she and Tom had gone together. But I never dared ask.

"She's sure the book's in the old Jessup house," he said, opening his suitcase onto his bed. "We'll be going in after it."

I stood up and began pulling on my clothes. I'd already heard Rochelle's theory: the book had been retrieved from the police by Jessup's occultist friends, who hid it in the dead man's house so his ghost could claim it at leisure. The part about our "going in" was new and ominous. I decided I'd better let it ride, concentrate on getting dressed and packed. Then I decided I'd better not.

"What do you mean, 'going in'?" I said.

"Just that. Going in. Without the current owners' permission. Without even their knowledge, we hope— Why are you gaping like that?"

"I really didn't think," I said, "that by joining the Super-Science Society I'd be embarking on a life of crime."

He sighed. "I wouldn't put it so dramatically. We're hardly talking about a life of crime, at least not at this stage. All we're going to steal is the annotated *Case for the UFO*, which the people who bought Jessup's house don't even know is there. We're not going to touch any of *their* property. Unless you've developed a taste for brass candlesticks? Ornamental clocks?"

"Well, of course I haven't—"

"Assuming the book really *is* there, of course. But that's Rochelle for you. Once she gets an idea into her head, she won't leave it alone until she's tested it. Whatever that may take."

"Julian, I know finding this book is important. But there are *limits*, Julian."

"Not for us, there won't be. Once we have it."

"Meaning what?"

"Oh, you know . . ." He mashed down the laundry bag where we kept our dirty underwear, preparatory to squeezing it into his suitcase. I reassured myself that probably I did know—had known, since we'd begun planning this trip. If Rochelle's recollections of the book were even partway accurate, it would be our portal to flight. Invisibility. Galactic journeyings beyond anything NASA could conceive, or the Russians either. That must have been the kind of thing Julian meant by "no limits." Wasn't it?

"But *burglary*, Julian?"

"Oh, *that*. Is that what you're worried about? No need. Rochelle'll be with us. She'll see to it the job's done right."

This was evidently meant as reassurance. It didn't feel that way. "You mean, Rochelle has done this kind of thing before?"

"Oh, dozens of times. Hundreds, maybe. . . . Close your mouth, Danny, or the bugs will fly in! Didn't your mother ever tell you that?"

"Rochelle is a *burglar*?"

"Not just her. Usually there's two or three helping her, though in a pinch she's been known to do it all herself. Fascinating modus operandi. But of course you already know it."

"How the hell would I know Rochelle's modus operandi?"

He closed his suitcase, sat on it to keep it shut, and clicked the latches into place. Then he slid off, planting himself on his bed like a teacher poised to lecture. Damn hot in here. With one of my socks I wiped the sweat from my forehead.

"She does the advance work," Julian said. "Picks out the target house, rings the doorbell some afternoon. Tells the lady of the house she's a coed, from whatever college happens to be in the vicinity. She looks mature enough to pass as a college student, especially when she's wearing her glasses instead of contact lenses."

"Coed," I said.

"Says she's doing a survey, for some kind of course—"

"Like a sociology course," I said. "At Temple University, for instance."

Lights going on inside, I see! More like flashbulbs, popping all over my brain. And Julian saw nothing, nothing at all. I sat down on my bed, opposite him; I didn't trust my legs to keep me vertical. He rattled on. "She gets the lady talking about herself. About her family, what kinds of lives they lead. The poor woman won't even notice she's broadcast a schedule of the times there'll be nobody home, sometimes for weeks to come. When they'll all be at the movies—"

"Or at their grandmother's in Trenton," I said. "For their Shabbes dinner."

"Yes, exactly. . . . Usually she gets a tour of the house. All sorts of fascinating information. Windows that tend to be left unlocked—"

"You, you, you—"

"Not that we need it most of the time. Me, I don't have Rochelle's charm.

But I've got a positive genius for locks. It was a talent that came in handy when I was younger, just in case people lost their keys to their home or their car. Or locked themselves out absentmindedly, the way people do—"

"*You son of a bitch!*" And I gave a howl that felt like it tore out my stomach.

Next thing I knew he was beside me, arm around my shoulders. "Danny! I'm so sorry! I didn't imagine—I mean, I thought you knew! I thought you'd figured it out ages ago!"

How was I supposed to have— But I wasn't going to give him one more chance to show how smart he was, how dumb I am. "You broke into my house! You *dirty, shitty, rotten*—"

I imagined his long fingers, now reassuringly grasping my shoulder, testing the lock in our doorknob. Transmitting to his brain the magic of how it might open without a key. I imagined Rochelle in my bedroom, a place I'd fantasized her more times than I cared to remember. But not *in this way*, an intruder, come to steal what was most precious to me. Tears rose in my throat; *this* time I would keep them safely within. I would take those fingers of his instead and break them one by one.

"You sons of bitches! All of you—you, Tom, Rochelle—" I paused to think whether Rochelle could be called son of a bitch, or "daughter of a bitch," or maybe just bitch, and this felt so absurd I almost started laughing. "You stole my book!"

"Your book?" Julian looked confused, as if I'd had some magic annotated book, like the one we'd driven to Florida to find. "Oh. You mean those typed-up chapters you kept in your briefcase. *Three Men in Black*, and all that. Your story about the UFO fluttering down on top of you, exactly twenty-nine days before we paid our visit. Pure coincidence, of course. But it gave us the idea for the phone call."

"The phone call! My God, my God—"

"Also some handwritten pages, by that friend of yours—what was his name? Jeff Dullard, something like that?"

"Stollard," I said, wondering if Julian had really got the name mixed up or if he'd intended a pun that did tickle me, furious as I was.

"We'd heard about that UFO Investigators group of yours. We wanted to find out more. What better way than to go into your house, borrow your files—"

"*Borrow?* When did you ever give them back?"

"We were going to mail them to you. Tom promised he'd do it. Don't blame me that his world history teacher had to assign a research paper at exactly the worst time. We all read what you wrote, with considerable interest. Especially the chapter on the three men. That was brilliant in parts. All wrong, of course. We don't know who the three men are either, but they're *not* the way you imagined them. But the manuscript showed originality. Considerable analytic ability too."

"So I get a B plus? Thanks a whole stinkin' lot, Julian. I'm just so flattered."

"We wanted you in the SSS with us. We tried to find a way to meet you. We knew you and that Jeff went on Saturdays to the Philadelphia library; your mother told Rochelle about that. We thought—"

"My mother," I said. I stood up from the bed. I walked over to the window and contemplated the eight-inch gash in the screen. Plenty of bugs here to swarm into an open mouth. I could hear the mosquitoes buzzing, revving themselves up for their big evening. What was I doing a thousand miles from home, freshly awake at six in the afternoon, in a ratty motel with a juvenile delinquent?

"We thought, how could we get you up to the Rare Book Room? And so—"

"I get a phone call. From my dear friend Julian. 'Count the days.' 'Follow the *moo*-woon.' And like the dumb sucker I am—"

"Wasn't me who phoned you. It was Tom."

"Of course! I knew I recognized him, the second we met!"

Not the face, it turned out: the voice.

"Only," I said, "I didn't—"

"Put two and two together?"

I nodded.

"Naturally. That's the part of your education we're now in charge of. Putting two and two together."

"You nearly killed my mother," I said. "That doesn't bother you?"

"No," he said, and at first I thought he meant, no, it doesn't bother me. "We would never have harmed your mother. Rochelle liked her. A kind lady, she said. Just horribly frightened."

Should I try to explain that my mother could have had another heart attack when she saw our violated home? She'd barely survived the first one.

The second would have killed her. "Frightened?" I said. I sat back down on the bed, keeping my distance from Julian. "Of what?" But of course I knew the answer: of death.

"Of being abandoned. By your father if she doesn't keep him placated. She knows how miserable he is, how the marriage was wrong from the start. How he rages against the both of you for what's gone wrong with his life."

And is this my fault? You could argue it either way. I looked down at my hands. I have good hands, veiny, with strong, well-shaped fingers. The hands of a man who will do great good in this world. A mosquito hummed in my ear. I didn't brush it away.

"Your mother turned to Rochelle," Julian said. "She asked, very timidly—she thought Rochelle was a sociology major, remember—aren't there societies where a man can take a second wife, a younger wife, and get his needs met through her? Those were the words she used. 'Get his needs met.'"

"I don't want to hear this."

"But you must. 'A younger wife,' your mother said. 'A *healthy* wife.' And then she looked at Rochelle, and her eyes filled with tears. 'But he'll love the old wife, won't he?' And of course Rochelle said, 'Yes, he will'; what else could she say?"

"Julian. If you don't shut up, I will walk straight out to the car, and—"

"Drive away? Leave me here? Your mother's terrified of that too."

"*What?*"

"Your father's not the only one she's scared will abandon her."

I turned my head; I looked toward the window. It's evening time in Kellerfield, I thought, just as it is here. "I won't abandon her," I said.

"Sure you will. You have to, to grow into yourself. But you can always say no; you have that freedom."

"I do?" I said, and felt a burst of hope. In my mind's eye I saw my mother, in her rocking chair in midafternoon, by the window in our kitchen, watching and waiting for me to come home from school. I could see her through the window, smiling, as I walked up the driveway. A glass of Pepsi-Cola and a bowl of pretzels—my favorite snack, since I was a little boy—would be ready on the kitchen table.

"Of course you can say no. Isn't that what you said to that pretty little girl when she got up the nerve to ask you to put your arms around her and dance?"

"That was a dream!" I yelled—for how unreal, impossible, dreamlike it was that it could ever have happened, that Rosa and I had come so close to holding each other in our arms.

"If you say so." Julian got up from the bed. He took his suitcase, stood it beside the door of the motel room. "Are you packed yet?"

"To go where?"

"Your choice. You can keep on with me to Miami. Or I can take you back into Jacksonville. There's got to be a Greyhound terminal there somewhere. You can go home and be with your mother. You don't have to join our life of crime, as you call it. No compulsion." He opened the door. "I'll wait in the car while you decide."

"How much time do I have?"

"All you need."

I don't know how long I sat on the bed. I could have measured the time by mosquito bites. I thought of my father and how he might take a new healthy wife by whom he could have a child of health, a boy he'd be able to love. Also of Rosa and what must have gone on in her mind before she left, and I thought, *It's not comparable. Her mother beat her, tortured her. Mine is only dying.*

I thought of the pain of growing. Of the guilt. Of how Rosa had the courage to endure both.

It was dusk when I went out to the parking lot. There sat the Pontiac, Julian in the passenger seat. This seemed natural, inevitable. I slid behind the wheel, turned the key in the ignition, shifted into first. "Where to?" he said.

"You sure you trust me with these car keys, Julian? Not to go running back to my mommy?"

"Drive," he said.

Sometime after midnight, about halfway to Miami, we stopped at an all-night diner. A waitress brought us cherry pie and coffee. She was very young, blond and petite, and heavily pregnant. Her face was set in permanent exhaustion. I had to look two or three times before I was sure she wasn't Rosa.

CHAPTER 13

IN MIAMI WE FOUND A SMALL HOTEL, CHEAP AND SHABBY BUT conveniently located, and slept until past sundown. We got to the airport at a quarter to ten that evening. Rochelle's plane was due in twenty minutes. There was no place to park.

"This is hopeless," Julian said as we circled past the terminal for the fifth time. "I don't want Rochelle to come and find nobody there. Why don't I leave you off here and you go to the gate? I'll be along in a little while. There's got to be *some* corner of this stupid lot that isn't full."

A few seconds later he and the car were gone. I marched into the terminal, straight to the arrivals board. Flight 257 from Albuquerque, due at 10:04, would be on time at Gate 19. It was just before ten o'clock now.

I hurried down a long, white, fluorescent-lit corridor. I was sweating all over. Would Rochelle come off the plane bare-shouldered, in the same evening dress she'd worn the last time I saw her? I ought to be wearing a suit and my best shiny shoes, not a checkered short-sleeved shirt with suntan pants and sneakers. I should be holding a corsage for her. My date, for my first prom.

Instead I carried a hardcover edition of Charles Fort's *The Book of the Damned*, which Julian had lent me. Something to read in case the plane was late.

The area around Gate 19 was crowded. There weren't any seats. I sat on the floor and leaned my back against the wall. A young Hispanic woman sat next to me, smoking. "Is everybody waiting for flight two-five-seven?" I asked her. She nodded without looking at me.

"May I have your attention please? United Airlines flight two-five-seven from Albuquerque, scheduled to arrive at ten-oh-four P.M., has been delayed. Currently anticipated arrival time is ten thirty-five."

Well, that was a pity. Julian would certainly be here before Rochelle arrived. I wouldn't need that corsage after all.

I opened *The Book of the Damned* and began to read:

> A procession of the damned.
> By the damned, I mean the excluded . . .

Yes. The damned are the excluded. The one lesson my idiotic school manages to teach. I'd learned it well, at the edges of conversations that didn't
include me, because I didn't talk like the others or about the same things,
and they knew it and so did I. Even Jeff. Now especially Jeff . . .

I snapped out of my reverie. Useless, this bitterness. The door from the
runway was propped open, people filing in. The Hispanic girl stood in a
corner of the gate area, passionately kissing a brown-skinned man with long,
slick black hair. I got to my feet, brushed off my pants, wondering if I'd even
recognize Rochelle when she came through the door. Twice I saw girls who
I thought might be her. But they weren't.

The line thinned to a trickle. Then it stopped. Plenty of seats now. I sat
down; there seemed nothing else I could do. I went back to Charles Fort.

> Battalions of the accursed will march, some of them livid and some
> of them fiery and some of them rotten. Some of them are corpses, skeletons,
> mummies, twitching, tottering, animated by companions that have been
> damned alive . . .

The words had turned meaningless. I closed the book. A stewardess
yanked at the door, and it swung shut. "Was this United flight two-five-
seven?" I asked her.

She nodded. She hurried away. I wanted Julian to be here. *Julian*, I'd say
to him. *Rochelle must have missed her flight. How are we going to link up with
her now?*

But there wasn't any Julian either.

I went back to the ticketing area. I couldn't remember just where Julian had
said he was going to meet us. The space around the ticket counters seemed
darker than it had before, and a lot more deserted. I was puzzled. With so

few people left in the terminal, there *had* to be parking spaces. What was taking him so long?

I wandered back and forth between the counters and the terminal doors, while a woman's voice droned announcements over the PA system. One of these began, very gradually, to penetrate my awareness.

"Albert Bender, meet your party in the baggage claim area for United Airlines flight two-five-seven. Albert Bender, meet your party . . ."

Albert Bender?

The Bender of the three men in black? The Bender to whom Julian had been charging his phone calls? Bender had to be a common name. Surely there were Albert Benders in Miami, just as in Bridgeport.

"Albert Bender, meet your party . . ."

A few nights earlier, while Julian was driving, I'd asked about those telephone calls. He'd given a very long answer that made very little sense. I may have dozed off for part of it. But I remembered his saying, more than once: "I send a message. By using Bender's name, I send a signal. You understand?"

I hadn't understood. A signal for Rochelle? A message for Tom?

But maybe I was the one the signal was for. And it was being sent right now.

I ran for the escalator.

The baggage claim area for United Airlines was deserted when I got there. At the other end of the hall a large group of people, apparently passengers on a TWA flight that had just arrived in Miami, milled around and waited for their suitcases to appear. But the belt for United flight 257 wasn't moving any longer. Only a few pieces of unclaimed luggage remained. Two dark-skinned men gathered the luggage onto carts and wheeled it off to some storage room. Both of them wore what I guessed was the uniform of the airport workers—black jacket and pants, black ties, black caps.

Cubans, they had to be. Refugees from Castro.

I bent over and examined the bags still on the belt. The light was pretty poor. But I could make out, on a tag attached by a small chain to the handle of one powder-blue suitcase, the name Rochelle Perlmann. There followed an address in Bala Cynwyd, Pennsylvania. A telephone number, with a Philadelphia area code.

I looked up. Through the plate glass window I could make out at least four taxis standing by the curb, presumably waiting for the TWA passengers. I could take the suitcase. I could get a cab to our hotel. I could wait there for Julian. Rochelle might have left a message for us inside the suitcase, explaining why she hadn't been on flight 257. I picked up the suitcase. I began to walk toward the doors.

"*Hey!*"

I stopped and turned around. One of the baggage workers was walking toward me, grinning amiably. He was a tall, powerfully built man with a swelling stomach and a large pockmarked face.

"That your suitcase, kid?"

I looked down at the suitcase, still in my hand. "I *think* it is," I said.

"Kind of a funny color suitcase for a fella to be carrying, wouldn't you say?"

Again I looked at the suitcase, a bit longer this time. "Yeah," I said. "I guess you might say it is."

His grin broadened. He looked like he was about to laugh. I prepared myself to laugh with him.

"What's your name, kid?"

He was at least forty years old. Yet I couldn't shake the sense I was facing some loutish kid from my phys ed class, getting ready to gather his friends against me, to taunt me for their usual stupid reasons.

"Albert Bender," I said.

"You got a claim stub for that piece of luggage?" came a voice from my left.

I turned to see the other baggage worker—small, wiry, snaggletoothed. I put the suitcase down and made a show of hunting through my pockets.

"I can't—I can't—can't seem to find it," I said. "I must have left it—"

"You must have left it on the plane," the tall pockmarked man said. "Isn't that right? You left it on the plane."

"Yeah," I said. "I left it on the plane."

"Let's have a look at that bag," said Snaggletooth.

Neither he nor Pockface had a trace of a Cuban accent, or southern for that matter. Seen close up, neither of them had any Hispanic features besides their dark skin. The color had a strange artificial quality about it, as if they both had decided to stain themselves brown for some reason I couldn't begin to fathom.

"Tag says Rochelle Perlmann," Snaggletooth announced. "It doesn't say no Albert Bender. Tell me, Al. What the hell you doing with Rochelle Perlmann's suitcase?"

"Rochelle's my sister," I said.

"Your sister?"

"My sister. I'm picking up her suitcase for her."

"Why can't your sister pick up her own suitcase?"

I thought of telling them she'd gone to get the car and had asked me to bring the suitcase out to her. But then they might insist on my taking them to her or waiting with me until she arrived with the car. "She missed her flight," I said. "I was supposed to come meet her, but she missed her flight. Seems like her luggage got on the plane, but she didn't."

"Thought you said you left your claim stub on the plane," said Pockface mildly.

"I did? I said that? I—I—"

"Now it sounds like you weren't on the plane at all," said Pockface.

"I was—I was—I must have been confused. I got all flustered, I guess."

"Flustered," said Pockface. He seemed to consider this idea. "You're a pretty nervous kid, Al," he said. "You know that?"

"Where was your sister flying in from?" asked Snaggletooth.

"Albuquerque," I said. "New Mexico."

"We know where Albuquerque is," said Pockface. "Been working at airports all our lives."

"What I don't understand," said Snaggletooth, "is what's a lady named Rochelle Perlmann doing being the sister of a guy named Albert Bender. How does that figure, Al?"

"She's married," I said.

"Married," said Pockface.

"To Fred Perlmann," I said. "In Philadelphia. About two years ago. Now she's flying in from New Mexico, to visit—to visit the family."

"Your family's right here in Miami, huh?" said Pockface.

"That's right," I said.

"What's your address?"

"Twenty-two-oh-eight Orlando Avenue," I said.

This was the address of our hotel and the only Miami address I happened to know. Snaggletooth took a small notebook out of his pocket and, with a nasty snicker, wrote something down. I realized I'd just made one more mistake.

"What does your brother-in-law do?" Pockface asked. "For a living, I mean. Up in Philadelphia."

"He's a lawyer."

"A Philadelphia lawyer!" said Pockface. He gave an odd snorting laugh. "It sure does figure. From his name, I mean."

"He sounds like a gentleman of the *Hebrew* persuasion," Snaggletooth said. "Am I right about that, Al?"

"Yes," I said. "You're right about that."

"Tell me the truth," said Pockface. "Doesn't that bother you, just a little bit? Your sister marrying one of them."

"No," I said. "Why should it?"

"Oh, I don't know," said Pockface. "Just, a lot of guys it would bother, that's all. You're a real liberal guy. I respect that."

"It'd bother the hell out of *me*," said Snaggletooth.

"Yeah, that's you," Pockface told him. "But Al's not like you. He's a liberal kind of guy. And he's right about that too! The Jewish, they're just like you and me. Isn't that right, Al?"

"Yeah," I said. "That's right."

"Fuck that," said Snaggletooth. "What I want is a closer look at that suitcase."

"*Good* idea," said Pockface. "Let's all go down to our office, have better light to see by. Al can sit down, take a load off his feet. Don't worry about the suitcase, Al, I'll carry it. What's that book you got with you?"

I handed him *The Book of the Damned*. He looked at the title as we began walking. It seemed mildly to surprise him. "Good book?" he asked.

"I think it is," I said.

"*The Book of the Damned*. All about you, right?"

I must have stopped walking. Pockface pushed me gently on the arm to keep me moving down the long white corridor.

"*Just* kidding," he said. "I'll read the book sometime. Always looking for good books to read. That's the way you broaden yourself, isn't that right, now, Al?"

CHAPTER 14

WE MADE TURN AFTER TURN, THROUGH A MAZE OF IDENTICAL corridors. I tried to keep calm, to remember every turn we took. There was no one in the hallways. The TWA passengers had left long since. For all I knew, we were the only people left in the terminal.

They led me to a small office. It was almost bare, except for a filing cabinet in the corner and a scuffed brown desk pushed against the wall. Fluorescent lights shone all around us. A third man, dressed in the same uniform as the others, sat behind the desk in a straight-backed wooden chair. His skin had the same strange brown tint as theirs.

"Hey, Corky!" said Pockface. "Got a young fella here. Found him walking off with somebody else's suitcase. Says it belongs to his sister."

Corky stood up and pushed the chair away from the desk. Pockface laid the suitcase on the desk. I set *The Book of the Damned* beside it. Pockface gestured toward the chair. "*Asseyez-vous*, Al," he said cordially.

I hesitated.

"Don't know much French, do you?" he said. He took me by the shoulders and pushed me roughly into the chair. It slid back a few inches as I landed. He towered over me.

"Let's get down to business," he said. "You got any ID on you, let's see it."

"I've got my driver's license," I said, getting up from the chair. "And I'll be glad to show it to you. But first I'd like to see some ID of *yours*, please."

"Yeah, sure," said Pockface mildly. And stood absolutely still for a second or two.

I didn't see him pull his hand back. I might have caught a glimpse of his large, hard palm swinging through the air toward me. My head jerked violently to the right; a burning pain flooded my face. Dazed, I sat back down. It took a few seconds before I could open my eyes.

Everything was a blur. My glasses had gone sailing off my face. Somebody was lashing my wrists together behind the chair, tightly, with wire. "Fun and games is over, Al," Pockface said. "You wanted to play I'll show you mine if you show me yours, you shoulda done it out in baggage claim. Where there were people around, so they could hear you when you hollered."

"What pocket you keep your wallet in?" Corky said from behind me. "Nev' mind, here it is. *Damn* if it isn't stuck tight." He poked his fingers into my hip pocket. I tried to squirm away. "No, no," he said. "Don't bother getting up. I got my razor right here."

Click! I felt my pocket pulled tight, then noisily cut away. I pressed my thighs together, hard. My wallet went flying through the air. Pockface caught it.

"Got it," said Corky. "No trouble at all. Didn't have to scrunch up your face so much, did you?"

"We ain't hurt you none, yet," said Snaggletooth.

"Hey, whaddaya know!" Pockface cried out. "This isn't Al's wallet. Belongs to some guy named Daniel Shapiro. In Pennsylvania, looks like."

"Bet that's another one of Al's brother-in-laws," said Snaggletooth. "Bet he's got *two* sisters, both of them went and married Jews. Then Al stole this guy Shapiro's wallet. Figured there'd be plenty of money there, didn't you, Al?"

"Hey, Al, you know what?" said Pockface. "Your brother-in-law's only thirteen years old. That's what it says on his license. Right by the photo. Damn if he isn't the *ugliest* kid I've ever seen. Glasses thick as Coke bottles."

"You got some weird family," said Snaggletooth.

"Where's my glasses?" I said.

"Right here on the floor," said Pockface. "Reminds me, we got to be careful. Might step on them just by accident. If we're not careful, I mean."

"How the fuck did this kid get a driver's license if he's only thirteen years old?" said Corky.

"Who knows?" said Pockface. "Maybe that's the way they do it up in Pennsy. Now, Al," he went on. "You listening to me? Corky is gonna play a little game with you."

I felt Corky's arm snake around my neck. His hand grasped my face. His finger lifted my left eyelid and held it open. There was a powerful smell of gasoline. In front of my eye something metallic gleamed, too close for me to focus on it.

"Corky's got a needle there," said Pockface. "He's gonna see how close to your eyeball he can get that needle," said Pockface. "Without touching it. He's gonna try *real* hard not to touch it. You got to help him not touch it."

"No," I said faintly. "No."

I tried to pull my head back. It was wedged firmly against Corky's shoulder. I jerked myself slightly from side to side. The metallic glint followed, only the tiniest distance from the surface of my pupil.

I began to scream. First a series of short loud yelps, then one protracted howl of grief and terror—for the pain, and for the pain that was to come, and the blindness that would follow. For the space of I don't know how many seconds, I felt myself to be nothing but that one extended howl.

"That was *real* good, Al," said Pockface. "Good and loud and all. Only trouble is, there's nobody can hear you. So you might want to do your lungs a favor, spare them all the hollering. Know what I mean?"

"I wouldn't jerk around like that either," said Corky. "All you're gonna do is get your eyeball stuck on my needle. You just stay *real* still. *That's* it. You're a good boy, Al. I got *real* close that time."

"What do you want from me?" I said. It was almost a whisper; I couldn't speak any louder. I didn't dare take any but the most shallow breaths.

"Just want to talk to you," said Pockface.

"Shit," Snaggletooth said. "What have we got to talk to *him* about?"

"You shut up!" Pockface yelled at him. "Got *plenty* to talk to you about, Al. Drugs, f'instance. What d'ya think about drugs?"

"Drugs?"

"Drugs. Like heroin. Like mary-*gee*-wanna. Haven't you ever heard of drugs? Don't you read the goddamn newspapers?"

Corky released my eyelid. I began to breathe again. I could not stop blinking.

"I think—" I really hadn't thought anything, until that moment, about either heroin or marijuana. People in the slums smoked them, or injected them, or whatever. They had nothing to do with me. "I think drugs are a terrible problem in this country," I said.

"That's right. And terrible problems call for drastic measures. Don't they?"

"Well, I don't know just what we ought to do about—"

My right eyelid was pulled up. Again I glimpsed the needle's shine. I moaned softly.

"*Don't* they call for drastic measures?"

I felt the point of the needle touch the corner of my eye, where the inside of the lid met the tenderness of the eyeball. I cried out. I tried desperately to pull myself back. "*Ooh*," said Corky. "Got a little close there, didn't I?"

"*Don't* they, Al?"

"Yes," I wailed. "They call for drastic measures."

"And how you think drugs get into this country, Al?"

"Get in?"

"They all come in from foreign countries. You knew that."

"I didn't know," I said.

"Sure you did, Al."

He began pacing in front of me as he spoke. "What happens is this. The Mexicans smuggle heroin across the border, into Texas, say, or New Mexico. Then your sister, or whatever the hell she is, gets it from them. Then she puts it into a suitcase, puts the suitcase onto a plane, and somehow manages not to get on the plane herself. Then you pick the suitcase up in Miami, and you got a million dollars in heroin in your hands. All ready to sell to the dealers, up and down the East Coast."

"*No*," I said.

"Oh, *yes*, Al. You know it, good as I do. In a minute we're gonna open this suitcase and find the heroin. And then you know what's gonna happen to you?"

"No, no, *no-o-o*."

"I keep telling you, *yes*, *yes*, *ye-s-s*. We're gonna find that heroin. And then we got the rest of your life planned for you. Don't care how many Jew lawyers you got for brothers-in-law, you ain't *never* getting out. We got you now, for good."

"Lookit him sweat," said Snaggletooth.

"There's no heroin in that suitcase," I said.

But deep down I knew different. At age fifteen, Rochelle was already an experienced housebreaker. Julian had told me that. Why shouldn't she have tried out drug dealing too?

"It's locked," Pockface said. "Let's have that screwdriver."

I saw his blurred form bend over the suitcase. I heard the latches snap open. Bitterness burned deep in my stomach. *Fifteen years old, and Lord knows how many boys she's seduced, how many homes she's robbed. How many trusting old sick ladies she's deceived—*

"What'd I tell you?" Pockface cried.

—and now it's drugs, she's dealing drugs, and now my life is over—

"Right there in the lining! There's the stash. You can feel it, sewed into the lining!"

"Oldest goddamn trick in the book," said Snaggletooth. "Don't know why they still think they can get away with it."

"Corky, you got your razor? Gimme your razor."

The lining ripped noisily, slashed open. Pockface reached in his hand.

"*Shit!*" he said. "It's a goddamn *book!*"

CHAPTER 15

THE THREE MEN CLUSTERED AROUND WHATEVER IT WAS POCK-face had in his hands. I glimpsed a slender blue-covered volume, so much like Julian's copy of *The Book of the Damned* that for a moment I imagined they might be the same. I struggled to stand up, to go over and look at it with them. I'd forgotten I was tied into the chair.

"A *book?*" said Corky.

" '*The Case for the UFO,*' " Snaggletooth read aloud, in a tone of disgust. " 'By M. K. Jessup.' "

"Look inside it," said Corky. "Maybe she hollowed it out. You know, cut the pages out, put the stash inside."

Pockface flipped through the pages. "Nah," he said, "it's all there. Some-body scribbled over it, is all. *And* doodled. Cripes, what weird pictures!"

"What'd she want to sew that into the lining for?" said Corky.

"Don't know," said Pockface, setting the book on the desk. "We'll go through it later, figure that out. Let's see what else is in this goddamn suitcase."

A pile of what seemed to be clothes began to accumulate on the floor. "Hey, hey, hey!" said Snaggletooth. "Take a look at this!"

"Wow!" said Pockface. He turned to me. "This sister of yours is one hot chickee, Al! Got *two boxes* of Trojans in her suitcase."

"Gonna have her a wild weekend," said Snaggletooth.

"And get a load of these underpants!" said Pockface. He held up against his face something that looked like a vivid red cloth. Then a black one. "All perfumed too." I could see his large body swaying as he began to chant, "All-the-*girls*-in-France, woo-woo-*woo*-woo-*woo*-woo-*woo* . . ."

"Find any heroin yet?" I said.

"*You shut up!*" he yelled. He turned back to the suitcase and again began rooting through it. The pile on the floor grew larger. "Well, hey, hey, *hey*. What do you know? What *do* you know?"

"What?" said Snaggletooth.

"Envelope. Got all her receipts in it, looks like. Hey, now *this* is something! For you, Corky. Seems like this lady rented herself a car in Albuquerque. August the nineteenth. 'Bout three weeks ago."

"Yeah?" said Corky. "What kind of car?"

"A 1963 Plymouth Valiant. So the little piece of paper says."

Corky whistled. "That's it all right."

"And what the hell's this?" said Snaggletooth. "A motel receipt. Monday, September ninth. *Yesterday*. At the Sunset Motel. Roswell, New Mexico."

There were other receipts, for other dates, all of them in Roswell, New Mexico. The three men tore at the slips of paper. They fought one another to see them. For a moment I thought they'd forgotten about me.

Then Pockface moved toward me.

"*Shit*," he said.

I saw the huge shape loom over me. I felt Corky's arm tighten around my neck. His finger forced my left eye wide open. I wanted to scream. I bit my lip.

"Awright, Shapiro," Pockface said. "You start talking, and you start talking fast. What was this cunt up to in Roswell?"

"I don't know," I said.

"*You lying little kike!* What was she doing in Roswell?"

"I tell you I don't *know*."

Pockface took a breath, lowered his voice. "Listen to me, Danny. I got the impression you don't see too good, am I right?"

"Yeah," I said. "You're right."

"You'll see a hell of a lot worse with a needle sticking into your eyeball."

"*Don't!*" I screamed. "For God's sake, please don't! I swear to God I'll tell you everything I know. But I don't know anything. I don't know what she was doing in Roswell. I never even *heard* of Roswell. I swear to God I haven't."

"Never heard of Roswell, New Mexico?"

"*No!*"

"Never heard of a disk that came down, crashed?"

"No, no!"

"Never heard of any little men found dead inside it? Or maybe alive, just *almost* dead?"

"No-o-o!"

"I count to ten," said Corky. "Then in goes the needle."

"You've got it all wrong!" I shrieked. "The crash was at *Maury Island.* That's in Puget Sound. *Not* New Mexico. *Never* New Mexico. It was Harold Dahl who saw it. Only he didn't see it, because it didn't *happen. Nothing* happened. It was all a *hoax.* You understand? A *hoax.*"

I babbled on and on, at the top of my voice, about Harold Dahl and Maury Island and its all being a hoax. I was obsessed with the idea they were too stupid to know what the word *hoax* meant. And because they didn't know what a hoax was, they were going to stick a needle into my eye.

Finally I ran out of breath. Corky didn't start counting to ten. The others were silent too.

Snaggletooth said, "Maury Island, *shit.*"

Corky's hand didn't move from my eye. But his muscles relaxed, and I found I was able to blink. He seemed to be trying to keep himself from laughing.

Snaggletooth said, "Harold Dahl, *shit.*" And snickered.

"Come *on,*" said Corky. "We gonna waste the whole night here, or what? This kid doesn't know shit about Roswell. He doesn't know shit about *shit.*"

"Danny," said Pockface mildly, "you don't know shit about shit, do you?"

"No," I said. "I guess I don't."

They were all laughing now.

"All you know is what Harold Dahl says, what Jack Shit says, what this other fella says. Isn't that right?"

I said nothing. My face blazed with shame and relief.

"You don't even know this Perlmann bitch, do you?"

I shook my head no.

"Just wanted to steal the suitcase, right?"

I nodded.

"Probably figured it was a girl's suitcase, right? From the color. Figured, a suitcase like that, there had to be girls' underwear in there. So you could try it on. That's what you like to do, try on girls' underwear. Am I right?"

I sat motionless, my eyes shut, my face flaming.

"Knew it the minute I laid eyes on him," said Pockface.

"Lookit him sweat," said Snaggletooth.

"Go ahead, Corky," said Pockface. "Show him the picture. Let our little friend know what he's getting himself into."

"Danny," said Corky, moving around to stand in front of me. "I want to show you a little something. Scenic photograph from Roswell, New Mexico. Think it might interest you."

He held the photo right in front of my eyes for just a second. Then he pulled it away. I had the impression of a metallic vehicle like a flying saucer resting on the ground, with a humanlike creature lying inside it, in some contorted posture, presumably dead. Corky held the picture about three feet from me. Without my glasses it was a blur. The wire cut into my wrists as I strained against the chair, trying to get a little closer, see the photo a little better.

"Hell," said Pockface. "Let's give him his glasses."

Snaggletooth picked them up from the floor and put them on my face. By some miracle they hadn't shattered. There was a long vertical crack in the right lens, from the top almost to the bottom. But the frame seemed to be holding it together.

I saw how I'd misread the photo. Yes, there was a vehicle; yes, it was resting on the ground. But it was an ordinary automobile. And there was a humanlike being inside, in the driver's seat, visible through the windshield, and yes, this humanlike being was plainly dead. He had died badly, his body twisted, his eyes practically bursting out of his skull with terror. But he was an ordinary human being.

He was Tom Dimitrios.

I blinked several times. I forced myself not to turn away.

"Looks to be a fella about your age, doesn't he?" said Pockface. "Only looks like maybe he could see without his glasses."

I said nothing.

"They found him first thing this morning, soon as the sun came up," said Corky. "The car was parked to the side of a road, two miles outside Roswell town limits. He was in it. Recognize what kind of car it is, Danny?"

I shook my head.

"A 1963 Plymouth Valiant," said Corky. "Same car this Perlmann rented in Albuquerque three weeks ago."

"He was smothered to death," said Pockface. "With a pillow, looks like. They must have gone out on the road, took a pillow with them. So they could fuck better. She must have killed him afterward. Then she walked back into town, or maybe somebody come pick her up. Took the pillow with her. It wasn't in the car."

I stared dully. The crack in the lens felt like it had always been there. Desolation blew through me like a desert wind. Of all the things I wished had not happened, I wished most of all I hadn't seen that photograph.

"How do you know?" I said.

"How do I know what?" said Pockface.

"That she was the one who killed him."

"That's what happens, Danny. It's the black widow spider. First she fucks, then she kills."

"How could she have held him down? Look at that picture. He knew what was happening. He would have fought her off."

"It was the fuck," Snaggletooth said solemnly. "She gave him such a blow-out fuck that all his strength went out through that fuck. Then she took the pillow and killed him."

"He would have fought her off," I said.

But I remembered how firm and strong Rochelle's handshake had been the night we met, how weak and flaccid Tom's was.

"She didn't kill him," I said.

"How you know that?" said Pockface. "You don't even know her."

"Wouldn't know what to do with her if he did know her," said Corky.

I looked from one to another of the three laughing faces. Some broad, some narrow. All of them stained that strange artificial brown. Stupid beyond stupidity.

"You don't know her either," I said.

The three of them rested against the desk. They looked at me with what seemed to be curiosity.

"She didn't kill him," I said. "*You* killed him. You and your goddamn creepy friends. How do I know you didn't?"

I wanted to gesture, point a finger, accuse them. My hands were still behind my back, tied tight with their wire. Corky sighed and walked around behind me. My stomach fell away in terror. I realized how very stupid I had just been.

"That's a real good question," said Pockface softly. "And I'm gonna answer it for you. It wasn't one of us killed him, because if we'd have killed him, we wouldn't have done it with a pillow. We'd have used the wire. Around the neck. That's if we were in a hurry. If we had time, maybe around the nuts first, then the neck. Allow us to give you a small demonstration."

"No. *Please.*"

"Don't mention it," said Pockface. "No trouble at all."

I felt Corky slowly put the wire around my throat, begin twisting it, tightening it.

"No," I said. "No, no, no."

"Don't worry," said Pockface. "We're not gonna hurt you. Not *too* much. Not *this* time."

The wire tightened more.

"Danny," said Pockface. "Lots of people talk bad about the Jewish. You know that, don't you? *Don't* you?"

I tried to breathe an answer. The wire was too tight. All I could manage was a feeble nod.

"But there's one thing I got to say about them. Their families are *real* close. And that's a good thing about them. This country'd be a better place if the rest of us were like the Jewish. That way."

He paused. I could say nothing.

"Especially Jewish boys. They love their families. Isn't that right?"

Another nod, barely perceptible.

"Do *you* love your family?"

I could not speak, could not move. The wire tightened again. I felt it slice into my flesh. I imagined the blood spurting from my throat. Images of red swam before my eyes.

"*Do* you, Danny? *Do* you love your family?"

"Yes, yes," I whispered.

"Say it."

"I love my family."

"*That's* right," said Pockface. Snaggletooth nodded solemnly. The wire loosened slightly.

"You love your family," said Pockface, "you ain't *never* going to talk about what happened here tonight. Isn't that right?"

"Yes," I said. "I'm never going to talk about it."

"You're not going to say a word about Roswell either, are you?"

"No. I promise. I won't say a word about Roswell, ever."

" 'Cause you know, Danny boy, we can find you now. Whenever we want. Wherever you go, we'll find you."

Corky began to untie my wrists.

"Say one word," said Pockface, "you're up shit creek."

"On my honor," I said. "I won't say a word."

I stood up, shakily. Pockface put his arm around my shoulders and drew me aside.

"Danny," he said. "I got a real special feeling for you. Just like you were my son. Know what I mean?"

I nodded.

"And I got a word of advice for you. Just like a dad for a son. You listening?"

"Yes," I said. "I am."

"Don't steal no more suitcases. You want to try on girls' underwear, take your sister's. Have you got a sister?"

"No," I said, "I don't."

"Well, then you gotta have a *mother*. Don't you?"

"Yes, but—I mean, she's sick, she's always been sick—"

"Then maybe you got a grandma. Ask her, she'll buy you some girls' underwear to try on. Have you got a grandma?"

"Yes," I said. "I've got a grandma."

"Good. You ask her. But don't go stealing any more suitcases. You promise me that?"

"I promise," I said.

"Good. *Real* good. And one more thing. You keep away from broads like this Rochelle Perlmann. Broad packs rubbers in her suitcase, she's nothing but trouble. Remember that."

"I'll remember," I said.

He took me by the shoulders, looked into my eyes, and smiled down at me. He began to sing, softly, with just a hint of an Irish accent. "Oh, Danny *boy*, the pipes, the pipes are calling. . . ."

I smiled back. I felt like I wanted to cry.

"Take care of yourself, Danny boy," he said, gently slapping me on the back . . . and then I was out of the room, into the long white corridor.

They had my wallet. I didn't care about that. I had taken the book from their desk; I had it safe in my hand. Only it wasn't *The Book of the Damned* that I carried, but *The Case for the UFO*, with all the Gypsies' markings. . . . From the room behind me, laughter erupted.

"Hey, Danny boy!"

I began to walk faster.

"Danny! You got the wrong book!"

Should I start running? If I run, I might be able to get away. But then they'll know that I know—

"Danny! You come back here!"

I ran.

CHAPTER 16

NOT CLEAR HOW LONG. THE CORRIDORS WERE ENDLESS, WHITE, empty; I don't know how many corners I turned. None led anywhere. I heard the men running after me. At other times I couldn't hear anything but the sound of my own footsteps, echoing around me through the hallways.

It might have been days and nights. Weeks, months, years. Once, I remember, I hid in a bathroom.

I hurried into a stall and climbed onto a toilet. There I crouched, my feet on opposite rims of the toilet bowl, my back against the wall, my head low enough it couldn't be seen over the stall partitions. It was all I could do to keep from slipping into the toilet. The men came into the bathroom. They looked into one of the stalls, but not mine. I held my breath.

"He's in here," I heard Snaggletooth say.

"No, he isn't," said Pockface.

"Shit," said Corky. "He's probably in the *girls'* room."

This was the girls' room I was in. Or rather the ladies' room. I suppose they were too stupid to realize that. They all burst out laughing at Corky's remark. They were still laughing when they closed the bathroom door behind them and went off down the hall. It may have been days and nights before I dared to move.

I could not get out of my head that Julian and Rochelle must be somewhere in those corridors, looking for me. They weren't. Neither was anyone else. Even the ticket counters, when I finally found my way back to them, were deserted.

I walked now. I didn't have the strength to run. Slowly I drifted toward the terminal doors, wondering how I was going to get back to the hotel. Or anywhere. Even if there were a cab outside, it wouldn't help. The three men had my wallet. They also, I remembered, had the address of our hotel.

"There he is!"

Terror gave me second wind. I tore out through the doors, into the thick humidity of the night. I began running down the curb. Several hundred yards down, a car was parked. The trunk was open. A man and a girl stood beside it, unloading suitcases onto the curb.

"Dad," the girl was saying, "it's no *problem*. There'll be *taxis* at the airport. I can take one straight to the dorm."

"You won't take a taxi," the man said loudly. He was bald and stocky, his sport shirt open in the heat. "You'll call Aunt Olga. She knows you're coming, she'll be expecting you. And you won't stay in the dorm either. You'll spend the night with Max and Olga."

"But, Dad, the plane won't get in till *two in the morning*."

The motor was idling. The key was in the ignition. I stood by the driver's side, my fingers on the door handle. The man didn't see me. The girl did. For a second our eyes connected. She may have nodded. She reached up and slammed the trunk shut. I jumped into the car.

My left foot groped for the clutch. There wasn't any. I turned cold, then recovered myself. Automatic transmission. The letters on the dial by the gearshift glowed in the dark. I guessed that *D* stood for *Drive*. I shifted into it, then went down hard on the gas pedal. The car lurched away.

"He's stealing my car!" the man yelled.

I heard the shots. I felt, as much as heard, the rear window explode behind me. Then came the blinding pain as the glass drove into my neck. I cried out, and for a second I closed my eyes. I almost let go of the wheel. The car almost went off the road.

But it didn't.

I tore through stop signs and red lights. Late; hardly any traffic. I tried to remember how to get back to the hotel, until I remembered I couldn't go back to the hotel. Sooner or later they'd be there looking for me. I hoped wherever Julian was, he wasn't there.

After a while there weren't any more traffic lights. No streetlights either. The road became a dark two lane, at first with a broken white stripe down its middle. Every few minutes I felt around the seat next to me to make sure

The Case for the UFO was still there. Twinges of pain shot up the back of my neck. Once I reached back there to touch it. My fingers came away bloodied, the pain so dizzying I nearly lost control.

Headlights in the rearview mirror, tiny in the distance. I jammed my foot on the accelerator; the needle went past seventy, then eighty. With damp, inexpert hands I clutched the wheel. The road, though not very wide, was even and straight. Thank the Lord. Julian had told me to expect that of the Florida roads.

Julian. Where have you got yourself to?

And Rosa—Rochelle?

Tears of loss, mingling with sweat, trickled down my face.

The headlights were gone. Alone once more. I slowed to sixty and glanced toward the gas gauge: quarter of a tank. Soon I'd need to find a town.

There had to be a map somewhere in this car. But I didn't dare stop to look for it, and besides, there was no place to pull over. Vegetation, thick and wild, crowded the edges of the road. Through its gaps I spotted something shining red, low in the sky at two o'clock my position, which I took to be the just risen moon.

So I was driving east or northeast? Made no sense. I ought to be in the ocean by now.

I couldn't remember when I'd last passed a road sign. I switched on the radio, pushed all its buttons, twisted the knob up to the highest frequency and down to the lowest. I did that twice more. Craving not just some clue to where I was, but the sound of a human voice, some human music. Nothing; just the roaring hiss of static. Which also didn't make sense. I couldn't have gotten so far from the city so fast.

I gave up, turned it off. The only sounds were the tires tearing down the now unmarked highway, much faster than I wanted to go; the tropical air from the opened window blew on my face. The reddish glow had disappeared. The moon must have climbed into the black sky, hidden now behind thick clouds. There were no stars. Only my headlights poked, feebly, into the humid darkness.

Needed to pee; nowhere to stop. After some struggle I let go. I dozed in the brief comfort of the warm wetness.

—I'm with my father, the two of us kneeling before a window, his hand on my

shoulder, gazing together into a rainy street. Headlights glare off the wet asphalt—

A dream? A memory? But of what?

Must have been a dream . . . and I snapped awake to see in the mirror a pair of headlights, huge and blinding, barreling up behind me.

I screamed, whether from the terror of the dream—which I'd felt to be deeply frightening, I didn't know why—or from this thing coming up from behind as if to ram me. My foot had slipped off the gas; I was hardly moving. I floored it but couldn't pick up speed fast enough. Just ahead the road forked, curving to the left, a sharp turn to the right. I hooked to the right, screamed again as the wheels beneath me lifted from the road. Almost wept as they slammed down once more.

The other car careened off to the left and was gone. Honking? With a shouted curse? Something like a beer bottle thrown out the window in my direction? I hoped so. But I couldn't be sure. I kept my foot heavy on the accelerator, even as the narrow, pothole-filled road began to twist and turn, for some reason I couldn't imagine. Even as I pushed my idle left foot hard against the floor, to keep myself awake.

The gauge hovered a tick above empty. I bounced, almost flew, over unpaved stretches. I kept away from the road's crumbling edge. Peculiar vegetation on both sides hemmed me in. Bushes, it seemed, tall as palm trees yet covered top to bottom with broad, thick leaves. Had this last turn carried me into the Everglades? Surely it was buggy as a swamp, the windshield covered with their bodies. I turned on the wipers, a mistake. All they did was smear insect slime over the glass.

I looked at the gas gauge. Empty. Yet the car kept moving.

What *were* these trees?

And what were the pairs of gleaming slitlike ovals that appeared every so often beside the road, eight or ten feet above the ground? The eyes of unseen animals, crouching amid the dark branches?

But how would animals' eyes have shone like that?

Farther away, off to my right: the red glow once more. Larger now, and brighter; but still close to the ground, and I knew it couldn't be the moon. While I pondered what it could be, what I already knew it must be, the engine coughed. The speedometer needle slid to zero.

The car plowed into a bushy thicket, a foot or two off the road, before stopping. Without gas I'd have to spend the night here, in the morning try to hitchhike. I left the lights on, so nobody'd come crashing into me by mistake. I thought it over, turned them off. There were worse things than accidents.

Two luminous slits, each swelling in the middle and tapering to points at the ends, hung in the air directly in front of me, some twenty feet away. Farther apart than any animal's eyes could be.

Hot as it was, I rolled up the window. Made sure both doors were locked. I slid over to the passenger side, bumping into *The Case for the UFO*, which I'd forgotten was there, and hunted in vain through the glove compartment for a flashlight. I turned on the radio, was greeted by a burst of static so earsplitting I switched it off. Through the fragments of what had been the rear windshield, mosquitoes swarmed. I tried to keep them away from my neck, let them feed as they liked on the rest of me.

Somewhere on my right the red glow dimmed slightly. Brightened. Dimmed. Brightened.

A car sped by. Down the road brakes squealed, doors slammed. I pushed open my right-hand door, grabbed *The Case for the UFO*, jumped from the car into the bushes. Crashed through the foliage, down an embankment, toward the red shining. From the road I heard running footsteps, then the doors to my car opening, closing.

"He's gone!"

Pockface's voice. The bushes thinned; I ran faster. Some animal, very close to me, gave out a loud ululating howl. "This way!" Pockface shouted, and I heard the crackle of branches as they pushed their way through.

Before me, a large clearing sloped down and away. At the bottom of the slope, resting on the ground, a huge disk, glowing fluorescent red. Last seen nine months earlier, a few yards from my home. Tumbling on me from the sky.

Just like then, a buzzing sensation, a tingling in my feet. Not holding me still; tugging me, rather, toward the disk. Yet I stopped. I resisted. "Promise me you won't get inside," Rosa had said. She'd known what was waiting. For that one moment the three men seemed inconsequential.

They leaped from the bushes, began shooting.

"Aim for the legs!"

My feet ran. I ran with them.

Any second I would feel the pain, the crippling. I would topple helplessly into the thick, tall grass. The disk would vanish like the mirage it had to have been. Instead it grew larger, more solid. As wide across, maybe, as three automobiles laid end to end. Silent, though somehow alive. At its top a dome-like protuberance pulsated. Along the rim a low dark oval, like an egg laid on its side.

A door?

I must have passed through.

Once inside, I had no memory of how I'd got in. I knew only that this was a place of fluorescent glow, white now and not red. A wall of pure whiteness gleamed before me.

Outside, the gunfire kept up. It sounded dim, remote. I should have heard bullets pinging against the shell of the disk. I didn't.

There were buttons. I knew which ones I needed to press and in which order. I don't know how I knew. I lowered my hands; the disk shuddered. It sank into the earth.

Down.

Down.

Down.

PART FOUR
MOONLIGHT BAY

(APRIL–MAY 1966)

CHAPTER 17

THE THIRST WAS WITH ME FROM THE BEGINNING—MORE AN annoyance at first than a torment. I had to find water, or something that could take the place of water, inside the disk. I was afraid to go outside; I delayed until I became desperate. By then it was almost too late.

Again and again I circled the disk's interior. I examined the rows of buttons and switches and small lights that surrounded me on every side, searching for something that might pass as a faucet. When thoughts skittered across my mind, frightening me, I calmed myself with acts of measurement.

Not of time. That wouldn't have been possible. My watch had stopped the instant I plunged into the earth. Weirdly, the moon was over my head. I could see it through the transparent dome at the top of the disk, always in the dome's exact center. It didn't budge from that spot, didn't rise or set. Always full. Three times its normal size. Since it was the same moon I'd always known—the same seas, the same craters—that meant I had to be three times closer.

But how could that be if I'd gone inside the earth? I had no clue; I didn't try to guess. Instead I measured space. I paced off the diameter of the disk, and although each time I did this, I got a slightly different result, it always came to about thirty feet. I did the same for the circumference and got ninety-five feet, which was close enough to 30 x pi. This reassured me. My physical circumstances might make no sense at all, but at least the laws of mathematics still seemed to work.

Meanwhile I was getting thirstier. Also, I couldn't see very well. The right lens of my glasses had a long vertical crack from what the three men had done to it. Through that lens everything shifted and shimmered and wouldn't stay in one place. When I felt too dizzy to stand, I sat on the floor. I closed my eyes. I could have sworn I had a canteen that I lifted to my mouth, tilted my head back, drank deep. I felt no relief; my throat was still dry. Then I saw what I had pressed to my lips: the book.

The Case for the UFO. Marked up by the Gypsies. Lost, then found; rescued or stolen by Rochelle, then by me. The book that revealed all secrets. Including the ones I needed to know if I wasn't going to die here? I started to turn the pages; I held back. I wasn't yet ready for disappointment.

The disk's inner walls and floor were blinding white, the kind that gives you a headache if you have to look at it for long. No seats, nothing that might be identified as furniture, except at the center a bulky object that reminded me of a closed sarcophagus. One solid mass, white like the disk, about three feet wide and long enough to lie on. In height it came to a little below my waist; it was like smooth, hard rubber to the touch. All around the sides, about three inches below the even rectangular surface, ran a series of small protruding knobs, spaced a few inches apart. I couldn't allow myself to imagine what they might be used for.

I tried sitting on it. Immediately I jumped off, as if I'd sat on a red-hot burner. Yet it wasn't hot. I just had the sense, ungrounded but very strong, that I mustn't be there. Something awful would happen on that table—altar, it occurred to me to call it—if I didn't get off at once. I leaped away, toward the control panel that ran all the way around the inner wall, with its oval buttons and tiny levers. I kept my hands glued to the wall, my back toward the table, until I felt safe again.

There had to be water somewhere in there. Living creatures of some kind must pilot these disks; all life needs water. That's why there can't be life on the moon. The moon is waterless; the "seas" people used to imagine are vast deserts, burning under the sun, freezing in darkness— But if there was water within those strange walls, I couldn't find it.

I had no choice but to go outside, and unless everything I'd learned was wrong, the dero or something like them would be waiting. Not to mention that I didn't know how to get out. The wall, as far as I could tell, was smooth, seamless. I sat cross-legged on the floor and slowly opened the book, willing myself to breathe steadily, evenly, deeply. With hands that would not stop trembling, I began to turn the pages.

First impressions were blurred, confused. I saw intricate diagrams drawn in the spaces empty of print, which I imagined bore some resemblance to the disk's control panel. My eye fell upon a sketch—which I hurried past, with a faint nausea—of a praying mantis and a pencil. The handwriting that framed these drawings was mostly illegible. A string of capital letters leaped out at me: "DO THEY NEVER INQUIRE INTO THE MANNER OF THE SEEDING?" In the surrounding scrawl I made out the words *Baby-Girl Christ, born of a Virgin.*

Religion, I thought. *All God and Christ, nothing about UFOs.* Certainly nothing about the one particular UFO that I happened to be trapped inside. I snapped the book shut and pushed it away. It slid across the floor, coming to rest at the foot of the casketlike altar. And a dreadful thought came into my mind:

This disk is the dero equivalent of a pressure cooker.

Placed at the surface as a trap . . .

I wailed and howled. My mind, my body twisted together within a spinning tunnel of terror. I beat my fists against the wall. "Please, please let me out!" I screamed, to whom or what I don't know. My brain switched itself off, and I lost consciousness.

I must have dreamed.

A lot like the dream that had come to me when I nodded off driving. Only a bit more detail; a sense of it lasting longer . . . *Night, and I'm with my father, and he feels like a giant, because I'm small. His hand is on my left shoulder. We look through a window into the street, and it's raining, and the streetlights and automobile lights glare off the pavement. I hear an engine start up. My father points and says, "Look, look," and I look as hard as I can . . .*

Someone stood up beside me, squeezed my shoulder—firmly, not painfully.

No. This had to still be part of the dream.

Dazed, blinking, I turned toward the wall and saw a crack. Vertical, nearly three feet high. It hadn't been there before. On the other side: blackness.

I squeezed both hands into the crack and pulled hard, in opposite directions. Slabs of the wall shifted, slid stubbornly apart. It was like prying open a closed metal eye. Forcing a window, long rusted shut. The edges of the crack cut into my palms. At last I made enough of an opening to crawl through, to the moonlit darkness outside.

Then I waited.

Half crazy with thirst, I flattened myself on my stomach, raising my head so my eyes were level with the bottom of the opening. Ten minutes I watched, maybe fifteen. No motion outside, nor any noise. The silence was absolute, unlike any I'd felt before. I heard my breathing like a windstorm. I heard the beating of my heart.

I dragged myself through the space I'd made. The wall of the disk was only inches thick—a foot at most. Yet passing through it, I felt myself half walking, half floating through a series of rooms, all of them empty, a dull white. Curtains, as though spun by spiders from ceiling to floor, waved softly back and forth in the breezeless passageway. I passed through them, or around them, without touching them. Drops of whitish liquid descended slowly from the ceiling, as though along milky threads.

Then I was outside, struggling to my feet, leaning on the slanted exterior of the disk. To the touch, neither hot nor cool. Yet it glowed a dusky red, like metal approaching red hot; and stepping away, I saw it was the only bit of color anywhere in this world to which I'd come.

CHAPTER 18

ASHES. MOONLIGHT. THAT WAS WHAT I SAW WHEN I LOOKED around. Right behind me, the disk. In front of me, I couldn't tell how far away, a shining, shimmering surface that might have been water.

The moon, huge and ferocious, hung over my head. I kept my eyes turned away from it. My shadow, cast narrowly around my feet, was as crisp as in noonday sunlight. Under my shoes the ground was ashes, or something very like ashes. It was slippery to walk on yet crunched like snow. The squeaking *t-ss-ss-t* of each footstep was the only sound in a silent world. It wasn't hot, nor was it cold. I felt no wind.

The disk lay in a clearing, about twenty feet in each direction. Beyond, solid vegetation encircled me, the bushes unlike anything I'd seen before. They were thickly planted; they came up to my waist. They had a stunted look, as if there were too many of them, too feebly nourished. The leaves and branches were gray. Everything but the disk was gray, or black, or silver in the moonlight.

How would I hack my way through all this shrubbery? But no sooner did I approach it, push at it with my hands than it softly crumbled into greasy dust. Faster and faster I crunched my way through the bushes, in the direction of the water. I began to run, treading branches and leaves and thorns into ashen fragments.

That was when the pain shot up into me, through my foot.

It knocked me off my feet, as if I'd been caught in an ocean wave. I sat down hard amid the crumbled bushes. I gave out a loud yell, which instantly I regretted. In a world so still, a sound would travel. A blackish liquid—my blood, darkened in the moonlight—oozed through my right sock, just above the ankle. On the ground by my foot, a long, sharp bone gleamed brilliant white, tipped by wet blackness.

I'd stepped into a skeleton.

I struggled to balance myself, squatting, on my feet. Pain washed through me—my whole body this time—and once more ebbed. I rummaged amid the jumble of bones. The remains of an animal like a medium-size dog— skull, and jaws, and teeth. Several broken ribs, one of which was the bone that had pierced me. And legs . . .

Six.

I counted, over and over, forgetting my thirst, until I was sure I'd made no mistake. Shakily I climbed to my feet. The zoology of this world was more than I'd bargained for. Six-legged creatures, big as dogs . . .

And where were the eight-legged things that fed upon the six-legged ones?

I stuffed my fist into my mouth. I tried to remember what the dero were supposed to look like. Basically humanoid, I thought, but warped and dwarf- like, their faces bestial and bizarre. I couldn't recall any mention of multiple limbs. . . . And I looked back toward the glowing red disk, to the white oval I'd left gaping on its edge. Anything might get in now.

I'll run back, I thought. *It's not too far. I'll find a way to barricade myself inside. I won't come out again.*

And survive how long without water?

No choice. I shuddered and took a few breaths. One advantage of the si- lence: if anything alive was slithering among these bushes, I was likely to hear it before it got too close. I began again, painfully and cautiously, to make a path for myself through the gray vegetation, toward the broad glitter ahead.

A lake, it seemed, as at last I drew near, praying it wouldn't turn into a mirage.

Yet it had currents, as if it weren't a lake but part of some vast river, flow- ing toward a place I couldn't imagine. Most of all, it was like a swampy marsh, with no defined edge. The bushes stopped abruptly, without first thinning, and a few feet onward the ashes of the land gave way to ashen waters. Before I knew it, I was up to my ankles. The water splashed, faintly, as I walked in it. My wounded foot burned at its touch.

I squatted, then knelt to drink. Immediately I pulled back. The water stank of rotting flesh, as if generations of animals had come there to die. It stretched before me, unending, no farther shore in sight. Once more I lowered my face.

Drink.

"Who said that?" I yelled, jerking my head up. I clapped my hand, pointlessly, over my mouth. The bushes closest to the water's edge trembled, as if in a breeze I couldn't feel, and I thought again of the dero and wondered where I might go to escape. No voice answered. Not even an echo. The voice that said *Drink* wasn't an echo either. It was a woman's voice, from inside me.

Drink, it said again.

"Who are you?"

The voice echoed back, *Are you, are you, are you*, and the surface of the water rippled as if something were stirring beneath.

She spoke again: *We were here before you*. And the echo said, *For you, for you, for you*, and again the water quivered.

I drank then, and the water tasted as bad as it smelled. I spit it back up. But I couldn't help myself. I drank again, and again—like an animal, my face and belly in the water, the pain in my foot forgotten—sickened by what I drank yet helpless not to drink.

The path back to the disk, which I'd cut for myself a short time before, was marked with my own outgoing footprints. They seemed soft and blurry, compared with the crisp prints I was now leaving, and I wondered why. I didn't stop to puzzle it out. I felt ill from the water, tired, aching to lie down even on the disk's hard floor. It was uphill from the lake, but the slope was very gradual. This was mostly a flat, level world to which I'd come.

The gap on the disk's side was wide open, just as I'd left it. No strange cobwebbed transit this time. One moment I was in the ash world outside the disk; then I put my knee inside and hauled myself in. Along the white floor I left an ashen trail, muddy with blood. My foot still bled and had begun to swell. I took off my shoe. Needed a bandage; an undershirt would do. I peeled off my shirt and set it aside—and stopped. My heart stopped also, for a second or two.

An ashen handprint on my shirt.

Tiny, not quite human. A thumb. Six fingers.

On my left shoulder. Exactly where I'd felt the grasping hand as I drifted up from my dream.

I heard high-pitched yelps, a whole string of them. They came from my own throat. I had to close that opening; never should have left it open. I yanked on the edges I'd separated, trying to pull them back together, join them once more into a solid wall. They wouldn't budge.

A dread of that empty hole in the side of the disk, such as I'd never known, came upon me. I backed away from it on my hands and feet, eyes glued to it, until I collided with the corner of the altar. Then, afraid to look into the blackness of the opening but afraid also to look away, I lay on the floor. Perhaps—surely—it was that crack in my glasses. But the blackness seemed to me alive, pulsating with multilegged, derolike obscenities that had once been inside and were certain to be back.

Once more I wailed and howled. If I'd had the strength, I would have torn off what remained of my clothes, gone stripped and naked. I lifted up my hands, pleading to the moon-ridden heaven for release from this place, yet knew, if I couldn't find a way to rescue myself, there wasn't anything on earth or in the black sky beneath it that would come to my aid.

CHAPTER 19

I TURNED TO THE BOOK BECAUSE I DIDN'T KNOW WHERE ELSE to turn. I trusted books; I always have. People will lie to you, betray you, abandon you. Books—never. And this *Case for the UFO*, which I imagined to be plucked from heaven . . . At the beginning I wanted to worship it. I placed it on the altar that might also have been a table, squarely in its middle, there to be bathed in the moonlight that streamed through the dome above. I knew I didn't belong on the altar, that I had no business there. The book did.

I paged through it, looking for some note from Rochelle, explaining why she hadn't been on the plane, where Julian had vanished to and why, how or if I would meet them again. Nothing. Only a printed book, every conceivable space—margins, blanks at the ends and beginnings of chapters, endpapers—packed with waves of scrawl in the Gypsies' three handwritings, their three colors of ink. Here and there a drawing.

Of a crater, for example. Like those on the moon, but with a tower jutting up from its center. A disk like a UFO rested at the tower's top. Other, similar disks approached the tower, departed from it.

Over the lunar maps and diagrams, which were part of the original printed text, there'd been drawn what looked like spiderwebs, the threads dotted with small, lopsided ellipses. The placement of these dots seemed to correlate with the patterns of buttons on the control panel, and I stood for hours by the disk's wall comparing the two. I didn't yet dare press the buttons.

Then there was the praying mantis. I stared at the blue-ink sketch in a margin near the middle of the book, of the long-bodied, long-legged insect impaled on a pencil. Its head hung at an awkward angle, unendurably painful. The thick eyes almost popped out of the face. The pencil entered between the lower legs; from the back of the neck the sharpened tip protruded. Stripes, drawn across the body in red ink as on a barber's pole, gave the impression of being wet like fresh blood.

Anxiously I searched through the sea of scrawl by the mantis's legs for some explanation of what the drawing meant, what it had to do with UFOs or with me. The words *THEY BURNED FOR 18 DAYS*, printed in block capitals, leaped out at me. No clue who "they" were, or why they burned, or what happened to them after the eighteen days were finished. On the opposite page, in another handwriting, I was able to decipher "And when the flesh is Burned shall Take Of The Fatty Ashes, and smear them upon the Altar. . . ."

Phrases from the Bible. I recognized them; by now I'd come to know the Bible well. I couldn't guess what this language was doing here. Yet it seemed strangely apt. I had walked amid the ashes barefoot now—the traction was better, and there was no way I could squeeze a shoe over my swollen right foot—and I'd been struck by their peculiar quality. They weren't dry and flaky, as I would have expected. Instead they seemed greasy, saturated with fat. What kind of burning would produce such ashes?

And why did my footprints vanish after I left them? Not instantly, to be sure, yet each time I left the disk to go to the lake, the prints I'd made in the ashes the time before were gone. Like markings in snow after a fresh fall. Were there ashfalls in this world, like snowfalls on the surface? Or did the ashes somehow ooze their way up from below? These were mysteries beyond my comprehension, unless the book should happen to explain them. So far it hadn't.

In the meantime I found good use for the oily, heavy ashes. I took one of my shoes and packed it full with them. It was a short, makeshift club, and not a bad one. I liked to stand amid the vegetation, the weighted shoe in my hand, and swing it low through the bushes. The leaves and branches flew into fragments at the impact. I knew the dero, or whatever else might come for me, wouldn't crumble quite so easily. But they wouldn't get me without a fight.

I knelt by the lake, prodding myself to drink. I couldn't. The water was disgusting. Vile. Putrid.

Drink.

It was the voice of the woman, speaking inside my head, as it had the first time I was there. I didn't know who she was.

"I don't like this water. I won't drink it."

Follow the moon. Drink from the moon.

"The moon? I can't reach the moon."

Her voice repeated back, in its echolike manner: *the moon, the moon.*

I realized then: the moon was in the sky. But it was also in the water, a few yards out from where I knelt. Its image rippled slightly and seemed somehow bigger than the original.

"I still can't reach it. I'm afraid to go out that far."

Go, she echoed back.

I knew the path from disk to water's edge. So far I'd had no stomach to explore further. In a place like this, fear trumped curiosity. But I'd begun to trust this woman, to think of her as a friend. I did as she said.

The water deepened as I walked. The ashes at the bottom sucked my feet into them, smoothly, past my ankles. The satiny touch soothed my swollen foot. When the water got to my thighs, I leaned forward into it and began half to swim, half to walk. I tried my best to keep the ash-filled shoe, which I carried everywhere I went, above the surface. The image of the moon withdrew from before me. Then it stopped, held still. Waited for me to catch up.

When I stood, the water came to above my waist. The moon shimmered beneath my face. I bent my face into it. I drank from it. And yes, it tasted cleaner, less foul, than in the shallows.

I gulped water, then more water. I stared into the silvery disk that quivered just below me, mirroring the moon in the sky above. And the shadow that passed across it—

IS THAT MY FACE?

What I saw had to be my reflection in the water. But it couldn't be. It had appeared suddenly, a darkness upon the moon's blinding silver. A triangular face, black or perhaps gray, with two eyes and two nostrils and a mouth. The face dwindled to a point at its bottom; the mouth was a short, lipless line. And those eyes—those blank dark ovals, slanting up from the center of the face—

Eyes couldn't possibly be that big.

I jerked my hand up and felt for my own eyes, realizing a second too late that I'd let go of my shoe. I felt my glasses and behind them the soft balls in their sockets. They were still my eyes. They hadn't been transformed into the black monstrosities staring up from the water. I clenched my fist; I smashed down hard into the dark face in the moon's image.

Waves rippled away. The face disappeared.

Surely I'd been seeing things. Still, it felt like time to start getting out of there. Then I remembered I'd lost my shoe. Without it I'd be defenseless. I closed my eyes, held my breath, and pushed myself down into the water. I began feeling with my hand along the bottom.

Felt the multiple legs twine around my body.

Felt the pointed nails dig themselves into my back.

I came up screaming, spitting out water. The thing that had got hold of me came up with me. Claws like ants' pincers crisscrossed my back. They made ribbons of my undershirt, my skin. The dark arrowhead of a face, hard and wet as a lobster's claw, pressed into mine. Its eyes tried to push their way into my eyes, through the cracked glass lenses that separated us. Deep inside each eye was a vertical slit, a crevasse, opening into an abyss. The legs felt numberless.

"Let me go!"

The face backed away. The uppermost legs—skinny, angled, brittle-looking—waved around my head, dripping their water into the lake. They gave off a loamy smell, like fresh-dug earth. Before I knew what I was doing, I had my hands around the thing's neck.

The lipless mouth barely moved. It droned a strange guttural language that seemed mostly to be the syllable *kha, kha, kha* in different combinations. I couldn't understand any of the words. Yet the meaning inside them hummed like a tuning fork in my head.

Until the seeding.

"What? What are you saying?"

I squeezed the throat, hard. I saw the leg cutting downward and felt a streak of burning pain across my forehead, down past my eyes. If it hadn't been for my glasses, I would have been blinded. I gave out a yell. I let go of the neck; I swung my hand and grabbed again. This time it was a leg I held.

"Talk to me, goddamn you!"

With its free legs the thing scrabbled at the surface of the water. My arm, as if on its own, gave a vicious twist; the leg came off in my hand. Like a water strider, wriggling its remaining limbs, the creature skittered off over the lake.

I stood, my feet planted on the bottom, gasping for breath. I thought my heart would burst and I would drown, choking blood. I forgot about my shoe. I imagined the water infested with these creatures. I waited to feel the jabs of their pincers. Half swimming, half running, I heaved myself shoreward, moving with the panicked slowness of my worst dreams.

At last the water fell to my knees, then my ankles. I marched forward. I lifted the creature's hard, slippery leg and waved it over my head. "Hyaaaaa!" I yelled at the top of my voice. I wouldn't use the leg as a club; it was too light for that. I wanted to say, to whatever might be watching me: this is what I did to your friend. I can do it to you.

The silent shoreline came alive. It hummed; it buzzed. Narrow shapes of gray and black slipped shivering into the ashes, as if sucked downward by a vacuum. Prairie dogs into their holes; trap-door spiders into their lairs. The bushes rustled from the movement. Then they were still once more. I dug my nails into my palms to keep from vomiting up the water I'd drunk. Slowly, very carefully, I began to walk.

Back in the disk, I examined my trophy. A severed leg, nearly two feet long—the leg of a monster-size insect or arachnid. External skeleton, which had looked almost black at the lake but in the disk's light was gray. One sharp joint where an elbow would be; from the spot where I'd torn the leg away, a thick black stuff oozed. But at the end, where the hand would be—not the arthropod pincer I'd imagined—

A real hand, with six fingers.

At the end of each finger a claw, mostly withdrawn into the crustlike skin.

I placed that hand against the print on my shirt. It fit perfectly.

My bare back leaked blood onto the altar's side as I sat thinking, wondering, staring. At the creature's arm, which lay on the floor next to my foot. At my own arm, the skin of which had begun to turn . . . gray, I thought at first. Looking more closely, I decided the color was a light brown.

From immersion in the lake's water, no doubt. The way your teeth turn brown when you drink too much tea. I remembered the stain-brown skin of the three men at the airport that had so baffled me. Had they been drinking, bathing, maybe even living in a lake like this? How? And where? And why?

Riddles chased mysteries, were chased by enigmas, around and around my brain. I must sleep; I could not possibly sleep. After a long time I got to my feet. I crawled out through the disk's opening, carrying my other shoe. I began to fill it with ashes.

CHAPTER 20

NO SUN EVER ROSE. NO DAWN EVER CAME. THE MOON HUNG
above me, always full, never changing.

I grew thirsty; I drank. Then I was thirsty again. I never felt the need to
eat, though, and guessed that the water by the lake's shore, foul as it was, had
something in it that kept me alive.

Gray shrubbery and in one direction the lake: these bounded my world,
unvarying as the monster moon in the star-barren sky. Every so often, in a
fit of energy and rage, I'd slam with my shoe at the bushes on the opposite
side of the disk from the lake, striking as hard, moving as fast and far through
them as I could. I thought: *They can't be endless. Sooner or later I've got to
come to something beyond.* I never did.

Yet they didn't grow back where I'd shattered them, and that gave me the
sense of some accomplishment. So did the feeling that my limbs had grown
longer, my stride wider. The fragments of the bushes flew farther at impact
than they once did; in the moonlight, my shadow stretched out beyond
where it once had. If my father could be here, I sometimes thought, how
would his and mine compare?

I never encountered anything alive, six- or eight- or many-legged. Only at
the lake.

From where I drank I had a clear view of several hundred yards of shoreline, on either side of me. None of it looked any different from the spot I'd
begun to think of as mine. Frequently now I saw the lake creatures, standing
in groups along the edge, and although they kept their distance, I could tell
they were the same as the thing that had attacked me in the water. Or maybe
not attacked, but just laid hold on me, with some desperate yearning that left
me bloodied and scarred and the creature mutilated, missing a leg, which I

now carried with me and waved above my head whenever the others showed
a sign of approaching. So they kept away. They stayed in their part of the
lake, I in mine, each of us bending to drink from the same filth.

I never understood why they didn't come for me inside the disk, while I
was sleeping and helpless.

I thought: *They're waiting for something.*

I took to sleeping with my ash-filled shoe under my fingers.

The lake's water soaked into my clothes, my underwear. They stiffened
as they dried. They cracked, fell away from my body in ribbons, useful at last
only to be piled into a pillow. Bare, curled into myself, careful out of habit
not to lie on my glass-riddled neck, I slept on them. I would have taken one
of the stones of the place to put under my head, but down here there weren't
any stones. Just ashes.

I dreamed of other places, which were the same as this one even though
they looked different.

> When I lie down, I say: "When shall I arise?"
> But the night is long, and I am full of tossings to and fro until the
> dawning of the day.

This is from the Bible, the Book of Job. Yet only a line or two later: "My
days are swifter than a weaver's shuttle, / And are spent without hope."

Time crawls snail slow, spins with blinding speed. Months and years
whirl by, too quick to grasp or even feel their passage. Yet the nights are endless. I know what Job meant; I've lain where he lay. The scraps of clothing on
which I've rested stank like his dungheap.

There the woman came to me, rising from the shards of my dreams.

She was the woman who spoke by the lake: *drink*; or *go out to the moon.*
Inside the disk, in the confusion of my sleep, she was no longer a voice inside
me. She'd begun to take form.

Mostly human. Not entirely so. Her eyes were cat's eyes, vertical slits for
pupils; her hair was white. She came shining in the darkness, naked like me,
and I tried to make out her shape, but all was filmy and vague. Skin rubbed
against skin; she was on top of me. Before I could stop myself, it was over.

She put her hand to her belly and smiled, maybe friendly, maybe mocking. "Is this the seeding?" I asked. She shook her head no.

Not yet the seeding.
Then she was gone.

Each time I returned from the lake, I dipped my finger in the ashes and made a mark on the disk's inner wall. When she first appeared inside the disk, there were twenty ash markings. Now . . .

Still twenty.

Sometimes a few more, or a few less. But always about twenty. Because after a while the ashen smears dry out, crumble to powder, drop from the wall without leaving a trace, and there's nothing at all I can do about it. So it's futile for me to make these marks. Yet I keep on.

Thirst is my only measure of time.

Ninth grade's gone by. Tenth. More than half of eleventh.

Pimples erupt on my face, burst in blood, with or without my father's assistance. There's stubble on my face, my upper lip. I shave and cut myself; more blood. "All young boys," my father smirks, "cut themselves trying to shave. . . ."

My journal, like me, is marooned outside time. The New Year's globe falls, explodes into 1964 . . . 1965 . . . 1966. It changes nothing. Spring comes to the calendar, not to the wind. Or to the chill inside.

Swifter than a shuttle. Without hope.

Beyond my bedroom wall she tosses to and fro. She breathes like an exhausted dog. She's going to die; I can tell from looking at my father; he's already got the funeral planned. I'm the only one who refuses to believe it.

Except, of course, her . . .

But in that timelessness mind grows, and its capacities. Like the hair on my forearms. Between my legs.

Slowly I mastered the handwritings in the Gypsies' book. I teased out the secret of their drawings. Abstract from them their details—grotesque, inessential. Patterns remain. These correspond to the buttons and switches and lights of the disk's control panel. Move the controls in accord with these patterns. Things will happen.

The disk might begin to hum, to tremble. Once, experimenting, I felt it lift a few feet above the ground. I looked at my hand and was amazed to see it turn transparent, the panel's lights visible through it. Lifting it toward the disk's dome, I watched moonlight sift through bone and muscle and skin.

This was flight. Invisibility too. If I'd dared, I would have kept on. I'd have raised the disk high, shot up into the black sky, and swooped out over the lake until I'd found the water's limit. I would have tested the edges of this world, no longer shackled by my swollen foot, by dread of the hands or tentacles or pincers reaching out for me. When I'd gotten beyond it—to a place out from under this awful moon, where there were colors again— I'd make the disk descend as UFOs do. Wobbling and trembling, like a falling leaf.

But I didn't.

The sight of myself disappearing filled me with dread. I hadn't forgotten the sailors on a navy ship, turned unreal in the experiment called Hell Incorporated. What happened to them was happening to me.

I fled the control panel. I huddled on the floor by the altar, trembling, my eyes squeezed shut. When I opened them, the disk was back on the ground, my body solid once more. Mostly I was relieved. Yet I was pained also, as if there'd been an opportunity and it had been missed, and I didn't know when or whether it would return.

I sat swaying over the book, poring over its words. I could make out nearly all that the Gypsies had written if I stuck with it long enough. The meaning was something else again. But that's the way of a scripture: it's often not meant to be understood.

> But what shall That Man do, when the Infant born of his Seeding is borne to him at Night, through the Neighborhoods of the Most Distant? How shall he Nourish her? How shall he keep Her from her death? And Woe to him if she should Perish! The Ashes shall be the Burning of His Own dear flesh.

The Seeding . . . the Ashes . . . There were clues here, if only I could decipher them, to what was happening around me. Perhaps a prophecy of my own future? And that "Most Distant," whatever it was: hadn't I been told of something like that, the night I first heard about the navy ship? I racked my brain to recall. In vain; and context didn't help. When I turned the page, the writer had lost interest in the subject and gone on to something else:

Such fools the Gaiyars are! They call us Alien, envision us as dwarves or monsters, search to the bottom of the sea or to the Edges Of The Galaxy for our home. Hah! as if we could ever be Alien to them! All the time we are within them, Bone of their Bone and Flesh of their Flesh. But they will not Understand, none of the Gaiyars will ever understand.

I knew "gaiyars"—a Gypsy word for outsiders, the way I'd sometimes hear my mother and grandmother talk about the goyim, the shiksas. The rest of the paragraph made no sense at all. I read on, hoping for explanation. At the bottom of the page I found a few lines in another handwriting, a different ink color, apparently in response.

But Jemi my Brother:
There is a truth in what the gaiyars say. True, we are part of them,
*   embedded in them, Spirit and Flesh, from the Day Of Their Birth.*
*   AND YET—*
From the depth of the sea to the End of the Stars,
Amid all the galaxies scattered upon the Great Disk,
From one edge of the universe to the other, and upon all its infinite
*   Planets and innumerable Moons—*
There is none more alien than We.

CHAPTER 21

I DOZED, IN THE MIDST OF A DREAM I KNEW EVEN THEN WAS more than a dream, when I felt the touch on my foot.

I'm in my mother's arms, and they're plump and strong like a healthy woman's. Her face is full and round, not peaky and withered, as I've always known it. She smiles down at me, without a trace of fear, the way she did before the sickness began and she and my father still had joy in each other.

She's teaching me the alphabet:

"Ay-bee-cee-dee-ee-eff-gee"

Suddenly she stops singing. Her face like the sky turns clouded and blank. . . . And the fingers touched me, light and gentle, and I awoke, crying aloud.

A moment later I was on my feet, shoe in hand, ready to strike. The silvery figure standing before me made no move, either toward me or away. I realized I wouldn't need the shoe and let it drop.

"Rosa," I said.

I'm not Rosa.

I repeated, "Rosa," although I believed her when she said she wasn't. She was taller than Rosa had been, and her silver-blond hair was longer. Her eyes never blinked. They were two broad slits, slanting upward from high cheekbones. They glowed yellow like candle flames. At their core was an oval of hot darkness.

Why do you call me Rosa?

"Because this is a place where names are forgotten. Especially my own."

She nodded as if she had understood. I waited for her to call me by my name so I could be real. The disk's fluorescent glare was gone, as if somebody'd at last found the switch and turned it off. The only light was the moon's, shining on her gleaming skin.

"There was a girl I knew named Rosa," I said. "A long time ago."

She did look a bit like Rosa. Her lips parted as Rosa's had when she'd stood before me, waiting to know if I would dance.

"I loved you all along," I said. "But Jeff told me first how he liked you, and he was my friend—I mean, I thought—"

How ridiculous this all was. But what do you expect of an eighth grader?

I said: "There was my mother too."

I had to protect her. She was afraid of the shiksas, and of their brothers, who, when she was little, used to waylay the Jewish kids and call them names and sometimes beat them up. Almost three years have passed since I saw Rosa, and even though I said no to that dance, my mother is sick beyond healing. Last Sunday we brought a chair for her out to the backyard so she could sit, bundled up, for ten minutes in the cold April sunshine.

Of all that's happened, not one thing can be undone.

The silver woman reached out her hand. After a moment I took it. I didn't think to notice whether it had five fingers or six. Moonlight spilled like heavy liquid from her hand to mine.

I tried to ask her name. The words wouldn't come out; my throat was so tight. Probably she had no name. She led me to the instrument panel, and there we stood as her fingers danced among the buttons and keys. I recognized some of the patterns I'd learned from the Gypsies' book, which I'd begun to try out for myself but so timidly, so clumsily. She wasn't clumsy or timid. The disk trembled; it vibrated. I felt it rise like an elevator.

In a moment you'll disappear, she said. *Don't be frightened. It's what has to be.*

I looked down at my body. Through it I saw the stars. Then we weren't rising anymore but falling—toward the moon, which grew larger, visible now from all sides because the disk had turned transparent just as I had. She too. I felt the warmth from her body, but I couldn't see her at all. Just the stars around us, through us, and everywhere the speckled blackness tumbling about us like an acrobat. The moon getting bigger and bigger; we were plunging toward it, weightless. Her fingers tightened around my hand. With my lips I groped for hers. She pushed me away.

Not now. Wait for the seeding.

"How long to wait?" I said.

Soon.

"Are we going to the place of the seeding?"

Yes. But not together.

I wanted to ask what she meant by that. Before I could speak, the moon exploded upon us, expanding, until its silvery glare was everywhere I looked. In those last few seconds I grew crushingly heavy. What would happen to me? Would my bones crumble under my weight? Would I lie, a helpless pool of breathing liquid inside my baglike skin? They didn't, and I didn't, and suddenly the pressure eased once more. I kept my eyes closed until I trusted myself to open them.

"Where are we?" I said.

Where do you think?

My head was in her lap. I felt weirdly light, as if I were going to sail off into space at any minute. I couldn't see her, but I didn't know if that was because she was still transparent or if my head was at the wrong angle. I wondered if the seeding was already past, if I'd been part of it and yet somehow missed it.

"Are we on the moon?"

Colored shapes streamed through the black sky above us. A flotilla of glowing objects, like the one that stopped over my house and hurled itself down upon me. Like the gas station signs, the evening before my mother's heart attack, when my father drove us home from a picnic in the country and I lay with my feet in his lap and my head in hers, and I watched the blazing disk of Gulf and the red star of Texaco and the winged, bloodred horse of Mobilgas stream through the sky beyond the car window. I was safe then and happy. For the last time.

Far beneath me I heard a faint murmur, which I took to be the lapping of tiny waves.

"We're in one of the towers," I said. "Aren't we?"

Just like in the crater that the Gypsies had drawn in their book. There must be many such towers on the hidden side of the moon—way stations for vast and thrilling journeys among the stars. The waves surely broke against its base.

"So there *is* water here," I said.

And I *could* drink from the moon, as she'd bidden me do. From water that was sweet and pure and good. I felt relief beyond anything I'd known.

I listened to the rustling, the humming. I began to doze. I slipped away. . . .

It's spring.

Today it even feels like spring—the first Monday in May. I come home from school under the newly mild skies. Mail stacked neatly on the kitchen table . . .

Wonder where Mom is?

She's gone to the bathroom, obviously, and this seems so obvious I don't even take the few steps down the hall to see if the bathroom door is closed. Normally she'd be in the rocking chair by the window to welcome me home, keep me company while I have my Pepsi and pretzels. I glance at the pile of mail, and at the top there's a thick rich envelope. Addressed to me. With a return address that for an instant stops my heart.

CONGRATULATIONS!!!

I've torn it open; I hardly believe what I'm reading in that letter. Good news, at last, at last . . . When I'd thought there was no possibility I'd ever get good news, ever again.

Your essay, "Passage of Time in the Book of Job," has placed among the finalists in the 1966 National Bible Contest. You are among the ten winners selected to come to New York City on Sunday, May 15, 1966, for the final round . . .

"Mom! Mom!"

So it was worth it after all. All the labor I'd poured into that essay, all the hope . . . First prize in the contest: trip to Israel this summer. I'll fly. I'll be out of here.

If only I win.

Once more I call out, "Mom!" as I head toward the bathroom, though if she's in there, I really oughtn't to disturb her.

The door is wide open.

No one there.

I start to be scared. I remember what my grandmother's told me, about the stroke that was the beginning of all this, a few years before the heart attack. I'd been very tiny; my mother had held me in her arms and sung me the alphabet song. Then all of a sudden her face had gone blank, and she couldn't remember what letter came after G.

"Mom?"

I find her lying on her bed, on her side, on top of the covers. I hear her soft snoring. Why is she asleep now?

Her legs. My father's right—I didn't notice, I didn't want to—they're all puffed up again, tubular, the way they were last summer, when she would have died, but the new drug drained the fluids and for a while she felt better. Her arms are a pair of sticks. And on her withered, graying cheeks—

Tears drying.

"Mom?"

Then I see it. A small envelope, typed, addressed to Mr. Leon Shapiro. Post-marked Long Island. No return address. Four of these letters have come for my father since last summer. She gives them to him and smiles as if to say "Won't you tell me who this is from?" But she doesn't dare ask, and he doesn't say anything, just puts them in his pocket, and we don't talk about them anymore. This one she's decided not to give him, because it's been opened; she's taken the letter out—

Archy S.—
Cheerio, my deario!
Me(g)hitabel C.

That's all it says. Handwritten, on a fancy-looking piece of notepaper. I don't know what it means. But I remember now who Mehitabel is. Mehitabel the cat. The alley cat. From that book Archy and Mehitabel *he gave her while they were courting. "Cheerio my deario!" was Mehitabel's motto; she ran with her tomcats, one batch of kittens after another, none of which she ever wanted. She left them out in the rain to drown—*

I don't know what this means. I don't know who lives in Long Island or why there's a g inserted into Mehitabel, or whether the C stands for Cat or something else. I'm scared, I'm terrified, I don't want this to be real. I want to turn around and get out of here, but I'm afraid I'll make noise, she'll wake up—

I tried to sit up. I couldn't.

"That's not water," I said.

No answer.

"At first I thought it was water, washing against something, very softly. But it isn't. It's louder now. Much louder. It's a humming, like the hum of a machine. And now it sounds like chanting, the chanting of many voices—"

I spoke to myself, not the moon woman. I knew she wasn't there anymore.

"And it *is* chanting, and it's getting louder. I can make out the syllables—"

Kha. Kha. Kha.

Again I tried to sit up, to see what was going on. Again I couldn't. I tried to move my limbs, any of them. I couldn't, not in the slightest, and I knew how dreadfully I'd been tricked.

CHAPTER 22

THEY SWARMED AROUND ME, OVER ME. THEY COVERED ME LIKE spiders.

The lake creatures. Inside the disk now. And I lay in the center, on the altar. The operating table. Of course that was what it was; I'd known all along. I stared, helpless, up toward the moon.

Cords crisscrossed my arms, body, legs. They cut into my naked flesh. I couldn't see, but I knew their ends were tied to the knobs along the table's sides. So that was what those knobs were used for. I'd known already. From the moment I first thought of it as the altar, I had known.

I pulled against the webbing. The cords yielded, very slightly. In that bit of give I felt a trace of hope.

They drew open my eyelids, placed clips so I couldn't close them, couldn't blink. They pressed their slit eyes against mine, and I felt my own eyes slitted top to bottom by the contact. I expected pain, but there wasn't any. Only the sense of membranes pulled open, tissues torn apart as though they were a fabric stretched against my skin, and deep in my stomach a faint nausea that might have been worse than pain.

Then they moved to my mouth.

My lips—forced apart. Fingers pressed against my tongue, down toward my throat. I tried to bite, but my jaws didn't work right, as though they'd been rusted. I let out a moan. It was drowned amid the creatures' chant, filling the disk like a mechanical hum.

This was what they'd been waiting for, why they hadn't come inside. I'd needed to become ready. I twisted myself against the cords; again I felt that minuscule yielding, no more. Tubes pushed up my nostrils . . .

Were they trying to kill me? I didn't think so. Probably didn't even want to hurt me. To them, my pain made no difference. They wanted to pry me open, to clean me out. Purify me of my filth and pus, my blood and excreta and tears. My human existence.

The six-fingered hands, claws projecting from the tips, moved downward from my throat. Across my breastbone. Down my stomach. I tried to press my legs together, as they dragged past my navel.

"*A-A-A-A-GHHHHH!*"

My cry was so loud, so jagged with fear I think every living thing in this burned-out, forsaken world must have heard it.

They flinched at the sound. Not much, but a little. Yet their cords held. And then I felt the probing, and then the cutting, and then the hollow needle sunk deep into my tenderest part. My body began to twitch beyond my control. With each spasm I cried out, "Let me die!" until that became a chant of my own, a counterpart to their *kha, kha, kha*. At each convulsion I grew emptier and weaker, the blackness in my eyes thicker and more like smoke.

At last darkness mastered me, and it was all I knew.

I expected them still in the disk when I opened my eyes. But there were only two. They stood on either side, helping me sit up. My hands were tied behind my back.

"That was the seeding," I said. "Wasn't it?"

My feet dangled over the edge of the altar. A large, transparent flask-shaped vessel sat on the floor beneath my injured foot, which was red and horribly swollen. I watched in disbelief as a thick drop, milky white, oozed glistening from beneath my big toenail and fell away toward the flask. For a moment it hung, quivering, at the end of a translucent thread. Then it fell with a splash into the liquid.

"You didn't have to do that," I said.

"If you needed this from me"—I gestured with my head toward the flask—"you could have gotten it . . . the normal way."

Like the Brazilian farmer with his she-alien, taken into her glowing red disk. With her wide hips and large thighs, she'd twice drawn his seed. But then I would have had pleasure, and that wasn't the plan.

I smiled in hatred. I played with my fingers at the cords that held my wrists together, probing for any bit of looseness.

"I would have given it to you. To *her*," I said, thinking of the moon woman. "Gladly."

They gave no sign they'd heard. One of the two bent nimbly to the floor. A thin jointed arm lifted the flask, whisked it away, disappeared into the darkness outside the disk. The other stood alone with me, looking into my eyes.

I looked back, into the two slitted pools of darkness. There I saw, or imagined I saw, my lovely moon woman, naked and far away and grieving. Caught in those eyes, like a firefly in a jar.

I made myself smile.

I beamed into the creature's eyes the thought *Raise your hand. Touch my lips.*

And it did. And I lunged—

"LEON!"

—and bit and heard the crunch of the exoskeleton as my teeth sliced into it. The creature gave a weak *hnnnnhh* cry and tried to pull away. But my teeth were as dug in as any dog's. With my legs I propelled myself off the table, sprang onto the creature, and together we crashed to the floor.

I kept it pinned under my body, working my hands loose. Then I grabbed the thing by its narrow throat. It felt smaller, weaker, more death-rotten than the creature I'd tangled with in the lake, uncounted ash markings ago. Or was I the one who'd grown? An unfamiliar strength blazed inside me, terrible and joyous, thirsting to burn off the dry decay from which I'd come. Like a conqueror, I crouched over my victim, my knee pressed into its body above the swollen abdomen.

"Who are you?" I screamed into its face. "*What* are you?"

It tried to answer, in its *kha-kha-kha* talk. I knew it was trying to tell me, to communicate its own pain. But I couldn't understand its language; I had no patience to learn. I turned it over, took it by the neck, slammed its face into the floor. Over and over I lifted that stony triangle of a head, pounded it down. I don't think I was trying to kill the creature or even hurt it. I just wanted to break open that damned mask of a face. Liberate whatever might be trapped inside.

It didn't struggle. It barely even twitched. By the time I finished, panting and sweating and weeping, I knew it must be dead. But the face wasn't even dented. It was harder than flint, that face. Even when the feeble neck frayed and gave way, and the sticky black stuff oozed onto the floor of the disk—

"LEON!!!"

—like a bad-smelling tar, and the body lay in a heap a foot or two from the now-detached head—even then I'd hardly made a mark on that face—

"LEE-O-N-N-NN!!!"

It's not my name my mother's calling. I run anyway.

CHAPTER 23

SHE LIES ON THE FLOOR, BESIDE HER BED. MY FATHER'S IN pajamas, kneeling. I wish it hadn't taken me so long to get here. That I hadn't been too wrapped up in the journal world to grasp she was crying for help.

She wails: "I *fell,* Leon! Leon, I *fell*!"

She's terrified. I feel her terror of her own crumbling body. She's still in her blouse and skirt; she must have been up late, about to undress for bed. Her large eyes stare blindly, focused on nothing. Where're her eyeglasses?

My father says: "Did you break anything?"

"I don't *know*," she says. And bursts out sobbing.

She cried in this room, this afternoon, reading the "Me(g)hitabel" letter from Long Island. She cried again in the kitchen when I showed her my letter from the Bible contest; she told me afterward those were tears of joy. All through dinner she was quiet, moody. She didn't say anything about the Long Island letter. She doesn't know I know about it.

I stand in the bedroom doorway. Should I come in, try to help? Or will I be in the way? Neither of them notices me. The yellow light of the bedside lamp surrounds her fallen body like a spotlight.

He takes her by the shoulders, gently, and raises her onto the bed. That's when he notices the covers aren't turned down. "Just sit a minute," he says. The small chair beside the bed has toppled onto the floor; he sets it upright. He helps her to the chair, pulls down the sheet and blankets, helps her back into bed.

"It *fell*. I leaned on it so I could get into bed, and it *fell*. I *always* rest on it when I go to bed and when I get up. It's never fallen before!"

She sounds hysterical. Also furious. Why has her chair betrayed her?

Will everything around her now play her false, abandon her? I feel the guilt stab at me that I want so badly to win this contest, to leave this summer.

I step forward. I say, "Can I help?"

Nobody answers. They don't even look at me. Maybe I spoke so softly they didn't hear. Now I see her glasses—on the floor, unbroken. They must have flown off her when she fell. I go over, pick them up.

She lies in bed, shivering, sobbing. She hasn't tried to cover herself; must be too weak, too frightened. He sits down next to her. She reaches for his hand, grabs it. He pulls away. Then he takes her wrist, thin as a stick, and holds it. Taking her pulse?

"Anything broken?" he says.

Tears glitter in her hollow eyes. I'm still holding her glasses; I don't know whether I should offer them to her, to him, to no one. He presses and pokes at different parts of her body, to see where she's been bruised.

"It hurts *here*." She points to her thigh.

He pulls up her skirt. On the left thigh is a huge ugly bruise, already turning purple. He presses with his fingers, and she moans.

He says: "I don't think it's broken. You'll be all right."

"Dad," I say.

He turns to me. He gives me a strange look, not angry, almost tender. But not really loving. Just strange. He takes the glasses from my hand and puts them on her face. She laughs.

"Archy," she says.

She's still laughing, even while tears drip down her cheeks. In that book of theirs Archy was Mehitabel's cockroach pal. Her scribe. Her confidant. Which didn't keep her from trying to eat him every now and then.

I know my mother's talking about the Long Island letter. From his face, I see my father doesn't know. She must never have given it to him; he can't figure out why she just called him Archy. I do understand. But she won't look at me.

Yet I see her. Her puffed-up legs. Her withered, strengthless arms. Her swollen stomach—like the bellies of naked, emaciated children, in news photos of African famines. I think, *She's hanging by a thread*, and suddenly I know what's going to happen. I tell myself maybe it won't. The horrible feeling—the despair and the grieving for her already, even though she's still here, still alive—passes after a moment.

"Leon. Will you stay with me?"

He nods to her. To me he says: "Go to your room. I'll be there in a bit."

She doesn't speak to me. When I reach the doorway, I look back. He's sitting on the bed beside her, holding her hand, singing:

We were sailing along on Moonlight Bay,
We could hear the voices singing, they seemed to say:
"You have stolen my heart, now don't go 'way"—
As we sang love's old sweet song on Moonlight Bay!

That song. Whenever I hear it, I think of spiders and sticky webs I can never get off my skin. I go to my room, start to slam the door behind me. Then I catch myself; I close it gently. I sit at my desk and wait for my father.

Passage of Time in the Book of Job
Essay—1966 National Bible Contest

Why is it history's cruelest tyrants who hold absolute power? Why do the freedom fighters, the boldest and most outspoken thinkers, die abandoned in torture chambers? Why, even in free lands, do the good and virtuous die young and suffer horribly?

Those are the questions posed many centuries ago, by the Hebrew writer of genius who gave the world the Book of Job—

My father knocks, then walks in. He glances at the pages of typescript I've read over and over while waiting—carbon copy on onionskin paper. The original is in an office somewhere in New York City. "That the essay you sent in for the contest?"

I nod.

"Guess they must have liked it."

"I guess."

He sighs. He sits down on my bed. He says: "When's the finals? This Sunday?"

"A week from this Sunday. May the fifteenth."

My heart beats faster. I know exactly what he's going to tell me, though maybe not right away. I have to drop out of the contest, my mother's too sick. We can't leave her alone, even for a day, to go into New York City. Certainly I can't be away from her all this summer if I win, which now I'm sure I don't have a chance to. I've heard about those finals: they ask you a million nit-picky questions about the biblical book you've chosen to write your essay about. Miss one question, you're dead.

My instinct is to cover my essay, hide it from him, find a way to slip it out of sight when he's not looking. No need. It doesn't matter if he reads this; it isn't the UFO journal. That's back in my dresser drawer, under my shirts, its usual hiding place.

He says: "What was all that stuff you were hollering to yourself in here? 'Who are you, what are you?'—something like that?"

So he was awake. We all were. In a death house, sleep comes hard.

I feel myself turn red. "I don't remember."

"You ought to know better than to go yelling like that in the middle of the night. With Mom so sick."

"I'm sorry."

He glares at me; in my mind I shrink to nothing. To keep myself from vanishing, I look at my essay, let my fingertips graze the edges of its pages. This isn't like the UFO journal, doesn't come from a special place of truth as the journal does. It's in school assignment style, though in school they'll never care about what the passage of time feels like when you're in pain. But like the journal, it might pass for grown-up writing. I suppose that's why I'm in the finals. I run my fingers over the thin, crinkly sheets, hoping that'll give me strength to endure what's coming.

My father looks up toward the bookshelves over my bed, where I keep my UFO books. He pulls one down, flips through it. M. K. Jessup, *The Case for the UFO*. "You still believe in this stuff?" he says.

"Yes. I do."

"I thought it was the Bible you were interested in now."

"That too."

"Jesus." He shakes his head. I feel his exhaustion, how badly he must have needed that "Cheerio, my deario!" I want to ask who Me(g)hitabel C. is; I hold myself back. "How do you do it all?" he says.

"I don't know. I find the time."

"You're not flunking out of school, are you?"

"You've seen my report cards."

"Well," he says, and I know what he's thinking. Of course I have time for this stuff. I don't have a social life: no friends, no girlfriends.

"How's your buddy Jeff Stollard these days?" he says.

I stiffen. "OK."

"What's he doing with himself?"

"He's in eleventh grade. Same as me."

"I *know* what grade he's in. But what's he doing? How does *he* spend his time?"

How should I know? We haven't been friends since our fight over Rosa, the summer after eighth grade. But that isn't really what came between us. Jeff just . . . changed. Taught himself the guitar. Found friends who have good voices, not like mine, so he can sing with them. When they're together, he acts like he doesn't know me. And I feel all over again the desolation of my solitude.

Just once, a November afternoon two and a half years ago . . . he came up to me, touched my shoulder. He said, "Kennedy's been shot." As if I needed to know that, and he had to be the one to tell me. As if the gravity of death were the one thing we still could share.

"He's interested in folksinging," I say.

"Folksinging. Not UFOs."

When Jeff and I were friends, my father wrote him off as one more "zombie" like myself. Now we hardly speak, he'll be the model of American boyhood. "Not anymore," I say, and it still hurts.

"Has he learned to drive?"

"He's got his license."

"That's good. Good for him."

I look away. I've had my learner's permit for the past four months, since the day before the journal started bubbling up inside me. It sits in my wallet unused, next to my UFO Investigators membership card. I can't ask my father to take me out for driving practice; I know the rage that'll erupt over my every mistake. So what am I supposed to do with it?

"Does Jeff go out with girls?" he says.

"Some. I think. Not much."

"Sure don't want to tell me anything." He gives a short laugh. "It's your mom you could always talk to. Isn't it?"

Not anymore. . . . I wonder if I should protest, try to soothe his feelings. He closes *The Case for the UFO* and puts it back on the shelf. "What I don't get," he says, "is why both? Why this and the Bible? What have they got to do with each other?"

I could go off, if I wanted, on how there are UFOs in the Bible. Ezekiel's vision of the wheels. What *really* were those angels Jacob saw going up and down the ladder? But this isn't the point. "I—I—they both interest me, that's all."

"You *believe* in the Bible?" he asks.

His voice has changed. Not using questions to prove to me how my life is all wrong, but like he's genuinely interested. Like he really wants to know.

"Sort of. I believe it's history."

"There are other history books. Why the Bible?"

Because it's the history that might explain me, and my parents and grandparents and that gray-bearded great-grandpa whose picture is in my grandmother's house, his name embedded in mine. Why all of us are the way we are. Why Jeff has his friends and I'm alone . . . But how do I say this?

"Come over here," he says.

I obey. He gestures for me to sit down next to him on the bed. When I do, he looks at me like he's about to say something really important. But all he does is reach out and touch my face.

"A new pimple?"

I nod.

"Still with those pimples," he says.

He sounds almost sympathetic, and I realize that this time we're not going into the bathroom to lance it. *Maybe it's not true, what I've always believed. Maybe he doesn't hate me. Maybe this is something complicated beyond my grasp, by things I don't remember, that happened before I was born. And that aren't written in the Bible.*

"Shhh!" he says suddenly, even though I haven't said a word. He jerks his face toward the wall. "You hear that?"

I didn't, but now I do. A faint moaning, from the other side.

"You go to bed," he says, jumping up. "I'll check on her."

At the doorway he stops, turns to me. He throws me a peculiar look, like when we were in her bedroom and I was holding her glasses. This time I know what he means: *I never walked out on you and your mom. Give me some credit for that, will ya?*

Yes, Dad, I will. I mean, I do.

"When's your contest?" he says. "This Sunday?"

I've already told him; already he's forgotten. I try not to sound exasperated. "The *next* Sunday. The fifteenth."

"You don't have to worry. I'll drive you there."

What? *He's on my side!* He wants to help me, let me fly, even collude in my flight; I don't know why. Whatever—I need to express some gratitude, don't I? *Thank you, Dad. That's really nice of you.* Easy enough words, aren't they?

Yet they refuse to come. I give a mute nod.

Later, in bed I fall into a hideous dream. I'm running, using all my strength, trying to gain momentum so I can hurl myself through a vast, tangled spiderweb spun in a tunnel through which I've got to pass. No stopping; no turning back; and if I don't hit the exact right spot, I'll be caught forever.

The spider is there, suspended, just outside my field of vision . . . and I wake, drenched in sweat. The words *She's hanging by a thread, hanging by a thread* run through my mind.

No more sleep tonight. I climb out of bed, retrieve my journal from beneath the shirts. For hours I write. When the room lightens in the dawn and my alarm clock goes off, I'm still hunched over that notebook, the pen twisting in my cramped-up fingers like something alive.

I knew I must leave this place at once, before the creatures realized I'd killed one of them and came back for revenge.

I write of sitting awake, fighting sleep for hours or days, poring over the Gypsies' book and what I remember of how the moon woman operated the disk's controls. Until at last I can work them skillfully as she, pilot the disk on my own.

Everything around me hummed and buzzed. I turned transparent, then invisible. I could feel my fingers, not see them, as they pressed, twisted, danced nimbly over the controls. The disk lifted off the ground, tilted at an angle. Then it shot off into the black, moon-ridden sky.

I climbed high, very quickly. If I wanted, I could have a bird's-eye view of the dark, stunted world I was leaving. But I didn't have the stomach to look at it too closely. I had an impression of vast desolate expanses, chalk white, dotted with clumps of charred, blackened vegetation. Brownish specks that looked like animals dragged themselves across the deserts. On the horizon, moonlight glittered off the endless lake.

Quickly it vanished in the distance. It was a tiny world, really, for all the strength of its gravity. Soon it was only a splinter, drifting in the blackness of space.

The stars surrounded me on all sides, above and below. Above me Orion swaggered. Scorpio crawled beneath my feet. I set my course for the unfamiliar brilliance of Canopus, and the Southern Cross—

I *will* win that trip!

For a minute, maybe two, I hung motionless in space. Behind me loomed the moon. It was the same moon anyone can see, that I've seen all my life. There were no towers, no waves, no waters of any kind. No place where a boy and a moon woman might rest from their journeys and thirst. Probably none of it ever existed in the first place. There were only the craters, and the mountains, and the broad burning wastes that were once foolishly called seas. Mare Imbrium, Mare Nubium, Mare Tranquillitatis.

Sea of Rains. Sea of Clouds. Sea of Tranquillity.

Somewhere in the blackness ahead of me, I knew, there was a slit wide enough for me to pass through. In the massed fabric of reality there's always a slit. You must find it. Then gather the power to force your way through, and shoot yourself toward that slit as though out of a gun. On the other side you'll be in sunlight once more. Where you were born to be.

Miss it, and you wander in darkness and endless thirst.

My heart beat hard as I thought of the chance I was taking, that I always must take.

A minute passed, maybe two. I waited for courage.

PART FIVE
A SONG OF ASCENTS

(JULY 1966)

CHAPTER 24

FROM BELOW MY FEET CAME A LOUD, SCRAPING NOISE. THE disk's momentum dragged it over the rocks until it ground to a stop. The impact slammed me into the edge of the control panel, and I slid to the floor and for several minutes lay there.

My leg: broken? But the pain ebbed, slowly, and at last I realized it was only a bad bruise. I listened in the darkness to what sounded like the waters of a stream beneath me, while I tried to remember how I'd gotten here. Only a few images remained. The disk hurtling forward into space, fast as I could make it go. Colored lights shooting past like meteors; white luminous globes flowing up toward what seemed a crevice, carrying me with them. Then the long, grinding drag over wet rocks.

The rocks at least weren't my imagination. I could see them glistening through the gaping hole in the disk's side. A stream, faintly gleaming, flowed among them. As soon as I felt strong enough to stand, I stepped cautiously out of the disk and looked around for whatever suns or moons this world might contain. There weren't any. I was in a cave, wide and high, but without any opening for light to come in. Only gradually did I understand that the water was the source of its own light, that it itself shone, as though light had somehow been made liquid.

The thing I'd flown was a dark, ruptured shell, its bottom and sides torn open in a dozen places. I'd never fly it again. I crawled inside to retrieve *The Case for the UFO*, then left the disk behind and limped my way upstream.

The grade steepened; the cavern narrowed. The noise of the rushing water grew louder. Walls began to emerge from the blackness, though their tops were too high for the water's light to reach. The stream tumbled into itself in small waterfalls, turning into rainbows as it fell from rock to rock.

Often I stopped to rest. Yet it wasn't long before I rounded the stream's last bend and saw before me an enormous round hollow like the inside of a globe. Bright water gurgled from a spot low on the rock wall.

I looked down: a clear, bubbling pool, fed by the spring, into which I longed to dip myself. I looked up and saw the dim outlines of a vast rock skull, its roof curving in a smooth arch, one cyclopean eye socket far up along its wall, barely visible in the lofty darkness. That was the opening of the shaft that led out of here, to which I'd have to climb sooner or later.

The Well of Souls.

All around were the souls, gathered to this place beneath the Rock in Jerusalem where the dead come to pray. I wondered if I was now one of them. But if I were dead, my swollen foot and bruised leg shouldn't hurt as much as they did. Nor did I much resemble the others. They were white and smooth and sexless, almost indistinguishable, all with puffy round limbs and faces like infants'. Yet some had been men and some women. Somehow I could tell them apart.

They bathed in the pool. They drank from it; they stretched upon the water-smoothed rocks by its edge. They paid me no attention, and I assumed I was invisible to them. The UFO, like the navy ship in that experiment, turns its riders invisible, and some recover afterward, but most do not. And I imagined the dead could not see me any more than the living.

Asher!

The voice cried out, in my mind rather than my ears. At first I thought it was saying "ashes" and speaking of the world from which I'd come. But then it called again, and this time I recognized that soul, and that I was the one being called.

So he did see me. But did he know who I was? Or mistake me for his own father?

I was four when he died. He taught me to read the year before, from the comic pages of the newspaper, me sitting on his lap, on the porch of the big old house that was his and my grandmother's, where on Sabbath afternoons he sat and read from his old Hebrew books. The Bible; other books too. But the Bible was the one I always remembered.

"I'm not Asher," I said.

Who are you then?

I would have told him my name, but I didn't remember it. In the place I'd

been, names are forgotten; that must be true here also. "You're my grandfather," I said.

He heaved himself up from the water and sat on a stool-shaped rock beside it. The stream had carved that shape, hundreds, if not thousands, of
years ago. He was pale and naked, a huge plump baby, his skin shiny as a
soap bubble.

I wanted to sit in his lap this once more, but I was afraid if I did, he would
burst. He motioned me toward a rock beside his. I sat down; with my body
I shielded *The Case for the UFO* from the water that splashed up from the
pool. I glanced toward my legs, stained an unnatural brown. They contrasted
oddly with my grandfather's paleness. The bright water would probably
wash away the tint if I bathed in it. But I wouldn't try that. I wasn't ready to
become a soul quite yet.

He said: *Why are you alone?*

What else would I be? I wanted to say. *I've always been alone.* Before my
mother got sick, I might have had friends. But I didn't, and then she did.

"You need to be proud of me," I said. "I won a contest. It was on the Bible,
and I read the Bible until I learned it better than anybody. I wrote an essay
on it, about how time can seem fast and slow at once. Then I went to New
York and answered questions better than anyone else could. That's how I
won."

I didn't tell him about the UFOs. I didn't think he'd understand.

"I read it in English," I said. "I don't know Hebrew, the way you did. But
I'll learn this summer. I'll be in Israel until the end of August. That was the
first prize."

I'd always wanted him to teach me Hebrew. I wanted to know those
strange-sounding words, that blocky script he pored over with such love. But
we never got beyond the newspaper comics and sometimes a few lines from
the Bible in English. Then he died.

Why isn't your mother with you?

"Beg pardon?"

I felt the rebuke in his words. I went on talking, a little bit desperately. I'd
loved him more than I ever loved my father. There were times I wished my
father had died and not him. He would never have tormented me over my
pimples; he would have taken me out driving and taught me, patiently, just
as he taught me to read.

"Don't you remember?" I said. "You always wanted to go to Israel. The night the UN voted there should be an Israel, you were so happy you cried. I wasn't born yet, but Grandma told me about it. And every year you saved money, and you would have gone, but that heart attack—"

Why isn't your mother with you?

"I'm only going for the summer, for God's sake! She'll be all right. She promised me—"

Yet what does it mean, an invalid's promise? "Don't you worry about me; I'll be fine!" Tears trickled from her eyes as she spoke, as though we were saying good-bye forever and not for eight weeks.

WHY ISN'T YOUR MOTHER WITH YOU?

Louder now, in my mind and possibly also my ears. I knew exactly what I was expected to do. Break down weeping, beg forgiveness, promise I'd leave at once and go home to sit beside her. Rage swelled my throat, strong as when I sat atop the lake creature, smashing its face into the floor.

"Why isn't she with *you*?" I screamed.

My body twitched at each thud of my heart, as my voice echoed off the walls of the hollow and I realized what I'd just said. I wondered if the souls would turn in unison to condemn me as the most evil of sons. Wishing his mother dead.

"I'm sorry," I said. "I didn't mean that."

Death comes in all seasons.

"It's only one summer," I said. "I've never been away before."

Silence. Then he sighed. He bent to the water and drank. At that moment he looked like one of the bubbles in the water. I knew he'd begun to forget me, and I became afraid. I'd waited twelve years to talk with him, and we would never speak again.

"I have a book," I said.

He looked up, with what I imagined to be a trace of interest.

A book?

"Like the old Hebrew books you used to read. There's text here, and there's commentary, and the commentary is more important than the text. There's a lot I don't understand."

He nodded.

"I want you to explain it to me. Like you did when I was little."

He rose from the waters and sat beside me. I wanted badly to touch him, but I was afraid. I opened the Gypsies' *Case for the UFO* to the page I hadn't needed to mark, I'd turned back to it so often I could find it in my sleep. I read aloud:

> Such fools the Gaiyars are! They call us Alien, when all the time we are within them, Bone of their Bone and Flesh of their Flesh . . .

—until I reached the words:

> True, we are part of them, embedded in them, Spirit and Flesh, from the Day Of Their Birth. AND YET—
>
> From one edge of the universe to the other, and upon all its infinite Planets and innumerable Moons—
>
> There is none more alien than We.

Again he nodded.

Death.

"Death?" I said.

Already I understood, just as he had. *Death*—the most essential and familiar part of us all. Born in us, bone of our bone and flesh of our flesh, the instant we're born. Yet also *death*—alien! Beyond all alienness! Through it I'm not *me* anymore; I'm nothing at all. Those Gypsies were right. Easier to conceive of the most fantastic star at the edge of the farthest galaxy, the most inhuman, unrecognizable form of life and intelligence than to conceive of death.

And who of all the people I know—Jeff, the kids at school, Rosa, wherever she is—can conceive of me?

The rock hollow, the radiant water spurting into it, the naked, babylike human bubbles swirling in the water: all spun before my eyes, as the meaning of the Gypsies' words sank in. I was sure I was going to faint. To steady myself, I reached for his hand.

"It's not true!" I cried.

It was too late to explain. I tried anyway. "I mean," I said, "*you're* dead. They buried you in the ground. And yet you're not alien. You're still my grandpa. I recognized you the moment I saw you. Don't you remember? You recognized me too."

Too late.

He'd burst the instant I touched him, like the bubble he was. I watched in despair as he flowed beyond my grasp, down the endless stream.

The rock wall was slippery with spray from below. Yet it was rough and tore my naked skin as I climbed. If I looked down, I'd get dizzy and fall, so I forced myself only to look up, toward the entrance to the tunnel. It must have been at least thirty feet up. I carried, as best I could, *The Case for the UFO.*

The hollow arched inward. My right foot, the bad one, slipped.

My body swung out from the rock like a door on its hinges. My foot kicked at emptiness; the book, in my useless right hand, waved in midair. *Must not let it fall.* The other foot pressed into its rock niche. With my left hand I strained to keep hold, pull the rest my body back against the wall. I looked down.

Saw the rocks on which I would shatter. Saw the soul bubbles, intent on their own eternity, indifferent to this flesh-bound man who swung, howling, in terror of death, a few dozen feet above them. Fall—and I'd lie forever, broken, on those rocks. No one would help. No one would notice.

With my throbbing foot I scrabbled at the wall, found a grip, lost it. My left fingers weakened. I felt them slip. I let go of the book.

In the second and a half it took to fall—my empty hand grabbing at a rock projection, my life, however precariously, back in my control—I felt all that had tumbled away with it. The secrets, the wisdom, the power. What was worse, the pain and blood that had gone into recovering it. Morris Jessup's, Tom Dimitrios's, possibly Julian's and Rochelle's; now mine. All futile, wasted, permanently lost.

I heard the splash. I knew what I'd see if I looked down: the souls scattering, the way water does when something heavy plops into it. Back a minute later, just like water, as if nothing had happened.

I wouldn't look. I closed my eyes, pressed my cheek against the wet rock. My dizziness passed. After a while I loosened my grip, started climbing again. I kept my eyes fixed on the tunnel entrance, now just a few feet away.

To give myself courage, I recited the psalms:

A song of ascents, of David.
I rejoiced when they said to me, Let us go to the house of the Lord.
Our feet are standing within thy gates, O Jerusalem . . .

CHAPTER 25

THE LIGHT FROM THE WELL OF SOULS DIMMED AND VANISHED.
For hours I scrambled upward through the tunnel's darkness. Then came a
light from above, which grew brighter as I climbed.

The last ten feet were nearly vertical. At the top: a thick metal grate,
bolted over the opening.

Useless, I thought. Hopeless. No way I was getting out of here.

Sink down. Slide back to the well. Drink its waters for eternity.

Who whispered those words?

My final message from the moon woman?

No matter; I knew better than to listen. I pulled myself up, braced my
knees against one side of the shaft and my shoulders against the other. With
both hands I struck at the underside of the grate. The screws, mostly rusted,
pulled free on the third blow. I pushed away the grate. I dragged myself up
into a small rock hollow, its floor paved with white marble. An electric light
burned weakly over my head. A short flight of steps led up and out.

Naked I came forth.

Like a pilgrim, I circled the Rock from which I'd emerged. The golden dome
arched over me; the carpet's softness comforted my bare feet. Huge gold letters, in a script I recognized as Arabic, ran in a band around the dome's base.
This was the wrong city—Jerusalem, *Jordan,* not Jerusalem, *Israel.* The city
and world of my enemies, where a person of my ancestry had no business
being. Yet a human city at last, where there were languages and things had
names.

I thought of the winged horse and the night journey. I thought of the
picture that hung in the Rare Book Room of the Philadelphia library, where

my own night travels had begun. I marveled that I was really here, that like the prophet on the winged horse I had flown. I imagined myself leaping over the ornate wooden fence that surrounded the Rock, clambering over the rough surface in search of his footprint. When I found it, I'd jump up fifteen feet and grab the end of the golden chain hanging from the center of the dome. I'd swing on that chain until I propelled myself into the sky. I was free, reborn. Anything was possible now.

It must have been late. The building was almost empty. A watchman, a huge man, dressed in a long gray caftan belted at the waist, sat on a folding chair by the entrance. His white kaffiyeh covered his head, flowed down over his shoulders. His fingers played with a string of beads in his lap. He looked straight at me.

My hands shot down to cover my crotch, and I let out a cry. Luckily he didn't hear. He yawned and shifted in his chair. He looked absently out the doorway, then back toward me. Then back to the beads.

Of course. I was still invisible.

Half a dozen men sat cross-legged in a small circle on the carpet, chanting something I supposed was a hymn. One man was older than the rest. He wore a small wine-colored fez, sparkling white linen coiled around it. His eyes were closed and hollow.

Ya nabee, salaam alaika, marhaban;
Ya rasool, salaam alaika, ma'a salaam.

"O messenger, peace be upon you, welcome. . . ." Somehow, I don't know how, I guessed at the words as they chanted them over and over. I must have drawn in my breath, softly but loud enough. The blind man, the leader, looked up. He called out to me in Arabic; he smiled in the most friendly way. He gestured to a spot beside him on the floor. I smiled back, though nobody could see me.

I shook my head no. The others looked toward me. Then one of them to the man beside him. He tilted his head and tapped it with his finger: *The old man's crazy.*

The setting moon bulged as though a little bit pregnant. It lit the stone platform around the Dome of the Rock, where I stood alone. The gnarled, scattered trees bent under their foliage, rustling in the night breeze.

Down a long, winding ramp I descended to the shuttered city. I moved through it like a ghost. I passed darkened shops, their fronts stone archways. Young men in slacks and open-collared shirts walked in groups, close together, laughing and talking. I pressed myself to the wall as they went by. I slid through a turreted gate with high flanking towers, past a tall white pillar as mute and solitary as myself.

Did I walk or float? I can't remember. Nor can I remember what was guiding me, how I knew exactly which street to turn into, which of the identical-looking buildings was hers. I went inside; I climbed two or maybe three flights of stairs. The button in the wall glowed like a dim orange moon. When I pressed it, I heard a distant buzz. I waited for her to come to the door.

CHAPTER 26

"DANNY."

She looked older than she had the night at the SSS house, when Julian introduced us. Her hair fell loose to her shoulders. Her breasts hung free and heavy beneath her flannel nightgown. Her brown eyes gazed at me, through the thickest glasses I'd seen on any human being.

"You're up late," I said.

"I don't sleep well these days."

Behind her, by the end of a wicker couch, a reading lamp was lit. In her hand she held a thick book, bound in a heavy paper cover. The collected stories of Guy de Maupassant, in French. She'd inserted her finger in the book to mark her place.

"I have terrible dreams," she said.

She stepped backward into the room. I followed; she closed the door behind me. A coarsely woven rug of crimson and white and black covered part of the floor, but where I stood the stone was smooth and creamy. Somewhere in the apartment a clock ticked loudly.

"You're naked," she said.

"I know."

"And your skin—well, never mind. You'll be in the sunlight now. The sunlight will heal you."

She extended her free hand, ran her palm down my cheek. Beneath her touch I felt on my face an odd softness, a springy furriness, as if she were caressing someone or something I'd never yet been. For the first time I grasped I wasn't invisible anymore.

"You've got a beard now."

"I'm older," I said. "Just like you."

"Of course. It's been three years."

Once thirteen. Now sixteen. Once 1963. Now 1966. And my face, once beardless, had sprouted, covered itself in hairs without my ever noticing. No wonder my grandfather had taken me for his own father, whiskered old Asher of Lithuania.

"But aren't you cold?" she said.

Only then did I realize, yes, I was cold. Where I'd been there was neither heat nor cold. I began to shiver and couldn't stop.

"Wait here a minute," she said. "I'll get you a blanket."

Almost at once she was back with a bulky wool blanket. She draped it around me. "Why is it so *cold*?" I said as soon as my teeth stopped chattering. "Isn't it summer now?"

"It is. But Jerusalem can be cold at night even in summertime. We're in the mountains, you know."

" 'As the mountains are round about Jerusalem,' " I said, " 'so the Lord is round about his people.' "

"Danny!" She laughed. "So you're reading the Bible now?"

"For the past three years," I said.

She stood close to me.

"That's how I got here," I said.

I held the blanket tightly around myself with both hands. I hadn't entirely stopped shaking.

"Would you like to see your daughter now?" she said.

The baby lay in her cradle, breathing noisily in her sleep. A network of very fine mesh hung suspended over her, from a hook in the ceiling. Its edges flowed down to the floor, enclosing the cradle on all sides.

Rochelle had taken a flashlight from a table in the hallway. "There's an overhead light in the room," she whispered to me. "But I don't want to use it. We'll wake her up, and then it'll take her forever to get back to sleep. She doesn't sleep, hardly at all."

"My God," I said. I could not take my eyes from the infant. "It was real."

Rochelle nodded. I think she knew what I meant. There really had been a "seeding" in that death-land beneath the moon, which now that I was out of it had begun to feel like a distant nightmare. Yet here was this tiny creature. Child of that land: my daughter, my burden. Whether I loved her I couldn't tell.

"You must be up half the night with her," I said.

"No, no. It's not *her* that keeps me up." There was an immense weariness and sadness in Rochelle's voice, and I remembered what she'd said about her dreams. "She doesn't cry. She just lies there with her eyes wide open, and you see her staring up at the ceiling. Or maybe at something else, I don't know what."

I took a bit of the mesh between my thumb and forefinger. "Mosquito netting?" I said.

"Uh-*huh*. You need it here, for the babies. They couldn't sleep in peace without it."

The silvery netting reflected the flashlight's beam and made it difficult to see inside. I had the impression of a tiny, frail form with spindly arms and legs, a swollen belly. A vast cranium, covered sparsely with fine, silky hair. Her ears were minuscule. Her eyes, which I most wanted to see, were closed. Behind their lids they seemed enormous.

We stood silently together for a few minutes, listening to the loud, labored breathing from the cradle. "Will she live?" I asked.

"We're not sure. She's got a chance, Dr. Talibi says. But not a very good one. He says she's hanging by a thread."

A thread. Spun only just now. Now about to be broken.

"Dr. Talibi?" I said.

"That's right, I'd forgotten. You don't know Dr. Talibi. He was our family doctor here, from back in the old days. He's got an office on Salah ed-Din Street. We'll go see him tomorrow, you and I."

She switched off the flashlight as she spoke. We stood in darkness. I gazed into the shadow amid shadows where my child lay and listened to her tiny lungs struggle for air.

"Her breathing," I said. "Why is it so hard for her? This Dr. Talibi—does he have any idea?"

"No, he doesn't. But I think I do. I think it's . . . the atmosphere. Theirs must be richer than ours. In oxygen. Not by much maybe. But enough to make a difference. I think their lungs aren't built to function in air like ours. And she's got lungs like her mommy's, poor little thing."

Another possibility occurred to me. Born of seed yielded in pain and fear, drained through a needle into a flask—how could she be anything but

warped, sickly, distorted? But then it would all be my fault, and I didn't want
to believe that.

"And hasn't this Talibi noticed? That— that—"

"That she's strange? Not entirely human? Yes, of course he's noticed. He's
not stupid."

She went on, more softly: "But I don't think he'll tell anyone. He'll keep
our secret. For Daddy's sake, if nothing else. He remembers Daddy. They
were *good* friends."

I wasn't entirely sure why she spoke in the past tense. From the sadness
in her voice, I thought I could guess.

"They came in the middle of the night," she said. "When they brought her
to me. Just like you tonight. They didn't have much choice, really. They were
wearing those long raincoats of theirs and those huge dark glasses that hide
everything. But still there was no way they'd pass if anyone had seen them
in the daylight."

"Three of them?" I said.

"Uh-huh. You know them by now; I can see that. There were three of
them, and she was the fourth, all wrapped up in her blanket. I said, 'Why
did you bring her to me?' I didn't understand; I honestly didn't. I hadn't had
anything to do with UFOs, ever since—well, you'll hear all about that soon
enough.

"They didn't answer. I don't know if they even understood me. I might
have been speaking English or maybe Arabic; I don't remember. They must
not have understood. They didn't say anything."

"They never say anything," I said.

After a moment, I said: "What about her eyes?"

"Her eyes? You mean, are they like ours? Or . . . *theirs*?"

"Yes. That's what I mean."

"Well," she said. "They do have an iris and a pupil. Just like ours. Only the
pupil is a lot bigger than ours. It's like your eyes, you know, when you've just
come out from the darkness. Hers are like that all the time. And the light
doesn't seem to bother her. At first I thought it would. But it doesn't."

She spoke slowly, as if she needed to choose her words very carefully.

"You could see how big her eyes are. Even with them closed. And it's a
funny thing, they're not just on the front of her face. The ends curve around

to the sides, just a little bit. They're slanted too. You can't see that so well when she's got them closed."

"And her hands?"

She looked puzzled. "What about them? They're just . . . hands. Five fingers. Four and a thumb."

"Not six?"

Rochelle shook her head. Relief flowed into me, like water down a thirsting throat. Now perhaps I could begin to love this child.

"Danny," Rochelle said suddenly. "Take off your glasses."

She turned on the flashlight and pressed its lighted end against my chest, muffling its light in my blanket. "Never mind," she said. "You don't have a free hand. I'll do it."

She reached up and took off my glasses. She raised the flashlight's beam until it was nearly in my eyes. I tried to see her face. But it was hidden behind the blinding eye of the flashlight.

"You're there!" she cried softly. "In her eyes!"

"I'm there?"

"The color. That beautiful brown, the little bits of green in it. I *knew* I remembered that color, the first time I saw her. The night they brought her here. You've got beautiful eyes," she said. "You know that?"

"No. I didn't know that."

"Well, you do. And so does she. She's got a little bit of you there in her eyes."

"Come on, Danny," said Rochelle. "We'd better see about getting you to bed."

We were back in the hallway now. The door to the baby's room was closed behind us. We didn't need to whisper.

"If we stay up much longer," she said cheerfully, "we'll hear the call to dawn prayers from the mosques. You've never heard that before, have you?"

She turned to me, smiling. At once her smile vanished.

"Danny! What's wrong?"

I couldn't answer. I hadn't known anything was wrong until I saw the fear in her face. All I knew was that I could hear the clock ticking, louder than before, as though echoing through a vast empty house.

That's what happens, Danny. It's the black widow spider. First she fucks.

Then she kills . . . and I saw in my mind the face of her murdered lover. Suffocated, fighting for breath; knowing he was about to die. And I would be next.

She reached for my hand. I pulled it away.

"What's the *matter*? What are you so *scared* of?"

Her voice seemed to come from very far away. I felt myself pulled backward, away, down the tunnel, toward the place where the shining, bubbling dead had gathered to drink. I imagined myself tumbling into that hollow, falling as my book had into the waters. And then, when I no longer existed, when I'd burst like one more bubble, everything would go on exactly as before.

"Rochelle!"

"What? What's the *matter*?"

"Rochelle!"

"Yes, Danny? What *is* it?"

I could speak. Or I could let myself be carried off, back to the dead. I chose to speak.

"Did you kill Tom Dimitrios?"

She shook her head no. She turned painfully from side to side as she kept on shaking her head no, without ceasing; and all the while she mouthed silently, over and over, "No, no, no, no, no" as the tears streamed from behind her thick glasses and down her lovely face.

PART SIX
ROCHELLE'S STORY

(JULY–AUGUST 1966)

CHAPTER 27

THE JERUSALEM SUN WOKE ME WITH ITS RISING. IT POURED through the open window with the morning breeze and bathed the wall opposite in golden light.

It didn't awaken Rochelle, at least not all the way. She stirred and murmured something in her sleep. Then she turned over, heavily, so that her back was to the window and her face rested on the edge of my pillow, close to my shoulder. I sat up in bed and reached over her to the night table, where our eyeglasses lay together, their lenses sparkling in the sunshine. I extricated my glasses from hers and put them on. The crack in my right lens scattered colors wherever I looked.

Her flannel nightgown, hanging on the wall, glowed softly in the new light. She'd apparently gotten up sometime during the night, retrieved it from the floor where she'd tossed it, and hung it up. As I watched, a tiny lizard emerged into the sunlight. In a series of jerky, hesitant movements it crossed the wall, leaped upon her nightgown, and hung there. Its body was dark against the bright cloth.

"Rochelle," I said.

"Unnhhh." She opened her large, myopic eyes and looked at me without quite focusing. "What is it?"

"There's a lizard on your nightgown," I said.

"A lizard?" she said groggily. Then she said: "Oh, Danny. For heaven's sake. They're all over the place here. There're more lizards in Jerusalem than there are people. They don't hurt anything. Can we go back to sleep?"

I didn't answer. All I wanted was that she not close her eyes. They were very close to my own eyes, golden brown in the morning light. I'd never seen anything more beautiful.

"Those glasses have seen better days, haven't they?" she said.

"They knocked them onto the floor," I said. "While they were slapping me around. I suppose I'm lucky they didn't stomp on them."

"I suppose you are." She took my glasses off, delicately, as she'd done twice the night before, the second time in her bedroom. "Don't worry about it," she said. "We'll get you new ones."

She cupped her hand behind my head and kissed both my eyes. I kissed her mouth. For a few moments our tongues caressed. Then she pulled her face away. "Oh, Danny," she said, "you are marvelous. But I think—I am so *very* sleepy."

"We could do it in our sleep."

"Yes, and what wonderful dreams we'd have!" she said, laughing. She added: "I'm a little bit sore down there too. It'd been *ages* since I'd done it, till last night."

"It's been ages since I've done it too," I said.

"Mmmm-*hmmmm.*" She turned over and nestled her back against me. I put my arms around her. She moved her rear end, gently, back and forth against my waist.

I awoke again, a little before she did. I lay on my back and tried to make out the blurred shapes on the walls. She laid her head on my chest and dozed there another minute. Then she began kissing my chest, while her fingers felt between my legs.

"Oh, dear," she said at last. "Where have all the flowers gone?" She sang: " 'Where have all the flowers gone, long time pa-assing . . .' "

"Isn't there something we ought to be doing?" I said. "To take care of her?"

"Her? Oh, you mean *her.* No, no. It's all right, honey. Jameela's with her now. She nurses her, sings songs to her. We'll look in on her after we get up. There's no hurry."

"Jameela." I thought about this for a moment. "What does Jameela think of . . . our little girl? Has she said?"

"Oh, yes. She loves her. She calls her 'my little strange one.' 'My little jinniyya.' That's what she thinks she is, Danny. One of the jinn."

"The jinn?"

"Oh, how to say? . . . The Other Ones. They're not ghosts, and they're not demons exactly, though some of them are. Demons, I mean. But there're also good jinn, who believe in the Quran and try to do right. That's what Jameela thinks the baby is. One of the believing jinn."

"Maybe she's right," I said. At the moment this seemed as good an explanation for the baby as anything I could think of. "She sings to her, you say?"

"The most marvelous lullabies. In her Galilean dialect. Jameela's from the Galilee, one of the refugees of 1948. It's a different kind of Arabic they used to speak there, not like here in Jordan. I listen for hours while she's singing, and I can't understand half of it."

She yawned. She stretched. She propped herself up on one hand. Her large, pillowy breasts swayed above me. In the morning light her skin seemed almost translucent. A very faint red line ran around her neck and down onto her chest. I guessed she normally wore something on a chain, under her clothes, hanging between her breasts, and she was slightly allergic to it. Someday I'd ask her what it was—after I'd asked about the thousand and one other things I'd waited so long to hear.

"It's so lovely lying here with you like this," she said. "I don't think I've slept so deeply for years."

"Neither have I."

"But I think we'd better be getting ourselves up. We've got a big day ahead. I've got to get you some clothes and a shaving razor, first of all—"

"That would help," I said. "If I'm not still invisible to other people, that is."

"Then to the optometrist, for some new glasses. It won't be much out of our way; he's just a block down from Dr. Talibi. And we'll see Dr. Talibi. To talk about *her*, of course. But also about you. You're not in such wonderful shape yourself, are you?"

"No. I'm not."

"That foot of yours could do with some antibiotics. And—and—is there anything else a doctor might help with?"

"The glass in my neck, maybe. They shot out the rear window of the car when they were chasing me," I said when I saw she looked confused. "Some of it went into my neck."

"Poor Danny. You *have* had a hard time. Turn over, will you?"

I lay on my stomach. I felt her touch, very tenderly, the back of my neck and winced in anticipation of the pain. But there was none.

"Does this hurt?" she said.

"Not at all. Feels good, actually."

"It's just scar tissue now." She kept on stroking, and the pleasant warmth spread from my neck through my body. "Three years have gone by, remember."

"I can't remember. I've never known."

Could I explain to her what it meant to be in a place without time? Or did she already know? She leaned over me, caressing with her open palm from the back of my head down to the bottom of my spine.

"It feels *very* good," I said.

I reached up, pressed my hand behind her neck. I raised myself from the pillow. Her mouth opened as I kissed her. She slid beside me, smiling. Her smile broadened as she lifted her thighs, took me in her hand, guided me in.

"Oh, *nice*," she said. Her voice quivered slightly. "Oh, *baby*."

CHAPTER 28

We sat side by side on a thick limestone disk that might have been a small UFO, while the sun poured down on the stones and the weeds, and Rochelle and I sat in the shade of the sepulchres.

And she told me her story.

"The first time we saw them," she said, "they were hitchhiking. By the side of the highway from Roswell to Corona—oh, maybe seven, eight miles out of town. I couldn't begin to guess how they'd got out there or where they were trying to get to. Just the three of them, in the middle of all that desolation.

"I said, 'Tom, did you see those three Mexicans we just passed, standing by the road?' Well, of course he'd seen them. Tom didn't miss much, though I don't imagine you knew him well enough to realize that. He said, 'They weren't Mexicans.' I said, 'Oh, no? What are they then?' And he said, 'I don't know, but they sure weren't Mexicans. They don't have the features. Maybe they're Gypsies, like the ones your friend Jessup got so excited about.' He said, 'Gypsies have dark skins, don't they?' and I said, 'Yes, I suppose they do,' and he said, 'Probably Gypsies then.'

"Well, no sooner did he get this idea than he wanted to go back and pick the men up. He pulled the car over to the side of the road and started turning it around.

"We'd gone quite a ways down the road by this time. Tom always drove twenty miles over the speed limit, wherever he thought he could get away with it. And out west they don't have speed limits once you get outside the towns. By the time he stopped the car the three men were—you could hardly see them anymore. Just three black specks, way back on the horizon.

"I said to him, 'Tom, you're insane! What do you want to do this for?' He said—oh, I don't remember everything he said, but it was all about how they might have interesting things to tell us. We might learn something from them if they were in the car with us, talking to us. Though just what he thought they could tell us, I don't have any idea.

"He said, 'Your friend Jessup always wanted to talk with the Gypsies, didn't he? Thought they had the secrets to the universe, didn't he?' And I said, 'Yes, and look what happened to Morris Jessup.' And he got real mad then and yelled, 'Jessup committed suicide, dammit!' And I said, 'Yes, and that'll be a good way for us to commit suicide too, letting those men into our car.'"

I stroked my cheek, freshly shaved. "Tom had courage," I said.

She looked at me thoughtfully.

"Tom had no sense of danger," she said. "That's why he drove so fast. I'm not sure that's the same as courage, exactly. He was never in a really danger- ous situation, not up till the very end. I don't think he had any feeling for what it might be like.

"He kept saying, 'You've still got your switchblade in your purse, haven't you?' And I said, 'Well, yes, of course I do. But there's no guarantee I'll be able to get to it in time. And anyway, there's three of them and only two of us.' And of course I didn't want to say this, Danny, but I'm sure you remember—Tom wasn't all that terribly strong. . . ."

We were at the Tombs of the Kings, off Nablus Road. Rochelle had given the watchman a few coins, and he had nodded to us, and we'd gone down the crude limestone staircase among the cliffs where the ancient Jewish kings of Adiabene had carved out their burial chambers. I wore the new clothes Rochelle had bought me that morning. Shoes too, though these had been a problem. She'd gotten them several sizes too big, to accom- modate my swollen foot. I had to wear extra socks on my left foot, while the right felt cramped and pinched, so I took the shoe off whenever I could.

The great circular stone, the size and shape of a tractor wheel, had once sealed off one of the burial caves. But now it had been rolled away from the door of the sepulchre and tumbled onto its side. Rochelle and I sat on it to- gether, while she talked and I listened, and every so often I stretched my bare foot out from the shade of the cliff into the sun's healing light.

———

"That was our first day in Roswell," she said. "We'd just checked into the motel, and we were trying to get the feel of the place. It wasn't till the end of the next week that we found anybody willing to admit the archive existed. It was another week before they let me see what they had. And sure enough, there was Morris's book. All ripe for the taking.

"It surprised me, Danny. It really did. I would have been ready to bet the book was hidden in Morris's house in Coral Gables, just like I told you, and the Roswell trip was one big wild-goose chase. Not entirely, of course. There were always the specimens. It would have been worth going to Roswell just for the chance to see the specimens.

"We spent three days in that motel. Travers Motel, it was called. I haven't forgotten any of the names, though I saw enough New Mexico motels during those three weeks to last me a lifetime.

"It was the morning of the fourth day that I went out to the car, just to get—I think it was a map we'd left in the glove compartment. I was thirsty, and I remembered they had a Coke machine in the motel office, and I thought, *Well, I'll go get a couple of Cokes for Tom and me.* So in I went. And there they were."

"The three men?" I said.

She nodded.

"You know that expression?" she said. "About how when you're scared suddenly, your heart goes down into your shoes? Well, right then I understood that expression real well. Because that's what happened to me.

"Three days before, driving in the car, I'd argued and argued with Tom till I persuaded him not to go back and pick the men up. And I was so relieved when he listened to me finally. And now it was as if the men had tracked us down and come after us."

"Had they seen your license plate, do you think?" I asked.

"I don't know. Maybe it was pure coincidence. Maybe they just happened to have stopped by the motel. All I know is, they'd made *real* good friends with the desk clerk. They were talking at the top of their voices and laughing, the big tall one slapping the counter while he laughed, he thought it was all so funny. He was the one with that awful face, with the pockmarks.

"The minute I walked in they got quiet. They were looking at me. Grinning. Looking me over, the way men always did. And the big one, with the pockmarks, called out to me, 'Hey there, little lady!' And they all started laughing again, doubled over with it, as if that were just about the funniest thing they'd ever heard.

"My heart was pounding so hard I thought it'd burst out of my chest. But I tried to stay calm. I walked over to the Coke machine, as slowly as I could manage. I put in a dime, and *choonk*, the Coke bottle came tumbling down. And then another dime. And all the time I was trying to look like I was ignoring them, and still hear everything they said. Look away from them and still see them out of the corner of my eye."

"Was the thin one there too?" I asked. "The one with the snaggletooth?"

"Snaggletooth. Yes, that's what you call it. I'd forgotten the word. He was there, all right. Meanest-looking man I've ever seen. And there was the third one. He was the only one they called by name. Jemi. They all called him Jemi. Even the motel clerk did. How the clerk knew those three men, I'll never begin to imagine."

" Jemi!" I said. "That's—"

"Yes, yes. One of the three Gypsies, or whatever they were, who wrote their notes in Morris's book. There was Mr. A. and Mr. B. And there was Jemi. . . . The minute I heard that name, I thought of Morris. I thought of how Tom was right, that Morris did want to find those three men, talk with them, learn from them the secrets of UFOs and invisibility and how it all fit together. Then I remembered Morris dead in his car. In the park in Coral Gables. Suffocated, his eyes bugged out in terror. And I knew they were here, and I had found them. Without quite trying to. And something awful was going to happen. To Tom. To me. To somebody.

"I took the Cokes and headed for the door. I was still trying to walk slow and easy. But you can't keep yourself from sweating. That's a fact, Danny, and it doesn't matter how hard you try. I was wearing my white summer dress, and it was all soaked, in two great streaks down from my armpits. Of course they noticed. The skinny one said something to the others, too soft for me to hear, and they all laughed. And the one with the pockmarks yelled, 'Don't get yourself all *hot*, now, little lady!'

"I marched out, and the screen door slammed behind me. I could still hear them laughing and laughing, all the way to the car.

"I only stayed in the car a few minutes. Just long enough to get hold of myself. I held on to the wheel hard, and I shivered and shook. I sobbed and sobbed. I had this awful impulse just to drive away, and not stop driving till I was back in Pennsylvania. I didn't, of course. I went to the room and said, 'Tom, we've got to get out of here.' And I told him why. And this time he didn't argue."

"So you didn't see them again?" I said. "Until the last night?"

"We never saw them again, Danny. Or I didn't anyway. I can't vouch for what Tom saw or didn't see at the very end. But they weren't among the men who stopped our car. I'm sure of that.

"They must have been in Miami by that time. Or on their way to Miami. And they couldn't be in two places at once. They're very strange, and they can do a lot of things you wouldn't imagine, just to look at them or hear them talk. But I don't think they can be in two places at once.

"We left the motel as soon as we thought it was safe and found another place to stay. From then on we never stayed in one place for more than two nights.

"The first week or so we spent most of our time just hanging around Roswell. Tom sat for hours in diners and coffee shops, pretending to read the paper, listening to conversations. At first I did the same thing, though in different places. But of course I couldn't just blend in with the background, the way Tom did. So after a few days I got a job waitressing, and then it was easier. The customers liked to talk to me. The men, I mean. At night I'd go to the bars and flirt like mad with anybody in uniform."

"From Roswell Air Force Base?" I said.

"Walker Air Force Base. Roswell Army Air Field was the old name. It was located just outside the town. They were young men, and there were lots of them, and they were lonely. Half of Roswell made a living off their loneliness. And I—well, I used to be pretty."

For just an instant her hand went to her eyeglasses. I wanted to tell her she was still pretty, the most beautiful girl I'd ever seen. I wanted to ask what had happened to her contact lenses, why she didn't wear them anymore. I only nodded and swallowed.

"Lonely people talk," she said. "That's something I've always known, ever since I was a little girl. They'll talk unless there's no one for them to talk to or unless they've got three men watching over their shoulders to make sure they don't. When that happens, the talk dies inside them, and they die with it.

"*That* I didn't know. I've had to learn it over these last three years.

"It paid off pretty quickly, my flirting. Though it didn't feel that way at the time. It felt like forever. I spent every minute of the day terrified that the next man who'd come into the diner or the bar would have pockmarks or a snaggletooth. Or be named Jemi.

"At the end, things moved very fast. You were with Julian that afternoon, weren't you, when he telephoned me? And I told him I didn't have the book, couldn't get the book, the whole trip had been a waste? That was three o'clock. By nine that night it had all turned around. I'd seen the book. I'd recognized it at once as the one Morris had with him when he died. That nice young boy, the lieutenant, had gone to the bathroom just long enough for me to do my switch.

"I took their *Case for the UFO,* the one with all the annotations, and left in its place a perfectly ordinary copy. Which, I'm sorry to say, I'd stolen from the Albuquerque Public Library a few weeks before. If you ever see Julian again, by the way, I'd be grateful if you didn't mention that part. That was the one thing that always made Julian livid, people stealing things from public libraries.

"By nine that night I had the book in my hands, and I was sewing it into the lining of my suitcase. I already had my flight booked for Miami the next morning.

"Tom wasn't going with me. He had business in southern California, and he was going to drive out the next day, after he'd left me at the airport. I'd tell you what his business was, but I honestly don't know myself. That was one thing about the SSS: we did keep secrets. Mostly to protect one another. Those were mean people we were tangling with. They could do some awful things to us if they got their hands on us. But you know that now, as well as I do.

"Anyway, it was mission accomplished, our last night in New Mexico, and we both felt pretty hilarious. We took a pillow from the motel room and hopped into the car. And the next thing I knew Tom was behind the wheel, and we were tearing out into the desert."

A party of tourists, two elderly women and a man, had appeared at the top of the rock-cut steps leading down to where we sat. They walked down a few steps, then stopped and looked around them, blinking in bewilderment. Then they went back up. One of the women, who seemed to have difficulty climbing, held tightly to the man's arm. We didn't start talking again until we were sure they were out of earshot. I watched two bright yellow butter- flies play tag with each other in the sunlight, around and around my wounded foot.

"Rochelle," I said at last, "you mentioned the specimens in Roswell. What did you mean by that?"

"Specimens," she said. "It *is* an awful word, isn't it? The people from the base used it all the time, and I suppose I just fell into the habit. We really ought to come out and say 'bodies,' shouldn't we?"

"So it's true?" I said. "There really was a UFO crash at Roswell?"

"Oh, yes." She nodded. "I've known about it so long it's hard to remember most people have never heard of it. Even the UFOlogists haven't, most of them. Or it's just a rumor, which they never know quite what to do with.

"I need to tell you one thing. I never saw the bodies. To get down into the vaults, you have to do more than drink a few beers with a second lieutenant. I did see some photos, though, in the archives, that they'd taken back in '47, when they first found the wreckage. And I must say—"

"What?" I said, after I'd waited for her to finish the sentence.

"They were children, Danny."

"Children?" I felt as though something spidery were crawling around the inside of my stomach.

"Uh-huh. You wouldn't think of them being children or even having chil- dren, would you? All this talk of little green men, or small humanoid entities, as the UFOlogists so love to say, distracts us from it. But I saw the photos, and now I've seen *her*, and it all fits together. It all makes sense—"

Again she stopped. She seemed lost in thought. "You needn't look so nervous," she said finally. "I haven't lost track of the time. Our appointment with Dr. Talibi isn't till five thirty. We don't have to stop by the apartment either. I told Jameela to bring her to the doctor's office, meet us there."

"I'm not nervous," I said. And since I didn't know what I was feeling and I sure wasn't ready to talk with Rochelle about it, I asked: "And this archive?"

"Top secret, in theory. In practice, even the junior officers—some of them anyway—come and go as they please. They like to use it, actually, to show off to their girls.

"I don't know just when it was established. Probably the late forties, a year or two after the crash. Somebody had the idea there ought to be a research center on the base, right next to the vault, so people could work from the resources to the specimens—sorry, there I go again; the *bodies*—and back again. Library and lab in adjacent buildings. You see what I mean?"

"I think so," I said.

"We'd had indications for some time that the air force was sending its most important UFO materials to the archive at Roswell. Not the Project Blue Book headquarters in Ohio. That was their official UFO project. But I think it was mostly window dressing, at least after the early fifties.

"So it seemed at least possible that the Dade County police—well, I don't know exactly what they did with Morris's book, after they took it away from me that morning. But somehow it got into the right channels and was forwarded to the archive. That was what brought me and Tom out to Roswell. That possibility, I mean. And it turned out—I was surprised; I told you that—to be true.

"If it hadn't, you and Julian and I would have gone after the book in Morris's old house in Miami. And Tom would still be alive."

The book had been found. Tom had died for it. Thanks to me it had been lost again, forever. "Rochelle," I said, "I'm sorry."

"I know you are. You'll always be sorry. And it isn't really fair, because it wasn't your fault. You couldn't have done anything but drop it."

"It was either the book or me."

"Which would have been—"

"The book *and* me."

"Exactly. Does it help that you know that?"

"No," I said. "Not at all."

"I didn't think it would." She looked down at my foot and mumbled a few words, something like "It never does help." After that she was silent for a very long time.

"Tom and I took the car that last night," she said, "and we drove out into the desert. And yes, we made love. The three men were telling you the truth, as far as that went. We did it outside the car, in the desert, under the stars.

"What was it you said they told you? That we'd had a blowout fuck, or something like that?"

"A blowout fuck," I said. I didn't want to say the words again and was sorry I had repeated them to her in the first place. This was not the part of her story I was most anxious to hear. "They said you gave Tom such a blowout fuck that he was too weak to fight you off when you smothered him with the pillow."

"Well," she said. "They do have an imagination, don't they? But we did make love, and it was lovely. Although one pillow wasn't enough to be comfortable on. Still, it was marvelous. Under that black sky, no lights within miles, and the stars sparkling everywhere above us.

"But I need to tell you, I'm sorry we did it. Because of what happened afterward. I can't see a starry sky now without feeling the most horrible sadness. Which is why, I suppose, I spend every night indoors. By myself. Reading. Just reading.

"We got our clothes more or less straightened out and got back in the car, and we headed back to town. We were both feeling pretty wonderful. Tom had found a country and western station on the radio and turned it up full blast. We were singing along at the top of our voices. Tom always loved country and western. And I—well, I hate country and western. But that night I loved it too.

"Then all of a sudden the music went off. In the middle of a song. All we could hear was static, very loud. And Tom laughed, and said, 'Goddamn transmitter has to go down right in the middle of "Honky-tonk Angels"!' And I laughed too, kind of sleepily—I remember I'd begun to feel sleepy—and I said, 'Let's see if we can't find another station.' So Tom started to turn the dial. But the static was everywhere, all over the band.

"I went all cold inside when I heard that. Because I knew what it meant: that we weren't alone. That we were being watched, and not for the good. That something very bad was going to happen, very soon, though I didn't know exactly what it was going to be. Tom had no idea. Lucky for him, I guess. He thought it was a problem with the radio, and he started cursing out the damn lousy radio, and the damn lousy car, and the damn lousy rental agency. As if it were all something ordinary you could curse and laugh and joke about.

"And then I heard our brakes squeal, and I almost went flying through the windshield. And we weren't moving anymore.

"The road was blocked, Danny.

"There was this huge wooden beam dragged across the road. It was so long you couldn't see where the ends were, to drive around it. It was pretty rough terrain anyway. I wouldn't have tried leaving the road to get around the block. I don't think we'd have gotten very far.

"There were six or seven men, wearing orange reflectors, moving around behind the beam. And behind them, farther back down the road, this strange light. It was kind of like a bonfire, only you'd expect a bonfire to be yellow or maybe orange. This one was white. I'd never seen a fire like that before.

"So Tom leans out the window and yells at one of the men in the reflectors: 'What the hell's the idea, blocking the road like this?' And the man looks at us and says, in this deep, peculiar voice: 'Road maintenance.' Just like that—like a machine talking. No expression at all in the voice.

"He was standing in front of our headlights. And the light reflected off his eyes, just like it would off a cat's. Not like a human being's at all. And don't tell me he might have been wearing glasses, because he wasn't. It was his eyes that reflected the light.

"I don't know if Tom noticed that or not. He didn't sound scared, just mad. He yells at the man, 'Well, how the hell are we supposed to get back into town?' And the man doesn't answer. He isn't even looking at us anymore, just moving back and forth behind that wooden beam of theirs, with all the other men, doing something or other. I couldn't for the life of me make out what.

"And then I noticed in the fire, that white fire behind the men, there were dark figures moving around. Very slender, very tall. I don't know if they were human. They seemed to be twisting and swaying, around and around and back and forth. In pain maybe. But there wasn't a sound from them. Or from the men in the orange reflectors. Or from anybody. Only that loud, horrible static from the car radio, which neither of us had thought to turn off.

"I said to him, 'Tom, turn the car around. We've got to get out of here.'

"I expected him to argue, Danny. To say something like 'And go where?' and I was going to say, 'Anywhere, just back down the road; with any luck we'll reach a town before our gas runs out.' But he didn't say a word.

"And then I looked at him. I saw his mouth was open. I saw something glittering on his chin, as if saliva were drooling out. I saw his hands moving over the steering wheel. *Feeling* the wheel. Like a blind man groping his way along a wall.

"I thought, *He doesn't know anymore how to turn the car around. He's forgotten how to drive.*

"So I said, 'Tom, honey. Take it easy. It'll be all right. I'll get out and come around to your side, and you just scoot over on the seat. OK?' He didn't answer. I don't know if he heard me. But I thought, *If only I can get us turned around, get us away from here, he'll be all right. We'll both be all right.*

"I got out of the car and started to walk around to the driver's side.

"I realized then there was a light somewhere above me. I didn't look up to see what it was. I looked at all of those clumps of—what do you call that shrub?—mesquite off to the side of the road, and I could see their shadows on the ground, all crisp and clear. The ground itself looked white, like snow in the moonlight. But I knew it wasn't the moon that was shining. It was much too bright for that. But I didn't look up; I didn't dare.

"That was the last I remember. Till I woke up and found myself lying in the dark, just off the road, with the pillow in my hands and the moon risen high. And the roadblock, and the men, and the white fire all gone. And the car, and Tom, gone with them."

"The pillow?" I said.

"Yes, the pillow. I was clutching it. Not lying on it. Holding it tight against my chest with both arms."

"And you hadn't taken it with you out of the car?"

"Of course not. Why should I have taken the pillow? Or the purse either. But when I woke up, the pillow was there, and so was the purse."

"But why should they have left the pillow with you?"

"I don't know. I have no idea at all. Some bizarre sort of gallantry, is the only thing I can think of. So I wouldn't have to take one of the stones of the place and put it under my head. But your guess is as good as mine."

I thought for a few moments. No explanation I was able to come up with made any sense. None of this made any sense.

"They left your purse with you too?"

"Uh-huh. That was one of the first things I did when I woke up, looked through the purse. I could see pretty well by the moonlight. Nothing was missing, as far as I could tell. My money was there. My keys. My airline ticket. And yes, my knife was still there. That was the scariest part. I was sure I was going to find it covered with blood. But it wasn't. Everything looked completely normal. Yet I could tell that they'd been through the purse. They'd looked at everything in it. And then they'd put it all back."

"And left the purse with you," I said.

"That's right."

"Why would they do that? Go through your purse and then leave every-thing? Not even take the money?"

"*That* one, I think I know the answer to. You'll understand too, in a min-ute. I had a lot of time that night to figure it out. I stood for hours by the side of that road, praying that sooner or later somebody would drive by. And shivering. I've never shivered like that.

"A little before dawn a pickup truck came by. All full of Mexican men. They worked in Roswell, in construction, I guess. I could hardly under-stand anything they said. They could barely speak English, and Spanish isn't one of my languages. But they were very kind. They saw how cold I was, and until they finally found a blanket for me, they were all ready to take their shirts off for me to wear. They even took me to the motel, once I managed to explain that was where I was going. It might have been miles out of their way.

"Hope is a funny thing, Danny. I'd thought it all through during the night, while I was out there hitchhiking. I knew I wasn't ever going to see Tom again. But when we got close to the motel and the buildings started looking familiar, I felt some part of me saying, 'No, maybe it's all right after all. Maybe it was all some joke, or misunderstanding, or something.'

"I thought, *I'll hop out of this truck, and the car'll be right there, parked by our room. Tom'll be inside, sleeping, his arm hanging out of the covers and breathing with his mouth half open.* The way he always did. I'd even started to work myself into a rage. I thought, *That little . . . turkey is going to wake up to the pounding of his life. You little creep, what'd you drive off and leave me in the desert for?* That kind of thing.

"But of course there was no car, and no Tom, and nobody'd slept in the bed that night. Nothing on the bed except my suitcase, almost all packed except for my toothbrush and a few night things. And Morris's book sewn into the lining.

"I wanted to throw myself onto the bed and cry. But I couldn't do that without moving the suitcase, and I felt too exhausted to pick up anything or move anything. Or do anything else. So I flopped into the chair by the bed and closed my eyes for a few minutes. And then I sat up and turned on the radio to hear the six o'clock news.

"I wish I could tell you it shocked me when I heard the announcer say it.

Or stunned me. Or something like that. But it didn't. I think I knew it was coming.

"They'd found him by the side of the road, outside the town, sitting in the car. In the driver's seat. Suffocated. Police said there were signs of a struggle. They were seeking his companion as a prime suspect in the slaying. Young white female, attractive, medium height, dark blond hair. And so on and so forth.

"I said to myself, *Old girl, it's time we got you out of here.*

"Five minutes later I was all packed, the room key was on the dresser, and I was walking downtown with my suitcase, calm and easy and slow. Dying with fear each time a car went by.

"But nobody stopped me. Nobody arrested me. The car rental office finally opened, after what felt like about a hundred hours. There was a moment of panic when I thought I didn't have enough cash to cover the rental. But they found me a cheaper car, and I was on my way. I drove straight to the Albuquerque airport, without stopping.

"My ticket was for Miami, but I knew I couldn't go there. There'd been a reason they left me with my money and my ticket. It had to be the same reason they didn't just take me off and kill me together with Tom, when they could have done that so easily.

"They wanted me in Miami. To be waiting for me when I stepped off the plane. I think they also wanted to catch whoever I was meeting there, along with me. They wanted to have the full force of the law behind them when they did it; that was important to them. And as far as the law was concerned, I was a murderess.

"So when I got to the airport, I went to the United Airlines desk. I got my ticket stamped for flight two-five-seven to Miami. I checked my suitcase through to the Miami airport. Then I walked off to Eastern Airlines and bought a different ticket for myself, nonstop to Idlewild.

"Idlewild, Danny. You remember Idlewild. That was what they used to call Kennedy Airport, back before the assassination. This was September 1963. The assassination wasn't going to happen for two months yet."

"No," I said. "I remember Idlewild. That wasn't what puzzled me."

She looked away from me. She looked very uncomfortable.

"You just told me you had barely enough cash to rent the car," I said. "Where did you get the money for another airplane ticket?"

———

Somewhere in the Tombs of the Kings, birds chirped.

"I lied to you," she said finally. "I didn't drive straight to the airport. I made a number of stops along the way. All in motels.

"Wherever I stopped I went into the front office. I asked about their rates. Twin beds or double bed. In season or off season. That kind of thing. Whoever was working the front desk would answer my questions, and I'd say thank you and go. And that would be it.

"But I knew that a fair number of the people in those motel offices would be guys, working alone. And sooner or later one of them would try to make time with me.

"The one who finally did was a nice boy. About twenty; tall, brownish hair, freckles. Bluest eyes I've ever seen.

"I asked him my questions, and we talked a few minutes, and he asked my name. His voice shook a little bit when he asked. I remember that. And I answered right away, without even thinking—"

"Rosa," I said.

"No. Not Rosa. Why did you say that? Do you know something I don't?"

"No. No. It's just . . . I once knew—I once cared about—"

"The name I gave was Rachel Partin. I don't know where that came from. But I knew, as soon as I said it, that I was Rachel Partin now. And I was going to keep on being Rachel Partin for a long, long time.

"We talked ten, maybe fifteen minutes. Him on one side of the desk, me on the other, and we were leaning toward each other. I'll never forget those wonderful blue eyes. He didn't take them off me for a second. Finally he said, very nervous, 'You know, there's not much business. I could put up a sign, BACK SOON, and we could go walk somewhere. Nobody'd mind. Nobody'd even notice.'

"And I said, 'Uh-huh,' and smiled.

"And he said, 'We've got some empty rooms here. We could go to one of those rooms, even, and we could—'

"He was blushing then, and he couldn't finish the sentence. I nodded, real slowly, and I said: 'Yes. We could.'

"But when he'd gotten the keys for the room, and he was fumbling with the BACK SOON sign, I said to him: 'One thing, Jason. There's something that gets me real, real hot. You want to know what it is?' I said: 'You go into the room first, by yourself. Then take off all your clothes except your underpants. Then lie down on top of the bed, so I find you in your underpants when I come in. Don't get under the covers. Just on top of the bed? OK?'

"He nodded. He couldn't talk. He just handed me a key and went off, his legs shaking, and left me in the motel office. By myself.

"I cleaned out the cash register, and I took off for Albuquerque. As fast as the car would go.

"Well, Danny. I imagine you can guess the rest.

"I got off the plane in New York about the same time the United Airlines flight was supposed to arrive in Miami with my suitcase. I phoned the Miami airport from Idlewild with that Albert-Bender-meet-your-party message. I'd arranged that with Julian as a signal, a long time before. He would have known what to do. I never dreamed you'd be all alone in the airport, with *them*.

"And no, I don't know what happened to Julian. I have no idea where he was that night. Where he is now, for that matter. I've not had any contact with him; I don't know what's happened to our lab or the observatory. For all I know, the old farmhouse isn't even standing. I haven't been in touch with anyone in the States. I haven't been back to the States since that night. I haven't set foot outside Jordan.

"I can't. I don't have a passport. And I'm wanted for murder."

"I wandered around the airport for a while. I didn't have any clear plan. I knew I had to get out of the country. I could have rented a car and driven down to the farmhouse and hidden there. But it would have been too risky. There was a real good chance they'd have thought of that too, and there'd be somebody waiting for me.

"So I let my feet carry me, and pretty soon I found myself in front of the Air Jordan ticket counter. There was one person working there, a young woman. It was already late at night, almost eleven o'clock, and there weren't many people around. I went up to her and started talking in Arabic, even though I guessed she was an American and wouldn't understand me.

"She said, 'I'm sorry, I don't speak Arabic.' And I nodded and smiled and looked very sad. And she said, 'I'll get the manager for you,' and I nodded again. And she called out, 'Mr. Makdisi!' and I felt my heart lift. Because the landlord we had in Jerusalem, years back, was named Khalid Makdisi, and it was a fair guess that this ticket counter manager Makdisi would be somehow related to him and they'd know each other. That's the way things are in Jordan.

"His name was Tewfik Makdisi. He brought me into his office behind the ticket counter, and invited me to sit down. He didn't ask who I was or what I wanted to see him about. He said, 'Please sit down,' and then he said 'Coffee?' and when I nodded, he poured me coffee.

"We talked. It turned out he and Khalid Makdisi were second cousins. He'd worked for Air Jordan, even back then. He lived with his family in Amman when he wasn't in New York, but he used to come to Jerusalem often and visit his cousin.

"He'd known Daddy. He'd known Mama too. He even knew me, though I'd been too little to remember. We'd all gone to tea one afternoon, in Khalid Makdisi's garden. The ladies let me serve the tea. I'd given him his teacup on the brass tray, and I'd said to him, *'Tafaddal,'* which is Arabic for *Please.* He remembered how well I pronounced the word. I looked like a solemn little blond owl, he said, in those thick eyeglasses of mine. But I spoke just like a little Arab girl.

"He asked me, 'How is your daddy? And your mama?' And I said, 'They've gone to the mercy of God.' And he said, 'Both of them?' And I nodded. And he said, 'God is the most merciful of the merciful.' And then he said, 'I'm very sorry.' And then he said, 'Please. More coffee?'

"I began crying, and he gave me a box of Kleenex and let me cry. When I stopped for a few seconds, he poured the coffee for me. And then I cried some more.

"Now you hold it right there, Danny Shapiro! I know just what you're thinking. *Never trust a woman's tears.* Isn't that right?"

I didn't know how to answer. The truth was I'd been thinking of poor Jason, lying on that motel bed in his underpants and how it must slowly have come to him he'd been tricked and abandoned and robbed. The thought of him wouldn't leave my mind.

"Well, you stop thinking that. It's not true, not at all. A lot of what I told Tewfik Makdisi that night I made up on the spot. I admit that. But I didn't make up the tears. They were real.

"I was fifteen years old, for heaven's sake! My . . . *friend* had just been murdered. If I'd been caught, that would have been the end of me for sure. You think any jury would have believed my story?

"I was about to leave my country. I wouldn't ever come back. I'd never be Rochelle Perlmann again. I saw all that, clear as the coffee in my cup. I would never see any of my friends, not Julian, not anyone. I wasn't going to see *you* again. I'd been having a few daydreams about what we might do together once we met in Miami, you and I. And not just a few either, if you want me to be honest about it."

"I didn't know that," I said.

"No. I guess you didn't. I guess you had no idea at all."

She looked straight into my eyes. "So what do you think?" she said. "Suppose you'd been in my place. Do you think you might have done a little bit of crying yourself?"

"Tewfik Makdisi asked me then, in the most roundabout and delicate way you can imagine, how he might help.

"I said, 'I'm a fugitive.' I said, 'They're trying to kill me. I have to get out of the country, tonight if possible.' I said, 'I don't have a passport. And I don't have any identification papers. And not much money either.'

"I gave him details. I can't tell you all the things I said. I talked about how cars would slow down as they passed me, people screaming things out the window, mostly in some language I couldn't understand. Then they started throwing things at me from the cars. Finally they'd started shooting. To scare me, it seemed, rather than kill me. So far.

"There were knocks on my door, late at night. Interrogations. Endless questions about all sorts of grotesque crimes that had taken place somewhere; they never explained just where or when. I'd say, 'I didn't do it. You must believe me, I didn't do it.' And they'd say, 'Who's accusing you? We're not accusing you. Are you accusing yourself?' They always ended by warning me not to say anything to anyone about what I'd seen. And I'd say, 'What are you talking about? I haven't seen anything.' And they'd say, 'If you tell anyone what you've seen, we'll find you. When we come back, we'll find you. We always find those we want to.'

"Most of this just came into my head while I was talking to him. But you want to know something strange? It all felt real at the time. As real as what happened in Roswell. Real as my sitting next to you now, telling you this. Realer, maybe.

"He kept his eyes fixed on me while I talked. I watched him too. His expression never changed. I couldn't tell whether he believed me. Finally he said: 'Who are these men? Do you know?'

"I said, 'I don't know.'

"He said, 'Are they the Zionists?'

"I looked away from him then. It was the only time while we talked that I looked away. I said, 'I don't know.'

"He said, 'Can you describe them? Tell me what they looked like?'

"I said, 'There were three of them. Always three. Though not always the same three. They all dressed in black, always. Black suits. Black ties.'

"He nodded very slowly then and looked at me, with a look of such understanding and compassion I have never seen on anybody's face before or since. He said, 'Yes. The Zionists. I've got to help you.'

"He stood up. He said: 'You'll tell me the rest another time. But now we have to move fast. The plane leaves in less than an hour.' I looked at my watch; it was already past midnight.

"He said, 'What name will you use?' I said, 'Rachel Partin.' He said, 'Rachel is a Jewish name, you know that.' I said, 'I don't care. It's my name now.' He nodded and said, 'I understand.' Then he said, 'It'll be all right.' He said, 'Excuse me. I have to leave for a few minutes. I'll be right back.'

"He wasn't, of course. I knew he wouldn't be. These things can't be done in a few minutes. It was almost forty-five minutes before he was back, with a manila envelope under his arm.

"He said, 'Hurry, please. We've got to go.' He handed me the envelope and said, 'There's another envelope, sealed, inside this one. Don't open it. Just keep it with you and give it to them at passport control in Amman. Everything else in here you can read,' he said. 'But not now. When you're on the plane. We have to hurry.'

"Later, after the plane had taken off, I read everything he'd put in the manila envelope. Except, of course, the sealed letter. I still don't know exactly what that was, although I can pretty much guess.

"There were recommendations. A letter in Arabic, to whom it may concern, saying what a wonderful tenant I am and how I take care of the property I rent as though it were my own. Two letters about how good a translator

I am, how fluent and effective a writer, how diligently and faithfully I work for my employers. One was a to whom it may concern letter, written for businessmen. The other was addressed to a friend of his named Rasheed Abdel Salaam, in the Jordanian Ministry of Tourism. He'd put two hundred Jordanian dinars in cash inside the envelope, just to get me started.

"He took my arm and led me past the stewardess who was taking tickets, down the jetway into the plane. He didn't leave until I was buckled into my seat. I never saw him again."

CHAPTER 29

THE DAY DECLINED AS ROCHELLE TALKED. THE SHADOWS OF
the evening stretched out among the mouths of the burial caves. The breeze
chilled my bare foot.

"Rochelle, who *are* they?"

" 'They'? Who are you asking about now? The three men? Those lake
creatures of yours? Who?"

How to answer? I tried to remember what I'd told her the night before—
things recalled between stretches of sleep and lovemaking, my hands drinking themselves drunk upon her cool, naked skin. They'd been fragments,
disordered and disjointed. Much, no doubt, I had kept to myself.

"All of them, I guess. And . . . *her.*"

Rochelle must have understood who I meant; she threw a quick glance
toward her watch. "We have a little time left," she said. "How's your foot?"

"Hurts. More than it has for a while. I don't know if that's good or bad."

She smiled faintly. "Swollen foot," she said, pronouncing it as though it
were some kind of name or title.

I asked what she meant by that.

"Never mind," she said. "You'll understand when you're ready. Now tell me.
What did you think of Tewfik Makdisi's theory about the men in black?"

"That they're Zionists?"

"Yes. Do you agree with him?"

"Do I—? That's the biggest crock I've ever heard!"

"Oh, really? Why?"

"Goddamn it to hell, Rochelle!" She smiled, more broadly now. It was her
smile, as much as anything, that was getting me angry. "Didn't I tell you the
things they said to me while I was tied to their chair?"

"Yes, you told me . . ."

The Jewish this, the Jewish that. The crooked Jew lawyers and the lying little kike who deserved to be blinded, a needle through his eyeball. Of course I'd repeated it all to her. How could I not?

"And you want to say they're part of some Zionist plot? I say: bullshit!"

"Say it quietly. We're in Jordan, remember."

"Total . . . horseshit! You want to know who's a Zionist? My grandpa! Or he was, while he was alive. And if there was ever a saint on this earth—"

"Shhh, Danny. Danny. Here the three men in black are Zionists. Not just 'seem to be.' Are."

"What?"

"Everything is Zionism and the Zionists. Everything you don't like, that you're afraid of. It was the Zionists who assassinated Kennedy. Did you know that?"

"How naive of me." My voice trembled, and I feared if I didn't get hold of myself, I might cry. "I thought it was Lee Harvey Oswald who killed Kennedy."

"Oh, Oswald pulled the trigger. But the Zionists put him up to it. Because Lyndon Johnson would then be president, and the Zionists figured Johnson would be more pro-Israel than Kennedy was. Which he has been, so that proves it, you see.

"There was a photo," she went on. "They sold it on the street corners here about two months after the assassination. It showed Lee Harvey Oswald and Ben-Gurion together, smiling and shaking hands. If you looked real closely, you could see the line where the two original photos had been taped together. But that didn't stop people from buying it. Or believing it."

"So Oswald and Ben-Gurion were buddies? That's what they think?"

"Not exactly. The Zionists used Oswald as a tool. They got rid of him afterward so he wouldn't talk. That's why they got Jack Ruby to shoot him right after he shot Kennedy."

"Jack Ruby was Jewish," I said.

"Yes, Danny. Originally Jack Rubinstein. You can't live in Jordan without knowing that. People here who don't know anything else about the United States know that: Jack Ruby was Jewish. And that proves the whole thing is true. You understand what I'm saying?"

That we pick our demons, maybe, and then build our worlds around them? Was it Julian who'd told me that? Or did I figure it out on my own?

"But the three men—what's this got to do with them?"

"Oh . . . how to say it? Take Albert Bender. Who were they, do you think, when they scared *him* into silence? Anti-Semitic bullies, like with you? Or Zionist conspirators, the way they would have been with Tewfik Makdisi? Of course not. Bender isn't Jewish, and he isn't Arab. I don't imagine Zionism, or Israel, or Jewish issues mean much to him. You understand?"

"I think so, maybe. But, Rochelle—"

"Tell me what Bender was afraid of. What he couldn't stop thinking about. What he wanted, more than anything in the world, and knew he couldn't have. Tell me all that. Then I'll tell you who the three men were when they came knocking on his door."

So that was why they were three? For fear, for want, for obsession? Yet they'd been real! "That skin of theirs, with the weird stain?" I said. Without meaning to, I looked down at my arm. It did seem that my own stain had faded since I'd been with Rochelle. "I don't think that was my imagination. You and Tom saw it—"

"And other people they've visited. I'm sure you didn't imagine it."

"But let me finish, will you? Where you're going with this, it sounds to me like you're saying they're nothing but a myth. Is that it?"

"Yes. The three men are a myth. That's exactly what I'm saying."

"So they're *not* real!"

"What are you talking about? Of course they're real." She bent toward me; she took both my hands in hers. "If they're not real, why those scars on the back of your neck? Why is Tom Dimitrios dead and not alive? Why can't I go back home?"

"I don't understand, I don't understand—"

"Listen. That place you went down to: where do you suppose that was? In this earth or out of it? In this solar system or out of it? In this universe or out of it?"

I tried to answer, stumbling, knowing I wasn't making sense. Rochelle kept nodding. I spoke of the earth, the moon. The point of gravitation neutral in between, yet close by the moon, where the UFOs' mother ship hangs motionless, not pulled either way. Where the mother ship is its own gravity . . .

But why had I gone down and not up to get there?

Why inward, not outward?

"It won't add up scientifically," I said finally. "I've run it a hundred different ways, a thousand times over. There's no way I can get it to work."

"Scientifically, no. But 'science is a turtle'—you remember that? Julian told me he wrote that on the back of our card the day he met you, just to tease you a little. To get you thinking."

" 'Science is a turtle that says its own shell encloses all things.' " I was surprised how easily I finished the quotation. "But tell me now. What is there that *isn't* a turtle?"

"Maybe nothing . . ."

"Not religion! Don't ever tell me religion is anything more than a turtle. I've been inside one religion, and it's the tightest, most suffocating turtle shell there ever was!"

I felt it strangling me even as I spoke. The thirst for chosenness that makes a lovely, spirited young girl into a thing forbidden and abominable. The suffering; the duty to the dead. All through your youth you bear them as a yoke, even as your days speed by like a weaver's shuttle. Yet how sweet and homelike it seems, while you're inside. A shiver of rage passed through me. From my hands into Rochelle's.

She squeezed them hard; she let them go. "Let me tell you a story," she said. "I came across it in one of my wee-hours-of-the-morning reading sessions those nights I couldn't sleep. In one of my 'quaint and curious volumes of forgotten lore.' I've thought about it a lot since last night."

I leaned toward her. My heart beat faster. This was going to be the answer, the explanation of what I'd been through. Or the nearest thing to it she'd ever give me.

"It's about a man named Timarchus," she said, "in ancient Greece. A friend of Socrates's. He went down into a cave by night, the way you went into that red disk. Only, three men in black weren't chasing him. Or maybe they were. I've forgotten a lot of the details.

"There were snakes in the cave. He didn't like snakes. He must have felt about them—well, the way you felt about being with those lake creatures.

"But here's the part I remembered, when you told me what happened to you. *The cave became the sky.* And when Timarchus went down into it, he found himself in the sky, close to the moon. The underworld turned out to be like a cone stretching through space, between the earth and the moon. And he was at the tip of the cone—"

"Point of gravitation neutral!" I burst out.

"No. No. That's science, remember. You're trying to force things back into that turtle shell. Just listen to me.

"The moon was covered with a fine white powder, which turned out to be made from the souls of the dead. Other dead souls were trying to land there, so they could come out on the moon's other side, to the Elysian Fields. . . ."

Her voice trailed off. She looked horribly sad.

"What happened to Timarchus?" I said. "Did he ever come back from the cave?"

"Oh, yes. He came back."

"And he told his story?"

"Yes. He told his story."

"And then?"

"He died. Three months later."

It's only a myth, I told myself. I felt a bit foolish. I'd let myself get so worked up by the portentousness of her tone, its oracular feel, that I'd really expected this to be something important. If science and religion are just turtles contemplating their own shells, then these old myths—what can they possibly be?

I looked away into the burial cave. Any moment I might see something monstrous rise from its depths, bearing the answers to all our questions—or, perhaps, itself the answer. I slid my good foot into its shoe. The other foot resisted.

"Swollen foot," Rochelle said.

All at once I knew what she meant. Oedipus. That's what his name means, because of how his feet were pinned together when the king his father left him to die on the icy mountainside. Oedipus, who jabbed out his eyes with pins torn from his mother's corpse when at last he found the truth he'd searched for.

Or it found him.

"Are they the same?" I said.

"Are they—"

"The lake creatures. The dero. Are they?"

"Danny. I told you the night we met: there's a continuum. We don't know how to put things into their categories. Most of the time we're better off not trying."

"But it *does* sound like the dero. What they did to me on that table—like what the dero do to their victims. Isn't it?"

"Yes," she said very quietly. "At the beginning. When they're getting started."

Getting started. How fortunate I'd been to have mastered the disk's controls just in time. "Why won't you look at me, Rochelle?"

"I *am* looking!" She stared fiercely, pleadingly, into my eyes; once more she took my hands. "Why do you need to *know*? What does the classification matter?"

"It matters . . . because of *her*."

She knew exactly what I meant. I saw it in her face.

"I don't know just how they took my . . . seed. Maybe on that operating table; maybe on the moon while I was blacked out. I don't know. Either way it was the lake creatures who took it. Who used it—"

"No use, no use to think this way—"

"And if they're the dero . . . and the dero are pure evil—"

Then I was father to a dero child. An infant demon, just human enough you'd want to shelter and nourish her like any baby. Until she'd grown too big, too smart, too powerful to be stopped—

"Should we kill her?" I said. "Or at least let her die?"

"*No!*"

Her cry echoed off the cliffs. Her face, in the shadow of the ancient graves, turned into something itself ancient—wrinkled, decaying, twisted in a pain beyond anything I could imagine. The vision I'd seen once on the SSS tower had been real. No trick of the moonlight, as I'd convinced myself it must have been.

The instant passed. She was Rochelle once more, her tears overflowing. She bent over me, threw her arms around me, pressed my face into her chest.

"No, Danny. Please. Don't even talk like that. We've *got* to keep her alive, and heal her, and protect her, and let her grow up. It's more important than anything we've ever done or will do. Take my word for that.

"There's a lot I don't know," she said. "I don't know if she comes from the dero or the Elder Gods or from something else, some race of beings that isn't either gods or dero, but a species like ours. Trying to keep their planet from blowing up, long enough to move on to their next stage. Just like us.

"Only they've crossed the threshold. At least some of them have. And now they've sent her—they've sent *you*—to help us across too.

"I don't know if that's true. All I know is, I like you a lot a lot *a lot*. And I didn't hurt Tom, and I will never hurt you. And I will never tell you anything I don't know to be true. This I know: that little child is a blessing, not a curse. For you and me. The whole world, in time. We need to give her a chance to live.

"We've got to go now. It's late. Dr. Talibi is waiting for us; Jameela's waiting. *She's* waiting. For all I know, her mind is already grown, it was grown from birth, and she knows everything that's happening around her.

"Don't worry about the shoe. You don't have to force it. I'll carry it for you. Walk on your good foot, and lean on me. Here. I'll help you up."

"Swollen foot," I said. Her strong hand reached out, took my arm, raised me from the burial stone where I'd been sitting. "Oedipus. You were smart to see that. But, Rochelle, it's only a *myth*."

"Myths are real," she said. "That's what I've been trying to explain. They have to be real. Otherwise they wouldn't stay around for centuries. They'd vanish like last year's top tunes.

"*That's* it, Danny. Take the steps one at a time. Keep your arm around my shoulder. Don't worry; we'll make it to Dr. Talibi's. He's only a few blocks away.

"Hold on to me, and walk on your good foot.

"*That's* it."

CHAPTER 30

THE MOON BLOSSOMED, SWELLED, THEN IT DWINDLED ONCE
more. When it became a pale sliver in the east, it was time for me to go.

Rochelle and I stood outside the Church of St. Peter in Gallicantu, on
Mount Zion, and watched the sun set across the Valley of Hinnom.

"There's where you'll take her across," Rochelle whispered. "Down into
the valley, then up the other side to that ridge, where you see those houses.
Keep to the right, though. The border runs between the houses. If you cut
too far to the left, you'll still be in Jordan."

Damn that Talibi, I thought. I held the binoculars to my eyes. I focused
on the tightly built cluster of limestone houses on the ridge opposite us, the
place called Abu Tor. The houses all looked the same, though Rochelle had
explained some of them were on the Israeli side, some on the Jordanian. The
border was all but invisible. I barely made out a barbed wire fence cutting
across a street, separating its two ends.

"And we can't just go to the Jordanian part of Abu Tor?" I said. "And sneak
over to the Israeli side from there?"

"Too dangerous. Too many guards. Better to go across the valley."

The valley wasn't exactly safe either. Rochelle had warned me about the
land mines planted there in 1948, during Israel's War of Independence, and
never removed. I turned the binoculars into the dark shadows of the valley,
looking for some trace of those mines. But of course you can't see a land mine
when you look at the surface of the ground. That's the whole point.

"*Hadassah*," Dr. Saeed Talibi had said three weeks earlier, when he was done
examining my baby. He spoke the word softly yet emphatically, with a
strange Arabic enunciation, ending the second syllable with a prolonged

hiss. In his white coat he hurried to his desk, began to write. Rochelle and I sat across from him, our hands touching. *"Hadassah,"* he said again.

"What do you mean, *'Hadassah'*?" I said.

I might as well not have spoken. A steady, cherubic smile lit his plump face; he covered sheet after sheet of office stationery with long paragraphs of English, which I soon gave up trying to read upside down. When he was done, he folded the papers and sealed them in an unmarked envelope. He handed it to Rochelle.

While Jameela, the peasant woman from the Galilee with her large gold-capped teeth and black embroidered dress, sat in a chair by the opposite wall. She smiled and crooned to the infant in her lap, a baby with a catlike face and huge black, slanted eyes. And tiny lungs, which struggled noisily to suck oxygen from our ungiving air.

The sun's edge touched the horizon. The church's bright mosaics glowed in its last rays. Rochelle and I spoke in whispers, though there wasn't anyone near. The acoustics of the place were strange. Every now and then we'd hear, coming out of empty air, a fragment of conversation or the drone of a tourist guide: "—this church, built in 1931 over the place where Peter denied Our Lord, the night he was brought before the authorities—" Then the voice faded away and we looked around, and sometimes we could spot the person who'd been talking. Sometimes we couldn't.

"I wish we could just cross at the Mandelbaum Gate," I said. "Like everybody else."

"I wish you could, too," she said, stroking my arm. "But you can't. You're not like everyone else. Other people have papers, at least a passport. You don't."

"And we don't want anybody looking at her too closely, I suppose."

"No, we don't. Try to bring her through the gate, and somebody's bound to realize she's not from this earth. If not the Jordanians, then the Israelis. And then the interrogations will start. Believe me, it'll be bad. The whole purpose will be defeated."

A priest, stocky, bearded, brown-robed, had led a group of tourists to a spot about twenty feet away. Some of them fingered rosaries and crucifixes as he read to them from the New Testament: " 'And immediately, while Peter yet spake, the cock crew. And the Lord turned and looked upon Peter. And

Peter remembered the word of the Lord, how he had said unto him, Before the cock crow thou shalt deny me thrice. And Peter went out and wept bitterly.'"

"Do you really think they can save her?" I said, once the group had left.

"I'm not sure. If she's got a chance anywhere, it's at the Hadassah Hospital on the other side. That's the best medical facility in the area. Maybe in the world. All the doctors here know that, and their patients do too, although of course they don't say it too loud."

She put her arm around my waist and rested her head on my shoulder. "I wish I were going with you," she said.

"Remind me again why you can't."

"If the Israelis catch you crossing, the worst is they'll hold you a couple of weeks till they get confirmation you really are Danny Shapiro, a nice Jewish boy from Pennsylvania who wouldn't do them any harm. They catch me, next thing I'm back in the States. Standing trial for murder."

I pressed my face into her hair. It smelled clean, of unscented soap. I'd never smelled anything finer in my life.

"So once I go," I said, "I'll never see you again."

"I wouldn't say that," she said. "Not at all. There's an even chance she may live. Better than even, Dr. Talibi says, if she makes it into the right hands. And if she lives, in a few years this world is going to be so different from anything we've known, we're not going to recognize it. So different we'll think we're living on another planet. Then I'll be able to come home. And you and I will be together again."

The voice came out of the air: "For what shall it profit a man, if he shall gain the whole world and lose his own soul? Or what shall a man give in exchange for his soul? Whosoever therefore shall be ashamed of me and of my words in this adulterous and sinful generation, of him also shall the Son of man be ashamed, when he cometh in the glory of his Father with the holy angels."

Then it trailed away, and I could not hear any more.

It's the priest, I thought. *The same priest who was here with the people a minute ago.*

The Valley of Hinnom began to darken. I looked toward the rocky, brambly slopes after which hell had been named. Once upon a time the people of Jerusalem had used this valley to burn their garbage, sometimes also their children, as sacrifices to pagan gods or maybe their own God. The stink of the place, the low growling flames, and the screams of children burned alive had made *gei hinnom*, "the Valley of Hinnom," into Gehenna, the Jewish word for hell. I winced and turned the binoculars upon the limestone houses of Abu Tor.

The barbed wire fence and the street the fence cut in two came into my view. Also a teenaged boy, walking down the street from the Israeli side toward the fence.

I kept my binoculars focused on that boy. I noticed, as he walked, how his clothes hung on his body as though they weren't quite right for him: suntan pants and a short-sleeved yellow shirt that seemed a little too large, a little too loose. He wore thick black horn-rimmed glasses.

I knew that boy.

I knew why his face sagged under the weight of sadness, of helpless worry, of exhaustion too deep to be slept away. I knew why he stepped so awkwardly, as though his body were a bicycle he hadn't quite learned to ride.

He's sixteen years old, but he might be twelve, or sixty. He's the son of a sick mother, of a father who's been cheated in life and marriage. He struggled so hard to win his contest and fly this summer, far away; but when he got on the plane, his grief and loneliness and fear got on with him, and wherever he goes they will find him.

—I can't stand him, I hate him, I despise him; with those thick glasses he's the ugliest creature in the world—

He's wanted a girlfriend but never had one. Close, close he came when wild, pretty Rosa reached out her hand to him, and who knows what would have happened if he'd said yes? But she'll not marry a man who's shy, for he'll run away when she winks an eye; and he did, he did, he ran home to his mommy. Who now is dying anyway.

He stopped at the fence. He stared at it, as if only now starting to grasp that this is the end of his world, that the border cuts through Abu Tor like a crevasse in the earth and there's nowhere more for him to go. He read about this in his guidebook. But it doesn't sink in until you actually stand there.

Tonight he'll write to Jeff back home, telling him about this place. He wants to convey with Abu Tor what he can't say in so many words, how it is to feel your difference separating you, bounding you, hemming you in. He imagines that if Jeff can only understand this and accept it, they might be friends again—

He opened his guidebook, to make sure this really was Abu Tor, that he hadn't made some mistake. He pulled a small notebook from his pocket and began writing, writing, while behind him two brown-skinned Israeli boys about his age, who a few minutes ago offered to buy the cheap box camera dangling from a cord around his neck, nudged each other and pointed toward him, and laughed.

—because Jeff doesn't care anymore about UFOs, and the book they were going to write will never get written. Jeff and his folksinging friends shout back and forth to one another in the hallways about the songs they're learning, the gigs they'll drive to this weekend. The mission, to search out the truth that lies beneath the shell of this existence—Jeff has abandoned it. So would this boy, if the choice were his.

But it isn't.

He chose his path long ago. Now he's become that path. If it leads to a dead end, to a border he can't cross, he must follow.

That's why he's so tired.

For this one summer he's had wings to fly. In a little over two weeks his summer will end. The people here aren't what he expected; they're warm and vital but coarse and rough, and everyone's Jewish, but it turns out that wasn't what his difference was about after all. Even here he feels the walls, the boundary, the pain of his oddness.

And since he got here, he hasn't had a letter from his mother. His father's letters hint at bad things happening with her but won't say what they are. Now he stands before a barbed wire fence, gazing into a place he can't ever go—

The boy looked up, straight at me.

I lowered my binoculars. I looked away.

CHAPTER 31

SHE TOOK ME TO DINNER AT A RESTAURANT ON SALAH ED-DIN Street. The upper chamber was carpeted; cushions were spread around the low tables; we had until midnight. We sat on the cushions in the candlelight.

I leaned against the wall as I ate. Rochelle leaned against me. We ate hummus with pita, and olives, and roast chicken served on pita. We drank bottled water and later tea. They served wine in that restaurant, but neither of us wanted any.

"You *must* give my best to Julian when you see him," she said. "I don't know when that'll be, or where you'll be. But whenever it happens, tell him his old pal Rachel says hello."

How will he know that's you? I wanted to ask. But she'd dipped a bit of pita into the hummus and touched it to my lips. I opened my mouth, and she fed it to me.

"If he's still alive," I said when I finished swallowing.

"Oh, he's alive. I don't know where he is, but he's alive. Julian's not so easy to kill. They've tried, more than once."

They brought dessert.

"She's going to live," Rochelle said.

"I hope so," I said. The dessert was sweet and heavy, something made with honey. I didn't know what it was called. I didn't expect ever to taste it again.

"She'll live," Rochelle said. "And then she'll grow. And when she's grown, she'll do what she was sent here for. Then you and I will be together again. And you know what we're going to do then?"

"What?" I said.

"We'll go to the old farmhouse, up to the second floor, and we'll make love. Real love. On the floor, that thin old carpet. The way I wanted to, the night I met you."

Outside, Jameela met us. She put my baby into my arms. Each time I held her I was astonished how light she was. She weighed less than the blankets wrapped around her.

Her eyes were wide open, as usual. She didn't cry or wail; no sound, except that dreadful breathing. Jameela kissed her eyes and wept and went off into the darkness. "*Ma'a-salaameh*," I called out, which is how you say good-bye in Arabic. But Jameela didn't answer.

We stood alone by the edge of the valley. The taxi's taillights vanished in the distance. No moon; only the black sky, the gleaming stars.

"Turn off the flashlight," Rochelle said.

The breeze, which had blown a faint odor of garbage from the valley, died down. The air was again still and sweet. I heard in the darkness the soft, familiar sound of her unbuttoning her blouse.

"Don't go yet," she said.

Perhaps I could begin to see her—perhaps I heard it, or somehow felt it—but I knew she was taking a chain off her neck.

"Give me your hand."

I reached out, and she took my hand, held it tight, pressed the chain into it. I felt against my palm the six sharp points of a Star of David.

"I've worn it underneath," she said. "From the day I got here."

"Rochelle. Oh, Rochelle—"

"You'll give it back," she said. "Next time we meet."

A rectangle of light glowed in the distance. A lighted window, somewhere in the Israeli section of Abu Tor. I took it as my beacon.

I heard the land mine explode a hundred times over as I ran. A thousand times I felt it. I felt my limbs, torn from each other, hanging bloody on the spiny bushes of Hell Valley. I saw the child I'd been carrying, naked and helpless, gasping out her life on the flinty ground as the sun rose over the Jordanian hills.

The light grew larger as I stumbled through rocks and brambles. At last I began to believe we were nearly there, nearly safe. When I heard the popping in my ears, I didn't grasp that it was gunfire. It took me even longer to understand I was the one they were shooting at.

I set my course toward that window.

Who are you that you sit up in your room in the dead of night?

Are you reading, perhaps, because you can't sleep? In your bed, do images come of your mother tossing back and forth like you, insomniac, her heart struggling to pump its blood, her lungs straining to draw in the air? Do you dream now, awake? Do you write in your journal to comfort yourself, to keep yourself from the worse dreams that will come when you slide off into sleep?

Whatever it is—please—stay at your desk.

Don't stop reading; don't stop writing.

Don't go back to bed.

Don't turn off the light.

PART SEVEN
THE CRY

(AUGUST 1966)

CHAPTER 32

"SHE'S GOT TO GO TO THE HOSPITAL," I SAID LOUDLY. "DO you understand? We've got to take her to the hospital."

I held up my hands—maybe to gesture, maybe to reach out toward my child. The handcuffs rattled on my wrists. The soldier on my left forced them back down. He pushed me, not very roughly, to keep me walking. Somewhere ahead, a ceiling bulb shone dimly.

"All right, all right, we take her," said the soldier on my right, whose name was Shimon. "Now you shut your mouth, OK?"

The soldier on the left burst out laughing. So he did understand English. The son of a bitch. When they first captured me, I'd babbled to him about how my child was terribly sick and needed to go to the hospital right away, and he just stared as if he had no idea what I was saying. Then he turned and spit on the ground.

As for the third man, the tall, muscular sergeant whom the others called Yehoshua, he seemed not to know any English at all. He carried my baby, still wrapped in her blanket, as he strode ahead of us down the dark corridor. The walls echoed the sound of her breathing. I would have called out to him, but I knew it wasn't any use. Again I tried Shimon. "*Hos*-pital," I said. "You understand? *Hos*-pital. She must go right *now*. She's *sick*. Very sick."

"You say that twenty times already," said Shimon. "Thirty maybe."

"It's *important*. It's very *important*—"

"Listen," said Shimon, "I know what is *hospital*, OK? I been in hospital myself. You be in hospital yourself now if we didn't find you. Dead maybe."

I knew what he meant. After they'd begun shooting, and I'd realized they were aiming at me, I had cried out: "Don't shoot. I'm an American!" They stopped firing. They shone a searchlight on me and used it to guide me up out of the valley. "Now left!" they screamed. "Now right!" And on more than one occasion, when I tried to walk straight ahead: "No, no, no, no!"

"You walk on *mokaysh*," Shimon said to me. "*Mokaysh* go *boom*"—he illustrated the violence of the explosion by stopping still in the corridor and waving his arms in all directions—"you go into hospital all right."

The sergeant turned and roared something at us. He waved his arm impatiently. Shimon started walking again. The soldier on my left pushed me to walk faster.

"You come out of hospital," Shimon said, "you got no legs. No *baytzeem* either, maybe."

"No *baytzeem*?" I said. "No eggs?"

That was the only meaning I had known for the Hebrew word until then.

The soldier on my left whooped with laughter. Shimon laughed too.

"Maybe he already doesn't have any *baytzeem*," the soldier on my left said to Shimon. "Maybe that's why he doesn't understand."

"Your new home," said Shimon. "You like it?"

It was a tiny, dank cell, about eight by ten feet. It had no window. We'd gone down a flight of steps when we first entered the building, and we were clearly underground. A small bunk bed, without pillow or blanket, lay against one wall. In the corner opposite the bed stood a bucket, its mouth covered by a flat piece of wood.

They took off my handcuffs. I stumbled to the cot and threw myself down; I was too exhausted to stand. They didn't try to stop me.

"You sleep good tonight," said Shimon. "Tomorrow you got a full day. *Lots* of talking to do."

He stood by the cot, looming over me. The sergeant and the third soldier leaned against the wall opposite. My baby breathed noisily in the sergeant's arms.

"You tell us all kinds of things tomorrow," Shimon said. "You tell us what the hell you doing in Jordan. Why you crossing the border in the middle of the night. Where you get that . . . baby."

"I told you. I'm an American citizen—"

"Then where your passport?"

We'd had this exchange a dozen times before. "What about *her*?" Shimon said, gesturing toward the baby. "She an American citizen too?"

I didn't answer.

"She an Arab, or a Jew, or what?"

The sergeant groaned and shifted his feet. This didn't seem to be a response to anything we had said, none of which he'd given any sign of understanding.

"Maybe to know what she is," said Shimon, "we need a—a—scientist." He groped for the words. "A *space* scientist. Don't you think?"

"No, *no*," I wailed. "She's just a sick child, is all. Horribly sick, and she needs—"

But the door had already slammed shut.

In the morning they were back. Shimon shook me to wake me up. There was no need. I hadn't slept at all.

"This baby," Shimon said. "She doesn't sleep. Isn't that right?"

"She's sleeping now," I said, pointing to her.

"She doesn't cry either. Not now, not before. I never saw a baby that doesn't cry."

"That's true," I said.

"Have *you* ever heard her cry?"

"I don't think so," I said.

"Tell me something." He leaned close; I smelled the coffee on his breath. The baby's eyelids trembled but did not open. "In the world she comes from, the babies don't cry?"

Outside, the sun had just cleared the horizon. The morning air was fresh and cool and soft. They led me to a small black car without official markings, into which I was invited, not pushed.

"Where are you taking me?" I said.

The sergeant drove. There was something familiar about the way he handled the wheel. I sat next to Shimon in the back seat, my baby against my shoulder. This time they hadn't bothered to handcuff me.

"Coming now to the corner of Yafo and Ben-Yehuda streets," Shimon announced jovially, like a guide on a tourist bus. "Heart of downtown Jerusalem. *Lots* of falafel stands here. Sell very good falafel. You want we should jump out, buy you a falafel to eat?"

I looked straight ahead. The third soldier, whose name I didn't know, sat in the passenger seat next to the sergeant.

"You hungry?" Shimon asked.

Yes, Shimon. I am hungry and very thirsty. I would give anything right now to have a nice orange soda. Let's jump out of the car, Shimon, you and I, and we'll get falafel and sodas for everyone. And then I'll be lost in a flash, and you won't find us.

"No," I said. "I'm not hungry."

"What's she doing?" said Shimon.

At first I didn't realize he was talking about the baby. She stirred inside her blanket. Feebly she pressed her oversize head against me. She'd never done that before.

"She sound . . . just like a cat," said Shimon.

Yes. Like a cat. Yet I had the sense the faint mewing wasn't coming from her throat, but from higher up, somewhere behind her huge black eyes. I didn't understand how that was possible.

"What's she want?" Shimon said uneasily. "What's she need?"

"I don't know," I said. The mewing was louder now, almost a squeal. In that cry I felt something strange and terrible. I peered into her face and saw no expression, any more than a flute or an oboe or a badly played violin has an expression. The sergeant briefly turned around. His mouth hung open. I knew that man; I'd seen him somewhere. I didn't have time to think where.

"Can't you make her stop that noise?" said Shimon.

It grew louder by the second. I pulled her to my chest and began to stroke her, trying to be gentle. "Shhh, it's all right . . ." The third soldier growled something in Hebrew and put his fingers in his ears.

She didn't clutch at me or resist. She felt in my arms like a bag of straw. Yet the wail she gave out was deafening. It was bigger than she was, than all of us, rising from below, splitting its way upward, filling the car and my ears and mind until I felt ready to explode.

"Make her *sto-o-o-op!*" Shimon screamed. I could barely hear him.

"Shhh, shhh, shhh . . ." I whispered in her ear.

The sergeant turned to stare. He let go of the steering wheel. A second later came the crash.

I don't know what it was we slammed into. We jerked forward; the doors flew open; there was yelling. The sergeant's voice was the loudest of many. No one noticed when I jumped from the car.

And began to run.

She lay in my arms, silent now as the dead. The breath cut into my chest; my swollen foot dragged behind me like an anchor. I ran beneath gray arches, among dingy buildings where the narrow stone-paved alleys twisted into one another and there wasn't any street or sidewalk. Rotting vegetable rinds squashed beneath my feet.

A narrow stairway, between high windowless buildings, led down to an alley. The steps were high and smooth and hard, also slippery where crushed watermelon fragments oozed their juice. I'd just started down when I saw the men gathered at the foot of the steps.

About a dozen men such as I'd never seen before. Not one woman. Pale and bearded; long caftans of greasy, fish belly white, striped with pale blue. They watched me with dead dark eyes, in which I expected hatred but saw only blankness.

My grandfather's fathers.

From half-opened lips came the hum of their chanting. *Kha. Kha. Kha—*

> *—b'shivt'KHA b'veyseKHA*
> *uvlekht'KHA vaderekh*
> *uvshokhb'KHA uvkoomeKHA—*

>> *—when thou sittest in thy house*
>> *when thou walkest in the way*
>> *when thou liest down and risest up—*

—thou must recite, thou must remember, the commandments of thy God. Thou must gather by the moonlit ashen shores of a dead book and a broken promise, quench endless thirst with waters of thine own rot—

I knew these men. I detested them, and for that hatred I despised myself, knowing I'd betrayed the generations that had borne me, allied myself to evil beyond imagining. My feet trembled. I stood still, not descending, not retreating.

The baby shuddered against my chest.

She began to make soft mewing sounds, the beginnings of that sirenlike howl I couldn't bear to hear again. I turned. I climbed back up the steps, careful not to slip on the watermelon. When I looked behind me, the men had vanished.

I drifted, strengthless, among the alleys. No benches; no stoops. No place to sit and rest. When I heard heavy boots running behind me, I didn't even try to get away.

The sergeant's powerful body thudded against mine, almost knocking me over. It swept me like wind at the seashore. His arm held firm around my shoulders, and once more I ran, as part of *his* running, and now I wasn't tired. Nor did my foot weigh me down. Swiftly we ran, faster than I'd have thought possible, and didn't stop until we'd reached a trafficked street.

He stood by the curb and held my arm tightly and waved his other arm in a great sweep. He shouted something, very loud. A taxi braked. He yanked open the rear door, pushed me in, and jumped in beside me. He spoke to the driver in rapid Hebrew. "Hadassah," I heard him say. "Hadassah."

I slumped in the seat. I stared at two huge foam rubber dice that hung from the rearview mirror, while I caught my breath. "*Todah rabah*," I said as soon as I could talk. "Thank you very, *very* much. *Todah rabah*."

The sergeant looked out the window. He gave a deep sigh. He said: "Oh, you're very welcome, I'm sure. But really, Mr. Shapiro, I'd have expected a *somewhat* more effusive greeting from you. We haven't seen each other since our drive to Miami three years ago, have we?"

CHAPTER 33

"JULIAN!!!"

"Sssh! Sssh!" He choked with laughter; his face was red from struggling to hold it in. "That's not my name anymore. Hasn't been for years now. They don't look kindly on Diaspora names in these parts."

"But how in the *world* did you—"

"I'm Yehoshua now. Or Joshua, if you really must. That's the way you say Yehoshua in English."

"I know."

His laughing fit had passed. He relaxed into the seat. "I've made aliyah. But surely you'd guessed that. You know what making aliyah means, don't you?"

"It's the expression for immigrating to Israel. Right?"

"Absolutely right. *May-achooz*, one hundred percent, as we say around here. Literally, it means 'going up.' You want to *go up*, my boy, this is the way to do it. Fine view from up here."

I supposed he meant that last remark figuratively. But it might have been literal too. We'd left the downtown streets behind, winding our way up into the barren brown hills around Jerusalem. Their slopes glared hot in the morning sun.

"Julian. I mean, Yehoshua. There's a lot of talking we need to do."

He nodded and said something I couldn't catch. His buckteeth, which I only now noticed, pressed into his lower lip.

"How did you happen to be on guard at the border at the time I was crossing? Was that just coincidence or what?"

"Coincidence," he said thoughtfully. He seemed to relax a bit, as though he'd expected me to ask a different question—like where had he been that night at the airport?—and now was relieved I hadn't. "That would be an awful lot of coincidence for one night, wouldn't it? Still, coincidences do happen. So it might have been coincidence, really. What do you think?"

"Don't be cute, Julian. I don't have the energy. I haven't slept since the night before last. And you and your friend Shimon weren't exactly good company, remember?"

"No," he said, "I guess we weren't."

"You and Shimon and that third character—what was his name? Somehow I never got his name."

"Itzig."

"Yes, that's right. Itzig the wit. Itzig the humorist."

"Now, take it easy, Danny—"

"Itzig, with his jokes about my *baytzeem*."

He fumbled nervously at a pack of cigarettes in his breast pocket. "Incidentally," I said. "Speaking of my *baytzeem*. What kinds of things would your—your *comrades-in-arms* be doing to me right now? If I hadn't managed to escape."

Out came the cigarettes. He looked toward the tiny, frail creature who lay in my arms, her breathing louder and more strained than I'd ever heard it. He put the cigarettes back into his pocket.

"Nothing very terrible," he said. "They might have roughed you up a little bit. More to scare you than anything else. You don't have to worry. I'd have found a way to stop it if it had gotten out of hand."

" 'Found a way'? Aren't you the one giving the orders?"

"Yes and no. Yes, I'm the sergeant, they're the privates. I'm the one who tells them what to do. But no, I'm not a free agent. There are limits. I'm under those limits, just as you are.

"Believe me," he said. "These are strange times. And my guess is you haven't grasped just how strange."

"Explain it to me," I said.

"You must understand, Danny, that Shimon and Itzig don't know a lot of the things you and I know. Neither do most of the people in the higher ranks. Some do. That's how I was able to get myself posted to Abu Tor. But most don't."

"Get yourself posted? So then you *did*—"

"No, no. Let me finish. They know there's something odd going on. But they won't let themselves think about it. For everything that happens there's an official explanation, and they believe it all. Just like the man in the street. Like back in the States when it came to UFOs. You remember that, don't you? They pride themselves on being very *practical*, very *matter-of-fact*. We're very much the *realists*, we Israelis. So *realistic* we can't see that the . . . *curtains* are fraying. They're almost worn away by now. Only a few threads left—"

"The *curtains?*"

"And those threads are already beginning to snap."

"Julian, what—"

"They've heard something about the Makhtesh. You can't be in the army and *not* hear about the Makhtesh, these days. They think it's all just rumor. There was a leak at the Dimona reactor, they think, and that's why the roads are blocked off—"

"Julian," I said, "what the hell are you *talking* about?"

CHAPTER 34

THEY PUT HER ON A COT UNDER AN OXYGEN TENT, WHILE THEY paged Dr. Zeitlin. Julian and I sat on vinyl chairs beside the cot. He explained to me why we had to wait for Dr. Zeitlin. Of all the Hadassah doctors, he said, only Zeitlin knew what was going on at this Makhtesh. Only Zeitlin would have some inkling of what the creature was that he needed to treat. Every several minutes there was an announcement on the public-address system, of which the only word I could make out was *Zeitlin*.

Dr. Zeitlin didn't appear. I sat slumped in the chair, going in and out of a doze, wondering from time to time what the Makhtesh was and what might be happening there.

Finally they found a cot for me, and I got a few hours of real sleep. We were up before dawn. Julian brought me a uniform.

"I forgot to tell you," he said as I followed him out the hospital doors. "You're honorarily in the army till this business is finished. Nobody's going to stop a pair of uniformed soldiers."

The stars glittered above us as, in the strange khaki clothing, I climbed behind the wheel of the jeep. Venus, more brilliant than I'd ever seen it, rose in the east. Julian showed me how to shift the gears.

I wish I could say it broke my heart to leave my baby in the care of strangers, that I could hardly bring myself to begin our journey, that my spirit stayed with her in her hospital bed. Truth was, I felt liberated and exhilarated as I guided the jeep onto the dark, empty road and saw the hospital's dim bulk recede in the rearview mirror.

"Did Zeitlin ever show up?" I asked.

"Oh, eventually," Julian said with a yawn. "Everybody shows up eventually. You just have to spend half your life waiting for them."

"He examined her?"

"Yes, he examined her. He also read the letter you brought across from that Arab doctor—what was his name?—Talibi. He read it very attentively. He's obviously got a lot of respect for Talibi. I have the impression the two of them know each other."

"How would that be?" I asked. "An Israeli and a Jordanian—how could they ever meet?"

"International conferences maybe." He yawned again. "Or maybe from the time before independence. Zeitlin's old enough to have been in practice back then, and I assume Talibi is too. In those days there wasn't any barbed wire border slicing Jerusalem in two, the way there is now."

"Jerusalem will be one," I said.

"*What?*" said Julian.

I gripped the wheel hard. My voice sounded as strange to me as it evidently had to Julian, and I was overcome by the feeling I was speaking and acting in a dream. I was afraid I'd run the jeep off the road.

"Who said that?" said Julian.

"I don't know. I think it was *them*. The aliens, the Elder Gods—I don't know what to call them. But *them*."

"Think, Danny, think." I could hear the fear and excitement in his voice. "Did they say Jerusalem was going to be *one*, O-N-E? Or *won*, W-O-N?"

"I don't know," I said.

It was a long time before either of us spoke.

"Is there hope?" I said finally.

"Hope? For what?"

"You know. For *her*."

"There's always hope," Julian said. "Even on the truck taking you to the gas chambers there's hope. That's one thing you learn every day, being in Israel."

"But is there hope for *her*?"

"Just drive, Danny."

The road snaked down from the mountains into the desert. The sun rose upon us as we passed Peniel.

I mean, Beersheva.

It was a dusty, ramshackle place, hot even at that hour. A few trucks lumbered through the rutted dirt streets. A few bedouin led their camels. By the edge of town, not far from the last rows of prefabricated apartment buildings, the bedouin had pitched their black goat-hair tents. Then we left these behind too, and we were alone in the flinty barrenness of the Negev.

"Like to switch drivers?" Julian said.

I did, very much. My swollen foot felt made of lead. I braked in the middle of the road. It didn't matter; we were the only traffic. We climbed out of the jeep and urinated on the stony ground.

At the Yeroham intersection we turned left. We kept on until we reached the roadblock. It took Julian nearly twenty minutes to talk our way through. I understood then why he'd wanted me to be in uniform.

"You're sure there's no radiation?" I said once we were on our way. The warning sign at the roadblock had been so emphatic I needed his assurance one more time.

"Of course I'm sure. The government had to come up with some plausible reason why all the roads to the Makhtesh are cut off. Everybody knows Dimona is only ten miles away. Everybody knows there's a nuclear reactor at Dimona. So, *voilà*, a radiation leak at the reactor, blown this way by southerly winds, danger to life and limb. Et cetera and so forth."

"And they went and evacuated everybody out of Dimona, just to make the story believable?"

"And out of Yeroham, for good measure."

"That's pretty extreme, isn't it?" I said.

"They're pretty scared," said Julian.

The Greater Makhtesh, he explained, was a huge crater that looked as if it had been scraped off the lunar surface and dropped into the Negev desert. One of the geological wonders of Israel.

For weeks now, odd things were happening there.

He spoke of white globes bubbling up from the crater's floor. The layers of ancient rock in its walls changed colors, even shapes. The bands of red sandstone, or the yellow or the white, might thicken. They might contract. They might shift their positions. They might change, in broad daylight, right before your eyes—

"That doesn't make any sense, Julian."

"It doesn't? Why not?"

"Layers of *rock*, in place for hundreds of millions of *years*, suddenly start shifting all by themselves?"

He shook his head.

"The curtains are fraying," he said. "The fabric is unstable. Something is bursting in on us, and we don't know what it is."

—and finally came the night of the red mist. It began as a shining red globe, swelling up, darkly luminous, like a balloon from the crater's floor—

"Or like that thing I saw through the telescope! Remember, Julian? That night in the tower, observing the moon—"

"The old SSS house," he said. "How I do miss it."

—then pulsating, then throbbing. Then exploding; and the Makhtesh filled with a thick red mist, a lake of luminescent blood. At dawn the mist faded. The tower remained, with the disk perched at its top—

It was the first thing I saw that desert morning as we drew near the rim of the Makhtesh. It looked exactly the way the Gypsies had drawn it in their book. The metal gleamed dully in the fierce sunlight.

"Julian! I've been there before!"

—*on the moon, my head in the moon woman's lap, listening to what I thought was the lapping of waves. She was real after all, and the moon tower was real, and here's one like it standing before me, in this moon crater in the middle of the desert—*

I think I fainted. I would have fallen out of the jeep if Julian hadn't grabbed my shoulders and held me all through the dizzy ride to the crater's floor.

Abandoned mining machinery lay scattered around the tower, like Tinkertoys at the feet of a giant.

CHAPTER 35

"SO," JULIAN SAID, "DO YOU THINK YOU CAN FLY IT?"

I looked around, still out of breath from climbing the tower. Outside, everything had seemed a bizarre chaos, as if this were the moon after all and not the Negev. Here in the disk it was all familiar. There was the control panel with its buttons and switches and levers, arranged as I'd come to know them beneath a swollen moon, in a time outside time. I knew it all, the way you know a home in which you haven't been very happy, perhaps, but where you've lived so long you can't imagine home anywhere else.

"Doesn't he speak Hebrew?" the lieutenant said to Julian.

Julian paid no attention. The lieutenant outranked him, but apparently that had stopped mattering. Julian watched me closely as I ran my fingers among the buttons, and I thought how I'd learned all this from the book we'd searched for so long and how I'd lost the book, and that didn't matter, for books are dispensable once they've become part of you.

"He's in the army," the lieutenant said loudly, gesturing toward me. "And he still doesn't speak Hebrew?"

"New immigrant," said Julian.

I walked around the disk, letting my hand trail along the surface of the control panel. Julian followed. The lieutenant leaned against the wall and watched us both.

"Julian," I said.

"Danny!" He saw my expression, and his face filled with alarm. "What's the matter?"

I didn't answer. I couldn't speak. I felt paralyzed with exhaustion and dread, and at first I didn't know why.

"Danny! What's wrong, buddy? Are you OK?"

I pointed to a small grayish smear on the wall, a few inches above the floor.

Julian crouched to examine it. He stood up, pale with rage. "Ohh . . . the *idiots*!" he burst out. "The damn idiots! Them and their cigarettes! You tell them, over and over . . . and they don't even have the sense to use a goddamn ashtray!"

The lieutenant stopped smirking. He ran over to us, his arms waving. He shouted into Julian's face. He jabbed his finger at the insignia on his own uniform, as though aggrieved beyond bearing. Julian shouted back, pointed accusingly at the spot on the wall. I dug my nails into my palms and waited for the nausea to pass.

"Julian," I said, "I don't think this is cigarette ash."

"Of course it's cigarette ash! What the hell else could it be?"

I knew what it was. I'd walked in it each time I'd gone to the lake. I'd wondered at its heaviness, its strange greasiness. Something had brought that ash in here; but when? And how? "Maybe a lizard tracked it in," I said, more to myself than to Julian.

"A *lizard*? Are you serious?"

I wasn't, really. I just wanted some way to make the ash smear into something normal, earthly. I hoped its resemblance to a six-fingered hand would turn out to be my imagination. That it didn't mean the things I'd left behind had followed me, were here to meet me.

"Well," I said, "it doesn't look like it's from a cigarette, that's all."

"What would a lizard be doing up here? Where would it have stepped in ashes? There aren't any ashes—"

The lieutenant had stopped shouting. "What did he say?" he said to Julian.

Julian translated for him. Then the lieutenant began explaining. He spoke earnestly and at considerable length, looking at both me and Julian, although it was all Hebrew and I could hardly understand a word. When the lieutenant finished, Julian turned to me.

"He says it probably was a lizard," Julian said. He'd mostly calmed down, though his voice still shook a little. "He says the lizards are all over the place, and they might even have climbed up this tower, and there's a dark, sandy soil in parts of the Makhtesh that looks a lot like ash, and— Well, that's what he says anyway."

"Yes," I said. My heart's pounding had eased, and I no longer wanted to vomit. "It probably was a lizard."

The lieutenant took a handkerchief from his back pocket and wiped the stain from the wall.

CHAPTER 36

"SO THE CURTAINS ARE FRAYING?" I SAID TO JULIAN THAT night.

"All around us," he said. "Wherever you turn, they've worn thin as tissue paper, ready to fall apart. Can't you see it? Can't you *feel* it?"

At that moment I couldn't feel it. The bottle of Maccabee beer I held in my hand seemed reassuringly ordinary. The stars shone above us in their old familiar patterns. They hadn't fallen. They showed no sign of being about to fall.

Those stars were the only light beyond our fire. We were camped just outside the Makhtesh, a few hundred yards from the rim, but after the sun set, the crater had vanished in the darkness. The beer was warm, but it tasted good. Julian had tried to teach me to smoke cigarettes—"Make a real Israeli out of you." After a few puffs I'd decided to pass.

"Why New Mexico?" I said. "Why not the White House lawn?"

Julian laughed. " 'If they're real,' " he said in a crackly old man voice, " 'why the dickens don't they land on the White House lawn?' That's what the UFO skeptics always say, isn't it? How many times have you had to answer that tired old argument?"

"Yes," I said. "Why aren't we going to land on the White House lawn?"

"I don't really know. It's just what they said you had to do: take the disk to southeastern New Mexico and land it there. They haven't given any reasons. They usually don't, you know."

"Any guesses then?"

"Uh-huh," said Julian, nodding. He drank the last of his beer, wiped his mouth with the back of his hand. He set the bottle carefully on the ground.

"From Dimona to Alamogordo," I said.

"What?"

"That's my guess. You can tell me yours in a minute. I'm guessing that me and my—whatever she is—"

"Yes. Don't we wish we could understand what that baby is?"

"*Whatever.* She and I are supposed to retrace the steps of the nuclear age. Right? Isn't that right?"

"Not bad," said Julian. "Go on."

"Nineteen forty-five we test the first atom bomb at Alamogordo, New Mexico. Fireball four times as hot as the sun. 'The radiance of a thousand suns . . . I am become as death, the destroyer of worlds.' That's what Oppenheimer said after the test, wasn't it? From that Indian book, the—the—"

"Bhagavad Gita," said Julian.

"Bhagavad Gita. I was about to say that. Quit interrupting me, Margulies."

"Margaliot. That's the Hebrew form of the name. Julian Margulies is past. All gone. I'm Yehoshua Margaliot now."

"I said, don't interrupt. *Anyway*, then comes Hiroshima, then Nagasaki—"

"And Roswell. Don't forget Roswell."

"Roswell?" I stared at him. "What's Roswell got to do with this?"

"It's where the Five Hundred Ninth Bomb Group was headquartered after the war. Those are the fellows who dropped the bombs on Hiroshima and Nagasaki. Don't tell me you didn't know that?"

"And now—" My mind had gone spinning off in a new direction; I struggled to bring it back to what I'd been trying to say. "Now it's twenty-one years later, and here we are in Israel, the newest country in the world, which is also the place of the oldest religion in the world, and there's a nuclear reactor at Dimona. They're building bombs, ten miles away from us, like the one Oppenheimer exploded at Alamogordo—"

"Only bigger. Better. Destroy more worlds," said Julian.

"And this is still a drop in the ocean, compared to the murderous stuff America and Russia have got—"

"Good," said Julian. "Very good."

"So we're off from Dimona to Alamogordo—or, I don't know, maybe to Roswell—to bring a message to the people of the world. From the—how shall we say it?—*the Others*. And the message is: *Stop it!*"

"Not bad," said Julian. "You're on the right track. But that's all very preachy, isn't it? Our benevolent space brothers appear on their flying disks. 'Peace, earthling! We come to save you from your self-destructive ways! Put away your swords, guns, bombs, live in peace and harmony,' et cetera and so forth. Straight out of a B movie, right?"

"Except I'm not exactly a space brother," I said.

"Don't count on that, Shapiro. But let it be. Don't you think a sermon like that is apt to be—well, of rather limited effectiveness? We earthlings have been preaching that stuff at one another for the past twenty years. Yet every year goes by, there's more nuclear bombs. Isn't that so?"

"And less than four years ago we nearly—"

We nearly used them. I stopped speaking. Almost, I'd stopped breathing. In the starlit darkness I felt myself back in that fourth week of October, when I was in eighth grade and the Russians sent missiles to Cuba, and Kennedy sent ships to stop them. All that week the dread of the bombs hovered over us, something monstrous in the sky, ready to fall and snuff us out . . .

And I became a UFO investigator.

"OK," I said. "We're not going to New Mexico with the message of peace. What *will* we be doing, then?"

"Death is 'the destroyer of worlds,'" said Julian. "Right? That's what the Bhagavad Gita says, isn't it? Right?"

"All right. I grant that. Let's go on."

"Well . . . suppose there's something that's the destroyer of death?"

"*What?*"

The fire had blazed up. I saw his face clearly. I said: "You're not joking, are you?"

He shook his head no.

"So who are you talking about?"

"Guess."

I could guess. Once more I heard Rochelle's voice:

She'll live, Danny, and grow, and do what she was sent here for. And in a few years this world is going to be so different from anything we've ever known we're not going to recognize it. So different we'll think we're living on another planet. . . . Once more I saw Rochelle's lovely, earnest face, her skin gold in the setting sun, planning with me how I would carry my magic child across the border.

And now she would live. The field telephone had rung that afternoon with good news. Zeitlin's treatment had worked. The baby was breathing normally. They'd give her ten days in the hospital—two weeks at most—to rest, heal, build up her resistance. Then they'd drive her down to the Makhtesh. Where I would be waiting.

I wanted, more than anything in the world, to hold Rochelle in my arms again. I took a swallow of beer.

Meanwhile Julian talked. About Einstein and his unified field theory, about the single web of which space and time are woven. What has been woven, Julian said, can also be unwoven.

"*So I'm unweaving time?*"

"Well, that's putting it a bit drastically, but—"

"I'm destroying death by unweaving time," I said. And when I saw him nod, I said: "That's what the UFOs are about, isn't it?"

No wonder the curtains were fraying.

"I'm rolling up the past twenty years," I said, "like a winter rug. The way you do before you stuff it into the attic."

Julian shook his head. "No," he said. "I wouldn't put it that way exactly. The twenty years will still have been here. You'll still have been born. So will I. At least I *think* we will."

"Then what exactly am I unweaving?"

"One thread from that rug, that fabric, that web—pick whatever image you like. One particularly dangerous, let's say *cancerous*, thread. Leave it be, and it'll destroy the rest. We'll all die, and be as though we hadn't been."

A meteor flared in the black sky.

"Julian," I said, "I don't think this is going to happen."

"Why not?"

"Because you can't *do* this with time. I mean, it's all very nice to make up these images, of threads and webs and whatever. But you can't pull out a thread from time, and save the rest or destroy the rest, or whatever you're going to do. I mean, time doesn't *work* that way."

"Doesn't it? Are you sure? Don't you remember . . ."

He spoke of an afternoon many years ago. Of a young boy who'd come to a library in a big city with his friends and stepped apart from them in that library—not for very long, that boy thought. When he went to find them again, they were gone. The library was empty: full of books, full of sunlight. But no people anywhere.

What did I think that was if not a thread plucked out of time?

" 'Science is a turtle,' " I said very slowly. " 'that says its own shell encloses all things.' "

"Charles Fort," said Julian. "So you do remember."

"Do you still read Charles Fort? Can you even find his books here in Israel?"

"In the libraries? The bookstores? Of course not. We're a practical people, we Israelis. We wouldn't waste shelf space on *The Book of the Damned*. They're still the excluded, as far as we're concerned. We've had enough experience with exclusion and damnation, thank you. We don't need any more."

"Abandonment too, Julian?"

I suppose it was his mentioning *The Book of the Damned*. Otherwise I don't know why I picked that moment to ask the one question that had hardly left my mind since the night he disappeared.

"I understand why Jeff left me," I said. "Rosa too—"

"Rosa? The girl who wanted you to dance, and you wouldn't?"

"I couldn't. You know why. And she had to move on—"

"Naturally."

"—and so did Jeff. And I wouldn't—I mean, I couldn't—because of—"

"Your dying mother."

"No, Julian. She's going to live."

The best medical care in the region, if not the world—how could she not live? "But *you*—" I said.

"But why did I leave you? All by yourself in that airport. To face whatever might be there."

"Yes. Why did you do it?"

He stood up. He brought fresh wood for the fire, which had been about to die out. Then he settled himself, slowly. I was patient. I waited.

CHAPTER 37

"THEY CAME AFTER ME THAT NIGHT," HE SAID. "DID YOU know that?"

" 'They'? Who exactly are 'they' now?"

"Yes. Who exactly are they? That's what we've wanted to find out all along. They came to our hotel."

And I'd given them the address. I blurted it out, in nervousness and confusion, and they wrote it down. "Twenty-two-oh-eight Orlando Avenue," I said. "Miami."

"So you remember that place?"

I nodded. "What a dump."

"Exactly. Rickety old hotel, all made of wood. One spark, it'd go up in flames. Remember that?"

I looked into our campfire. "I remember. So?"

"It did. Three-thirty that morning."

He picked up a scrap of wood from beside his booted foot and tossed it into the fire. We watched together as it flared, blackened, crumbled.

"Of course," he said, "I wasn't there at the time."

"Three-thirty A.M.? You weren't in the hotel? Then where?"

"Miami Beach. There was a Cuban coffee shop open all night. I went there after I left you at the airport. I sat and drank coffee and read Charles Fort and listened to the Latin music on the radio. All night, until the six o'clock news came on, and they reported the hotel fire. That was the first I heard—"

"*So you left me alone in the goddamn airport, so you could go to some goddamn stupid Cuban coffee shop and read your goddamn stupid Charles Fort?*"

"That's right. And you don't understand why I did that?"

"No, I don't. I haven't got the slightest fucking idea."

"Fucking idea," he said. It was the saddest I'd ever heard his voice. Fire-light flickered on his long face.

"I broke every speed limit there was," he said, "as soon as I heard the news. I had to get back to the hotel, find out what had become of you and Rochelle."

"Me and *Rochelle*?"

"That's right. You and Rochelle. What's the matter, Danny? Haven't you understood yet?"

Of course—me and Rochelle. Two's company, three's a crowd. The tactful thing for number three to do is vanish. Give the young lovers their privacy, a room to themselves.

How was he to know Rochelle wouldn't be on that plane?

"They don't control destiny, those three men," he said. "In my bad moments sometimes I've thought they do. I would've committed suicide then, I suppose. Except I was afraid they'd be on the other side, waiting to have me."

"We'd better pray they aren't," I said.

"*You* pray. You're the Bible scholar. Me, I'm interested in this world, this life. And here they don't rule. Not entirely at least."

Proof: Julian wasn't at the hotel when the three men showed up in the middle of the night, tied the night manager to a chair, found our room, doused it with kerosene, and set it on fire. Neither was I. Nor Rochelle.

He got there in the morning, just before seven. He saw what was left of the building. He spent nearly an hour. Then he drove straight to Philadelphia, not stopping to rest. He emptied his savings account, headed for the airport, bought a one-way ticket to Israel.

"And that's how Julian Margulies became Sergeant Yehoshua Margaliot?" I said.

He nodded. "The switch went on in my brain after what I saw that morning. The little voice told me I'd had enough Diaspora for one lifetime."

"Enough high school too?"

"Diaspora, high school. Same shit."

He posed as a reporter. The policeman, keeping people from the building, looked at him real close when he said he wanted to see the remains of our room. "You're a Jew," the cop said. "Right?"

"Yeah, that's right. I'm a Jew."

"Then maybe you don't want to go in there."

He went in anyway. Everything was black: ceiling, walls, floor. The wires in the light fixture in the ceiling had burned or melted, and it had come crashing down to the middle of the floor.

The two beds were charred and shapeless, stank from the kerosene—

—and I said, "Go on, don't stop," though of course I wished he would stop and say, "That's all, Danny. That's all the story there is"—

—but he could still see, they'd bunched up the sheets and blankets into two humanlike shapes, tied together with wire, one in each bed. Me and Julian. Or so they were meant to be—

"My God," I said.

Then I said: "There's more, isn't there?"

"There's more."

They'd taken two Stars of David. Each a foot and a half across. The stars were made of some very solid metal that didn't melt. Julian didn't know what the metal was, whether it was of this earth. It had turned all black, and he was afraid to touch it.

They fastened one star to each of the two dummies, where our chests would have been. They poured on the kerosene.

"The stars got red hot in the fire," Julian said. "They burned their way through the dummies into the mattresses. Among all the charring, I could still see their mark, in each mattress. Two six-pointed Stars of David, side by side."

I was sick with dread. I wanted to vomit. I felt as I had that morning when we were inside the disk with the lieutenant and I'd seen on the wall a smear of gray ash that I knew hadn't been tracked in by any lizard.

There was more.

"They'd brought a can of spray paint with them," Julian said. "They left a message on the tile wall of the bathroom. They must have figured that was where it was most likely to stay legible, even after the fire. Can you guess what it was?"

The voice came through my mouth, but it wasn't my voice. I think it was Pockface's—looking upon me and Julian as I'd looked upon the lake creatures in caftans at the foot of the steps, loathing them with all my soul.

"Dirty Jew, stinking Jew, bloodsucking motherfucking kike"—and I felt my jaws as his jaws, my tongue as his tongue, as the string of obscenities rolled through my lips. "Hitler never should have let you live, should have killed you all—"

Julian shook his head.

"It wasn't that," he said. "Not like that at all."

What the three men had sprayed on the bathroom wall, in huge block capitals, was this:

WE WILL FIND YOU

WHEN WE COME BACK WE WILL FIND YOU

WE ALWAYS FIND THOSE WE WANT

CHAPTER 38

TEN DAYS, IT TURNED OUT, WEREN'T QUITE ENOUGH FOR THE baby's recuperation.

It was nearly two weeks—just past midnight, the last day of August—before the phone rang in my rented room in Beersheva. Julian, who'd also received a phone call, came to pick me up.

And so we ate breakfast with the soldiers by the first light of dawn, at the bottom of the crater, near the foot of the tower. There was bread, and leben out of plastic containers, and hard-boiled eggs, and tomatoes and cucumbers, which we sliced with our knives on our metal plates. The sounds of Hebrew conversation washed comfortingly over me as I ate. As the sun began to press itself over the horizon, the baby arrived.

At first we didn't notice the jeep winding its way down to the crater floor. I became aware of a hum of astonished voices, moving toward me down the long tables. There was applause also, and cries of "You're the father?"—to which I nodded.

I don't know who carried her to me and eased her into my arms. But it was Shimon who brought the bottle.

"Here," he said to me. "Take this."

It was the first time I'd given her the bottle. I stood awkwardly, feeding her, while her blanketed head rested against my shoulder. The men sat around us and watched. Some of them stood, leaning against the tables. They talked and pointed. Often they laughed. Maybe it was my clumsiness that amused them. But I didn't hear any malice in the laughter, only warmth and kindness and friendship.

The dawn had been chilly. Now the rising sun began to warm us. The tower's shadow stretched across the crater; the shadow of the disk at its top lay on the crater's rim. My little girl breathed easily and softly as she sucked on the rubber nipple. She smiled, not at me particularly but at the world at large. She was bigger since the last time I'd carried her, and heavier.

It's true, I thought. *They do grow faster than we do.*

"Excuse me, mister," one of the soldiers said timidly in English. He was a small dark-skinned man, with a rumpled uniform and a day's growth on his cheeks. "Excuse me that I ask. But the mother of that one—from where is she?"

"I don't know," I said.

"You're not mad at me that I asked?"

"No," I said. "I'm not mad. But I just don't know."

"Eyzo chamoodeleh," he said finally, stroking her enormous forehead with the tips of his fingers. "What a cute little girl."

We went up in a helicopter. They let down a rope ladder, its end trembling in the air just outside the disk's entrance. Julian went down first, carrying the baby. I followed, taking care not to look toward the ground. "There, Danny! I've got you!"—and I felt his strong hand gripping my arm, pulling me after him into the disk.

"Julian," I said once we were inside, "why don't you come with us?"

"Really, Mr. Shapiro! I'm in the army now. The Israel Defense Force doesn't look kindly on its soldiers trotting off on foreign jaunts, in the middle of their service."

He patted me on the shoulder and laughed. "I'll be along soon enough. Don't you worry."

The helicopter hovered outside. The dangling ladder jerked and quivered. Julian reached out, grabbed it, swung himself onto it.

"Julian!" I called after him.

"What?"

The helicopter was making such a racket I barely heard him. "Your old pal Rachel sends regards!" I yelled.

"My old pal *who?*"

"Tell you later," I said.

I held my baby against my chest as I stood, moving back and forth, pulling switches, touching buttons. Her tiny fingers grasped at the collar of my shirt.

She squealed with joy as the disk trembled, as my body and hers turned transparent and the disk became transparent around us. She laughed out loud and clapped, as if to say, "Daddy, show me more!"

We lifted from the top of the tower. For a full minute I let the disk hang motionless over the crater. The soldiers watched from below. They must have seen it from the outside as a silvery platter, brilliant in the morning sunlight. Then suddenly I made us flutter down, almost to the ground, in a wobbling motion like a falling leaf.

The soldiers scattered. When they saw it was all right—I was in control; we weren't going to crash—they turned and cheered. They clapped wildly. Some of them danced, strange dances I'd never seen before. Some put their fingers in their mouths to whistle. I shot the disk off at an angle, into the liquid blue of the morning sky, while a baby's laughter gurgled against my chest.

The sparse clouds fell away beneath us. The horizon began to curve. If we kept on like this, in another minute the blue around us would turn violet and then black. The world would turn into a blue and green globe, shining in the blackness, its surface flecked with ragged smears of white. No need to go so far. I arched the disk down toward the blueness of the Atlantic.

The sun glinted off a silvery cylindrical object, tiny in the distance, far below us.

A jetliner.

"Ladies and gentlemen, this is your captain speaking.

"If you'll look out your right-hand windows, ladies and gentlemen, you'll see something very unusual. Something most air travelers don't get to see. At least, not up close like this.

"There's no reason to think it's dangerous. Because, you see, this flying saucer has been keeping us company for several minutes now, and if it were going to blast us with a death ray, we figure it would have done that already. And it hasn't. So there's no reason to think it's going to do it now.

"We don't know where it's coming from or what it is. At first, when it came shooting down from above and behind us, I thought it might be a falling star. But it stopped in midair, a few miles ahead, like it was waiting for us to catch up. And we did catch up. We went right past it. And when we passed it, I saw it trembling, like a big silver leaf in a strong wind.

"And then I thought we'd seen the last of it. But what does it do but come curving up like a boomerang, and there it is ahead of us, not moving, just off our right wing. In a couple of minutes we're going to pass it again."

—he's on the plane, that boy, the boy from Abu Tor. Flying home to his sick mother, so when he gets there, he'll see her again and make everything right.

Through the window I can make out his face—

"It's flying with us now, ladies and gentlemen. It and us, together. Like two good old friends. Like boyfriend and girlfriend, holding hands.

"It looks different now, seems to me. At first it was silvery, metallic. Now it's got a liquid quality. Whiter, more pearly. Like a teardrop, shining on your cheek.

"Tilting a little now . . .

"Looks to be about fifty feet from the wingtip.

"Less than fifty, really . . .

"Coming closer now . . .

"Thirty feet . . .

"Less than thirty feet . . . more like twenty. Now less than twenty—"

"SHE'S FIBRILLATING!"

"SHE'S FIBRILLATING!"

A jolt, as of electricity, shot through the plane. The passengers leaped against their seat belts. The disk, which had touched the plane momentarily, darted away at terrific speed, as though it and not the plane had been stung.

CHAPTER 39

FOOL! I SCREAMED AT MYSELF AS THE PLANE TURNED INTO A silvery pinpoint and then vanished. I heard the cry echo from every corner of my skull. *Idiot! Half-wit! Numskull!*

You couldn't leave it alone, could you?

You had to move in, closer and closer, trying to see. Trying to grasp—

What was that sudden flash that cut my eyes like a knife, stabbed into them like a needle?

My eyes hung open, gaping. They dripped darkness.

The sky turned purple around us. The sun glared in its center, ferocious, malignant. The ocean, and the entire planet, fell away in the distance.

It's all dark. Everything around me is dark. No sound, either, except occasionally the noise of thunder.

It was a dream but not just a dream, like the dreams that had come to me in the underworld. It erupted inside the disk, and I was in it, wide awake, and there was no escaping. Outside was emptiness. Absolute blackness, speckled with points of light.

I'm alone, and little again, and we're in my grandparents' house. In my arms, a stuffed bear. The bear once had a name, but now he has none, because I know he isn't real; he's only a piece of cloth sewn together around other pieces of cloth. He's nothing at all.

There must be others somewhere. I think I can hear their voices down the hall—distant, behind closed doors. Or maybe it's just the thunder.

We spun off into space. I knew what was happening in that dream that was no dream and all the things that have happened because of it. I couldn't stop them.

—

I get out of bed. I'm in a hallway, and it's dark, and I can make my way only by keeping my hand on the wall. Ahead of me is a faint strip of light. I set my course toward that light.

It's coming from beneath the closed door.

I feel my way around the door. There's the cut glass knob. I know that doorknob; I've been here before. Now I turn the knob and push the door open. Only an inch or two. I'm very scared.

My mother is lying in her bed. I know it's her, though I can't see her. For a moment I'm not sure if it's a bed she's on or an operating table. But then I know it's a bed. My father stands by her, his back to me. Two other men. One of them is Sy Goldfarb, who was our family doctor even before I was born. Who warned her she'd better abort me, her health wouldn't stand her having a baby.

The third man must be a doctor too. Suddenly he says, in a loud, worried voice: "She's fibrillating! She's fibrillating!"

The lightning flares. The thunder crashes.

Then I'm by a window, and my father is with me. Sy Goldfarb and the "she's fibrillating" doctor must be gone somewhere. We kneel together, my father and I. We look out on the rain-soaked street, the cars swishing back and forth and their lights glaring off the wet pavement. The lightning has passed, and the thunder is a faraway rumbling, but it's raining hard.

My father doesn't say anything. But he squeezes my left shoulder, and I know he wants me to look, because there's something very important happening in this street, something that will change all our lives and I must see and remember it. And at first I can't see it. But then I do.

Backing out of the driveway. Turning into the street. Speeding away from the house. Hurtling like a spaceship into infinite blackness.

The ambulance. My mother inside.

CHAPTER 40

WE CAME BACK.

Where else could we have gone? I don't know the other solar systems, and in this one there isn't any other planet where we might live. On Mercury you melt in the heat; on Venus you suffocate beneath the clouds. Mars is cold, and you can't drink the water. The others are monstrous chunks of rock, where there's no water at all, and your own weight crushes you the minute you land.

The moon? Once I'd been to the moon, in a time out of time. But you can't live there except inside a tower, and there aren't towers on the moon anymore. So we came back.

I held my baby tight as we flew and tried not to see her face. Her eyes had turned strange. The pupils had swollen into opaque blacknesses. Within the blackness of each eye was a slit, running from corner to corner. Beyond the slit: blackness beyond blackness.

I wrapped her in the blanket and held her with both my arms, close against my chest. Her mouth hung open, drooling, while she gasped for air. "Here," I said to her as I held her small heart to mine, "take breath from my lungs. Breathe with my lungs, and you'll be able to live."

But I knew, even then, it was impossible.

We flew over ocean. Then over land. It was nighttime; many must have seen the disk passing overhead. Some teenage UFO investigator must have written in his journal that it was *a luminous disk . . . deep red, darker at the edges than near the center. . . . It moved westward at a leisurely pace. . . .* And the story begins all over.

Westward. Not pausing, this time, to bring the disk down. I was exhausted, desperate to land. Yet—*from Dimona to Alamogordo* was the plan, and Alamogordo lay still to the west. Westward rides the sun.

Catch up with the sun, keep pace with it, and we'd have light. A single day, an hour, would go on forever.

One endless minute, in eternal sunshine.

The disk's inner light began to dim. These mechanisms wear out, just as ours do. They fail by degrees and imperceptibly. When at last they've worn away, you're surprised to find yourself in the dark.

Shadows appeared around the disk's edges. At first they were mostly transparent, like the floaters that pass across your field of vision—unnoticed, unless you choose to notice them. At first I chose not to notice.

She saw them. I know she did. That must have been why she began to sing.

"Ay-bee-*cee*-dee-ee-eff-*gee* . . ."

Her song rang pure and clear and sweet, not in my ears but in my mind. With my ears I heard her gasping as she sucked air through her mouth, trying to fill the emptiness in her lungs. But in my mind, sometimes even now I hear some echo of her song. I can then believe, if only for a second or two, that she's still with me.

I held her in my arms, the way she once held me.

And the shadows thickened, and the sound of *kha-kha-kha* chanting around us grew louder, until at last I had to admit the truth. It was the lake creatures. They were inside the disk; they'd been there from the beginning. That smear of ash on the disk's wall that I'd so wanted to believe was a lizard—it wasn't. It was them.

Their handprint. Their mark, their warning. Their way of saying: *We are inside.*

We will always be inside.

"Don't stop," I said to her.

She stopped on the *G.* I'd hoped she wouldn't. I'd hoped this time she would remember, go on and sing me the rest of the letters, and everything would turn out all right.

"Please don't stop."

I must have sounded panicked. She must have picked that up in my voice, and it frightened her. Except for her breathing, she was silent as a stone.

"Listen," I said. "It's not so hard."

—but her eyes were turning blind, her pupils solid shells of blackness—

"I know the letters. I'll teach them to you."

I tried to sing: "Aitch-ai-*jay*-kay . . ."

Silence.

"Come on!" I pleaded. "Sing *along* with me.

"Aitch-ai-*jay*-kay-ell-em-en—"

Desperate, I searched her eyes. All black, unrelieved black. Not even a split in them. Not even the dark crevasse.

The disk flew wild, rudderless, without a pilot.

She twisted in my arms. She mewed like a cat.

"No," I said. "Not that cry again. Please."

—careening through the night sky, a few thousand feet above the flinty desert—

The mewing. Louder. Ready to transform itself into a shriek. To spew out the pain and horror that lay hidden behind the black eyes.

"Shhh. Quiet. I can't bear it. You understand? I won't be able to bear it."

—arching downward, downward—

Then came the cry. Just like in the car, with the soldiers, and Julian at the wheel. Such a cry I'd never heard before. I'd hoped never to hear it again.

It filled the disk, every cubic centimeter, every space curved and angular. With all the grief, rage, abysmal fear she'd carried inside that frail body all the days of her brief life. It howled through my soul and body, and I knew I'd go crazy if it didn't stop. To save her, and me too, I had to make it stop.

That was why I pulled her to me, pressing her tiny face into the softness of my shirt. Why I felt her struggle like a fish against my chest and held her even tighter.

Why I stopped noticing if she was breathing.

It was night in the desert. I can't remember if there was a moon.

I don't remember the impact when we struck the ground. What I remember is a blinding white flash, engulfing us all, the radiance of a thousand suns. We all turned transparent, ghostly, almost nonexistent. Then the glow faded, and we faded with it.

Very far away a coyote wailed.

It was cold, but at first I didn't feel it. My chest was crushed so tightly I couldn't move. My right arm was pinned between my chest and the instrument panel. I tried to use my left hand to free myself. The first wave of pain washed up from below my waist, and I fainted.

The front of my shirt was wet. Something warm and sticky had dampened it, seeping slowly through the cloth, until my chest was soaked. It began to dry as the night passed. The cloth stuck to my chest.

Time and time again, as the hours passed, my left hand crawled toward the source of the wetness. It moved almost on its own, as I lay half conscious, sliding in and out of delirium. Then the agony from below blossomed in my brain as an endless series of fungoid smears: angry, glowing red mushrooms of pain, each one following upon the last. I jerked myself into consciousness and pulled my hand away. I then felt the pain with all my mind and knew the absolute and unbearable dominion that pain has over the mind when it's fully conscious.

Sometime before dawn, my hand won out. It went where it was trying to go, where I was trying to keep it from going. I felt my fingers palpate the crushed and ruined smear of flesh and bone and blood and tiny, twisted organs—the *it* that had once been a *she*—

That oversize head of hers—trapped, caught between my body and the metal—

Crushed like an egg—

Her shattered skull, that delicate eggshell, smashed—

Her pain and my own, so mingled now I could not tell them apart, filled my empty lungs. I howled them out into the desert night, and at once I filled with them again. And screamed, and screamed some more.

The coyotes answered me with their yelping, until the desert echoed with our cries.

Julian?

We did it, her and me.

We flew the disk to New Mexico. We unraveled time. *Unspun* time. Rolled time up like a winter rug.

Only it didn't work out quite the way we thought it would.

Did it?

Julian.

Do you even exist anymore?

The jeeps came first, with the dawn. Then the long line of trucks, olive green, with the words *Roswell Army Air Field* stenciled on their sides. They began, very carefully and methodically, to dismantle the wreckage of the disk and load it into the trucks. The tall, pockfaced lieutenant, who directed the operation, guffawed as he looked down on us.

The snaggletoothed sergeant looked closely into my face and snickered.

"Cripes," he said to the third man. "What *eyes*!"

The third man, who stood just outside my field of vision, didn't answer.

"What *eyes*!" Snaggletooth said again.

They loaded us into a truck, with the last of our shattered disk. The trucks' engines started up, in the stillness of the desert morning. We began to move.

PART EIGHT
THE BURNING

(SEPTEMBER–NOVEMBER 1966)

CHAPTER 41

TUESDAY, SEPTEMBER 6, 1966. THE DAY AFTER LABOR DAY.
First day of senior year in high school. My last year; my strangest.

Final bell has rung. We're out of the building, scurrying for our buses—
me trying to get used to being here again with the kids I've known so long;
how odd it is, everyone around me speaks English—when who do I run into
but Jeff Stollard.

He greets me warmly, friendlier than he's been in years. For a few seconds
it feels nice. "How was Israel?" he asks.

"Pretty good," I say. "Did you get my letter?"

"Letter? Yes. The one you wrote me about that place—what was it, Abu
Tar?"

"Abu Tor."

I suppose I should ask: "And how was *your* summer?" But his answer will
be about all the folksinging he and his buddies have done, are doing, will do,
and I can't stand to hear that right now.

"Yes," he says. "Abu Tor. It sounded very interesting."

He looks at his watch. We have ten minutes from the bell to catch our
buses; the drivers won't wait. The engines are running. Their exhaust climbs
into the hot afternoon sky. "You know," I say before I can stop myself, "my
mother died."

He knew my mother, from back when we were friends and he used to
come over my house sometimes.

"When—when—" He looks, he sounds shocked. "When did it happen?"

"August. About three weeks ago."

"Did you come back from Israel when it happened?"

"I didn't know about it until I got back."

—and my father picked me up at the airport, and neither of us mentioned her until we were in the car, driving through the humid night, and I said, "How's Mom?" and he said, "Well, my boy, I'm afraid I've got bad news," and I said, "Very bad?" And he said—

"She was a nice lady," Jeff says.

There's sorrow in his face. His body relaxes a little bit, as if he's thinking, *It's not the end of the world if we miss our buses.* As if our bikes were standing between us once more, as in the old times; I can almost feel the handlebars under my palms. In a minute we'll hop on them and zoom off somewhere. Talk and talk until all this begins to make sense, and the years of silence between us will be like they never happened.

"It's really—it's really—" Jeff says.

I nod.

"I wouldn't have thought . . . this would happen," he says.

"I didn't either."

—and afterward, after he told me, my father said, "You don't know how I've dreaded this moment," while all I could think was: The sword has fallen, finally, finally, fallen—

"But I don't understand," Jeff says. "Why didn't your father let you know when it happened? They've got telephones in Israel, don't they?"

"Sure. It's a modern country, just like here."

"So why did he wait for you to get back?"

"I don't know," I say. And I really don't.

CHAPTER 42

ALL I KNOW IS THIS:

I was not judged before I came to this place of torment. There was condem-nation, yes, and pain beyond bearing. But no judgment. There's never any judgment.

The lamp blazes over my desk. The journal lies open before me. It's a warm night, early September. I haven't touched my calculus, my physics, my English lit. I keep expecting somebody to remind me, gently or angrily, that it's past midnight and tomorrow I'll be up early for school. No one does. Sometimes I hear my mother moving around the house the way she used to, but it can't be; it's my imagination. In the bedroom next door my father's snoring. He must have moved back there sometime during the summer, after she died. Or after she was taken to the hospital.

I write:

First there was the ride in the truck. Then the high-ceilinged building into which she and I were brought. Then we rode the elevator, down down down, deep into the earth, then on the wheeled carts through endless tiled corridors. Nowhere in all this was there any judgment. They never even spoke to us.

They laid us on the table, under the white fluorescent light. They attached a tag to my wrist and another tag to hers. I couldn't see what was written on the tags. They separated us then, but not as the sheep are separated from the goats; we were just separated. They put her in one drawer, me in another. They closed the drawer, and all was darkness. I thought I might see her again on the other side. But there is no other side to the darkness.

There's only the smoky air and the burning, bloodied stake that runs through my body and up through my throat and digs with its pointed end into the roof of my mouth. And the low hills around me, blackening in dark red flames.

Now I know who they are, the three men in black. I knew the moment my father spoke the words *Mom is dead* and their darkness filled the car, blotting out the headlights and neon signs and even his face behind the steering wheel. And I knew: *they've won.*

Always they will win.

In every life theirs is the victory.

They set me on the table and stripped me. They peeled the cloth from my crushed and mangled body.

"It's dead all right," said Pockface.

"What do you mean, 'it'?" Snaggletooth said. He flicked with his forefinger between my legs. "It's a 'him'."

"It's an 'it'!" Pockface roared at him. "You don't believe me, look at those eyes!"

The third man worked with his needle, trying to force it into my eye. It was useless. My eyes had turned broad and hard as shells washed up on the seashore after a storm.

"He looks so fuckin stupid now, doesn't he?" said Snaggletooth.

"He'd look better with a smile," said Pockface. "Let's see if we can't give him a smile."

They tried with their fingers to twist my lips into a smile. It didn't work. My mouth was set firm in death. It was smaller than it had once been, and the lips were thinner. Only my eyes had expanded, swelling in great ovals to cover most of my face.

"They fly these fuckin disks all over the sky," said Pockface. "And they look so stupid. How do you figure that, now?"

Snaggletooth turned to the third man. "You got your razor with you?" he said.

"What you want a razor for?"

"See if we can't give him a nice big smile," said Snaggletooth.

—and I would have twisted in pain, in anticipation of their cutting, except that I was already dead, and the dead can't move, although we can feel everything, everything—

"Uh-uh, uh-uh," said Pockface, holding up his big hand. "They open the drawer, they see we been cuttin at him, and then there's trouble. We don't want no trouble, do we?"

So they didn't cut me, not where anyone could see. But they stood around the table where I lay, and solemnly they recited, looking into my face: "FOOL. FOOL. FOOL." They took the six-pointed star Rochelle had given me and heated it in the flame of their cigarette lighter, until the metal began to glow. Then they pressed it into my chest. The skin bubbled and blackened, and at last I was branded.

Maybe that was the judgment. There was no other judgment.

CHAPTER 43

JEFF HAS A GIRLFRIEND.

It's October, and I see them together everywhere. In the halls, the cafeteria. The auditorium after school, where Jeff and his folksingers go to rehearse their music and clown around together, and his girl sits on the stage, watching, laughing, applauding.

She's tall and blond and pretty in a kind of prim way. She's a junior. I've heard him call her Janet.

I pass them in the hallways while they stand together, laughing and talking and touching hands. At first I thought he might introduce me, so we could all be friends. But whatever relic of friendship there was that first day of school, it didn't last. Not after he met Janet. If he sees me when he's with her, he nods to me very cautiously, as if to say: "Yes, I know who you are. But don't come over and talk right now. This isn't a convenient time, you see."

And Janet looks at me, sort of bemused. As if I were a strange little dog she and Jeff spotted while out on a walk together—deformed, but in a way that's harmless. As if, say, one of my legs had been lopped off, but I go on trotting on my three little legs almost the same as other dogs do on four.

In the dark ceiling, over the bed where I can't sleep, I see Rosa Pagliano's face. She laughs, not kindly, not graciously. She sings, "I'll not marry a man who's shy, for he'd run away when I winked an eye," and now I know for certain she's mocking me. I curse my God, my tribe, my family. And at last myself, for having been so slow, so timid. Such a good boy for my mother.

If after a few hours I haven't slept, I get out of bed. I turn on the light. I pull out my old UFO Investigators membership card, with the *DS & RP* heart on the back. I tell myself: I'll tear it into pieces. That's what Jeff surely did.

Why do I have to carry this burden—of feeling, of remembering—year after year, while my youth is sucked away and I turn old and stooped?

The UFO Investigators

Member _____

shall be accorded all privileges

pertaining to that post

I shove the card back into my wallet. From the other side of my bedroom wall my father snores. He sleeps well these days.

If he hates me, he doesn't show it. Since I've been back we've had a peace pact, the terms unspoken but understood. I will not ask why he didn't call me in Israel when my mother went into the hospital and he knew she wouldn't come out alive. He will not ask why I didn't pick up a phone myself, even though it was clear from his letters that something was badly wrong. We each carry our guilt.

I don't ask, "Did she leave a message for me before she died? A letter? Anything?" I know she didn't. It feels right and appropriate that she didn't. I don't know why.

I don't ask who he was phoning while she was in the hospital.

I've seen the bills; he left them out on his desk in the den. I suppose he figured I wouldn't notice. More than two hundred dollars for long-distance calls the last week of July and all through August, starting the day my mother went in. All to one number. In a town I'd never heard of but, when I checked the atlas, turned out to be on Long Island.

Those are, as they say on TV, "the facts, ma'am. Just the facts."

A few more such facts:

Jeff never went out with Rosa Pagliano in eighth grade, any more than I did. I think maybe he asked her out and she said no, and he was too embarrassed to admit it. When we had our big fight—after the eighth-grade dance, and after she'd left town and school was out for the summer—I tried to find out from him if that was what happened. He told me to mind my own blankety-blank business.

She never went to the Philadelphia library with him and me. Actually, Jeff and I went to Philadelphia together just once. After that I always went alone, because once we'd handed in our science paper and gotten a B+ on it—with a few compliments about our "originality" and "analytic ability"—Jeff didn't care anymore about UFOs, though he went through the motions of working on a book with me and I nagged him into writing a few pages. The bus didn't stop in Braxton. It never did. I doubt it ever will.

But this much is true: Rosa did ask me to dance with her.

I did say to her, "Never touch the stuff."

And the next week she ran off to Florida. Maybe there was a connection, maybe not. I couldn't ask her mother because even if Helen Pagliano was sober and sane—a big if—she sold her house in Braxton and left soon after Rosa did. Nobody knows where she went.

That fall I did search the Florida phone books in the Philadelphia library, for listings for Pagliano. I did find a "Pagliano, Joseph" in the Jacksonville directory. I did call that number from a phone booth, stacks of quarters by my side and my heart in my mouth, and the man who answered did say to me, "You got the wrong number, mister." To this day I don't know if he was telling the truth or lying.

Most people, I find, are liars.

So I have only one way to be in touch with Rosa. It sometimes works. But only very late at night, between 1:00 and 2:00 A.M.

I take the UFO Investigators membership card. I hold it in my hand, lightly rubbing it as if it were the pocket-size disk Albert Bender's spacemen gave him, or the Delta Device Jeff and I used to tell each other we'd make in metal shop someday. I say, "Kazik, Kazik." When I do that, I feel perfect certainty that Rosa—wherever she is, Florida or New Mexico or (who knows?) Wisconsin; married or pregnant, or alone with her children by whoever'd been the last to betray her—still has her card, the one I gave her. She takes it out and looks at it in her despairing nighttimes, just as I do. It reminds her how vast and teeming and rich the sky seemed, how it called to her. To me.

This is our only contact. She never appears in my UFO journal anymore. Neither does Julian or Rochelle. That journal still flows within me, but in brief, sudden spurts, with weeks sometimes between entries. And when it comes—

For centuries I hung on the stake—

When it comes, it is wholly dark and terrible.

It really was Braxton kids who broke into our house when we went to my grandmother's for Shabbes dinner. Less for the money, apparently, than for kicks. They got caught three weeks later, in another burglary down our street. They stole our TV—yes, they did, not like I wrote in my journal—but they couldn't sell it, so the police brought it back, and it's still in our living room, just like when my mother was alive. It'll probably be there when I graduate from college.

And yes, they did take my briefcase. They must have thought it was something valuable. When all they found inside was typewritten pages, straight it went into the garbage.

My father leaves my pimples alone. He doesn't fuss at me however late I stay up. At six-thirty he wakes me for school. If I'm half dead from lack of sleep, I comfort myself there's only so many more days until the weekend. Then he makes breakfast.

Scrambled eggs and toast with grape jelly; it's very good. Now I notice, as I never did before, that he wears an apron when he cooks. We don't talk much. He turns the radio to a station that plays old-timey songs, and we listen while we eat.

> *The bells of St. Mary's, ah hear! they are calling*
> *The young loves, the true loves who come from the sea*
> *And so my beloved, when red leaves are falling*
> *The love bells shall ring out, ring out for you and me!*

Outside the window, red leaves are falling. I want to cry, from the beauty and sadness of it. I look away.

The red, the yellow leaves turn brown. Then they're gone. October becomes November.

Hardest part of the day is lunchtime.

I sit at a table near the back of the cafeteria, with the other kids nobody wants to eat with. Two small, skinny, homely girls with bad complexions, who I think are sophomores. A fat, ugly boy, also a sophomore, with a crew cut and widely spaced teeth. They're all morons. Each day at one o'clock, the fat kid pulls out a transistor radio and turns on the news.

"In the Gulf of Tonkin this morning, at least forty-three men died and sixteen were injured when the U.S. aircraft carrier *Oriskany* suddenly went up in flames. . . ."

"My brother's in the 'Nam," the kid with the radio says to me. Every day, Monday through Friday, he says that exact same thing. I nod, while behind us the cafeteria murmur of boys and girls together, laughing and flirting as they eat their lunch, ebbs and flows.

"Sister Rosa, a sixty-four-year-old Vietnamese nun held prisoner by the Vietcong, told her harrowing tale of ten months in captivity . . ."

Sister Rosa?

Suddenly I see before me Rosa Pagliano's grave, sweet, almost feline face. Not singing, not laughing now, but solemn and tender. Her full lips slightly open, as if to tell her own story of captivity and torment and exile. To hear mine.

Rosa, I'm sorry.

Rosa, I'd love to dance with you.

Rosa, don't go—

A burst of laughter, from behind. I recognize the voices. I turn around. Jeff and his pals and his girlfriend, all cracking up together. One of them starts singing; the others, as soon as they're able to quit laughing, take up the song. Loud enough the whole cafeteria can hear.

It's the Kingston Trio song, about poor ol' Charlie. The man who went to ride on the MTA and couldn't get off again and never returned. Who rides forever in underground darkness, maddened by thirst and rage and betrayal. Whose wife once a day goes down to the station . . .

> *And through the open window she hands Charlie a sandwich*
> *As the train comes rumblin' through!*

They sing that line superfast, "through-the-open-window-she-hands-Charlie-a-sandwich," and when they're done, they're almost rolling on the floor, they think it is so funny. I know it's not me they're laughing at—they don't remember I even exist—but that's what it feels like. I jump up from my chair.

"Hey! Where you going?"

It's the fat kid, the one with the radio. Nobody else seems to notice. "To hell!" I call out.

No one stops me. Not even the teachers. How could they? I'm invisible. When they find out, I'll be suspended. Maybe even expelled. I don't care. Already I'm condemned; why should I care?

I burst out of the school, into the pale wintry sunlight. It's cold; my coat is back in my locker; I don't care. A few minutes later I'm beside the highway, striding northward against the traffic.

The cars pour toward me, past me. Ton after ton of metal, unceasing, relentless.

Must be miles I've walked. Slower now. When I charged off the school grounds, I thought walking fast and fiercely might purge my fury and pain— my rage at my aloneness, the irretrievable waste of my life. All it's done is make me tired.

The sun hangs low above the horizon. The wind blows cold.

Cars come from everywhere. They dizzy me, fill my ears with their murderous noise. The sun's light—feeble, waning—is deeper darkness even than that damned cafeteria. Life stretches ahead of me in unending futility, like this car-choked highway.

This is the world, in which I am condemned to live.

All I have to do is step out there.

One second—it'll all be over.

If there were anyone to hear me, I would scream. I hear the squealing of the brakes; I feel the splintering of my bones, my head crushed like an egg. I run to a chain-link fence beside the road, grab it with both my hands. I will not release these cold twists of metal, to save my life.

The sun's about to set. I can't spend the night here.

I let go of the fence. I begin to walk back, slowly and carefully, like an old man crossing an endless sheet of ice. I try not to hear the automobiles.

CHAPTER 44

FOR CENTURIES I HUNG ON THE STAKE. MY FLESH CLOSED around it, formed and reformed itself upon the splintery wood. All those centuries long, I remembered the agony of the first piercing.

My belly, my bowels, my intestines tore themselves away from the wood that had penetrated them. But how could I hold myself apart? It wasn't possible, fixed as I was. The muscles grew exhausted and limp; the tissues pressed themselves against their mute tormentor. In pain they fused. And so I hung, sometimes screaming but for the most part silent, while the dark flames writhed on the low hills around me and the years silently passed by.

Somewhere above me, some exile might trudge through the heavy, fat-soaked ashes. He might wonder, as I once did, what burnings could have produced them. Now I know. They're me. My own burning flesh.

From immemorial times the dero have had their hells in the underworld, and it has never ceased. You see, you surface Christians are not so far wrong in your pictures of hell, except that you do not die in order to go there, but wish for death to release you once you arrive. There have always been hells on earth, and this is one of them.

The Elder Gods . . . God . . . the dero. It's all the same.

The three men arrive, to attend to me. They come from bathing in some lake of rot like the one I've known. It stains them an inhuman brown. It also makes them live forever.

At first I feared they'd come to wound me, to add their torments to those of the stake. No doubt those were their orders. But after so many millennia they'd grown bored with torturing. Instead they lounged beside the stake and lit cigarettes, gazing at the dimly burning hills. They began to offer me their cigarettes. Since with my stumps of arms I couldn't take them, they put them into my mouth and helped me smoke.

For hours they stand beside me. I think they're glad for my company, after their own long loneliness. They and I together look upon the dark, smoldering hills and the smoky valley in between, and because I'm fixed on the stake and can look in only one direction, they look in that same direction with me.

If I'd been judged, I would know why I've been sentenced to this place. I'd grasp how I merit this suffering. But there was no judgment. There never is.

Sometimes, though, the smoky darkness of the sky seems to part. I think then that I can see through to a place that's in the heavens, yet so close you could almost come fluttering down from it to stand beside me.

My little girl is there.

She sits in the lap of a gray-bearded old man whom I've never seen except in a picture. It's Asher, my grandfather's father. The rabbi, the saint. He holds a glass of ice water to my little girl's lips and tenderly lets her drink it.

She seems happy now.

I realize: she's given water to drink because she was a good girl, that little daughter of my grandfather. And I am left to burn with thirst because I was supposed to keep her alive and I let her perish. I was supposed to comfort her, and I left her to die alone.

I killed her.

She smiles down at me, very lovingly, and I know I am forgiven.

So I cry and say: *Great-grandfather Asher, have mercy on me, and send this little girl to dip her finger in water and cool my tongue, for I am in torment.*

But he only shakes his head. I remember then that I've seen all this, said all this, done all this a thousand times before. He rattles off his speech: *Son, between us and you there is a great gulf fixed, so that those who would pass from here to you cannot, nor can you pass from there to us. . . .*

He's lying. I know these holy old men—goddamned liars every one. I crossed greater gulfs than this in a second and a half when I had my disk to fly. I could do it right now, if only I could get myself off this damned stake.

I look away, insofar as that's possible for me. I wait for the three men to come back. At least they give me their cigarettes.

Meanwhile my mother sips her water and smiles graciously down.

There is something, I think, she doesn't know. None of them knows it. Not even the three men, who have been everywhere and know everything but are too stupid to know what to make of it.

My arms have rotted to stumps. But stumps will grow.

I will pull myself free. Then I will burst forth.

The prison can hold the body—not the spirit, not the mind. *I will burst forth.*

I will smite the door; I will shatter the bolt. *I will burst forth.*

I will cut through the fence; I will break through the wall. *I will burst forth.*

I will cross the gulf; I will abolish the border. *I will burst forth.*

I will stretch out my hand; I will raise myself from hell. *I will burst forth.*

And meanwhile I recite this over and over, as my incantation—to ease my thirst, to cool the burning. To smooth the roughness of the stake that pierces me.

I will burst forth.

The drawer—that place where they shut away my body as if I were some damned lab specimen—yawns open on its rollers. Its latch and lock are broken. It won't hold me again.

I climb out. They want to stop me, but they can't. They're too frightened.

They stare at me. They gape. They turn sick with horror. The kids from school, the teachers, my father, that woman he's going to marry now that my mother is out of his way: they're all pale and speechless. They don't have to tell me what it is that so horrifies them. I know better than they do how I've been mutilated.

When I speak, it's not in anger. I don't want to hurt them or frighten them. They're scared enough as it is. Instead I speak calmly, with grave sadness:

You must look at me, I tell them. *You must listen. You cannot look away.*

I am come from the dead; I am come to tell you all. I will tell you all—

PART NINE
TO COOL YOUR TONGUE

(AUGUST–SEPTEMBER 1967)

CHAPTER 45

August 20, 1967

Dear Julian,

It's taken me awhile to write. Believe me, I haven't forgotten you.

I thought of you back in May, when we started hearing about the Arab armies massing around the borders and saying they were going to push you into the sea. I remembered what you said to me last summer. "There's always hope. Even on the truck taking you to the gas chambers, there's hope. That's one thing you learn every day, being in Israel."

(That's what you said, wasn't it? It's what I had down in my journal.)

Then I thought of you after the fighting started, and a day or so later I passed a newsstand and saw the headline ARAB ARMIES SMASHED IN BLITZ—ISRAEL PROCLAIMS TOTAL VICTORY. And the next few days I read everything about the war in my father's *New York Times*, and I saw the photos of the soldiers praying and weeping by the Western Wall, where no Jew was allowed to set foot for nineteen years. I looked for you in all those photos, even though I knew you wouldn't be there.

Then when I saw this headline, at the end of June—

ARABS AND ISRAELIS MINGLE GAILY
IN UNITED JERUSALEM

Thousands of Residents Move Between Sectors
as 19-Year Barriers Go Down

—as soon as I saw it, I cut the story out so I could send it to you if I knew your address, which of course I don't.

I wanted to ask: Were you there on that day, when the Arabs from East Jerusalem poured into Israel and hugged everybody they saw?

I know you're all right, that you weren't killed in the war. It's not so easy to kill you. Rochelle told me that, the night we said good-bye.

Yehoshua. I still call you Julian. I can't help it; I'll always think of you as Julian; the name Yehoshua doesn't mean anything to me. Just a guy in the Bible who was a great conqueror and killed a lot of people, and they named the Book of Joshua after him. It makes me sick, to read about those people being massacred. A lot in the Bible now makes me sick.

When I was so wrapped up in the Bible, it gave comfort to my mother. I think it reminded her of my grandfather, made her feel he wasn't entirely dead. But I'm living with my father now, and my father doesn't care. He doesn't even care anymore if I spend my time researching UFOs. All he cares about is Meg Colton.

That's right—you don't know about Mrs. Colton. I didn't know either, until a few months ago.

"I simply cannot *understand*," she says to me over the phone yesterday, "why you wouldn't let me and your father send you back to Israel this summer."

"It's too late," I said.

And then, even though she's calling long distance from Long Island, she starts arguing with me. It may be too late *now*, she says. But it wasn't too late back when they first offered me the trip, the night of my high school graduation in June. I got dragged into the argument, even though she doesn't understand at all what I mean by "too late." Namely, that being in Israel doesn't mean anything to me anymore.

Hard to explain what it was before my mother died. Maybe the promise of a country where the world might be made new and I'd have a place in it, and now I know that's never going to happen. Even though Jerusalem has been won and become one, just as I said in my journal, and the Arabs have come with laughter and hugs rather than knives and hatred. It's nice, but it's nothing to me. I'm not part of it. It's too late.

Yet I do wonder: Were you there when the walls came tumbling down? When people crowded back and forth through the Mandelbaum Gate without passports or papers or anything? Did you see them tear down the fence at Abu Tor?

And what about Rochelle?

Did you see her the day the two Jerusalems merged into one? Did you recognize each other, call out to each other in the street? Then afterward did you go to talk over coffee? Tell each other your stories, the way last summer each of you told them to me? Did you then—this hurts to ask, but I need to know—did you go to bed together?

If you did, don't worry, I'm not mad. But I have to know.

It should have been you and Rochelle, from the beginning. Not her and Tom. Not her and me, even. Her and you.

I graduated from high school in June, with honors but not highest honors. I was glad to graduate at all. In November I thought I was going to be expelled for walking out of school in the middle of the day. I wasn't even suspended. The principal called me into his office and gave me a long lecture on not letting myself and my family down; that was all.

The night after graduation, I went to a party at a friend's house. I stayed until three in the morning. I figured Jeff and his girlfriend, Janet, would be there, and I was curious to test myself, whether I could be with them now without envy, without bitterness. I think it would have been OK. But Jeff's group had a paying gig in Philadelphia that night, so I didn't see them. Probably I'll never see them again. Before long I found myself on the couch with a girl named Sandra Gilbert, from my English class. She's tall and good-looking, with long, smooth coppery hair, and she always made a big point that she was *Sandra* and nobody was supposed ever to call her Sandy.

(Which reminds me: I'm not Danny anymore. My name now is Dan. Could you remember that when you answer this letter? Thanks.)

Sandra and I sat on the couch, while Sergeant Pepper and his Lonely Hearts Club Band played on the stereo. There wasn't any alcohol at the party, but I felt drunk. I told Sandra that even though I don't believe in God, I wish there could somehow be a Day of Judgment, so I'll know there's justice in the universe and whatever I get will be what I deserve.

I said to her: "Even if I was condemned, I would want to be judged."

Which is better than the alternative, being condemned without judgment, but I didn't tell her that because I didn't think she'd understand. I let my hand rest on her arm, and she didn't move hers. After a while I kissed her, as a lot of the kids were doing around us. At first she kissed back. Then she pulled away.

She said, "I have a boyfriend."

He's a sophomore at Rutgers. She met him while waitressing the summer I was in Israel, and now he's gotten her involved in the anti-Vietnam War movement. We got to talking about Vietnam, which was easier than talking about her boyfriend. We agreed the war there is wrong, all wars are wrong, they never accomplish anything. Even a war like yours, which I know you had to fight because otherwise the Arabs would have killed you all. Even if the war can be won and over with in six days, like yours was.

Yet it must have been so wonderful when the two cities became one, and Jews and Arabs hugged and danced in the streets. Tell me: Were you there that day? Was Rochelle?

I must have looked unhappy. Sandra must have seen how bad I looked. I'd just tried to kiss my first girl and got told she was going with someone else! After a while she took my hand.

"Don't worry," she said. "You'll have a girlfriend in college. The girls there will appreciate you."

I sure hope so.

Soon August will be over. Three and a half more weeks, my father will drive me up to college, and I won't live at home anymore. I've got my license finally, so I may share some of the driving if he doesn't make me too nervous.

I'm going to Carthage University, in upstate New York. That's the same college my parents went to, where they met before the Second World War. Mrs. Colton went there too. Her name wasn't Colton in those days. I think she and my father were boyfriend and girlfriend before he met my mother. I think they must have kept something up even after he got married, even after my mother got sick. Maybe especially after she got sick.

Did I ever tell you about the letter that came for my father the spring

before my mother died? The one signed "Me(g)hitabel C." that she opened
and that sent her into tears, her last spring on earth? Of course "Me(g)-
hitabel C." was Meg Colton.

I suppose, out of loyalty to the dead, I ought to hate Mrs. Colton. But
mostly she just bores and irritates me.

First thing, when Dad introduced us last March, she squeals at me:
"Why, you're the spitting image of your mother!" I think she's imagined
ever since that I *am* my mother, come from the dead to judge her for what
she did, fool with my husband while I was dying. That's why they were
so eager to send me back to Israel this summer, to get me out of their way,
so I won't make them feel guilty for what they're doing. *Were* doing—

Of course.

That's why he let me go last summer.

So I wouldn't be around, so I wouldn't know about him and Mrs.
Colton.

He could have stopped me. He knew she was going to die. I knew too,
but I couldn't admit it, I wanted so bad to get out of that house. He could
have sat me down, said, *Son, you won your Israel trip fair and square,
but you can't go. Not this year. Next summer you will, yes, I promise you
that, but now you can't, because she's very sick, and if you go, you'll
never see her again, and I won't let you carry that guilt, that pain.* I
would have been mad; I would have hollered; I would have argued. But I
would have stayed if he'd said so. He didn't. Now I know why.

I'm a cynic these days, Julian.

You would have appreciated that when we first met. You were pretty
cynical yourself, if my journal is any witness. But I don't think you are
anymore. Now I think you'll be disappointed in me. I can't help it, though.
This is how I am.

Amazing. This letter has gone on for pages, and I've hardly mentioned
UFOs.

I haven't stopped believing. UFOs are real. I know that, as truly as I
know you're real, Rochelle's real, the three men are real. It's just that I no
longer believe—how can I put this?—that they're accessible. They're in
the sky; I'm on earth. I used to think, if I researched them, investigated
the sightings, learned the physics of how they fly, I might be transported

with them into the skies. Last summer I *was* transported, sort of. I flew, I really did, to Israel and back. But then I crashed. I'm still digging myself out of that wreckage.

Maybe UFOs will work for you. They won't for me anymore. I have to find another way.

A few nights ago I had a strange dream. It's still with me; I can't get it out of my head. Maybe that's why I'm writing to you now, after putting it off for so long.

It was the night of August 17. That's one year to the day after my mother's death, though it was two weeks later I found out she'd died. The three men in black were in the dream, threatening me, warning me. Saying over and over, "Fog, thy name is UFO!"

Their faces were covered with black silk. No trace of any eyes or nose or mouth underneath. I realized, even in the dream, they must already be dead. It was one of the scariest dreams I've ever had, but I wasn't scared. Not then, not afterward. The first thought that came to me when I woke up was how appropriate it is, that *fog* and *UFO* share two out of three letters.

Well, Dr. Freud, what do you make of that?

Here's what I think: when we watch the sky, we're looking in the wrong direction. The real mystery is right here, among us. It's the mystery of boys and girls who become men and women, whether they want to or not; and sometimes they don't marry at all, at all—as in that silly old song Rosa and I sang to each other. But mostly they do marry, sometimes the right person but most often the wrong one.

Then they get sick. Then they die. And the rest of us go on living, because we have to.

What do you think, Julian? Shall I take my UFO books with me to Carthage? Just on the off chance I might change my mind, find I still have energy for UFO work, when I'm not studying or writing papers or—what the hell, why not?—trying to find a girl to go out with?

No. I'm not going to take them. But I'm not going to throw them out either, the way my father wants me to. They stay right here in my room, on the bookshelf above the bed where I've slept since I was five years old and we moved into this house. They're clumsy books, even silly most of them. But they're part of me. I won't deny them.

You're part of me too, Julian. That's why I'm writing to you now, before I leave for college and become a different person, someone I can't imagine.

I don't have your address, so I don't know how I'm going to send this letter. Maybe just: "Sgt. Yehoshua Margaliot, Israel Defense Force, Israel." Sort of like "Santa Claus, North Pole" don't you think? Yet the letters always seem to get there.

I think this one will too.

Be well, Julian. Take care of yourself. Write soon.

When you see my old pal Rachel, tell her I said hello.

Your friend,
Dan

CHAPTER 46

September 14, 1967

Dear Dan,

Or "Mr. Shapiro," as I like to think of you. Don't worry—I won't try to call you Danny.

You needn't have worried, either, about your letter reaching me. Whatever you write, whatever you say, whatever you think will always find its way to me if you want it to. And you needn't concern yourself with whether I'm real, as your allusion to Santa Claus would perhaps suggest. I am entirely real. So is Rochelle. You've always known that.

In other words, yes, Virginia, there is a Yehoshua Margaliot.

Still a sergeant in the Israel Defense Force, unscathed by this awful war, which I'm delighted we won but bitterly sorry it happened at all. It shouldn't have happened. That night by the Makhtesh when you and I drank beer together and talked about plucking the cancerous thread from the fabric of time, I would have sworn nothing like this would ever happen again. But the Makhtesh is empty now. Not only is the disk gone—you know better than anybody, you were the one who flew it—but the tower it rested on has vanished. In a red mist, just as it came. The Makhtesh is nothing anymore but a crater in the desert.

And we've been through one more war.

Your friend Sandra Gilbert is right. They're all wrong, all terrible. They don't accomplish anything except that if you're lucky, you're still alive when they're over, which is a real, if transitory, achievement. I was at the Wall with the paratroopers the day we took the Old City, and I saw all the praying and the crying. I did some of it myself, though I've never been what you call a religious man. But of course, as you say, you won't find me in any of the photos. I'm not the sort of fellow who tends to appear on film.

And yes, Rochelle and I are together once more. (Though I think I will discreetly dodge your question about our sleeping arrangements.) We didn't meet on that splendid day you wrote about, of Jews and Arabs dancing together in the streets of Jerusalem. I wasn't even in Jerusalem that day. I'd been assigned to guard duty in Nablus, one of the Jordanian towns we've conquered and now are going to have to occupy, for longer than any of us cares to think. Nobody's dancing in the streets there.

How Rochelle and I found each other—well, I'll get to that in a minute. First I need to tell you this. My hat is off to you, that you didn't let your father and his gabby fiancée send you back here this summer. When you came last year, you were on a mission, something only you could have accomplished. This summer you'd be one more tourist among the crowds of tourists, and I'd be delighted to see you, but we wouldn't have one damned thing in common except UFOs, which you've stopped believing in even though you don't know it yet and probably won't for a long time.

I also need to say congratulations on that kiss.

Do me a favor. When you head off to college, don't forget to take Sandra's address. Write to her. Sooner than you write Rochelle, sooner than you write me. Yes, I know, she's got a boyfriend, a college man. But you'll be a college man yourself in a couple of days. And boyfriends are not always forever.

Only what we carry in our hearts is forever.

One morning, just about four weeks ago, the phone in our barracks rang, and it was for me. I think it must have been the exact same time you had your dream about the three men. Remember, the sun rises earlier here than where you are. It's morning in Israel, while back in the States you're still in dreamland.

It was Dr. Zeitlin from Hadassah, the one who treated your baby. Who found for her the healing none of the others could. He said: "Go across the old border that isn't there anymore, *borukh Hashem*, thank God. Find Dr. Saeed Talibi." And he gave me the address of Talibi's office.

I said: "Why? You want me to bring him a message?"

"No message," he says. "Just go. Find him."

Probably you can guess the rest of the story. Who should I find in the good doctor's office with him when I get to Salah ed-Din Street in East Jerusalem? You already know. You already can guess—part of it.

Talibi and Rochelle, just beaming, delighted as can be. And there's a third person with them. A fourth, counting me.

This is what gives me hope. An impossible hope, a hope that shouldn't be there. I think, if I hadn't seen that little girl with my own eyes—

A toddler, I would have called her. Except she could barely toddle. Hardly had the strength to walk; couldn't do it at all without Rochelle's helping, holding her hand. She breathed hard every step she took. But just her walking was a miracle.

She shouldn't have grown so much since you flew with her in the disk. She wouldn't if she were a human child. But their physiology is different; Talibi kept insisting on that.

Her eyes are still enormous. Rochelle has to put huge sunglasses on her whenever they go outside, so she won't attract attention. Talibi seems to think they'll shrink as she grows, in proportion to her face, so eventually she may be able to pass among human beings.

She speaks.

She held out her hand to me and said, in perfect English: "You must be Julian. Mama's told me so much about you."

Who she meant by Mama, I don't know. I don't think it was Rochelle; she knows Rochelle's not really her mama. I shook her hand, very gently. I said to her, in Hebrew, "*Koreem lee Yehoshua*," I'm called Yehoshua.

She answered in Hebrew, "*Naeem me'ohd*." Pleased to meet you.

I couldn't believe it. I had to plop myself down into one of the office chairs, I was so flabbergasted. Talibi's belly shook from laughing, he must have thought I looked so funny.

He said: "Arabic too."

French also, Rochelle tells me. Those are all the languages we have among us, so we don't know how many she knows. All that are spoken on this earth, I suspect. And even beyond.

She had a message for you.

She said to tell you she loves you. She doesn't blame you for what happened; she knows it wasn't your fault. She said, when you thirst, she will always dip her finger in water and cool your tongue. I don't know what she meant, but that's what she said. Even if there's a gulf between you and her the size of the galaxy, she said, she'll find a way to bring a cup to your lips—

Why, Mr. Shapiro! You're crying!

CHAPTER 47

I KNOW I'M CRYING. I CAN'T STOP. MY TEARS SPILL ONTO the paper, onto Julian's letter, onto the pen through which his words pour out. By the dresser my suitcase is packed, my journal inside, though I'm leaving all my UFO books here in the bedroom of my childhood.

"Danny!"

It's my father. He knows I'm not Danny anymore. Sometimes he forgets. I don't say anything. It's hard, but I wait him out.

"Dan!"

"What, Dad?" I call back.

"Ready to go!"

So this is good-bye. I won't live here anymore. All summer I've looked forward to this, getting out of his and Mrs. Colton's hair, living in a dorm, going to bed whenever I please. Leaving this soiled, tattered cocoon behind me. But now—

"Five minutes, Dad! OK?"

"OK. Five minutes."

I said five minutes; I meant five minutes. That's all it'll take.

It's a bright, blowy day, warm for September. The windows in my bedroom have been open until now, when I shut them. I go to the bookcase over the bed to say good-bye.

One by one I touch them, the odd, disreputable books that shaped and consoled my teenage years, kept over my bed so I could reach for them when sleep wouldn't come. Albert Bender, *Flying Saucers and the Three Men.* Charles Fort, *The Book of the Damned.* And of course M. K. Jessup, *The Case for the UFO.*

I pull *The Case for the UFO* down from the shelf. I flip through the pages. Plenty of annotations. All of them mine.

No Gypsies passed this book hand to hand, writing into it the secrets of UFOs and invisibility. Maybe that wonderful book, that special copy, really exists. Maybe someday I'll find it. But this isn't it. Just an ordinary book, by a UFO investigator with fifty-nine years of loneliness behind him, more than three times my seventeen. Who finally couldn't face any more years. So he went to his car, ran a tube from the exhaust pipe into the window, turned the ignition . . .

I shudder. My fingers curl, as if to grasp at a chain-link fence. I promise myself: never again.

It may be better at Carthage; it may be worse. I will never let myself come near that again.

I close my eyes. Once more I feel myself climbing the wall from the Well of Souls, toward the entrance of the tunnel that leads from death into life. I hold the book tight, so it won't fall from my hand. Below me are jagged rocks; if I slip, all my bones will be shattered. Amid the rocks I can see the bursting bubbles that are the souls of the human generations—

One of them my mother's.

I clutch hard at the book, so I won't start up again with the crying. But it's too late; they're already flowing, those tears—

"Danny! Dan!"

—and in the act of clutching I swing out from the rock wall and nearly lose my grip. I don't think twice. I let go the book, grab on to the wall. The book falls with a splash into the waters below, scattering the crowd of departed souls—

It tumbles onto my bedspread.

There I leave it.

I hurry out to the car, on a windy autumn day, clouds blowing across the empty blue sky.

ACKNOWLEDGMENTS

Many have helped me along this road. First and foremost, my wife, Rose Shalom Halperin, my earliest and in many ways my best reader, who saw the first sentences of the first draft (long since discarded) in January 1997, and said, "It's good. Keep going." And I did keep going; and when I grew discouraged with the length of the journey and its difficulty, she was there to encourage and sustain me. This book, and my life as a writer, I owe to her.

My friend and former colleague, Professor Yaakov Ariel of the Religious Studies Department, University of North Carolina at Chapel Hill, read an early draft and gave me encouragement and valuable suggestions. He drew upon his experience growing up in Jerusalem, in the Abu Tor neighborhood along the old border (before the 1967 war) between Israel and Jordan, to show me how I might handle the end of what is now Part Six; his comments inspired me to locate a crucial scene at the Church of St. Peter in Gallicantu. Novelist Lee Smith, with the warm generosity that has always been characteristic of her, read part of that draft and gave me her feedback and encouragement, along with my first guidance into the unfamiliar world of the publishing business.

Several years later, novelist Ann Prospero read part of a later draft that had been much revised and tightened but was still far too long. She said, "You've got two stories here, and they keep getting in each other's way. The UFO story is the more exciting of the two. Keep it; get rid of the rest." I did as she suggested. Thus was born *Journal of a UFO Investigator* in its present form.

Novelist Peggy Payne was "book doctor" to an early draft, and I'm indebted to her for the care and sensitivity she poured into this task. I am indebted to the writers' group established in 2001 by Charity Terry-Lorenzo, which has helped me over the years with one novel after another. The membership of the group changed over the years; those who worked with me on *Journal of a UFO Investigator* were Mike Brown, Vicki Edwards, Sylvia Freeman, Bryan Gilmer, Jessica Hollander, Jennifer Madriaga, Susan Payne, Dave VanHook, and Robin Whitsell. I'm grateful to them all, and most especially Bryan and Dave, who, even after we were no longer in the group together, generously read complete drafts of the novel and gave me their invaluable criticism and warm encouragement. So did novelist Joyce Allen and my friends Elaine Bauman and Jonathan Tepper.

My current writing group, under the incomparable leadership of novelist Anna Jean Mayhew, has given me the most immense help with this and other projects. Its members have included Gabriel Cuddahee, Ron Jackson, Deborah Klaus, Kathryn Milam, Susan Payne, Elizabeth Schoenfeld, and Sarah Wilkins. Special thanks to Gabe, who gave me the title for Part One, for which I'd searched for many months.

Danny Shapiro's story owes a great debt to the mythmaker extraordinaire of Clarksburg, West Virginia, Gray Barker (1925–1984), and his forgotten 1956 bestseller *They Knew Too Much About Flying Saucers*. The "three men in black" may not have been Barker's invention—there probably is a nucleus of fact in the story of Albert K. Bender's frightening brush with mysterious visitors in the fall of 1953. But it was Barker who gave the legend its powerful and enduring formulation. He did much the same for the "Shaver mystery" that unfolded through the second half of the 1940s on the pulp pages of *Amazing Stories* magazine, with its "Elder Gods" and "dero" and underground caves. A few years after the publication of *They Knew Too Much,* Barker moved on to promoting the legends surrounding the death of Morris K. Jessup (1900–1959) and their link to the ever elusive Philadelphia experiment.

(The second of the two quotations at the beginning of chapter 4 is adapted from Shaver's story "Thought Records of Lemuria," in the June 1945 issue of *Amazing Stories,* the first from a column of Barker's in the June 1957 issue of *Flying Saucers* magazine, reprinted in 2003 by Rick Hilberg. The "Shaver" quotation on page 73 is in fact Barker's formulation of Shaver's ideas: *They Knew Too Much About Flying Saucers,* pages 62–63. The passages quoted by Rochelle and Julian on page 63 are from an actual letter sent to Jessup in 1956 by the eccentric drifter Carl Allen, and the description of the moon-tower picture on page 125 is inspired by a cover illustration drawn by Albert Bender for the November 1953 issue of Barker's *The Saucerian*. Other details of the "Gypsies'" book are my own invention.)

The best exploration to date of Barker's enigmatic life and tangled motivations, his real sincerity and freewheeling approach to truth, is Robert Wilkinson's brilliant 2009 documentary film *Shades of Gray*. Barker's papers are housed in the Gray Barker Collection of the Clarksburg-Harrison Public Library. There, doing research for this book in September 2004, I was welcomed and given every possible assistance by curator David Houchin.

Danny's experience in the Philadelphia Library, in chapter 5, draws upon an incident reported by folklorist Peter Rojcewicz in *Journal of American Folklore*, vol. 100 (1987), pages 148–161. Others who've inspired this book's treatment of UFOs include the late Karl Pflock, whose *Roswell: Inconvenient Facts and the Will to Believe* (2001) is the definitive account of the Roswell legend, and Jerome Clark, my friend from the distant days when I was myself a teenage UFO investigator. In his magnum opus *The UFO Encyclopedia* (1990–96, second edition 1998), Jerry has gifted us with an inexhaustibly rich source of knowledge, which no one with the smallest interest in UFOs or UFO belief can afford to do without.

The North Carolina Writers Network, through its annual conferences, helped me learn that literary agents are not necessarily figures of dread. Through its critiquing service, it allowed me to make use of the "book-doctoring" of poet and short story writer Ruth Moose, who gave me the right feedback at the right time.

And speaking of agents . . . I'm lucky to be represented by one of the finest, the supremely savvy and sensitive Peter Steinberg. Not only did Peter find a splendid home for my book—it's his genius, for taking a story and making it better, that I have to thank for three plot alterations that raised the novel to an entirely new level. For all the good things that have happened to this book, I'm deeply grateful to him, his wonderful assistant Lisa Kopel, and his overseas colleagues at Intercontinental Literary Agency (Sam Edenborough, Tessa Girvan, Nicki Kennedy, and Jenny Robson). Also to Bill Martin and Beverly Swerling Martin of Agent Research and Evaluation, whose expertise first guided me in Peter's direction.

At Viking, I've been blessed with two of the finest editors I can imagine. Kendra Harpster, who shepherded the manuscript from acquisition to production, persisted in asking exactly the right questions of the book and refused to be contented with any answer that did not move it toward becoming all it could be. Josh Kendall has taken it from there, bringing his panache and sound judgment to the book's benefit in a multitude of ways. Thanks also to Amanda Brower and Laura Tisdel, for their careful reads and penetrating suggestions, and to Maggie Riggs, Josh's tirelessly helpful assistant. And to Carolyn Coleburn, Gabrielle Gantz, Alex Gigante, Pearl Hanig, Daniel Lagin, and Jennifer Tait.

I thank novelist Philip Gerard, for a conversation more than six years ago which helped me see unrealized potential for the book. I thank reference librarian Barbara Harris of the Roswell (New Mexico) Public Library, who helped me research the history of the town and the air force base when I visited Roswell in September 2006; and the staff of the Free Library of Philadelphia, who helped me get the details of the library scenes just right. I thank writers Paul Cuadros, Alison Hill, Jake Horwitz, John Kessel, Duncan Murrell, James Protzman, John Reed, Howard Schwartz, Daniel Wallace, Allen Wold, and the late Professor Martin Lakin; readers Ayesha Coleman and Benjamin MacLeod; and our family friends Shirley Bullock, Gina Mahalek and Jackie Wilson, Steve Eubanks and Steve Mullinix, for help that they themselves know best. And I thank our "beloved community" of faith, the Eno River Unitarian Universalist Fellowship (ERUUF) of Durham, North Carolina, which has given Rose and me a place of worship and inspiration, amply fulfilling for us the promise of one of our favorite Unitarian Universalist hymns:

> *Come, dream a dream with me . . . that I might know your mind.*
> *And I'll bring you hope when hope is hard to find,*
> *And I'll bring a song of love and a rose in the wintertime.*

Durham, North Carolina
July 2010